RHYMER

BAEN BOOKS by GREGORY FROST

Rhymer

RHYMER

GREGORY FROST

RHYMER

A Baen Books Original

Baen Publishing Enterprises
P.O. Box 1403
Riverdale, NY 10471
www.baen.com

ISBN: 978-1-9821-9266-2

Cover art by Eric Williams

First printing, June 2023

Distributed by Simon & Schuster
1230 Avenue of the Americas
New York, NY 10020

Library of Congress Cataloging-in-Publication Data

Names: Frost, Gregory, author.
Title: Rhymer / Gregory Frost.
Description: Riverdale, NY : Baen Publishing Enterprises, [2023] | Series:
     Rhymer trilogy ; 1
Identifiers: LCCN 2023002616 (print) | LCCN 2023002617 (ebook) | ISBN
     9781982192662 (hardcover) | ISBN 9781625799173 (ebook)
Subjects: LCSH: Thomas, the Rhymer, 1220?-1297?--Fiction. | LCGFT: Fantasy
     fiction. | Novels.
Classification: LCC PS3556.R59815 R59 2023 (print) | LCC PS3556.R59815
     (ebook) | DDC 813/.54--dc23/eng/20230202
LC record available at https://lccn.loc.gov/2023002616
LC ebook record available at https://lccn.loc.gov/2023002617002645

Printed in the United States of America

10 9 8 7 6 5 4 3 2 1

DEDICATION

To Terri Windling and Ellen Datlow,
partners in folklore, fairy tales, and balladry.

ACKNOWLEDGMENTS

As with most novels, various people played a part at various stages in the development of *Rhymer*. The author would like to thank a few who played significant roles in its gestation. First, Jonathan Maberry, with whom the original "T. Rhymer" tale was concocted. Although this version has journeyed a long way from there, none of it would exist at all had it not been for an initial idea discussed over beers, lo, many years ago. Second, my thanks to author/translator Craig Williamson for all the Anglo-Saxon riddles in his *A Feast of Creatures*. Neither Thomas nor Taliesin would exist as they do without you. A special thank-you to Oz Whiston, proof- and beta-reader nonpareil. I cannot imagine getting feedback from anyone else as reliable and helpful as yours. You are the "True Thomas" of this text. Finally, to my agent, Marie Lamba, for doggedly representing the project through its various permutations.

PART ONE:
TRUE THOMAS

I. On Huntley Bank

"Ya understand?" Onchu asked, and Thomas realized suddenly that his brother had been speaking to him. He looked up, mouth agape, lips slack as a drunkard's. He squinted. He pushed dirty fingers through his unkempt hair. Shook his shaggy head. They weren't at home, their mother and father weren't here, their sister, neither. What was Onchu saying?

"God, he's gormless." Baldie laughed. He stood behind Onchu, halfway to the river. The river . . .

Onchu shushed Baldie and tried again. "You stay here now, Tommy. It's dry an' ye ken sleep in the grass while we fish upriver, right, little brother?" He tenderly brushed back Thomas's hair.

Thomas took in the tall, reedy grass around him, the glimmering of the river ahead; then he twisted around to see the trees behind him. Black alders. He knew where he was, remembered they had come here from home, the route Onchu, Baldie, and he always took, though the specifics of the journey itself eluded him. So many things eluded him. They'd been walking, but anyway he wasn't allowed on a horse. He closed his eyes, saw his feet, plodding, plodding, plodding along a path, following it from their big wooden wall with the keep upon its scarp, past sties and the well, across countryside past Oakmill on the Tweed to the Yarrow where it met the Ettrick Water—Onchu's fishing path.

The weight of his brother's hand slid down and pressed upon his shoulder. "Sit," Onchu gently ordered, and he opened his eyes again. Memory slipped away like a school of minnows.

Thomas Lindsay Rimor de Ercildoun, half-witted fourteen-year-old son of a locally powerful family, did as he was bade and squatted down in the grass. He was lean and black-haired, and his fierce blue eyes could pin you sharp as blades if you could get him to focus on you for longer than an instant. Had it not been for the fits that plagued him and the simpleness of his mind, he might have been a fine catch for most any girl in the town. The trouble was, everyone there and for miles around knew of his *peculiarities*. Some thought him possessed. Others were certain he was touched, perhaps even divine. Weren't the sibyls of ancient days similarly cursed? And the poet Taliesin as well? Opinions varied widely.

Those closest to him—his father, even his mother (privately), and definitely his brother—believed him to be a harmless idiot. His sister, Innes, alone thought him blessed by God in a way no one yet understood. Which wasn't to say that Onchu didn't love him, he did; but Thomas was more often than not a burden to him.

Pushed down, he sat cross-legged among the reeds. He smiled to Onchu.

"Hey-o," Baldie said, "there's a relief." His thick mouth smirked beneath a nose bent crooked ever since the first time they had brought the idiot with them.

That morning, Thomas had been seized by a fit, fallen face-first into the Ettrick Water, and would have drowned if Baldie hadn't waded in quick and grabbed hold of him. But Thomas, unaware of everything including his savior, had flapped and windmilled and swung his head wildly back, cracking the bridge of Baldie's nose, getting himself dumped facedown in the water again, until Onchu hauled him out. Baldie, cursing and spitting, refused thereafter to touch him for all the treasures of the fay.

When Onchu had flung him safely onto dry land, he'd rolled about and babbled, *"The teeth of the sheep will lay the plough to rest!"* and then fallen quiet and still. As his "predictions" went, it made about as much sense as any.

There were no fish caught that morning. Spluttering Thomas had scared them off.

Since then, Baldie continued to give him a wide berth. If he'd set himself on fire now, Baldie would only have nodded in appreciation of the blaze from a respectful distance.

"Ye don't follow us now," Onchu told Thomas. He knelt close, rubbed Thomas's back. "Ye stay here and sleep till the sun's down. Or, I don't know, count the leaves on that black alder."

Thomas tilted back his head and looked at the nearest tree upside down. "Two thousand nine hundred sixty-eight," he said.

"Leave him already!" Baldie called. Boots off, he was wading into the water, hissing at every plashing step from one big and precarious stone to another.

"Christ yer," Onchu cursed. "Then count the damned bulrushes."

"Eighty-seven. I could see more were I standing." He started to get up.

"Well, you're *not* standing, Tom. Lie back now, count birds flying over, count clouds, count catkins till we come get ye and then tell me all of what you've seen, hey, sweet boy?"

He did as he was told, and stared into the sky, all but forgetting that Onchu was there.

"Come on," insisted Baldie. "It's feckin' cold and I'm not gaunny stand here till meh balls crawl up inside me!"

Thomas heard Onchu, laughing, tug off his boots, and wade out after his friend. Plump Baldie was generous (though he would never admit it), but Thomas saw him as true as the tenderness in Onchu's heart for himself. Heard them on the far bank then, Baldie chattering about the harvest.

Their voices faded into the world where birds sang songs—no two alike, a conversation he could very nearly understand as he tracked it back and forth—and the reeds sizzled now, waving accompanied by breezes, and thoughts jittered and split and swarmed.

Every moment took him off somewhere. He hardly noticed when the sounds and sensations of the whole world absorbed his brother and Baldie like soil soaking up rain. Time isolated him from before and after, cause and effect, sealed him off from human communication, from meaning. It could be sunrise one moment and night the next; such discontinuity was just how the world was to Thomas. He was quite used to losing most of it. What was lost wasn't important, wasn't noticed.

After awhile, he tilted his head back again. "Two hundred seven catkins," he said of a goat willow, "larger than my fingers." He held up his hand to study those fingers. Dirt encrusted the broken nails. The sun was hanging to the west now. Afternoon had arrived—new shadows, different lines, angles, and slices out of the light.

He placed his hand over the sun. The edges of his fingers glowed red-orange and he smiled.

A breeze blew and the reeds hissed all around him. An alien scent rode on the breeze. It drew his attention away from admiring his glowing fingers. He recalled every smell ever, though many had no name and simply came with images, moments cut out of a dark dough and scattered. This one was new, strangely sweet, like wildflower honey.

At that moment the sun went into eclipse, or had it begun to set? His hand was just his hand again, held up against darkness. He lowered it.

A strange shape sat upon a beast right beside him, silhouetted black against the sun. The shape seemed to have two heads. He squinted, but that didn't help. Odd spikes festooned the figure and the horse it rode; but he saw immediately that it wasn't a horse. It had a snout too long and too sharp, though it pawed the ground as impatiently as a horse. It carried its rider out of the sun's way, and brightness flared into his eyes again, making them tear up. The air tinkled musically. The sweetness enveloped him and the bees making it buzzed within his brain, realigning his thoughts. Two tiny things like bats dove and flitted about the silhouette.

Thomas sat up, wiped at his eyes, streaking dirt across his cheek like some warrior Pict preparing for battle. He was no longer staring into the sun.

Peering down upon him was the most extraordinary woman he had ever seen. She wore a green cape, the hood fallen back to reveal her resplendent red hair beneath a pointed cap. The beast was revealed now to be a stallion of pure white bedecked in a fine blue-and-gold caparison. How had he seen it differently? It also observed him coolly, but he hardly noticed that. The second head belonged to Onchu, who was seated behind the woman on the stallion. Onchu's expression was as dull as if he was asleep with his eyes open.

"Onchu changed his mind about fishing with Baldie," Thomas said aloud without noticing. "Why?"

Something like invisible fingers seemed to prod and push at his head, creating a pressure not unlike what he felt just before a fit struck. But no storm raged through him. Instead the bees buzzed about his thoughts again.

"Majesty," said a deep voice. Thomas followed it to a retinue of two men on their own horses behind her. Knights in black armor. They had plainly crossed the river together. "Shall we—?"

"No, Adalbrandr," she answered. "Look at him. Poor broken toy, and such a pretty one, too. What a waste. I wonder, should we swap him for this other?" Odd that her cherry lips didn't move as she spoke, though the words rang in his head, clear as New Year's bells.

The Queen of Heaven, he thought, but could not remember where he had heard the title. Was it a song? Wasn't someone playing a hurdy-gurdy?

She smiled then with the magnanimous pity of a monarch, and in that smile lay her decision that would change her world and his in ways unimaginable. She would not take him in place of the other boy, but instead leaned down and brushed her long, slender hand across his face. Her blood-dark nails traced his forehead. His whirling, buzzing thoughts slowed, stilled. Desire plucked at him.

For the first time in his life, Thomas experienced a silence inside himself.

One thing was clear. "Onchu changed his mind about—"

"Shhh." The lady shushed him with the sound of the reeds. Urged him to lie back in the grass again and sleep. To her retinue she said, "We will leave this one. Let him forget we passed. I've snatched his puzzle-thoughts from him."

He did lie back as commanded, but neither slept nor forgot. He could see in his mind the fifty-nine silver bells woven into the stallion's mane, and the twelve stars along the reins, the way the shining barding across its forelock poked up as if the horse had horns, just as he could see the odd gold shape of the lady's eyes, which made him think of both buttons and spiders—the way her six pupils seemed like a circle of pinpricks within her bright irises. She pulsated with desire. He wanted to go with Onchu. They went everywhere together.

The bells tinkled as she rode off.

The other two passed beside him, and like her they each crossed the ball of the sun; and as they did, they changed. Spines as sharp and polished as thorns projected from their silhouettes. Their mouths became fanged, and the beasts upon which they were seated turned into things carved from dark skeletons but not of horses. He had never seen anything like them, and was too awed to be terrified. Close by came the gray riders' thoughts, matching the cold regard in their eyes—*they* wanted to kill him, nor cared that he saw their true nature. But their queen had been clear in command, and they passed him by, becoming men and horses again.

He watched them, upside down, riding toward the black alder, until the swishing tall grass hid them.

He lay still awhile longer, wondering about things, his thoughts assembling in ways new to him, in orderly patterns. The great roar of the world had quieted, letting him perceive his thoughts before he spoke them. Eventually he arrived at a troubling question that brought him to his feet: Why hadn't Baldie been with them, too?

By what new instinct he couldn't say, Thomas walked down to the strand of pebbles and small rocks where his brother and Baldie had crossed the river. The big stepping stones out in the water led to a path up the opposite bank. They always fished in the same spot, across the peninsula of woodland.

As he stood there, a long wooden pole swept past. Pulled along by the current, it clacked against the stones in the middle of the stream, rotated, and slid between them. It was unmistakably Onchu's dapping pole, tied with strips of leather at the handle and the juncture in the middle.

Floating along the river as if in pursuit of it came a bundle of rags, but soon enough he identified a forearm, the back of a head, legs. The rags became a body.

He waded in. It was icy cold, the water. He jumped from stone to stone to intercept the body. It floated up beside him and he squatted, grabbed onto a sleeve and tugged.

Baldie rolled over like a log. Faceup, his blank eyes stared wide as if beholding something terrible in the sky. There was no wound, no blood to be seen. Sodden and heavy, he was too much for Thomas, and the current had its way, prying the body from his chilled fingers into the main channel, and dragging Thomas in with it.

He splashed, choked, hammered the surface with his arms, finally clutched onto the big stone again and pulled himself back to safety.

By the time he could look, Baldie was well down the river, a flowing clutch of rags again.

Thomas managed to work from stone to stone and finally washed himself up on the pebbly strand. Crawled out and lay, gasping.

Pressure filled his head again, streaks of lightning fractured his sight. He heard his voice as he always did—as if it was another's: "A teind *for hell, they arrive, they take, all greenwood their enchantment!*"

He mewled and rocked and rocked on the strand. Unlike every riddle he had ever babbled before, this one opened to him like a flower. His thoughts quieted, coalesced around it.

The knights had killed Baldie to take Onchu. But why, and where were they going? No war hereabouts, no fighting. No village, no habitation on that path, in that direction, either. Only the old abbey, and they were no monks. *They arrive, they take.* Fifty bird calls trilled on the wind, like tinkling bells. *All greenwood...*

Thomas jumped to his feet and ran.

II. The Teind

The riders easily outdistanced him, but the moist soil made their tracks easy to follow—three-toed hoofprints belonging to no horse he'd ever seen. It seemed reckless, as though the lady and her knights did not care if anyone saw or followed after them.

He'd thought it was the new abbey under construction toward which they headed; but once they'd forded the Tweed, they diverted east, and east was the graveyard and Old Melrose, as people were already calling it—the six-hundred-year-old abbey ruin where the Cistercians used to live. It was a holy site and had been one for a long long time, *before there were even monks.* Who had said that? Someone speaking to his father, once upon a time when he was younger, because people would say anything in front of him, he didn't matter. But look how he did now!

He jumped with excitement as he ran along the path. Look how he was able to sort things that he'd seen and heard!

There was a war in the south—a king named Stephen and a queen named Matilda, but they weren't married to each other. Didn't like each other. How was that important to know? He could not remember, if ever he'd known, couldn't even be sure that the war was something current or yet to come.

Some things remained jumbled and obscure after all.

Up ahead on a bend of the river and near the bridge to Ercildoun lay the ruins of Old Melrose. He would be upon it soon.

He slowed his step and walked on through the trees with more care. The Queen of Heaven might not like it if he intruded. Maybe she had descended to reward Onchu for looking after him. His brother certainly deserved a reward, just for all the times he'd stood for Thomas, defended him. There were so many people who couldn't tolerate his weakness, his confusion. It seemed to make them angry or afraid. He didn't understand why. He asked for nothing from them, yet they accused him of being a demon or of being guided by demons, which was funny in its way, since *guided* was something he definitely wasn't.

Ahead stood a thicket of downy birch, past which he saw the first of the sixty-seven grave markers along the north side of the old abbey. It was a small rectangular building with no door in its doorway and half its roof thatch rotted and gone, nothing like the majestic structure that would be built to replace it. Dozens of circular stone huts in various states of decay dotted the rocky ground beyond it.

He could not see the Queen of Heaven yet, but he could feel her, the pressure in his head so like the storms that lashed him before a riddle fell from his lips.

Crouching low, he worked his way from marker to marker, some misshapen and grown over with moss, others covered in lettering, none of which he knew how to read. He reached a stone on a small knoll and peered over the top of a gravestone.

The two knights sat on horseback still. Around them stood seven people on foot. They weren't monks. The five men wore doublets or tunics rich with embroidery. One of them he recognized from Ercildoun—an alderman named Stroud, distinguished by his dark beard and the scar that interrupted it on his right cheek, who had come to his father's hall many times. The two women wore crowned wimples and long satin gowns of blue and gold respectively. People of wealth, they all appeared to be.

In the center of their loose circle, both the Lady and Onchu sat upon her horse as if basking in their admiration.

Thomas took to hands and knees to steal closer still, behind one mossy stone that looked as worn and ancient as the ruins.

The people on foot closed in upon the horse. They gathered to one side of it, reached up. Hands grabbed Onchu's leg, arm, his shirt. They pulled him down among them. They made an excited noise that seemed to emerge from inside Thomas's head, a weird chirring as if fierce beetles were crawling out his ears. He could not help swatting at himself, the sensation was so overwhelming.

The Queen uttered a command, but her words were foreign and queer now. He could not see Onchu between the people, but it was clear he was the object of their efforts as they worked, buzzing like a hive of bees—only not bees, not anything he knew or understood.

After some minutes, the noise abruptly stopped and the people backed away. Onchu, upright, stood naked in their midst. He didn't move, nor seem at all self-conscious as he'd been the one time that Innes caught them swimming naked. Then, Onchu had covered himself with his hands. Now they hung loosely at his sides as if being naked no longer mattered.

The Queen made another statement Thomas didn't understand. Strange that he'd comprehended her words before without difficulty but could not decipher the strange noise she made now.

The alderman strode up in front of the Queen and her horse. He raised his arm high above his head. His fingers held something dark and about the size of a small skipping stone from the river. Onchu and Baldie skipped stones on the Ettrick all the time. This one twinkled.

The alderman brought his hand straight down, and where it swept, the air seemed to sizzle with green smoke. The smoke became a kind of fire that spread, eating away from the center outward, becoming a circle. It was like nothing so much as a great round Catherine window—like the great round hole where the window would go in the new abbey. The green edges continued to flicker like fire, but the circle contained something other than the view of the old ruin now. Two creatures stood on the far side, black in polished armor, spiny, and with yellow eyes. They looked the way the mounted knights had against the disk of the sun. It might have been an illusion, but the two seemed to stand at the head of two lines, which receded into some foreign distance, into eternity for all Thomas could tell. Seven tiny creatures like dragonflies or bats darted in and out of the opening.

The six besides the alderman closed ranks to either side of Onchu and together they all paraded toward the circle. Onchu walked under his own power, if sluggishly. The Queen and her knights followed, the whole of it seeming like a great ceremony.

Why Onchu had agreed to go with them, Thomas could not fathom, but it wasn't—could not be—a good thing. He stood up and jumped over the low marker. He needed to bring Onchu back home.

The three horses carried their riders into the circle.

"Wait!" Thomas shouted.

Alderman Stroud swung about, shocked until he saw who had yelled.

"Stop!"

The alderman smirked and stepped through the circle after everyone else, then turned and for a moment simply stared at him as if too astonished to react.

Thomas ran for all he was worth, weaving around the stones, straight at the man. He didn't have a weapon, but then he'd hardly thought how he intended to rescue his brother. The alderman went down on one knee to cut the air upward on a diagonal even as Thomas sprang.

As the alderman rose, the circle collapsed toward a single seam, and Thomas merged with it, halfway through. The world around him flung green jewel shapes—lozenges, diamonds, shards—flickering facets shifting into new sharp-edged forms too fast for him to comprehend. They coalesced, flared bright as the sun. The great roaring of a tempest filled his head, searing voices, shrieks and shouts. Green turned to red, the roar rushing over him as if he was drowning in a sparkling, spinning ocean of blood, while sun and moon whirled and whirled and whirled about him.

Then the colors burst and hurled him away like an angry child throwing a cloth doll. Out of the glare, he flew back into the world again, struck the nearest grave marker so hard that it tipped halfway out of the ground; he flopped behind it, insensible.

The seam was gone, leaving not a trace upon the air.

After a while, when nothing moved, the birds began to sing again. Thomas heard nothing. The sun, no longer whirling, steadily descended. A dragonfly lit on his cheek, considered his eyelash for a moment, and then flitted away.

III. Waldroup

"Hey, little brother. Hey, wake up now." Hands shook him gently.

"Onchu," he muttered, then tried to reach out.

"Is that supposed to be your name or mine?"

He opened his eyes. A bearded face he didn't know grinned down at him, features fluttering in torchlight. *It's nighttime.* With that he realized that what he thought inside he no longer had to say aloud; he could contain thoughts, keep them to himself. He recalled all at once inhumanly long fingers that played across his head, seeming to pierce his skull, the sensation so intense that he wiped a hand across his face to see if there was blood from the sharp nails. None, but his body shivered as if beset by an ague. The stranger looked concerned. It was an expression Thomas had beheld most of his life, mainly in response to something he'd said, but right now it didn't matter.

He sat up, clutched at his side where it twinged, and stared past the man. *Green fire.* Gone, everything was gone, everybody. Onchu, too. His eyes welled with tears.

"Boy, what is it?" The man twisted to follow his gaze.

He shook with weeping, tried, then sobbed, and tried again to explain. "Queen of Heaven. She's took—she's took Onchu."

The bearded man's expression furrowed, which puckered the scars across his cheek and forehead. His gaze shifted to the tilted gravestone beside them, and he grunted with apparent understanding. "That so, little brother? Then I am most sorry for your loss. Which one is his?"

"No," he answered, wretched and despairing. He rocked back and

15

forth, put his hands on his head. How was he to explain? "She *took* him," he said again. In his head he heard the voice of a neighbor, Mrs. Duncanson, speaking of someone's stillborn baby: "Not lost but gone before, poor dear."

"Gone," he managed. "Gone before." He shook his head. It was impossible to tell it. She had taken Onchu and left him behind, when it should have been him. He tore at his hair, slapped himself, unable to sit still until the man stabbed the torch into the ground, then grabbed his arms and anchored him in place.

"Go ahead and rage, boy. Get it out, but not by harming yourself."

The strength of those arms kept him in check, kept his hands at his sides while he kicked and twisted and yelled, until finally his fury broke, leaving him empty in his weeping. The man knelt patiently, as if he'd nothing else to do in the world. He wore a light tunic and loose, checked trousers. A satchel lay beside him, made of heavy cloth and patched in a few places. A cord was tied to the points of it, front and back. It must in some manner unfurl. Thomas's interest in it carried off his misery. The man hesitantly let go of him, and he wiped at his runny nose and wet face.

"Your family live hereabouts?"

Thomas nodded. "I—my . . ." He stopped, unable to locate the knowledge. Where was the name of his family, his town? What was that neighbor's name that had just been in his head?

The man must have read confusion or terror in his expression. He patted Thomas's shoulder. "Well, let's be up, then. This ground's soggy after the rain." As he stood, he offered his hand. Thomas took it and the man drew him upright, not letting go until it was clear Thomas could stand unaided. "Odd that you're not soaked from it. Ya can't have lain there long." He lifted the cord of his satchel over his head and onto his left shoulder with the satchel resting on his right hip. "Can you share at least your name, then?"

"Thomas." He said it without thinking, then skried the name as if it would reveal the thoughts he couldn't find. When that failed, he walked straight past the man to where the green fire had been.

"And lovely to meet you, Thomas, my own name's Alpin Waldroup," the man said as if still conversing with him, adding in a singsong voice, "'Oh, and that's grand, sir, thankee for not leaving me on the wet ground to rot.'"

The jibe was lost on him. He muttered, "Onchu?" and waved his hands in the air as he stumbled around in a circle.

Alpin Waldroup shook his head, picked up his torch, and walked over. "Boy," he said.

Thomas dropped to his knees, pushed his palms across the rough ground. "Where are they? They're gone, just gone." Looked up. "Where are they?"

"Thomas, lad." He reached to squeeze Thomas's shoulder reassuringly, but the touch jolted him. He lurched to the side, where he sprawled on his back, arms and legs windmilling wildly.

"*Horses but not horses, knights but not men!*" he cried out. "*The Queen took all through fire green! Say their name!*"

Waldroup had drawn back from the flailing limbs. "What fire you talkin' about?" he asked, but Thomas's eyes were rolled up in his head, his back arched. He clawed at the dirt. Then, as quickly as it began, the fit ended, and Thomas sighed shakily, blinking and confused. Spit and foam trickled from the corner of his mouth. Waldroup repeated his question.

"Green fire," he answered. "A ring of it right here." He pointed to the empty night.

For the first time, Waldroup looked worried as he cast about them. The heap that was the abandoned abbey seemed to move and shift at the edge of the torchlight. The eye sockets of the skulls carved on the stones seemed to look their way. He hauled Thomas upright again. "We'd do well to quit this place, I think."

"But, Onchu—"

"Onchu's not coming back, lad."

Thomas looked to where the fire had been. "It should have been me, not him."

"Be glad it wasn't. Come now, come on." He lifted the torch and strode forward. Not wanting to be left behind in the dark, Thomas hurried after.

They walked through the black night, the torch throwing just enough light to reveal a few yards of the path they trod.

"Listen, then," said Waldroup. "I think we should give you another name for now. Maybe no one will come looking for you, but it's best if we don't assume anything. So, what would you like to be called?"

"Don't know." He had only just become Thomas.

"Let's call you Fingal, then, since you're a stranger even to yourself."

"Fingal," he repeated, trying it on.

"Now, we're heading for the Abbey of St. Mary that King David's having built. You know of it, yes?"

Thomas turned the words over, finally shook his head in defeat. "I don't remember anything but me and Onchu and Baldie."

"Baldie, eh? Well, your memory's improved by one. You didn't remember him the last time."

"He drowned. In the river."

"Hey-o. Well, *he* won't be looking for you, anyway."

They walked on. It was a two-mile trek on the path. Waldroup said nothing more and Thomas strained to remember more, but the memories he sought remained just out of reach. Moments did rise up before him—the reeds and catkins, a silhouette against the sun, lifeless Baldie floating away.

Eventually a light flickered in the distance. At first he took it to be a reflection of the torch, but it grew ever larger until it became a campfire surrounded by various lean-tos and half a dozen small huts. The wet night was warm but men and boys sat near the fire, where a set of three upright poles supported two bowed crosspieces from which hung a large ceramic pot.

One of the men, holding a wooden bowl, watched them approach. "Thought maybe you'd fallen in the quarry, Waldroup. What you got there? Another apprentice?" He pointed his large wooden spoon at Thomas.

"Runaway, name of Fingal. Needs work."

"You try to pass him off as a carver, I'm leaving."

"You'd do best to pack now, then, Seumas McCrae."

"You're having me on."

"I am, and you're doing all the work." The men around McCrae laughed.

Waldroup wove a path through them to the largest hut. A man with stringy gray-and-black hair leaned in the doorway, watching their approach. He wore only a linen tunic, apparently ready to sleep, but was chewing idly on a yellow-flowered stem of tansy. Behind his hut, a pale wall full of arched windows and chimneylike buttresses stood out against the black night. To the right stood an odd, immense framework with a treadwheel in the center of it.

Impossible how much had been built. Why, surely not a month earlier, only the cloister and nearby priory had been finished. The monks had new dwellings but little else stood here. How did he know this? Onchu had led him past here repeatedly to fish in the ... the Tweed. That was the river. They'd seen these men and the structures at a distance. No more than a week earlier, there was hardly anything erected here. How had this happened? Waldroup put a hand on Thomas's back, shoved him forward, which brought him back to the moment with this man eating the raw flower. "Lachlan Clacher," Waldroup said, "this is Fingal."

Clacher took the stem out of his mouth, then spat. "You digging up boys at the quarry now, Alpin?"

"One more *for* the quarry. And we could still use a few." He gestured at the four boys seated by the fire.

"He's all sinew," Clacher complained.

"So was I once."

"Maybe as a bairn. Not in my employ." He pointed the plant at Thomas. "You ever work stone, Fingal?"

Thomas shook his head.

"Well, there's a ringing endorsement."

"He's an *apprentice*, Lachlan. None of these Selkirk boys knew anything at the start. I'll teach him."

Clacher thought, shifted his gaze from Waldroup back to Thomas. "Sure, we're short a few, and with Lenox dead under that putlog scaffold ..." He grimaced. "I'll try him. But you're responsible for him, Alpin."

"Oh, agreed."

Clacher tapped the tansy stem a bit, then chuckled. "Maybe you can get him running one of the treadwheel cranes before winter."

"You don't even have *me* working one of them."

"And why would I? You're too good at the quarrying." He then retreated into his hut.

Waldroup gently turned Thomas around. He said, "Come, get some broth now. You have to be hungry." They walked back to the fire. From one of the lean-to structures, Waldroup grabbed wooden bowls and spoons, handed one of each to Thomas.

Staring at them in his hands, he said, "I don't understand."

"It's simple, really. The master mason has just approved you to work the quarry with me. I thought he might. King David wants this abbey completed in a decade. We currently don't have enough men and lost a good one a week ago to an accident." He ladled some broth into Thomas's bowl. "Quarry work is hard; the other boys'll tell you that. You get good enough at cutting, you'll move up the ranks and maybe work here, shaping the stone. Put your mark upon this abbey." He ladled broth into his own bowl. "More to the point for you, maybe, each day you work the quarry gives you an excuse to look in upon the ruins where your Onchu was took. Mind you, don't you say anything about that to the others. Right?"

He glanced over his bowl at the four pairs of eyes that watched him approach.

The broth wasn't terribly good, but Thomas found that he was ravenous, as if he'd been starved for a week. They joined the loose circle of men and boys. The men sat on broken chunks of stone, the boys on the damp ground. While Thomas slurped at the broth in his bowl, Waldroup introduced the other boys as "Iachan, Kerr, Lachie, and Shug." All of them hailed from Selkirk and seemed to know one another. He felt he ought to know where Selkirk was but only nodded, saying nothing rather than display his ignorance. Lachie inquired where he was from, and Waldroup answered for him. "Oh, Fingal? He's a runaway from Otterburn."

"Yer father beat ya?" sandy-haired Iachan asked. "Mine did. Nuffin I did were right."

"Well, you're not beaten here," Waldroup promised.

Thomas noticed he was looking at the other men as he said this. Most of them nodded. Two wouldn't meet his gaze. His rescuer seemed to wield a certain amount of authority.

"Lachie here works the treadwheel. He's been with us longer. Started at the quarry same as you will tomorrow." He grinned at some thought. "You'd better have another bowl of broth, little brother. By tomorrow's end you're gonnae be too sore to eat." He clapped him on the back and nudged him toward the ceramic pot.

After he'd finished his second serving, Waldroup took his bowl and spoon, pulled him to his feet, and led him to another of the huts.

"That mat there belonged to Lenox. You take it. Everybody understands. The other boys have theirs, anyway. You drag it into *that* hut. You'll be sleepin' with the Selkirks."

He picked up the straw matting Waldroup had pointed out and hauled it into the other hut where four mats were already laid out. He placed his at one end of the hut and sat down on it. The mat didn't seem terribly comfortable but it was dry. The other boys came in together.

The one called Lachie said, "I was you, I'd move to the other end. That's Shug next'a you an' he farts in his sleep."

The boys laughed, including Shug. "An' when he's awake," added Kerr, the tallest, muscular one. Shug punched him in the shoulder, then laughed again.

They all sat down on their respective mats. Thomas lay on his back. He didn't know who he was but his name now was Fingal, and in the morning he was going to go off and cut stone. The shifting new reality left him dizzy.

Onchu was gone. *The Queen took all, knights but not men.* He clung to the words of his riddle as if he had the slightest idea what they meant.

IV. Cleaving Stone

✠

Waldroup supplied him with tools and an off-the-shoulder bag to contain them. Like the mat he'd slept on, the tools had belonged to Lenox, the man who'd died and who, as it turned out, was the first marked grave in the new cemetery north of the abbey.

Thomas proved to be a fast learner. By the second day, he had absorbed the idea of there being cleavage and bedding planes, and was able to identify stress points in a slab of limestone and drive his copper wedges along a line with the precision to split it into blocks. Waldroup remarked, "Anyone would think you'd done this before." Iachan and Shug were impressed, too.

He hadn't, of course, but something about the work was akin to counting things—patterns opened to him in a kind geometry. Striations in the stone revealed themselves as lines and angles, almost as if drawn upon the slabs. Focusing on the work kept his thoughts from straying to Onchu and how *he* should have been taken instead. He was the damaged one. Nobody would have missed him, would they? Even if he ever remembered more people, they would all say that Onchu had mattered, had been of worth.

The one aspect of quarrying he had trouble with was carrying cut blocks to the oxen-drawn carts to be hauled to the abbey site. The other boys were stronger, and even they grunted and groaned at the sledges they used to pull the rough stones onto the carts.

The first day proved Waldroup true: He ached nearly to where he didn't want to eat, just to crawl off and sleep. But Waldroup wouldn't allow it and made him eat the mutton and bread and mashed-up turnips.

He was going to sit alongside the other boys, who seemed just as exhausted, but Waldroup led him off a ways.

It turned out he was ravenous—too hungry to care where he sat.

Waldroup asked, "Anything new come to you, today, Fingal? Remember more?"

It took him a moment to remember that he was Fingal. He shook his head.

"Well, let's give you a few days, hmm? Can't elude you forever." He chewed on a chunk of bread awhile. "You always suffer from those fits?"

"Yes." He bowed his head as if to ward off a blow.

"Anything you ever gabbled out before make any sense?"

Waldroup seemed to be teasing him. He glared through his brows. "Sometimes. Maybe. My sister thinks it's prophecy."

"A sister, then, you have a sister. See? You did remember something new."

Waldroup was right. *Innes.* He had a sister named Innes. It was as if she had been hiding. He could see her face, and didn't want to lose her. "Innes," he said.

"All right, then. We got Innes, your sister. And Baldie, that was Onchu's friend. That's good. We'll figure you out, name the whole of your family before long." He reached over and gripped Thomas's shoulder. "Just be careful who you share this with. *Fingal.*" He gave a nod of his head at the other boys.

"You think someone's coming after me?"

"I think it's better that we assume so."

"Why?" He scratched at his cheek, then set down his bowl, watching Waldroup all the while. "The green fire—it meant something to you, didn't it?"

"Here, more meat for you, little brother." He snatched the bowl, got up, and returned to the ceramic pot, ladled more into both Thomas's and his own bowls and brought them back. "Eat another portion, you worked hard." He sat down and returned to eating as if they hadn't been speaking at all.

Thomas waited for an answer. When it didn't come, he ate the rest of his own food. He'd have tried again, but by the time he'd finished, all he could think of was crawling into the hut. Inside it, he clambered right over Shug, who didn't even budge but did fart.

Falling asleep, he realized that he hadn't gone to the abbey ruins at day's end as he'd intended.

In the morning, he hurt everywhere. The taller, more muscular Kerr smiled and told him, "It'll get better. Few more days, an' you'll think ya done this yer whole life."

"I don't think I'll live long enough for that to happen."

Kerr just laughed.

They cleaved block after block that day. He and Iachan assisted Waldroup and another man, who seemed the best at placing the wedges, while a third man directed the other boys with hauling the cut blocks on the sledges.

Thomas drove one of the carts back to the abbey. Beholding the site in full operation amazed him. Dozens of men crawling about on scaffolding, some—including Lachie—working treadwheels to raise blocks into the air, the stones held in place only by giant calipers—Waldroup told him this was called a *lewis*—others mixing mortar, climbing up ladders while balancing their hods, working in seeming peril as the shaped blocks were guided over to them and lowered, all of it coordinated with whoever worked the treadwheel. They were ants lifting grains of dirt above them as they swarmed over a mound, raising its height with each grain they placed.

That second night, he still felt as if his joints were being separated. His hand trembled as he lifted the food the monks had prepared to his mouth. He sat with the other boys for most of the meal, but eventually crouched down beside Waldroup, who asked, "How is it for ya, now, Fingal?"

He thought a moment. "I'm an old man today," he said. Waldroup and the other men nearby all laughed.

Clacher went off. Others turned in. He remained beside Waldroup, not exactly certain as to why.

But at the point where he started to get up, Waldroup abruptly said quietly, "I've seen your green fire. Once."

Thomas eased back down.

"On a battlefield in France. Your spiky knights and queen, alongside people what looked like anyone else." His food eaten, he set down his bowl. "Believe me when I say your brother had no choice. They picked him for her tribute and that was that. Once picked, you're done. So stop thinking it should've been you. If it had, you wouldn't be here."

"But the Queen of Heaven—"

"Not who she is, boy. There's more heaven in my compass." He patted his satchel. "Your brother's took by the Queen of Ailfion as a *teind*, though don't ask me what he's a tenth part of. No one who knows that is still on our side of the veil. But you can be sure they'll come looking for you next if they want to keep it in the family, cover their traces. All the more reason for you to be Fingal, my apprentice. 'Tis nobody looking for *him*."

"*Ailfion?*"

"Or sometimes Elphame or Elfheim. It has dozens of names, so I been told. Seems anywhere you go, they've a name for it."

Worn out, Thomas sat with his head lowered, his face a mask of confusion.

Waldroup tousled his hair. "Yeah, I know. Too much, isn't it? I tell ya, your best move is to let it go."

But he couldn't let it go. At least once each day, Thomas took the opportunity to visit the ruins. He didn't know what he was looking for, exactly: some sign of Onchu, or at least an indication that someone else had been there. But there were no such signs. The only footprints in the dirt and mud were his own. Even so, he expanded his search, looking around the piles of rubble, even creeping into the old abbey crypt, which was dark and uninviting and, as a crypt ought to be, lifeless.

Every night he went to bed with a full belly, which was about the only part of his body that didn't hurt. He would eat whatever meal the monks in their beehive huts had prepared (some were decidedly better cooks than others) and then collapse. That changed only gradually.

Every morning, he and his Selkirk friends walked alongside Waldroup and other quarrymen, beside the ox-drawn carts. He and Waldroup didn't discuss what Thomas hoped to find, or what he should do if indeed he came upon another group of those elvish knights and their victim.

Days dragged on, became weeks, and he realized one morning

that his fits had left him, as if they had taken wing along with his memory. But that didn't fill in any further, either: He knew only that he'd had a brother and a sister, but no family name nor where he hailed from came to him. As they dared not seek for answers to the mystery of him without possibly endangering everyone working on the abbey, the matter was left for another time, Waldroup saying only that he expected the memories would return—he'd known plenty of soldiers who'd been knocked so hard that they were like chunks of wood, but always sooner or later some of what they'd lost returned. "Or else they died," he added. Thomas couldn't tell if it was intended as a joke.

After a while the subject of his past seemed to matter less. The exhausting routine of quarrying became his life and filled up the vague part of him that had been scooped out. His leanness filled out, too. He was shorter than Kerr, but his shoulders were broadening, his arms and thighs thickening with muscle. A light beard softened the sharp line of his jaw.

His daily visits to the abbey ruins might have tapered off, but then came the night Iachan disappeared.

V. Iachan's Departure

Well past the meal, and everyone had turned in. The boys slept together, and it wasn't uncommon for various of them to get up in the night for a piss, movement that barely caused Thomas to stir if he heard it at all. That was true for all of them in their exhaustion.

If it hadn't been for Shug, no one would have noticed the absence before morning. But Shug wasn't given to assessing a situation before voicing his thoughts, and, returning from pissing, he asked himself aloud, "Where's Iachan?" as he noticed the empty mat.

The whole hut stirred. Lachie said, "Leave off, Shug," rolled over, and went back to sleep. Kerr looked up, saw the empty mat, and replied, "Gone for a piss, same's you," and lay back down. Kerr said nothing as both of them had covered his opinion.

Thomas nearly did the same, but sitting down beside him, Shug added softly, "Well, 'e were gone when I went out and ain't at the piss hole neither." Then he lay down and promptly farted.

Two minutes later, Thomas was still awake and Iachan hadn't returned. He leaned up on his elbows to stare at the unoccupied mat. There was nowhere to go, and why would Iachan wander off anyway?

He got up and padded out of the hut. If anyone heard, they thought he was also going for a piss after being awakened by Shug. Outside, he put on his shoes. He hesitated to wake Alpin, fully expecting Iachan to reappear momentarily. Still, where would he be? Wandering around the abbey in the dark? Too dangerous, and there were plenty of stones to perch on out here if he needed a think, but

nobody was sitting there. Not even Clacher munching on some tansy
to cure his gout.

He knew that what he was thinking was a ridiculous leap and that
by the time he got back everybody might be looking for him, too.
But he argued that if he went to the ruins, at least he would confirm
that events there weren't the reason for Iachan's absence.

Thomas carefully picked his way past the huts and stones and
piles of rubble to the downriver path, then increased his pace until
he was quick-marching through the deep darkness. The path had its
treacherous tree roots and stones, and he was careful of each.

Even before he'd come in sight of the ruin itself, he became aware
of how the distant trees seemed to be lit and shifting back and forth
in a flickering green glow. Cautiously, he left the purlieu of the trees
and sneaked into the plot of grave markers. On the far side of them,
dark figures moved before a spitting, flaming ring. He counted four
people standing close together: a bearded man, a woman wearing a
wimple and glittering headband, a taller man, and one who was squat
by comparison with the others. They faced the ring, backs to him.
He scrabbled on hands and knees to get closer.

Out of the hole in the air, two imperious black knights rode. It
might have been that they were riding black chargers but they
seemed to him immense in their slick, reflective armor. He
remembered the two who'd accompanied the beautiful queen. These
could be the very same two. Then one of the people said a name,
"Adalbrandr," and he knew they were those knights.

The quartet parted to let the knights pass, and for a moment
Thomas glimpsed another, smaller figure, shed of its clothes, in their
midst. He gaped, his mouth went dry, and he nearly stood up and
shouted. But he'd done that before and was no more prepared for it
now than he had been then.

The riders turned their chargers about to flank the naked victim,
and the three of them crossed back through the ring. Once inside it,
they turned again to face the four people on this side, and Thomas
saw Iachan's slack-jawed face clearly for a moment. Then the bearded
man stepped forward and, extending his arm to the green fire, sealed
up the circle. The last bit of flame vanished. Iachan and the knights
were gone.

The people muttered in conversation, walked closer to the ruin, where he realized now they had horses waiting. The men assisted the woman onto her palfrey, then mounted their own.

He lay flat as they departed, only the woman riding past him. The others went off in different directions.

When they were gone, he crept to where the ring had been, the exact place where Onchu had been taken. Now he knew for certain—knew and was unable to do anything. His hands curled into fists. He couldn't do this, couldn't stand helplessly by and just watch again.

Thomas ran to the Abbey of St. Mary, to his hut, but didn't sleep the rest of the night. In the morning, when it was clear to everyone that Iachan had vanished, Clacher shrugged it off, insisting that the boy had just run back to Selkirk. He'd employed any number of apprentices who found the work too difficult and ran away.

Waldroup seemed to sense that something more had happened, but it wasn't until they were off away from the others at the quarry that Thomas told him everything he'd witnessed. At the end of the day, Waldroup accompanied him to the old abbey ruins, where footprints and strange animal tracks not belonging to horses confirmed the story. Past where the ring had been, the prints all ceased.

"We have to do something. They've taken another. What can I *do*?" Thomas asked.

"I don't know," Waldroup replied with an imposed calm. But from his expression it was clear that these creatures snatching someone from their group with such ease had shaken him badly.

That evening, the two of them sat on cut blocks delivered in the final cartload of the day. The three Selkirk boys sat well off to one side, huddled away from everyone else. Their conversations all day only reiterated that none of them believed Clacher's claim that Iachan had run off. As Kerr put it, "He'd ne'er go back where his old man'd beat him some more, and he don't know no place else." Nods all around.

Thomas hunched over his own bowl of lamb and turnips and bread, limiting the breadth of the world for which he was responsible to this small wooden bowl. Waldroup hadn't spoken a word since the ruins.

Without looking up, Thomas said, "You were on a battlefield

when you saw them, you said," as though they had been conversing about this just moments before.

Waldroup hardly slowed his eating, as if he hadn't heard. A moment passed, and he simply replied, "Norman battle," and went right on eating, only glancing around to make sure no one else was within earshot.

"Which one?"

"Has it a name? I never heard it. I fought with King David against Stephen for possession of Northumbria. We lost, I suppose, though the king got to keep Carlisle and his boy's got a title still in England. It was over quick and hardly any pay in it. So I went and hired on with Stephen's mercenaries, following into Wales, where he retreated. Then joined with Waleran de Beaumont on his behalf and sailed off to Normandy. Stephen showed up eventually and brokered a peace, but by then I'd already been brought down." He pointed with a fistful of bread at the puckered scar over his shoulder. "Broadhead right in the joint, nearly snapped off 'tween the bones. When I was done screaming, I thought I'd lost the arm for sure." He winced at the recollection of the agony.

"So, there I lay among a lea of dead archers as the sun went down, when three people come into view, walking across the field as if on a casual outing. Must have walked into the aftermath from a nearby town. I could tell from the way they dressed they were people what know a fair amount of comfort in their lives. The way they turned over the bodies like looking for the tastiest one, I thought them witches. Then one of them made some sign in the air, and a circle of green fire split everything wide." He looked Thomas in the eyes. "Your black knights just rode right out of it like magic. Was two of 'em, maybe e'en the same two."

"They let you see?"

"I was lying in among the corpses, blood, and dead horses, myself a dead man too pigheaded to die. The witches had caught themselves a livelier boy, a foot soldier who'd been clipped above the ear, hardly more than dazed and confounded, really. They stood him up, swaying, glancing around at the sky like he'd never beheld it before, and then the knights led him to that green blaze. *She* was waiting there on the other side, everything shimmering red like a waterfall of blood behind her, as if her red hair was grown out and plaited into the whole world there. I could only watch them. But I think they didn't care whether or not any of us saw. We were just dead men to them. The knights and the lad—well, they stripped him first, same as Iachan and your brother—they all went through, and then one of those three people knelt before the green fire and as he stood up, the fire vanished, until nothing of it remained. It was like he'd poured it down his sleeve."

"But what's on the other side?" Thomas asked.

"Now, how would I know that? They didn't take me. If they had, we wouldn't be discussing it now."

"But then it could be heaven? It *could* be?"

Waldroup knocked his wooden spoon against the bowl. "Those thorny soldiers—you recall them thinking how they should kill you? Sound like the thoughts of angels to you?"

Thomas squirmed. "But now they can come after us here? And you can't shoot anymore, on account of your shoulder."

For a moment, Waldroup just stared at his own scar, then he snorted. "Have you not noticed me hauling blocks of stone, boy? My shoulder healed fine. Not perfect but better than it should have. Hurts in winter, sometimes in the rain. It was my luck that day they didn't search my side of the field instead of the other one. Your brother and Iachan . . . whatever you think—and whatever *is* on the other side—it's better they were chosen than you. I don't have to follow those black knights to know that I don't want to." He concentrated on his lamb, finishing it in silence. When he looked up, he found Thomas eyeing him still. "What, is there something else?"

Now was the time to say what he'd lain awake thinking this morning, what had been working at him all day. "I thought . . . I thought you'd maybe be willing to teach me what you know. You know, soldiering."

"*Soldiering.* Oh, you think soldiering'll help?" Waldroup set down his bowl. "So, here's what you need to know about soldiering: It's all a great mess every time, two sides fighting for some sort of supremacy, and you're to contribute your skill—and your life, if needs must. At the end of the day, whatever castle you've stormed or village you've sacked and burned, it's all for them, the people of comfort and power. And the next day, if you live, you're expected to do it over again. There's pay in it most of the time if you can keep your gorge down. Almost everyone does at first, and some for a long time, but they get to like it, can't do nothin' else. Plenty don't make it past the first skirmish, the first minute. And some kings lose their nerve and sell you out, giving back all that you've taken for them in order to make a truce or bargain to capture whatever prize they really sought, which you weren't privy to because nobody tells common soldiers anything. Here's the rules of soldiering for a mercenary: embrace the fight, fight to win, and ignore everything else. Just know that when a king wins, most of the time it means you're unemployed again."

"But that's what you did."

"That's what I did, yes. With a warbow. More chance of survival as a bowman. Aren't charging at crazy men in a mess of blood, shit, carved-out livers, and muck, not as likely to get trampled. But an arrow can still find you, same as yours finds them. And those Ailfion knights . . . we don't even know what it takes to bring them down." He tapped the wooden spoon against his scarred shoulder. "Stick to the stonework, and don't be wandering off by yourself again. Then you can live a full forty years like other men."

"Iachan didn't wander off. They took him from right here," he said. "What if one of these men helped them? What if Clacher did it?"

"What? Clacher's not helping *elves*." But he glanced at Clacher as if to make certain, then got to his feet. He started to walk away with his bowl. Thomas got up and stalked him like a shadow. Abruptly, Waldroup turned about and dragged him away from the cooking fire. Everybody was watching and everybody would have been able to hear.

Finally, Waldroup let go of him and said, "Listen to me, son. What I told you the first night is the truth. Your brother's not any place you can pursue him, not any place you *want* to pursue him. The best soldier in the world can't bring him or Iachan back from Ailfion."

"*I* will."

Waldroup hissed through his teeth. "*Nobody* goes into the world of the dead and comes back. And that's what Ailfion is for our like. Nobody knows what's on the other side of that ring. I didn't understand what I'd seen on the battlefield, and I asked and I asked, told my story to whoever would listen, until somebody warned me I should shut my mouth if I didn't want the elves coming for me, too. Because they have done for others, and you never know when one of them's listening—that was my warning. Don't know who they are, the helpers of the elven. Look like anybody, smiling and friendly, so you won't realize who you've told until you wake up in your bed and they're already around you, dragging you off, never to be heard from again. I paid heed. I shut up. And I'm still here. If there *is* one among us, and you poke at this, you're poking a stick into a hornet's nest that you can't even see, what can open up beside you and drag you right in." He shook his head and walked back toward the thick of the huts.

Thomas ran after him. "Alpin! Teach me things! *Fighting* things!" he yelled.

Waldroup came about. "Lad, you do not know what you're saying."

Miserably, he replied, "That describes my whole life."

Seumas McCrae, sitting nearest, turned at this and goaded Waldroup: "Ah, go on, then, Alpin. Teach the boy the bow at least. You made us listen to your jabber long enough about how grand you are with it in your hand. Prove it."

From the doorway of his own hut, Clacher yelled, "You do it at day's end if you do it at all! I won't be losing quarry time over this, especially as we're down another pair of hands. And by that I mean you drag any more of them boys other than him into this at all and I'll send you packing, Alpin Waldroup."

Waldroup scowled at McCrae, then faced Clacher. "Lachlan," he said, "I wasn't even—"

Clacher only repeated, "Day's end!"

Waldroup finally bowed his head in capitulation and shook it slowly. "Fine," he told Thomas. "Day's end. I guess if you're training with me, at least you won't be off by yourself somewhere they can snatch you, too."

VI. Learning the Bow

True to his word, end of the day every day unless the rain was so torrential as to be blinding, Waldroup trained "Fingal" in the art of the bow, using broken scaffolding planks for targets. They practiced in the quarry, which, because of its closed shape, kept misaimed arrows from disappearing into the landscape. And despite Clacher's threat, they usually had an audience of three Selkirk boys, who were occasionally allowed to draw a bow themselves. Iachan had never returned and that trio now never went anywhere except together.

By fall's approach, "Fingal" had learned to hit the plank with nearly every shot. He proved to have a gift with the bow: He saw the shape of every arrow's flight before he let go, and it wasn't long before his hypothetical arc and the true one aligned almost every time. More than that, it seemed that, once shown something, Thomas couldn't forget it. Waldroup proclaimed him an excellent *target archer*. "Now you have the distance, we'll see how you handle firing on the run. Master that, and you'll truly be formidable."

His extraordinary memory also assisted in studying McCrae and the other craftsmen as they wielded mauls and chisels and scrapers to shape the mullions and intricate trefoil designs at the top of the openings, and to smooth the curves defining the arches until they almost mimicked folds of drapery. While the masons mixed mortar, passed hods up to the scaffolds, worked the treadwheels and lewises, Thomas practiced detailing in imitation of their work, using cracked or split pieces that lay scattered about, duplicating delicate tracery in cast-off chunks of stone. Amazed, Clacher proclaimed, "If t'was carpentry, I'd name ya Joseph." It was as if he'd been shaping stone since he was five. Thomas told an increasingly dumbfounded Waldroup that he thought his empty mind was just hungry to be filled up with everything.

Transforming as both bowman and mason, he was changing in other ways as well.

His fifteenth summer had seen a growth spurt. He stood now a full head taller than the spring day when Waldroup had found him—shorter than the unnocked bow, but nearly equal with Waldroup. They were close enough now in height and color that they might have been mistaken for a father and his sinewy, shaggy-haired son. The boy Waldroup had found among the graves had transformed.

In those five months, the new abbey had transformed, too. Its entire ambit was framed now, the south aisle built higher than the running mold around it, and higher than the lancet arches of the first four of its windows. When it was done, it would have eight of them.

The south transept extended higher than the door, and the east entrance had risen nearly to the height of its rose window. Clacher predicted that, with a few more men, they might finish the abbey in less than the ten years King David had required. He hoped to hire six more over the winter. But work would go slower next spring as they came to rely completely upon scaffolding, treadwheels, and lewises to place every stone.

It was on one cold autumnal day that a party of five influential men and women arrived at the abbey to behold its progress. Thomas, working with a brace and shell bits to grind small pock marks in the stones for the pincers of a lewis to grasp, glanced up and saw them on horseback. He was wearing a heavy shoulder cape with the hood up against the cold, and so half of his face remained concealed. It covered his look of shock.

"The helpers of the elven," Waldroup had called them, and here they were—the very ones who had taken Iachan. Had they been hunting for him?

The lead man wore a dark beard. Close up, Thomas saw that it was gashed on one side by a florid scar. One of the women was she who'd ridden past him as he crouched in the dark. She wore a wimple and the same headband, glinting with precious gems. She sat loftily, and held her fur-lined cloak tightly around her as she looked them all over. Thomas quickly bowed his head and pretended to concentrate all the more upon his work with the brace.

Clacher had left whatever he was doing, and walked past Thomas to intercept them. "Good sirs!" he called. "Alderman Stroud!"

The name was like a slap. It rang in his ears. Memories that had eluded him for all these months broke open. He heard his father call out the same way: *Alderman Stroud!* Welcoming the man to their home ... He could see home now, its stone walls, tapestries, the overhead beams. His mother, and Innes, his sister. He remembered them, knew them, knew his family's name. *Rimor de Ercildoun.* And this man, with the scar through his beard, had been a friend of his father's, or had pretended to be, in order to select Onchu for the elves.

Where was Waldroup? At the quarry probably or somewhere in-between with the cart and the oxen. The enemy had arrived, and he was nowhere about. Thomas looked for a direction to escape. If only he had his own bow. ...

The alderman was telling Clacher, "We were passing on our journey and wanted to see how the abbey is progressing."

He sighed. So they weren't here for him at all. Thomas lay down the shell bits. He sat still and listened.

Clacher had launched into a windy declaration of the magnificent design of the new abbey, praising the skills of his group of workers—how he had personally selected each of them, and how they hoped to complete the work in less time than even the king anticipated. He groused that he could certainly do with more workers, but, as they all knew, skilled masons were scarce.

The alderman replied, "You'll see some soon enough, I wager, now that the Battle of the Standard's resolved. Archbishop Thurstan raised an army, if it's all to be believed, and despite a determined campaign, the king lost against Stephen. Everybody's being sent home, save for Earl Cospatric. He's dead." He tittered as if at some private joke. "This winter will see any number of men returning, and none singing a paean to 1138, the year when King David was repelled."

Thomas's eyes went wide. He'd not thought to ask what year it was and nobody had said. But how could this be? It was 1135. The Year of Our Lord was one of the few things that stuck in his head back before the Queen had touched him. He knew the year with absolute certainty.

"Now, please, lead the way. We want to see how the transept is coming," Alderman Stroud said as he dismounted.

Clacher escorted the quintet past where Thomas sat upon the block of stone. From beneath his hood, he watched the alderman, followed by the woman and the one who had to be the taller man from the ruins, and another woman unfamiliar to him, her dress as green as summer. Then a third man walked up from behind him, and Thomas couldn't help glancing around. A heavy figure wearing a gray tunic under a heavy red cloak with gold-trimmed shoulder cape. His belly half obscured his belt. He slowed as he neared. Stopped.

The oddness of it made Thomas look up.

The reddish beard was thick. In the wind, where everyone's cheeks were pink and chafed, his remained so colorless it seemed no blood reached the skin. His expression remained almost vacant, as though the muscles of his face connected to nothing any longer— almost as empty as the last time Thomas had seen him, floating away in the river.

Baldie stood there, eyes as shiny and soulless as buttons, staring down at him, seemingly perplexed. More jowl and fat than at the river, but unmistakably Baldie.

Within the beard his mouth worked, as if uncertain of what he wanted to say. His voice grated like an old hinge. "Know you, do I?"

Thomas lowered his head and shook it vehemently. He kept his hands gripping the block of stone so as not to tremble.

In the distance, Alderman Stroud called, "Balthair, come along!"

Thomas stared down at Baldie's brown leggings and muddy shoes. If they stepped toward him, he would flee, but finally, and unsteadily as a drunk's, the legs walked off toward the abbey, followed by the horse.

Thomas lifted his head only enough to watch Baldie's red-draped back as he joined the alderman and the others. The five followed Clacher inside the abbey walls.

Setting down the brace, Thomas slid off the stone.

This surely couldn't be. Baldie was dead. How had they resurrected him? What had they turned him *into*?

That this Baldie nearly recognized him terrified Thomas. He wanted to find Waldroup's bow, string it, and kill them right now. But how would he ever explain to Clacher and the others what he'd done? Those five might conspire with the elven but they would die like anybody else, and he would be hanged for it. Who would listen to his claim that one of them was already dead, drowned? Even Alpin couldn't save him from being hauled before a reeve. In any case, Waldroup had taken the bow with him that morning. He wouldn't be using that.

Thomas paced around the stone. His head threatened to crackle with lightning, and he knew what that meant: a fit was coming. It had been so long, he'd thought himself free of them. But a fit here, now, and all of Stroud's party would realize who he was. He didn't dare remain.

He struck out, walking swiftly, not daring to run, around the eastern end of the abbey, away (he hoped) from where Clacher would regale the visitors with stories of the abbey's construction—off in the general direction of the quarry. He was just going off to help Waldroup. Was Baldie paying him any mind? He had to hope not.

He grit his teeth, balled his fists, fighting back the imminent seizure, muttering, "Not yet, not yet, not yet" in rhythm with his quick walk as he climbed the heights beyond, until he was halfway down the other side of the hill and out of sight. Then he gave in, let the lightning and the roaring fill his head. He dropped onto hands and knees and drowned in the blanketing wave of it. He thought he heard himself shout, bark, no idea what words if any poured forth.

When he came to his senses again, it seemed nothing had changed. Minutes not hours had passed. The light was the same or near as. He wiped at the foaming spittle at his lips, then unsteadily he got up. No one was watching. No one had heard him. All right, then.

He walked on, clumsy and slow, in the direction of the quarry.

The year was 1138. Waldroup confirmed what the alderman had said. Three whole years had somehow spun by without him. He was fifteen, but he ought to have been eighteen. The green fire had swallowed him and spat him back out in a different time.

"Lucky for you it did," Waldroup told him. "It's probably the reason you're still alive. If that very alderman and your drowned friend bestride the land now, you can be sure they'd have done for you if they'd caught you on the day."

Was his soul imperiled? Shouldn't he make some sort of confession to one of the monks who dwelled in the priory? Maybe get some blessing to repel them?

Waldroup advised against sharing the story with anyone. "Any one of those monks could be like your Alderman Stroud. If you've something to say, take your troubles up with God directly, as He won't share it with anyone. See it this way: Right now no one's looking for you. Or me, while we're about it. And I'd prefer they didn't have cause to. Now, come on, help us get that slab into the cart and then we'll head back to the abbey and have a look at them. I've never yet beheld a dead man who talks and rides."

But by the time they returned to the abbey with their quarried stone, the five visitors had gone. Clacher had abandoned his fawning attitude. In his opinion, they had come here just to pass some idle time, and hadn't really cared about how the work was going at all. "Very odd people," he said. "All they wanted to see was the north transept, what's hardly built and failed to impress. Didn't care about our work otherwise, and nary one smile between 'em, like strangers who had arrived together by accident."

When the first snow came, the workmen changed tactics. Instead of cutting and placing more stones, they piled a layer of straw and thatch on top of the highest row they had finished to protect it from moisture, and then lay one more row of stones on top of the thatch. Once that had been accomplished, there was no more quarrying to be done, no more work.

The abbey was going into hibernation for the winter.

VII. Ercildoun

The high street was a swill of snow and mud and rotting foodstuffs as the two men trudged into Ercildoun from the south.

Nothing much had changed in Thomas's three-year absence. Wood houses and buildings were laid out on both sides of the high street, one and two stories, in some places so tightly packed as to form a rampart of house ends with shared walls or, at most, small lanes between, leading to the narrow backland strips called rigs that extended out behind each house. Some rigs contained separate sties and stalls where byres weren't built onto the back end of the houses; on other plots it was kilns and ovens—fire sources and cooking hearths separated from main houses and shops to protect the entire town from accidental conflagration. On this cold day their smoke combined to haze the air blue. The street smelled of wood, bread, hops, manure, pottery, and hot iron. The mingle of smells shifted as they walked toward the bowyer's shop near the top of the hill. Nobody paid them much mind. They were dressed like any other men in their caps, heavy cloaks, and loose trousers.

Thomas counted windows, doors, footprints in the slush and people about. He watched for any of his own family, but saw no one he recognized, neither parents nor sister. Only four of the seventeen people looked at all familiar. He suspected he'd met them somewhere, sometime, but in his fuddled former life identities hardly ever stuck and everyone seemed strange. Those who glanced his way didn't give him a second look. *They don't recognize me at all.* It was both thrilling and disheartening, and he felt like a ghost wandering up the street.

His own family, when they did see him, would they know him? Would they believe him when he explained who he was? They had lost their sons already, three years gone.

Three years gone.

His brain seized upon the phrase, and a flash of lightning ripped through his head, a vision of Onchu riding behind the Queen, but he managed to wrestle this fit down, throwing himself against Waldroup, who held him upright. Through clenched teeth, he muttered the riddle so that only Waldroup heard: *"Three are dead, but only one gone, and two still striding in Ercildoun."*

Bracing him until he could stand, Waldroup eyed him askance. It was his first encounter with a fit since that night he'd found Thomas. "Is this going to happen a lot here?" he asked.

Thomas squeezed his eyes shut and concentrated on driving the lightning out of his brain. It shrank, dwindled as if rushing away. "I don't know," was all he could reply. "I thought the fits had left me until Baldie reappeared. Least, I—I didn't shout it. That's a first time, I think. And I pushed it away. Didn't used to know how to do that." After a moment he gently shook off the support.

"Still, your Baldie's from here, isn't he? Could be the place, the memory of it, sets you off. We'd best do our business, take a room, and lie low this night," Waldroup said. "Now, where's the bowyer's?"

Thomas pointed to the building beside the ironmonger's, noticing for the first time a wooden sign hung over the door—the carved image of an upright bow and vertical arrow side by side. That was new. There had been no such signage three years past. Glancing about, he saw another over the brewster's door, a wooden slab on which were carved what looked like a sprig of yellow gorse beside a rabbit. He couldn't figure how that represented anything at all.

"Let's see if your man at least has staves. You can pick one out and retrieve your bow come the thaw." Thomas followed him to the door, but Waldroup turned and put a hand on his chest. "What's your name then, stranger?"

"Fingal—" He paused and thought. "Fingal Coutts."

"Good." Waldroup opened the door. "After you, Squire Coutts."

"Squire?"

"Would you rather be my page?"

❈ ❈ ❈

Inside, the building was divided into a small workshop in the front, with the residence beyond a tapestry at the back. A bench occupied the center of the workshop, positioned to sit in the light from the window had the shutters been open. Along it were scrapers, a two-handled draw knife, assorted feathers, and arrows—some without fletching, some without tips. Wood shavings covered the floor like flakes of snow. It all smelled of freshly cut wood and oils.

One of the posts supporting the right-hand wall had two large pegs driven into it near the top. A bow lay across the pegs and would have formed a cross were it not for the cord strung from tip to tip and the large stone hanging from a hook at the cord's center, the weight of which pulled the bow down. In the low light it made the wall seem to be frowning at them. The bow was polished, and crisscrossed with sinew on either side of its the center.

The bowyer emerged from behind the tapestry. Warm air from the back arrived with him. He was thin, and all of his hair grew around the sides of his head. Thomas had seen him before, but it was clear he did not recognize Thomas.

"How may I assist you gentlemen?"

Waldroup explained, "My young squire here needs to acquire a bow."

"Ah, apprenticing in the art of warfare?"

"Cutting stone mostly, but, yes, a bit of that, too."

"Oh, you are from the abbey?" the bowyer guessed.

"We are, but winter's set on displacing us and it's time to hone other skills."

The bowyer looked Thomas up and down. "You're tall, young man," he said as if Thomas did not recognize that about himself. He walked to the bow that was being tugged upon by the stone weight. "This one might suit you well. I've been tillering it awhile now, driven out the flat places, the bit of warp. It's good yew."

"It isn't made for someone else?" Waldroup asked.

With closed eyes, the bowyer raised his brows. "It was, in fact, commissioned. But he has quite forgotten about it." He lifted the weight off the string and set it on the floor, then lifted the bow from the post and turned it upright.

"Who forgets ordering a bow like this?"

Now the bowyer stared straight at them, relishing the opportunity to gossip. "It is for a local man who came into wealth when his father and brothers died. He hardly remembers from week to week what he wants."

To Thomas it sounded almost as if the bowyer was describing him; but that couldn't be, as he had no other brother but Onchu. His sister, yes, but . . .

The bowyer continued, "He might recollect it by the time summer comes 'round again, so there's plenty of time to tiller him another, assuming you're a customer who pays." He compared the height of the straight bow to Thomas. "Yes, this will be a good fit for you, young man." He held it out.

Thomas took it. "Thank you," he said, then as Waldroup had shown him, he laid it across his palm. The slight curve floated on his hand.

"I see you *have* been training him, Sir Mason." He retrieved the bow. "You'll want arrows?"

"Yes," Thomas said. "I owe him two that shattered practicing."

The bowyer smiled. "Only two? Well, then, Squire—?"

"Coutts. Fingal Coutts."

The bowyer nodded. His eyes took in the purse hung on Thomas's belt, the larger one on Waldroup's. "Squire Coutts. If you return in the morning, I shall have it, and a dozen—that is, fourteen—arrows for you as well."

Waldroup patted him on the back. "This man knows his business. That's a fine bow to take with you."

The bowyer bowed his head in recognition of Waldroup's praise. "Then you're traveling?" he asked.

"For the winter," Waldroup said. He opened the door.

At the threshold, Thomas abruptly turned about. "The man you made this bow for. What might his name be?"

"Balthair MacGillean. Most folk hereabout call him—"

"Baldie," said Thomas.

The bowyer gave a look of mild surprise, but he was already out the door. Waldroup smiled ruefully to the man and said, "He, ah, visited us at the abbey. As you say, seemed distracted." Then he closed the door after him.

Thomas was headed across the wet mess of the road toward the brewster's. "So, a coincidence, the bow of the man who almost recognized you at the abbey," Waldroup asked as he caught up.

"But none of this is possible," said Thomas. "I told you what happened to me. Baldie was—"

"The one that drowned, aye, I know."

Thomas nodded grimly.

"Drowned three years past in a river, but he's viewing the abbey and ordering a bow?" Waldroup shook his head. "We know he's one of these servants of the elven, but even so—"

"His family's more than the equal of mine. They've land to the west of Ercildoun. He has two brothers, just as the bowyer said."

"Who also said he doesn't have them any longer. So perhaps, after all, he didn't drown. Maybe he was stunned, and swam to shore farther down. Someone rescued him after you gave chase for your brother. It's an easier explanation." He said it with the tone of someone waiting to be convinced.

"*Three are dead, two still striding in Ercildoun,*" he recited again, this time with understanding of his riddle. "One of those is me."

"You were dead as well?"

"I am to Ercildoun." He stared into Waldroup's eyes. "And Baldie's joined up with the alderman. He wouldn't have done that before."

"All right, but say for a moment he survived." Thomas started to object, but Waldroup held out his hand. "His family dies from some plague, he inherits all, and by the bowyer's description, it's left him in a bad state. The alderman's still an alderman for all that he may oversee the elven and their *teind*. You said your own father knows him. Why shouldn't Balthair MacGillean's relationship be the same as your father's, now that he's head of his family? What if he doesn't know anything about the alderman's service to these creatures?"

Adamantly, Thomas said, "He *didn't* swim to shore. He was dead in the river. I couldn't hold onto his body and he floated away, belly-down. He was drowned when the river took him."

Sloshing through the muck, Waldroup said, "So, what, then? He and the alderman are dead men? The servants of the elven are all of them dead men? What about the people I saw on the battlefield?"

Thomas made as if to respond but gave up.

"Elven have powers, and they're cruel, I'll give ye that. But can they revive the dead? I'm not ready to grant them the attributes of the Christ just now." He fell silent as they passed three other men. All nodded at one another. Once beyond them, he added softly, "Let us therefore strive not to call attention to ourselves tonight and be gone in the morning wi' your bow. Dead *or* alive, I don't crave their scrutiny."

The brewess introduced her alehouse as The Gorse and Hare, which explained at least the symbols on the sign over the door. They bought wooden tankards of ale from her and sat at the far end of a long central table that could accommodate twenty. She did have two curtained chambers at the very back of her establishment next to where large pots hung over a low fire, which were available for a night's stay at a reasonable price. The humid, smoky air smelled sourly of mash. Waldroup and Thomas chatted with her while she showed them the tiny sleeping arrangements. "We done all right 'ere. Used to be the byre was attached t'the back. But we went and built a second shed for stock. Turned the first into a threshing barn. 'usband tills a field farther out, but not now a'course. He's at mill today, down on the river."

By late afternoon, half a dozen locals had gathered around the long table with their tankards, talking of this or that. The bowyer himself arrived and sat among them, and Waldroup bought him a tankard.

The bowyer made introductions to the others, telling them that Waldroup and Thomas were stonecutters working on the abbey but that Waldroup was a sometime knight and "Fingal" his squire. One of the men asked how long they'd been on the job, and Waldroup replied that he'd arrived after fighting too long in France, while "Fingal turned up early this summer and has been working the quarry since." It was the truth, and if anyone in that group was looking for news of someone who'd vanished three years ago, those facts should have put them off the scent. It was clear that none of the men recognized Squire Coutts.

After a while, Waldroup leaned close to the bowyer. "I have to ask again. That fella whose bow you're selling us—you're *certain* he won't mind? Don't want to stir up trouble with a local laird."

The bowyer laughed. "Balthair? I don't even know why he wants one. I doubt 'e's ever as much as braced a bow. It's what I said to him, too. I swear, unless I remind him, he won't even take notice that he ordered one. If he purchases it, it'll just lie there and rot in the castle."

"You said his family all died?"

"Oh, yeah, yeah. Troubled clan, the MacGilleans, and God's smited Balthair in particular. Three years back, lad was fishing with two friends—well, a friend with a half-wit brother—and those two drowned. Devastated their family, the Rimors. Never recovered the bodies, even. River took 'em and probably washed them out to sea. Baldie did all he could to save 'em, but the idiot one pulled his brother under. Some as thought that boy had the gift of prophecy, but really, he didn't know up from down."

Thomas made to stand, but under the table Waldroup grabbed his wrist and held him in place.

"That's terrible," he said, "to have your children die before you."

"True enough. Family didn't want to believe it. For a long time they held out that the boys would return somehow. But that sort of hope is like a purse with a hole in the bottom. Sooner or later, you got nothing left."

Waldroup nodded. "That would seem to be a terrible fate dealt to the *Rimor* family, not this other fellow."

Thomas kept his eyes downcast, not daring to look up just then for fear of them flooding with tears.

"Oh, it was," the bowyer said. "Near broke their mother. But Baldie, now, he survives that, and we're all saying how lucky he is, you know, when not two months later his father falls into a well, breaks his neck. One of his brothers is so distraught he hangs himself, and the other—so far as anyone knows—drowns himself in the same river that Baldie crawled out of. History's repeating wheel of tragedy, innit? The perversity of things."

"Turned all around," agreed Waldroup. "I can see how with all that going on, he might forget about ordering a bow."

"Oh, well." The bowyer glanced aside. "I'd not quite come to that yet. There's still more to the tale. Ya see, our Baldie went and got married last year. To the daughter of that family what lost their sons."

Thomas couldn't help himself from saying her name. *"Innes?"* His horror was plain. The others at the table stopped their conversation and stared at him.

The bowyer said, "That's right. Innes Rimor. So, you *do* know these families, then."

"I . . ." He gave Waldroup a painful look, then got up and walked into the back.

Expectations swung slowly to Waldroup, who replied, "He's a sensitive lad, our Fingal. I believe he encountered that very girl on the road to the abbey. I know he was watching everyone on the street when we came into town today, hoping to see her again."

"Last summer, was it? Turned his head, I imagine. She *was* a beautiful girl, would hae been with child then, though."

"*Was* beautiful?"

The bowyer looked at the table, displaying the few remaining hairs on top of his head. The other men glanced away as if they had other things to consider. The bowyer tapped the edge of his tankard. "I shouldn't be saying all this. She lost her newborn just this month. Three weeks old when it withered and died. Midwife says it was a hard birth, too, so she'll have no others. Daren't even try, and the poor girl only seventeen. Gone mad, she has."

"Jesus have mercy."

"Indeed, I expect it's only prayer to Him that's kept poor Balthair sane amidst all that death. It's a curse for sure. But now you understand why he won't notice if the bow goes elsewhere. Somewhere far away is better."

Waldroup drank his ale down and stood. "Don't think I'll tell young Fingal that, as I know he did fancy her." Now the men looked up at him, nodding, agreeing that anybody would have fancied her. To the bowyer, he added, "In the morning, then, sir."

"Oh, yes." The bowyer emptied his own tankard and stood. He smiled. "Small beer in my case. Can't afford to muddy my faculties, can I? Not tonight. Arrows still to fletch, hmm?" He turned and headed for the door. The others pretended not to watch Waldroup retreat into the back, and whatever counsel they kept, they kept it to themselves.

VIII. Innes

Waldroup was snoring in the brewster's, completely unaware that Thomas had stolen out the back, through the barn, and between the buildings. He strode swiftly across the high street, up the hill, and out of the town. All he wanted was to see his sister and to know she was safe—at least that was his rationale for sneaking off on his own.

Innes had never been the least attracted to Baldie. Of that much Thomas was certain. He knew of no discussion between his parents on the subject of her marrying into the MacGillean clan, either, though admittedly they might have had discussions where he wasn't present, in body or in mind. There *could* have been plans to marry her to one of the older MacGillean boys. The union would have been considered a good one for both families, not a step up but certainly a doubling of holdings, of prominence. In truth he—the idiot son whom everyone dismissed—knew nothing of that, did he? It wasn't as if his opinion would have been solicited. Nobody had ever planned to marry him off to anybody. Even the Church wouldn't have him. Still, his parents had no reservations speaking of that in front of him; why would they not have spoken of such a profitable union? But *Innes*? Innes had been quite obsessed with another boy entirely.

He had to find out the truth.

The home of clan MacGillean, northwest of the town, was a square stone keep on a motte built inside a rectangular palisade wall with towers at the corners and an entrance that was a single large gate with a drawbridge over an enclosing ditch. To his knowledge, the bridge had never been raised. As a child in his brother's company,

51

he had spent days and nights inside the walls and in the keep. It was the first stone keep he'd ever seen—every other castle he knew had keeps made of wood. It had recesses in its walls with holes above them, so that fires could be lit in every room, not just in the center of the great hall. As a result of all the burning for warmth, he smelled the castle long before he reached it.

Baldie and Onchu had shown him secret entrances in various rooms and led him along subterranean passages and into chambers, sometimes to see if they could lose him, because such dark mysteries were what boys invariably sought out. Once, the two of them had locked Thomas in a dark cell deep below the tower (there were three), but when he didn't scream or cry, they'd let him out. It was useless trying to frighten someone without enough sense to know they ought to be scared.

An escape tunnel led under the palisade and ditch to a small mound overgrown with saxifrage east of the house; only he, his brother, and Baldie had seemingly ever set foot in it. No one had ever attacked the MacGilleans; no one walked the ramparts at night. No one used the tunnel. He saw no reason to claw his way in through it now. Instead, he crept through the gate, then pressed to the shadows of the palisade, and stood awhile to observe the yard. The stables and byre were at the far end of it, against the north wall. Not far from there stood a hall, workshops, and barracks. Close by stood a kitchen hut, and beside it the well where, presumably, Baldie's father had fallen in.

Smoke drifted out the holes in most of the roofs. The moonlit yard itself lay abandoned, still; no one appeared to be walking the parapet or manning any of the towers.

Shutters and sheets of parchment covered the windows in the small buildings and those of the keep. It was a drafty old keep, colder than any of the houses in the town if the fires weren't tended, even though its walls were almost as thick as the abbey's. He ran across the yard, then dashed up the steps of the motte. At the top he turned and watched the walls and yard. Nothing stirred.

The main door was not locked, but it groaned and shuddered at his touch. It had always been creaky. He pressed it open only enough to let him slide through. He stood still again, listening for footsteps, for any sound that he had alerted someone to his presence. They might think a wind had pushed at the door, or perhaps some ghost was creeping about. How many people would be in the keep as opposed to the other, warmer buildings across the yard?

He hurried up the first flight of steps, which led to a gallery above the empty, uninviting ground floor. The entrance had a trapdoor that could be dropped and bolted in an attack. The gallery contained windows overlooking the entrance that Baldie claimed were for shooting down at any enemy that made it through the doors. Beyond the gallery stood the great hall.

It was dark, all torches extinguished; the low fire still burned in the shallow hearth, but its heat was being drawn out through the hole above it. Shadows danced like goblins over the walls and hangings. Someone had tended to that fire sometime within the last hour, but he saw no sign of them. He crept into the smoky hall.

Years earlier, Onchu and Baldie had picked him up and tried to stuff him up into the hole that overhung it. But the exhaust holes were hardly more than slits, and he'd hung from one of them instead, perfectly content to be smeared with grease and soot, again frustrating his tormenters. Now he crossed to the projecting slab of stone and crouched to warm his hands over the low flames. He could see his breath in the air. He recollected the layout of the other, chambered floor above.

Warmed, he rose again, ready to move, when there came a pounding at the door below. Fast as he could he scampered across the room, past a table that could easily seat a dozen, and behind a large decaying tapestry that hid one of the secret passage entrances. He had just ducked out of sight when, overhead, footsteps thudded across the beams. Someone spoke down below. Apparently a servant had been sleeping there. Somehow Thomas had missed him.

He knelt, and squinted through a section of the tapestry all but devoured by moths; the remaining threads made it like observing activity through a dense screen.

Shortly, the servant ushered someone up across the gallery and into the hall. Cautiously, Thomas drew the edge of the tapestry aside.

It was the alderman, Stroud.

"Thank you," the alderman said to the servant. "I shall wait here for your master."

The servant had hardly taken a step to go fetch him when Baldie appeared. He was fully dressed and wearing a heavy robe against the chill. Given the footsteps above and how quickly he'd arrived, it did not seem he had been sleeping.

The servant bowed before him and then hurried to the hearth, tossing two more logs onto the fire. Thomas drew farther back behind the tapestry, almost flat against the wall so that no hint of him would be visible.

The servant began poking at the crackling logs, and the flames jumped. The room grew brighter. Baldie called out, "Leave us!" The servant laid down the poker and scurried away like someone who'd been kicked before for not moving fast enough. Baldie's voice was that same raw croak as at the abbey.

He and the alderman crossed to the long dining table and sat down at one corner. The alderman said, "Two men are in the town, masons they claim to be, one an apprentice who seems to know of you and Innes in a way that concerns me. He is perhaps fifteen. Dark-haired, lightly bearded. I'm told he reacted strongly to your names."

"You think it's he?"

"It is just possible, though he wore his cap all the while and never babbled nor suffered a fit. By description he sounds too steady and too *young* for him, but we cannot be sure. And you mentioned there was someone among the laborers at the abbey."

"Memory too vague to offer proof. More a whiff than a recognition. How does yours come to know our Innes?" asked Baldie. "When might she have made a mason's acquaintance?"

"It's claimed he encountered her last summer upon a path to the abbey and was smitten by her beauty. Perhaps he walked through the town and down to the river? No one would have noticed."

Baldie shook his head. "I think it improbable he could have met her. We'd bound her to us before summer—before even we dispatched the last MacGillean brother."

"But she did pass from here to her family home on occasion. She did travel through Ercildoun."

"Twice, but since the arrival of the changeling, the glamouring, she's remained spellbound to her chamber. No, I think we do not believe this story as it's being presented."

"I thought as much, too, Elgadorn."

"So it must be he, else he's a puppeteer."

"If not one of these cutters, might he have sent them to test our vigilance? It seems—"

Baldie shook his head. "You'd give him the wits for subterfuge. He's hardly any wits at all. The Balthair knew him very well."

The alderman made a gesture of bewilderment. "Then, we are confounded. A boy too young to be him, asking after your wife, probing. Mayhap someone from this household has said something—one of those you dismissed? And, yes, we know you dismissed them early, but still, if even one gleaned some hint of the changeling before we placed the nurse ... Thinks me we've no choice but to meet these two before they return to the abbey and share their story further." He made a gripping gesture with his fists. "We must twist the truth from them."

Baldie considered a moment before asking, "Where and when?"

"The bowyer says they intend to go south tomorrow. And here's an irony—it's your bow they're collecting."

Baldie smirked lopsidedly, as if one side of his mouth was not working. "We believe the Balthair wants it back. Clearly, they're thieves."

"Clearly. They'll certainly take the corpse road across the river to the old abbey ruin. They brought nothing with them—no provisions or travelers' packs—so they must be returning to the new abbey site. They'll have to pass our spot."

"We shall bring reinforcements," said Baldie. "Whatever their story, well, it won't matter once they're on the other side. Just two travelers waylaid by the road. Who will even notice? Come spring, they'll be forgot."

The alderman closed his eyes as if imagining it. Then the two of them rose and left the hall.

A minute later, the rusty groans and thunder of the main door closing below echoed up the circling stairwell. Thomas waited behind the tapestry until Baldie had walked past the hall again and up the stone steps to the third floor. The servant did not reappear to stoke the fire, which burned brightly now in the empty, smoky room, giving off some measure of heat. Overhead, footsteps clumped about once more, and then there was silence.

For a moment he relived the experience of creeping up the hidden passage to the corridors of the upper floor and going from chamber to chamber in search of his brother and Baldie. Directly overhead was the patriarch's dwelling, a large room comprising great beams and uprights and a huge curtained bed. His wife maintained a separate, smaller chamber—or rather, she had—across the hall. He knew the secret way up, through the wall, but all would be pitch black in the passage and he had no torch to guide him. Besides, it would dump him in the patriarch's chamber with Baldie. That was not where he wanted to go.

Thomas stole out from the tapestry and across the gallery. He watched down below for any sign of the servant, but there was no one. He guessed the servant might have exited with the alderman. He climbed the stone steps fast, bent low, slowing as he reached the second floor, his eyes at the level of the narrow corridor floor. The doors hung closed on each side.

He stepped into the corridor, waited, then crept along it until he arrived at the point where the patriarch's door was to his left, the uxorial chamber to his right. There was nothing for it. If Innes was spellbound to her room as Baldie had described, then she must be in there and not with her husband.

Pressed to the door, he tried to hear over the roar of his own heartbeat in his ears. Nothing. If she screamed or was possessed, then in a moment he would be running for his life. But he had to know.

Cautiously, he pushed down the handle of the door and eased it open. Firelight played upon the walls of the room as it had the great hall, though in a far smaller, shallower fire pit. The narrow windows were covered in parchment, but the smoke was drawn out through them, leaving the upper part of the room thick with it, like a fog.

Although the alderman had mentioned a nurse, he hadn't counted upon her sleeping at the foot of the bed.

Was it Innes under the bedclothes and furs? It must be. Still—this nurse was an unanticipated problem, surely another enemy.

He cast about for something to subdue her. He had brought nothing, no weapon.

A small log stood upright beside the little hearth, ready to be added to the fire if needed. He crept to it and took it with him to the bed. At the foot, he stood, hefting the log, but unable to strike the sleeping servant, a thick-bodied girl of perhaps twenty. She might

have been the second woman in the group that visited the abbey—
he couldn't be sure. What sort of misplaced chivalry kept him from
striking this creature? He did not know, and had no time to consider
it. He leaned in close and whispered to the nurse.

Before she was entirely conscious, she sat straight up, saying
"M'lady?" and Thomas clubbed her with the log. She fell against the
footboard and slid back into her own small berth. One arm dangled
out of the bed, and he gingerly laid it back across her, then set down
the log.

When he turned, his sister was sitting up and staring wide-eyed.
She hadn't screamed yet, but she looked about to.

"Innes," he said. He moved slowly, unthreateningly along the bed,
and had the presence of mind now to remove his cap. His shaggy
dark hair spilled out around his face. He reached toward her. "Sweet
sister."

He knew his voice was changing, deepening, but she replied with
"Thomas?" A question, yet she seemed to know—her expression
wondrous—and he hurried to embrace her then and let her see his
face clearly.

She reached out, and he took one of her thin hands, pressed it to
his lips, looked into her darkly sunken eyes. The smell off her was
unwashed and sickly. Her cheeks that had been full and flushed were
tight upon her bones and waxy pale. Her dark, matted hair hung
lank. It was as if she were being kept in a pigsty.

Innes studied him just as intently, no doubt seeking the signs of
her brother, who ought to be older than she, not to mention simple-
minded, unlikely to sneak successfully into any room or move with
any grace or skill. Yet in the end she broke into a wide smile and said,
"It *is* you, isn't it? Oh, my dear Tommy." She clutched him to her and
he embraced her. His fingers counted her ribs. "Where have you
been? Is Onchu alive, too?"

He sat upon the fur. "He's been taken."

"Taken?" Her expression shifted in confusion. "Then he is with
God?"

"No. The elven took him while he was fishing."

Her expression flowed then from doubt to judgment: He was still
her mad brother, who spoke in riddles that rarely made sense. He
could not let her settle upon that conclusion.

"I know that Baldie claims he saw us drowned, but it's not true. *He* was the one who drowned; I saw him, Innes. Onchu was taken by the elves' queen. When I tried to chase them—I would have brought him back!—something happened to me, and three years passed me by as if I didn't exist. I can't explain it."

"Balthair drowned?"

He nodded furiously. "I know how it sounds. Men in Ercildoun told me how he came back alone with his story of both of us dead." Her glimmering gaze held his, rapt. "I'm not a ghost, Innes. And I didn't drown Onchu."

"But how is—how is *he* alive, then?" She gestured at the door.

"I don't know. But he is in league with Alderman Stroud, who helps the elven select their victims. He was on hand the day they took Onchu. I saw him plain."

She looked away from him then, her brows drawn together. "The alderman . . . He took an interest in the family after—after you and Onchu were gone. He consoled Mother, gave her a potion to calm her. He's been advising Father ever since. It was he who made this union with Balthair. And they meet often, the two of them. I hear them."

"They've met just now below. The alderman intends to take me on the road this morning, as he did Onchu. You mustn't tell Baldie that I was here."

"But Thomas, Mother and Father need to know you're alive!"

He shook his head. "No. You can't—" he began, but lightning shot through his head and he pitched against her. Heard his own voice recite: "*Who am I, brings calamity like weather? Best you don't know me, else drown in the torrent, your blood or theirs.*"

In the spangled darkness that followed, the pressure retreated slowly, until he became aware of his body again. The words stayed with him for once. It was himself he'd described, he was sure. He brought calamity: on Alpin, on Innes if anyone knew he'd been here, on the masons at the abbey if the alderman thought for a moment he'd shared any stories with them. He smelled Innes in the linens pressed to his face. Her hand was stroking his head and she was shush-shushing him as if he was her child.

He pushed up onto his elbows. Had he shouted the words? He twisted about to watch the door, but nobody opened it, and Innes said, "It's all right, Tommy."

"No, it's not. I imperil everyone here. If Baldie learns you've spoken with me . . . You can't tell him. Nor Father and Mother, not yet. It would put you all at risk now."

She dropped her fingers from his hair. "Sweet brother."

The servant at the foot of the bed moaned vaguely.

"I need to be gone. I don't want to hit her again."

Innes held his forearm tightly in her small and bony hand. "When will I see you next, then?"

"Let's learn first what the alderman has in mind for me." He leaned forward and kissed her forehead, whispered in her ear, "I'm so very sorry for the loss of your child, but promise me you won't die because of it. Live to make another."

Her eyes filled with tears. She said, "But what are you saying? He's not lost. He's there, Thomas." She pointed to a cradle across the room past the nurse's bed. "Little Dougal."

He rose and looked at her, at the cradle, at the nurse, who did not stir. Uneasily, he crossed the room.

"Is he sleeping?" Innes called softly. "He's so good and never cries at night."

Thomas bent over the cradle. In the firelight he saw it quite clearly and it saw him as well. *The changeling.*

He gasped and drew back.

One green-black creeper emerged from the misshapen bundle of sticks and twigs, and slid up over the edge of the cradle as if to reach him. The eyes were holes between the woven twigs.

The nurse groaned and her head lolled.

Thomas backed away from the cradle, turned to his sister.

Spellbound to her chamber. Was it the room itself, glamoured for her? She had no way to know and could not tell him. No doubt Baldie had put it about that her baby had withered and died, and that she was mad in her grief. People would give a madwoman a wide berth. But his parents? How were they kept away?

If the room was glamoured for anyone who entered . . . then how was it that he saw true? He could not fathom the magic, but knew without doubt that the thing would shortly alert the elven servant when she came to her senses, and Baldie as well.

He could not remain another moment. "I will come back," he told Innes. "I promise."

He ran to the door. Innes reached for him, called to him. He shushed her and opened her door. For an instant the flames in the hearth fluttered, painting her drawn, wet face fearfully against the darkness. He took with him that final image of her and of the vegetative thing beyond her rising up out of its crib.

Something thumped in the patriarch's chamber, and he flew down the corridor, the many steps, and out the ancient door. If anyone saw him scurry across the yard and set off at a dead run for the dark distant myth of Ercildoun, they didn't raise an alarm or race after him. His sister wasn't mad, but she would be if Baldie and Stroud had their way. Whereas, he, a ghost, could do nothing here but escape.

IX. Corpse Road

Early in the morning, at the bowyer's they collected Thomas's bow and a belt quiver filled with a mix of both target and war arrows, fourteen in all. Waldroup bought two knives. His own bow he'd left back at the abbey, a decision he now regretted.

They paid the bowyer and headed south out of the town. Beyond the snow-topped trees and grasses, the Leader Water wove in and out of view on their left.

They had no sense of being followed along the road, but then they knew already where their enemy intended to confront them.

As they walked, Waldroup commented, "If it were me, I'd choose the bridge over the Tweed."

"Why there?"

"We have to cross it, and once we're on the bridge they have only to arrive at both ends to trap us. No choice then but to capitulate or jump into the river and drown."

"But the alderman said they want to take us at their *spot*."

"And we think that's where they carried off your brother, where I found you," Waldroup said. "Well, it does have convenient ruins to hide among, and we'd best make use of them ourselves if we do get across that bridge. If they haven't arrived first. Our only advantage right now is that we know they're coming. And if they've opened that ring of theirs, let those spinose knights in, I fear we're finished."

They trudged on through the muddy snow awhile before he added, "Remember all you've learned."

❊ ❊ ❊

61

Near where the Leader fed into the Tweed, the woods grew thicker, offering plenty of cover for anyone to waylay the passing traveler. The area had a reputation for occasional thievery, but usually in better weather. Heavy branches here would spill snow on anyone trying to sneak among the trees this morning.

They soon reached the top of the final hill descending to the Tweed bridge, and paused to study the landscape all the way to the far side. Even though between them they had come to the old abbey many times, from this side of the river everything looked different to Thomas.

The scattered graves looked like a cut-down young forest, like stumps poking out of the snow, dotting the way, eighty-two of them. The abbey's thatch roof was itself half-rotted. The stones of the nearest corner were fallen in, leaving a dark, gaping emptiness. He'd looked in there the once, into the crypt, not a place he cared for; then again, that hole amidst the rubble might make an excellent defensive position if the two of them could reach it. Beyond the ruin, the remains of the round monks' huts stood like close-pressed hillocks across the rocky landscape. Most of them stood roofless, a few half-collapsed. It all seemed exactly as abandoned as the evening Waldroup had found him. Maybe with their early start they were ahead of the alderman and Baldie.

Thomas stared at the spot where Onchu had ridden out of the world—no burning green fire on display. Not yet.

The bridge ahead was large enough for a stone-laden ox cart to cross, rutted and slushy from someone's recent cart wheels.

"The alderman called this a corpse road. I remember my father calling it that, too."

Waldroup nodded. "For the bodies carried straight from Ercildoun to the graveyard. Likely why the bridge was built. And in time it becomes the main road, to the abbey, then to Roxburgh and Selkirk. Everything passes this way. Didn't give it a moment's thought when we set off to buy your bow, did we? It's just the way to town."

"We should have taken Onchu's fishing path instead."

"To avoid them? But who's to say they'll ride to Ercildoun first? You don't know where they'll catch up to you, only that they *will*. Me, I'd rather choose where. It's that much advantage, a luxury that may yet save your life."

Thomas shook his head. "I'm not very good at strategies."

"And yet, you're the reason we know we're expected." He nodded at the way ahead as they descended to the bridge. "The half-melted snow doesn't help. Hides any tracks a full snowfall might have revealed." He stared off in silence awhile. "You notice anything peculiar?"

Thomas squinted, shook his head again.

"What animals you see? Hear any birds?"

Silence and stillness. "But there are *always* birds."

"Mmm-hmm. And when's the last time you crossed that plot of graves without spying a hare or two?"

"When Onchu . . ."

Waldroup patted his shoulder. "Come on. Pretend you suspect nothing, and let's try and get set in amongst the graves at least before they reveal themselves."

They walked over the bridge without incident.

"Your alderman's not much of a strategist, either," he muttered. "Too certain of his cleverness."

Across, they walked through river sedge and soon reached the outer ring of graves. Thomas continued to find his attention drawn to the spot where the hole between worlds had burned in the air. Maybe a corpse road arrived on purpose at a place where the wall between worlds was thin. Maybe it had led here before there was an abbey. *Before there were even monks.* He'd thought that about Old Melrose itself before—that it had been a sacred, maybe haunted, site long before the monks had come. Onchu would be just on the other side, seemingly only a few steps and three years away.

A premonition settled upon him like a chill. He held the strung bow straight down against his hip, but with his other hand he drew three arrows from his quiver one by one and fitted the fletches between the knuckles of his bow hand. He hadn't yet mastered holding them in his drawing hand the way Waldroup did.

By now they should have turned and been heading along the path to the new abbey, but instead they continued in amongst the graves. By now anyone watching would have recognized the deviation.

The riders emerged from behind the old abbey. Two rode out from behind the monks' huts, three around the ruin itself, past where the stones had fallen in. Alderman Stroud and Baldie rode together.

The other three men seemed like regular soldiers, like ... Alpin Waldroup.

Thomas kept the bow down, though they would have seen it, knew he had it, but perhaps he would not seem much of a threat to them. He'd never been much of a threat to anyone ever. Fear burned sharp in his belly. He would fail. He should hand the bow to Waldroup now while there was time. But when he offered it, he realized that Waldroup had moved off to the side, putting distance and several gravestones between them. The alderman guided his horse as if to intersect Waldroup's path. Thomas threaded his way between the skull-headed stones.

One of the five men on horseback had a bow, too. The other two soldiers were armed with swords.

The alderman called to him. "Squire Fingal Coutts, we arrest you and your companion for the theft of that bow, which by all rights belongs to Balthair MacGillean, for whom it was made."

It was the accusation they had rehearsed the night before. He answered it directly. "I paid for this. Ask the bowyer in Ercildoun. He sold me it and the arrows."

The alderman smirked, clearly amused that Thomas even bothered to offer a defense against the pretense of a legal charge. In the face of such dismissal, Thomas's fear of him turned hot. "Take them, then." He held the bow above his arm, as if offering it to the trio of soldiers. They came ahead faster, arriving at the graves.

The one bowman among them had to guide his horse around a large broken marker. For a moment he looked down to navigate as he tugged at the reins.

Remember all you've learned.

Thomas turned his bow and fired. No doubt the movement made the soldier glance up, but he was only in time to take the arrow in his breastbone and not his skull. His head snapped back. His arms, guided by some instinct, fired his own nocked arrow. It skidded wide, in among the graves. The soldier fell from his horse.

With drawn swords, the other two kicked their horses to a gallop. Thomas had already nocked his second arrow, and he shot the nearest soldier from his horse. But his third passed over the horse's mane and under the soldier's hand gripping the reins, and sword raised he rode Thomas down.

Instinct deserted him. He froze, unable to do anything but watch his death arrive.

Then from nowhere a knife caught the soldier in the temple, embedded to the hilt, and he seemed to spring from his mount, losing hold of his sword as he fell. His panicked horse hauled him straight into the horse in front of him, and he fell under its hooves, though it was doubtful by then he noticed.

The alderman and Baldie sat their mounts side by side, chestnut and skewbald, and made no move to attack. The alderman was animated, but Baldie's dull expression never changed, like a mask over his real face. Thomas nocked another arrow.

Alderman Stroud considered the bodies around him, as if none of the deaths meant anything. He raised one hand in acquiescence. "Very well. Further shooting is unnecessary. We sought you gentlemen of the road and we found you. Answer our questions and you can leave. You can even keep the bow. We will not seek retribution for the loss of these . . . deputies."

"You might've said that first instead of threatening us with arrest for the theft of something you well knew we didn't steal. Then your deputies would yet live," said Waldroup.

The alderman looked between them as if uncertain where to start, who to address.

Waldroup grunted. "Have ye any real questions at all?"

Baldie interjected, demanding of Thomas, "Tell me how you know my good wife."

Thomas opened his mouth but made no answer. Inside his head lightning sizzled. *Not now, please, not now!* He began to choke, and doubled over. He glimpsed Waldroup turning toward him, then looking at the other two as if they'd provoked the fit with their magic, but this had come like all the others before it. He dropped to his knees. The new arrow he'd drawn spilled from his useless, twitching fingers. He gasped raggedly, heard himself stammer:

"N-no union is sacred,
no couple be bound,
when a wake be their joining,
death shares their bed."

He sprawled onto his side, his legs jerking.

Baldie sat stricken. "Thomas Rimor?"

"Then it *is* he," said the alderman. "O, glorious day. We account for him at last." He paused only an instant before he charged Waldroup, so fast and close that it was all Waldroup could do to spring aside; a hoof struck him a blow in the hip and spun him in a new direction, where he landed hard against the edge of a gravestone.

Thomas heard it all. With all of his will, he made himself rise to his knees.

The alderman rode past him, and like a man half his age he leapt from his horse. It only took him two steps to reach the spot where Onchu had been taken, raise his hand as if to command the sky, and then begin to draw downward, leaving a crooked line of green fire burning in the air.

Waldroup sprang clumsily off the gravestone where he'd fallen, both hands raised over his head. As he dropped he plunged his remaining knife into the alderman's shoulder. Stroud howled, and dropped a small black object he'd been holding. The green fire burned like a puckered scar but no portal expanded from it. It was too small and malformed. Waldroup tumbled to the ground and Stroud kicked him in the head.

Thomas reached for the spilled arrow, dragged it to him, and slapped it against his bow. From his left, Baldie charged, and he barely rolled away before the hooves could strike him.

Instead of coming for him again, Baldie kicked his horse faster to ride down Waldroup, sword now drawn for the kill. Thomas rolled to his knees again and with the bow laid horizontally fired his one arrow. It struck Baldie square in the back and threw him against his horse's neck. The sword flew from his grasp and his horse ran on past Waldroup, nearly knocking down Stroud.

The alderman fled on foot. He wove among the graves and ducked through the opening in the broken corner of the old abbey before Thomas could scrabble to nock another arrow or stand up.

Baldie's skewbald horse had come to a stop. It turned, backed up, sidestepped, responding to confused signals from its rider, until it had come about. Baldie tried to sit upright. The gory head of the arrow pushed out from between his ribs. Hunching, he held both hands wide in a gesture of surrender. "Now, wait, Thomas, wait."

Thomas held another arrow ready for his bow. "You told everyone I drowned my own brother."

"We had to offer *some* story that would be believed. You were both gone."

"You took my sister, stole her will, swapped her baby for a . . . a *thing*."

Behind him, Waldroup groaned. He gasped out, "'A wake be their joining,' hey?"

"I'm *Balthair*. Listen, I'm your brother-in-law now, Thomas." He wrapped one hand around the shaft of the arrow and tried to pull it, but it was slick with blood and his hand slid around the tip. It must have cut him, but he didn't react. He kept attempting to pull it to no avail.

"Baldie drowned. I saw him. E'en held him for a moment."

Blood was trickling from Baldie's mouth, bubbling and foamy on his lips with each labored breath. His skin was pale, gray. He squeezed his eyes shut in pain, though even then his expression remained cold and uncanny. He leaned forward until he lay against the horse. When he opened his eyes next, for one brief instant he was Baldie again, a friend behind his boasts. "Hey-o, Tommy," he wheezed. "Thankee." His body began to shake then. A red mist burst into the air as if erupting from his pores. It was like nothing Thomas had ever seen and it evaporated in an instant. Then Baldie's face went slack and more than slack. His mouth seemed to slough down toward his chin. The skin around his eyes, his cheeks, the flesh on his outstretched fingers, all melted like candlewax, and he pitched sideways and fell. He landed in the wet snow like a rupturing winesack and lay still.

Waldroup managed to pull himself up against a gravestone to view the corpse. Mud and blood smeared his face. "Sweet Jesus. What *was* he?"

As if in reply, from the depths of the old abbey behind them came an inhuman screech.

"He was Baldie, but he wasn't anymore. Only at the very last . . ."

Waldroup tried to stand, but almost stumbled, and clung to the gravestone, wincing. "I'm going to need a minute or two. The alderman, Thomas. He has our answers. We have to stop him escaping, can't let him bring others."

Thomas got up, gathered his arrows back into his quiver. Then, cautiously, he approached the line of green fire. Close, it hissed like fatty meat dripping on a spit. He crouched and retrieved the black thing the alderman had dropped. It was a peculiar stone, the same one he'd used to open the way before the Queen of Ailfion. It was circular, polished, and black with greenish-gray pebbling. One edge was scalloped, something like the way a flint ax head might look, but much more precisely cut. Indentations ran from between the scallops, and each one seemed to glow a deep glittering blue, a crescent of jewels. It fit his hand, and was warm as if it had been set near a fire.

He glanced at Waldroup, balanced on one leg and warily watching; then he touched the stone to the bottom of the fire, drew upward back along the line. The fire vanished as if he'd wiped it away until there was nothing but a thread of smoke.

Waldroup sighed with relief. "I thought sure 'twould kill you if you touched it."

"So did I."

"Brave or foolish lad you are, Tommy."

"If we can close it, then probably we can open it again, too."

"Well, leave it closed for now. I don't want to face more of them. Save opening for another time." He gestured to the abbey door. "The alderman."

"What screamed?"

Waldroup shook his head. "He maybe let something loose in there. Wait for a moment and I'll come with you."

Thomas smiled but proceeded.

"Be careful, then, little brother." It was what he had called Thomas the first time they'd met on this spot, the same thing Onchu had always called him. "I'll be right behind you, if a bit slow."

Thomas crept to the ruins, bow at the ready, and peered around the edge of the hole. Then he stooped and ducked inside the abandoned abbey.

X. Among the Ruins

Light poured down into the abbey, most of it through the open sections where the roof thatch had rotted away. Some thatch lay upon the floor, covered with unblemished snow, no footprints to indicate that anyone had fled to the far end. The only footprints descended the stone steps to the dark crypt beneath what had been the nave.

Thomas stood at the top, motionless, taut as his bowstring. Then came the sound—a faint, grating, scraping sound. Stone against stone.

He went cautiously down the nine steps, knowing he was vulnerable, visible in the one large shaft of light, the narrow space confining him to pressing his bow close, no way to fire it.

New pressure grew in his head. He stopped, ready to fight off the seizure, to lurch back up the steps, but no fit manifested and the pressure remained. As his panic subsided, he took stock of the sensation, recognized how it was different, yet familiar. He knew it now: the pressure of the Queen and her soldiers as they'd passed him by on that summery day—the chirring whispery words of a language he did not understand. Where was it coming from now? Had the alderman opened a new gate to his world after all?

Thomas descended cautiously. The chirring grew louder. It was if he were entering a field full of crickets.

The crypt was significantly dimmer than above—enough so that he held his position on the bottom steps, bow drawn, while his eyes adjusted to the gloom.

Six funnel-shaped pillars supported the ceiling in two rows of three, while eighteen recesses lined the long side walls. These looked to contain bones—the remains of monks, or perhaps abbots. Down the center of the crypt stood four stone vaults, which appeared to be identical at first. But the lid on the last one was askew. He crept the rest of the way down, but kept his attention on that last box between the pillars.

Nothing moved, though surely Alderman Stroud knew he was here. The alderman must be behind one of the pillars or crouched behind one of the vaults. Or else he had climbed into that last vault but not had time to pull the lid straight in order to hide. Thomas remained at the base of the stairs, where he could see all of the space. Impatiently, he waited for his enemy to show himself.

The crooked lid of the last vault lifted and budged slightly, the grinding sound of it almost painful. It wasn't being drawn closed. It was sliding open.

Thomas crept to the nearest pillar, bow raised now. He edged around it and stole to the next. Leaned out enough to watch the fourth vault.

A pale, iron-colored hand with long insectile fingers and growths like thorns dotting its knuckles reached out of it, grabbed hold of the lid. Another hand clutched the lip of the vault itself, and a figure sat up in the opening, head peering out. It was sharp-faced, sheathed in chitinous black—spiky and unnatural all over, it seemed. Like its fingers, the face was abnormally long. The creature pulled itself up, one arm seeming to bend the wrong way, and stood unsteadily, surveying the vault. It stared right at the pillar behind which he hid. Too late now—he'd been seen.

Thomas stepped out and loosed his arrow. It struck the creature solidly in the chest, but instead of killing it, the arrow only knocked it off-balance; the arrow bounced off the hard black armor, and the creature caught itself against the vault before it could fall. It hissed and its golden eyes fixed on him.

At the same moment, he saw his error. It hadn't been him the creature spied. The alderman lunged around the pillar and struck him from behind, a hard blow to the head that drove Thomas against the side of the nearest vault. He doubled over it, fell to his knees, then scrambled away as something struck the stone where he'd been, sending up gravel-like bits. He embraced the second vault, head still ringing, then turned around.

The alderman wielded a thigh bone in his good left hand, raised now to bash in Thomas's face, but a sharp whistle from behind made him whip about defensively.

Waldroup crouched halfway down the steps. He had grabbed the dead soldier's bow and quiver. He shook his head at the alderman, who obediently lowered the leg bone. Then with the slightest movement, Waldroup adjusted his aim, and fired his arrow between the two of them, and straight into the waking spiky creature's unprotected forehead.

Stroud gasped, almost a whine. The creature squealed—the same noise they had heard at the death of Baldie. It collapsed upon the lid, then slid back into the vault, leaving one arm outflung in the opening. Waldroup already had another arrow nocked and aimed at the alderman. He gestured that Stroud should let go of the bone.

He complied, darkly. "You've killed a great one," he said sourly, "killed an immortal. You've no idea what this will bring down upon you."

"Well, I expect you'll tell me, since we're going have us a wee conversation."

"I'll tell you nothing," the alderman sneered.

"And will you still say that after I've pinned your other shoulder to a pillar and put arrows in both your knees? There are many ways for you not to die, you see, and no one and nothing is comin' to rescue you now. All your men are dead. As well as your . . . what was he, the immortal?"

The alderman glared his refusal to answer. As promised, Waldroup shot him through his good shoulder. The arrow spun him around. He collapsed, falling onto the shaft itself, which made him squeal with pain.

Thomas, unsteadily—and though he could feel the wetness of blood trickling down the back of his neck—almost went to his aid. He had known the alderman most of his life, though only as part of the local landscape, a figure who engaged his father in conversations, given to, or perhaps mimicking, laughter and camaraderie. Had he always been turned? Waldroup seemed to sense something of his empathy and stepped in his path before coldly standing over the alderman.

"I'll ask you again," he said. "What was he? Elf? *Fae?*"

"Yvag," the alderman replied through clenched teeth.

"Which is what?"

"Your mangled word is 'elven.'"

"So then it's true." Waldroup looked amazed. "The black-armored things *are* denizens of Ailfion."

"Ailfion. Elfhaven. Álfheim. Ildathach. So many of you have tried to own it by naming it. You know nothing still."

"We've gotten it wrong, have we?" The alderman shrugged. "So what name do *you* give it?"

"Yvagddu."

"Sounds like it ought to be a village in Wales."

The alderman smirked. "The Welsh would be tywyllwch llwyr. Is it important to you to know all of this?"

Waldroup sighed bitterly. "Whatever they're called, you help them, against your own kind."

The alderman met his gaze and laughed. "You've no idea."

Thomas interjected, "What was Balthair MacGillean?"

Stroud seemed to have lost interest in them and was gazing around as if he might find a weapon or an escape. Waldroup made as if to aim at his knee, and he snapped back to attention.

"There was no Balthair. There was Elgadorn." With his chin he gestured toward the vault and the protruding arm.

"Meaning?" Waldroup asked.

"He was the same."

Thomas replied, "The same, how? I don't understand."

"A conveyance," Stroud snapped. "A lich."

Thomas and Waldroup exchanged a look, neither quite understanding. Waldroup said, "Explain."

"Ask me something else—something you might understand."

Waldroup's eyes narrowed, but Thomas had gotten to his feet, and came around him. "What is this?" he asked. He extended his hand toward the alderman. On his palm lay the strange stone with blue etching.

The alderman failed to hide his eagerness to have it, though he tried. For a moment he hesitated and in his glance was calculation: of distance and his chances of avoiding an arrow if he jumped to grab the stone.

Seeing the look, Waldroup told him, "You won't make it."

Stroud scowled at him, but his eyes were still drawn to the stone.

Waldroup pointed the arrow at his knees again, and Stroud answered quickly, "It's called an ördstone."

"It cuts open a way between here and Ailfion?"

"Does it? I've no idea," Stroud feigned.

"Do you ever speak without lying? I thought the *fae* had to tell the truth."

"Ha-ha! You people invent such tales."

Thomas said, "You used it to open the way when you took my brother. I watched you."

The alderman calmly explained, "Your brother volunteered for the greater good."

"No, he never," said Thomas.

"We were going to take you but he told us how worthless you were, that you couldn't even hold a thought in your head."

"He *didn't*! He never would have!" His eyes teared.

"It should have been you, shouldn't it?" the alderman said. "You've thought that every day ever since. You know it's true."

Waldroup took a step and pinned the point of his arrow against Stroud's cheek. "That's just about enough of that if you don't want to die here and now. Whose greater good did he sacrifice for?"

The alderman turned his face, looked again at the motionless hand extending from the farthest vault. "I've answered your questions. Now let me go. Both my arms are gone numb. I'm wounded, I'm dying. I can't hurt you."

"Can't you?" asked Waldroup. With his head he gestured to Thomas, who picked up his fallen bow. Sparks danced before his eyes when he raised up again, and he leaned against the vault for support before he took aim at Stroud.

Waldroup turned, saying, "Watch him. I'll be only a moment." He walked to the half-open vault at the far end.

Thomas said, "I know you're lying about Onchu. You had no qualms about tormenting my sister, you and Baldie."

Stroud gazed at him as at a simpleton. "Oh, you refer to the changeling? That is nothing so special. There are many, many of those. They are how we populate our world, especially when your like harm an Yvagvoja. You owe us another even now." He watched Waldroup leaning over the side of the fourth vault, licked his lips. "If you gave me that ördstone, boy, why, I could take you there and you could see your brother again. Ask him yourself if he didn't dissuade us from picking you. You could join him in *paradise*."

"You knew us, both of us. You've known my family for years. But you didn't hesitate to destroy Innes."

Stroud shook his head sadly. "Not how it was at all. She had a most difficult birth, nothing to do with us. The baby...was stillborn. We protected her from that knowledge, giving her something to believe in, and removing the infant from this world. The midwife—"

"You stole my *brother* from this world."

"He was the *teind*!" Stroud snarled. "Chosen, do you understand? We *needed* him! He died as an offering that we immortals may all live on."

"Died?" The word caught in Thomas's throat. He had almost believed the alderman's enticement that he might see Onchu again. It was clear from Stroud's expression now that he'd said more than he'd intended.

So at last Thomas knew: Onchu would never be rescued by him. He drew the string taut on the bow. "I think I want to hear no more from you."

Even before he'd spoken, the alderman had begun humming, very softly, a queer tune that wormed into Thomas's brain. The chirring pressure was back and the tune became a murmur flowing from him, but did his lips move at all? It did not seem so, but the murmur, the sound, became whispered words echoing in his head: "Wait, now, wait. Listen to me, listen to my voice, Thomas Rimor. Listen and let it calm you, soothe you. Soothe you, calm you." He made a shushing sound like wind in reeds, the sound the Queen had made a thousand years ago.

With effort the alderman rose up. He snatched a glance at Waldroup, who had his back to them as he worked the lid back onto the vault.

Thomas swayed where he stood. The string relaxed in his fingers. They uncurled. The arrow tipped.

"I promise you power and wealth, Thomas Rimor—just let me in, let me possess you for a minute. Your family already is the equal of Balthair's. Now that he's gone your sister inherits all. You'll own land on both sides of Ercildoun as it grows. Your mind which troubles you, it has almost healed in the three years of your wandering—"

"Not healed, the Queen's gift," he muttered. Brow knitted, he swung his head to drive out the webs entangling it.

"Nicnevin?" The alderman spoke her name in surprise, spoke it aloud.

"She . . . stilled me."

Stroud wasted no time in capitalizing on this new information. "There. See you how kind we are, Thomas Rimor? Not the villains you'd have us be. You have misinterpreted all you've seen. Your *brother* understood us. Let me in and you will be stilled again, you will sleep in dreamlessness, no fits, no—"

"Where is the knife?" called Waldroup. He had quietly come around the pillars and now stood in the middle of the crypt, behind the alderman. "I left it in your shoulder, man. Where is it now?"

Stroud continued to stare at Thomas as he answered with sham weakness. "It must have worked loose, fallen when I . . . ran." And silently for Thomas only: "Come, son. I've always called you son, remember? Now, the one you should kill is the one who brought you here." Stroud backed aside so that Thomas faced Waldroup. He pointed, and his unspoken words swelled in Thomas's head. "Kill *him*. Kill the one who brought you here."

"Stop moving about now," Waldroup said. He raised his own bow at the alderman.

Thomas quaked with the effort of fighting the alderman's ensorcellment. The words compelled him. The pressure pounded inside his head again. *Brought me here.* The power behind the words like vines grew tight, encircling him with confusion.

He stumbled back, and he was aiming now at Waldroup, watching as though he and his body had parted ways, while his fingers trembled at the cord.

"Little brother, what's this?" Waldroup said, confused.

The alderman grinned in triumph. The bloody knife he claimed to have lost glinted in his fist. *"Kill the one who brought you here!"* The order screamed in Thomas's head.

Squinting now, writhing, Thomas grimaced as the words twisted him up. His arm shook, his arrow scraping against the bow.

"Little brother?" asked Waldroup.

He fired.

The tip of the arrow split those grinning teeth and thrust the alderman back. Stroud's look of triumph turned to horror. The fletch of the arrow projected from his mouth, and he pawed helplessly at his lips, his face. He shivered violently and a red mist erupted from him like smoke out of a chimney hole, gone in an instant. Left behind was a shell. Unlike the wet dissolution of Baldie, Alderman Stroud in an instant withered to parchment—to a desiccated corpse the equal of those ancient bodies lying in the recesses around them, save that it was dressed in fresh finery. Waldroup's knife clunked to the ground, while the weight of the clothing pulled the alderman, bones clattering, after it.

The spell he'd woven lifted. Thomas, weak-kneed and sweating, clung against the nearest pillar, the bow dangling from his fingers.

"Tom?"

"He played it wrong," he explained. "Kill the one who *brought* me here. But that was he. You told me to wait for you."

Alpin Waldroup laughed with a kind of horrified relief. "You would have *shot* me?"

"He tried to get me to. He was in my head, ordering me—" He was interrupted by an inhuman screech like the one they'd heard following Baldie's death. It issued from the sealed third vault.

For a few minutes nothing happened. They waited, watchful, half certain of what was about to occur.

The lid shifted slightly, rose up, and clattered; then with a drawn-out scraping it began sliding slowly, roughly down. Waldroup gestured for Thomas to move, and they took up positions behind two pillars.

Long iron-colored fingers curled around the lid of the vault with nails like talons and pushed until it tipped and stood at an angle against the foot of the tomb. The creature sat up slowly, its skin a greenish gray, mottled where it showed, webbed with the same black carapace including a helmet that shadowed its eyes—the armor of the Yvag.

Thomas raised his bow to kill it. Waldroup whispered, "Wait."

They watched from the shadows as the Yvag climbed unsteadily out of its vault. It glanced at the tomb beside it, but Waldroup had replaced the lid so that it looked sealed.

Tall and reedy, the creature shuffled across the dim crypt, working so hard on staying upright that it kicked apart the dusty bones and clothes of the alderman without slowing. Its legs bent oddly, as if with additional joints. Its breathing seemed labored, and as it passed, the noise of its exhalations seemed to emerge from its side. It was desperate to get out.

The Yvag hauled itself up the steps. In one hand it held something small and dark and glittering.

The moment it ascended, Waldroup said, "Now. Before it has time to slice the world."

"Why didn't we just kill it?"

"I wanted to know what it would do. It was *buried* with one of them stones. I'll wager the other one was, too, maybe the lot of them. Your alderman came down here for a reason, and it wasn't to marry Elfland into the church. Come on!"

He raced out the door with Thomas close behind him, and thinking that Waldroup's curiosity had almost got him killed.

Outside, two horses remained, searching for grass to eat beneath the thin snow. They looked up at the creature as it lumbered to the same spot as all the others and raised its arm to cut open the air. Two arrows struck it at the same time. One bounced off its armor but the other pierced the narrow space just under the helmet. The creature went up on its toes, flinging the ördstone without control, then crumpled to the ground and lay trembling, still alive.

Waldroup walked up to twist the spiked helmet off its head, but before he could, like a live thing the helmet snapped away from him and retreated into the suit of armor. A spray of silver hair spilled out around the blotchy, batrachian face, but nothing like human hair or animal fur. It was strange and metallic, like tightly woven wires. The creature hissed at him with its needlelike teeth. Points as sharp as thorns grew from its iron-gray face. Like the Queen, its eyes were peculiar, having no central pupil but a ring of black dots circling enlarged golden irises.

"Yvag," Waldroup said, and the creature stared at him hatefully, black blood flowing around and down into its armor. "You want to go home." He walked to where the ördstone had been flung. Held it up. "I promise I'll send you if you'll tell me why two men died and two of you waked."

The Yvag tilted its head as if not sure it understood, but then it smirked. "Skinwalkers, we," it wheezed with something like pride.

"*Yvagvoja.* Great . . . honor." The words echoed inside Thomas's head as if in a well. It glanced at him. "'See how we are kind, Thomas Rimor?'" it quoted in a rusty version of the voice of the alderman. Then it laughed, cold and humorless. Its torso heaved. Black blood bubbled from its lips, and its head drooped, chin against the arrow.

"Damn it."

"Skinwalkers?" Thomas said.

"He told me I was wrong accusing him of working for the elven. He *was* elven, your alderman. Two deaths so unnatural," said Waldroup, "and after each, one of these things stirs to life. That's no coincidence. 'A conveyance,' he called your Balthair."

Thomas's eyes widened. "The alderman wanted me to give myself over. He promised me paradise."

"The sort you don't return from, I'll wager. Look around you, little brother. Your friend and the alderman both—one drowned, an empty vessel. The other taken who knows when? Long ago from the look of it. Maybe all the time he visited your family, he was this. As he's down to dust, he might have been dead longer than you've lived. They aren't liegemen for the elven, they *are* the elven. Them's I saw on the battlefield—wealthy, influential people, who had no business wandering in gore and guts among dead and dying soldiers. Why else were they there? Skinwalkers, weren't they, looking for their *teind*?"

"*Yvagvoja*—the alderman used that word and so did this thing," said Thomas.

"Mmm. Your friend Baldie drowned, but maybe no accident. Maybe that was always their intent, having him on hand to explain your brother's disappearance. Stroud knew anything you said would be dismissed, so they could blame you. Only, you vanished. They moved onto their larger plan, and one by one, all his family conveniently died, leaving him to inherit."

"And left for Innes."

Waldroup nodded. "He and the alderman could have planted the idea in your father's head, the way he planted shooting me in yours. They would have had all your property if you hadn't returned. They *would* have killed your family next."

"They snatched her baby, took it away."

"Same as Alderman Stroud would have done with you."

They stood a moment looking each other in the eye. Then Thomas said, "The other two vaults. The ones who visited the abbey, who accompanied the alderman to view our work. They're still asleep."

Grimly, Waldroup faced the ruins again. "Well, then. What happens, d'you suppose, if the leech dies before its host?" he asked, and strode back to the ruins of the crypt.

The second of the four vaults in the crypt contained a sleeping Yvag as well, which proved to be a problem. It was one thing to kill the elven when they were animated, dangerous—no different from cutting down a rampaging soldier in battle—but the idea of cold-bloodedly murdering the creature while it slept caused them both to hesitate. Waldroup even said, "This is ridiculous," but remained standing over the vault they'd opened, staring down at the inhuman, armored knight, and clearly confounded by his own reluctance. "Maybe it's protected and we're spelled against harming it. How would we know?"

"We should wake it up," Thomas suggested.

Waldroup reached in and tugged at the helmet. It receded, and the silver hair spilled out like brushed metal threads, finer than any metal they'd ever seen. It half covered the sharp, weirdly granular face that could have been male or female, and that remained severe and threatening even in sleep. The creature's head rocked as the helmet came away, but it did not stir. "If we *can* wake it up," he said.

Pushing the lid further out of the way, he leaned in and drew a strange thin dagger from a sheath in the armor. The blade edges were scored and oddly notched so as to present a barbed surface. The whole of it was dull black, not like metal at all; but the slightest touch of its edge sliced his finger. "Jesus." He licked the cut.

He held it up vertically to show Thomas.

"If you got stabbed with this, it would take half your entrails with it coming back out." Then he balanced the dagger on one finger. "Perfectly made. It's as light as rain." He flipped it up, caught it, and carefully tucked it back into its sheath, then worked the sheath free. It came away with a quiet click. "Better than mine, and they're good." He nodded at the first of the four vaults, nearest the steps. "We might as well open that one, too, see what treasures lie inside. You should have one of these knives yourself, lad."

Thomas turned and shoved the heavy lid. It grated and rumbled, sliding open enough to reveal the sleeping creature in the darkness below.

He just had time to acknowledge that when something tiny and glistening flew out of the opening. It was smaller than a bat, green and skinny, and made a wild gabbling noise as it flitted past his face. It hooked his hair and shot toward the ceiling. His head snapped back as if tied to a horse, and he cried out. As if in reply, the little monster let loose a high horrid squeal.

Waldroup plucked his newfound knife and without hesitation vivisected the thing. Its two halves plopped onto the lid in front of him and continued squirming. It still clutched a fistful of Thomas's hair.

In the vault out of which it had flown, the sleeping Yvag came awake. It hissed and blinked up at Thomas through the small opening.

"Waldroup!" shouted Thomas.

But Waldroup had his own trouble. The other Yvag was awake now, too. Disoriented, it grabbed at the side of the vault and tried to pull itself up while also clutching for its missing dagger.

The pressure of a hive of bees swelled inside Thomas's head. The creatures were angry and talking to each other.

Waldroup's Yvag lunged at him, caught him around the back of the neck and pulled him halfway over into the vault with it. He drew his arm back and stabbed its own knife hard into its throat.

Thomas backpedaled furiously as his enemy pushed the lid aside as if it weighed no more than parchment, and sat up. The stone lid hit the floor and broke in half.

He grabbed his bow, pressing against the nearest pillar as the Yvag stood. It pulled its dagger and bent into a crouch, about to spring. He shot it through one eye and it flipped backward over the lip of the vault and crashed down in shadows and billowing dust. He had another arrow drawn and ready, but saw that Waldroup had dispensed with his, was in fact holding its severed head up by the shimmering hair. "That knife's very sharp, indeed," he said. Black blood had spattered his face and clothing.

"What happened? Why did they suddenly—"

"The little monster." Waldroup wiped the blade of the dagger through the hair of his dead Yvag, then leaned forward and used the tip to flip the gelatinous bat thing over. It had ceased wriggling.

Still holding the bow, Thomas edged over and peered down at it.

It had goggle eyes and prominent little fangs in a mouth full of tiny sharp teeth. Its ropy arms ended in circular spheres sporting claws all around. It appeared to be sexless, its jointless reedy legs resolving in vestigial two-toed feet. Tiny leathery wings lay twisted under its back. It had a tail like a mouse.

"It looks like something made out of a nightmare," said Thomas, but he had a vague recollection of having seen its like before. He pushed the fingers of his drawing hand into his hair, winced. He was bleeding. The little monster had torn hair out at the roots.

"Homunculus," Waldroup replied. "Or maybe it's a *fae*, a hob for real, hey?" He poked at its body cavity with the dagger. "But look at this now."

A whitish fluid spilled from its torso, and the dagger caught shiny strands of metal, as if its organs had been woven from the hair of the Yvag. Its green jellylike flesh was already melting into a puddle on the lid; shortly, only the spun wiry metal remained, like a miniature skeleton. In moments all of that had turned to rust and disintegrated.

Thomas was perplexed. "Why do you think only this one had it? Was it a pet?"

"Nasty little excuse for one." He dragged its gooey carcass off the lid, dropped it inside the vault. "I think it's a sentinel, like for any army. All of them sleep here while they ride their human hosts. Didn't wake for intruders, nor even the alderman, before he died. This thing was in the first vault in order to sound the alarm, but we started at the other end because that one rode your friend Baldie. I wager the idea is, the one nearest the steps is likely to get opened first should someone come looking, so this thing sounds the alarm and wakes them all. They came full-on very quickly, didn't they?" He turned and gazed down the row of opened vaults. "All of them, sleeping in our tombs, in graves, alive. How many queer tales of undead things this explains," he mused.

"So two more will have died now, just like the alderman?"

"I expect so, but I'm not staying to find out. It's time we were gone. This won't be the only place they keep the puppeteers. Come on." Waldroup led the way up the steps.

"But shouldn't we wait to hear?" Thomas asked him as he followed. "They might be anybody."

They emerged from the ruin.

"Oh, not anybody, I think. They're selective, aren't they? People of influence. Perhaps your sister's nurse *was* one, but maybe she's just spelled alongside your sister. I mean, lookit. Balthair and Stroud and those others who visited the abbey—all influence and wealth. The nurse has got neither."

A possibility suddenly dawned on Thomas. "My father?"

"If they'd had him, they'd have used him. You couldn't make yourself kill your father."

"But they didn't know Fingal was me until just now."

"That's a fair point," Waldroup agreed, and pondered for a moment. "No, it's like I said—they had plans to dispense with him, same as Balthair did his own family. He'd have inherited everything again, wouldn't he? You've just saved your father for the time being, lad. And that's all you can hope for right now."

"Yvag." Thomas scowled as he said it.

"Dwellers in *Ailfion* or *Elfhaven* or whatever they want to call it. Hidden on the other side of this." Waldroup held up a black stone he'd taken from the Yvag he'd killed. Glancing around them, he added, "We need to collect our arrows from these bodies, gather our belongings from St. Mary's, and get well away from here. Very, very *far* away." He gestured with his head. "So pick a horse."

"Why?"

"Because who knows what alarm's been sounded. That screech maybe can be heard across boundaries. Stroud made it clear there would be retribution, and that was just for the first one we slew. When they learn all four are dead . . ."

Thomas said, "I have to see Innes. I have to know if the sorcery lifted with Baldie gone, that she can see the world aright."

"Listen to me, Tommy, you *can't*. However much you want to, you have to leave her now. They're gonnae want our blood, little brother. And what will you tell her she doesn't know? Either the glamour's lifted and she can already see things right, or she never will. And you can't fix that. You've done all you can."

Thomas shook his head violently.

Waldroup said, "You go to her now, you'll focus the Yvag on her.

But you won't be here to save her, because you'll also tell them it's us who killed their sleepers here. Right now there's no one left who knows that. We don't know how many places these things are sleeping. We have maybe enough time to collect our things, but we're riding for the coast this night and a ship to Calais. And not a word of it to Clacher, either, not even him." He walked over to the body of the Yvag, leaned down and picked up the blue ördstone the creature had dropped. He knelt beside it and, raising the stone above himself, cut a diagonal line down through the air. The line glowed a spitting, hissing green, and as the tip of it touched the ground, the green line parted, unfolding into a darker circle. Cautiously, Waldroup peered in.

Behind him, Thomas beheld nothing but a weird distorted reflection of his friend as if framed in a mirror of running blood.

Waldroup rolled the dead body of the Yvag through the opening. Then he cut upward from the ground, which closed the circle again. The fire sputtered, vanished.

"Why?" Thomas asked.

"I promised to send it home. And I hope it'll serve as a warning to the rest of these bastards that things are different here now. They don't need to know we're scarpering. Let them be afraid for once."

Thomas thought about it. "That's a good message. Things *are* different."

"So long as we're careful. We'll be long gone across the water, and none left from this encounter who can tell them true, Thomas. At least I hope so. No guaranteeing there aren't crypts in Selkirk or Gallae, but they won't learn of us from Stroud or his men, hey? Now, here," he said, and flipped the second ördstone to Thomas. "One for each of us."

Thomas looked at it. For an instant a tiny ribbon glittered between the two stones, like a straight sprinkle of dewdrops linking him to Waldroup. Then he closed his fist over the stone and the glowing line vanished.

He walked around the site, tore his arrows from the soldiers' bodies, hunted up the one that had missed its mark. He thought of the first Yvag in the crypt, and the arrow that had bounced off its armor. He said as much to Waldroup, who replied, "You stay here, I'll go find it. That green fire shows up again, be prepared to shoot whatever comes out." Then he descended once more into the crypt. Thomas was more than happy not to have to go down there again.

At the point where Thomas began to worry something had gotten him, Waldroup emerged and handed him the single arrow. "Ended up underneath the Yvag in its vault, that did. So, that's all of them, we're certain?"

Thomas nodded.

"All right, then. Let's go."

As Waldroup had once put it, the Yvag had feasted on Thomas's heart: They'd murdered his brother, driven his sister mad, cruelly plucked her child from her and left a bundle of living twigs in its place. He wanted them to know they had an enemy who would dedicate his life to paying them back if that's what it took. He opened his fist and stared at the weird black stone. "Thomas Lindsay Rimor de Ercildoun, Your *Majesty*," he said to it. Then he dropped it into his quiver and grabbed the reins of his new horse.

One day he would tell her his name now that the alderman had provided hers—Nicnevin—but not before he'd cut down a whole army of her kind. Alas, that would not be today.

He swung up into the saddle to ride past the grave markers and after Alpin Waldroup.

PART TWO:
TÀM ŁYNN

XI. The Knight

The knight arrived at the home of the tenant-in-chief, whose name was Cardden, on a fine spring afternoon. The knight was dirty and tired as were his two horses. Outside the palisade gate, he dropped down from the saddle and then, leading the horses, walked across the immense open yard to the keep. Seven people in the yard paused in their duties to watch him pass by. One, nearest the keep and with a face that reminded the knight of a peregrine, turned and hurried up the steps and inside it.

The knight wore a worn leather shoulder cape over his brown tunic. He was bare-legged, and the ragged edge of a pair of braies showed just below the tunic's hem. He left a sword, two bows, and two quivers on the second horse, along with a bedroll and an old weathered satchel holding his mason's tools. The weapons, his bearing, and the way his blue eyes, heavy-lidded with fatigue, took in everything around him bespoke his lethal occupation.

The tenant-in-chief met him at the steps up the motte well before he reached the keep. Dressed in a lightweight belted tunic and rolled-down boots, Cardden had bowed legs and the hunched posture of someone who had spent his life bent over the moldboard of a plow. He was balding in the center of his hair, but he still had most of his teeth.

The knight nodded deferentially as he drew from his tunic a small parchment, which he held out to Cardden, who unfurled and read it. It was simple and clear, a document of scutage that assigned Cardden responsibility to make good on a debt owed by King David to the knight for his service in the defending of the Empress Matilda. The king's seal was affixed, testament to the pledged fealty.

Cardden lowered the document enough to study the weary knight more carefully. No more than twenty or so years of age surely, with strands of black hair across his eyes, which shone like chips of sky seen through the naked branches of winter trees. Although he was smiling vaguely, doing his best to seem unthreatening, the young knight had about him the air of someone used to the unexpected, the violent, and the quick... someone who had survived by instincts for so long that he no longer noticed he had them—even here, where there was no situation to threaten him. Plus, he had a scar along the hairline on the right side of his head, mostly hidden beneath the shaggy hair.

He is dangerous, Cardden thought, and for a moment considered sending for Gospatrick, the sheriff of Roxburghshire.

But the document was real. Cardden *had* promised to pay scutage as a form of tax on behalf of up to three men who had fought for the king. This was the first who'd ever applied. Most, as he well knew, did not survive to take advantage of the offer. While he hadn't exactly depended upon it, admittedly he'd half expected never to have to pay any scutage at all.

"Two oxgangs of land, a virgate," he said, handing the parchment back. He owned a ploughgate himself, much of it lying fallow this year. A virgate was not a lot, and anyway, the knight as tenant would be expected to share some of what he grew and raised with Cardden. Aside from that, it might not be a bad idea to have a young and skilled soldier about, and much nearer at hand than Gospatrick who, if sent for immediately, might arrive in a few hours if it suited him. "Very good parcels I have, both fermtoun on a slope near the Teviot, and shielings that include huts higher up where you can graze your livestock. I imagine, in order to plow you'll be acquiring at least a few oxen?" Purchased perhaps from him.

The knight nodded somewhat uncertainly, as if the actuality of farming had not occurred to him before now.

"What's your name, then, husbandman?"

"Tàmhas, sir. Tàmhas Lynn."

"Welcome, then, Tàmhas. Lynn, you say. Are you from Peeblesshire?"

"Eh, no. Ayrshire, sir."

"Ah. Well, I shall ride along with you and your plot we'll choose and mark out between us right away." He went back up into the keep.

The knight stood awhile observing the keep and the walls, and the various wood outbuildings: the main hall where the family would live, and beside it the cooking house and well, a weaving shop, a stable that looked to include a smithy's or at least a farrier's workshop. So intently did he contemplate the thirteen buildings within the palisade that a girl carrying a basket of eight eggs almost collided with him. She jumped back, startled, as quickly as he did. She wore a blue gown with flared sleeves, and an embroidered waist belt and hip girdle. Her brown hair was braided. The tips fell past her waist. He counted sixteen braidings on one side and seventeen on the other, but restrained the urge to mention this.

"You should be careful, sir," she said sharply.

"Forgive me, I do try to be." He looked upon her with his head slightly bowed. Her face was flushed as if with fury. She glanced at his horses, at his weapons.

"You're a soldier, then."

"I have been before now." He tried to make out whether she was truly angry with him, though he couldn't fathom a reason. Finally, he added, "I think you walk very quietly." Her eyes flashed for a second meeting his, and her cheeks reddened darker.

"And you, I think, daydream," she said.

He stepped aside to let her pass. She curtsied, then started across the yard to the cooking house. To her back, quietly he said, "If I'm dreaming you, may I never wake up."

She could not have heard, and kept walking, but then paused just before she entered and looked him over once more, whether or not with hostility he couldn't tell.

Cardden, emerging by then, came down the steps, and although the knight asked nothing, he said, "My daughter. Janet."

Cardden returned to him the parchment. Tucking it back inside his tunic, the knight felt that he was tucking away that name for safekeeping as well.

"So, you must have been a good soldier, then," said Cardden as they rode along, paralleling the path of the Teviot Water. The land on their right turned from marsh to grassland, and soon they entered woods. The waters sparkled between the trees and shrubs.

Tàmhas Lynn replied, "I was a lucky one is all. Doesn't matter how good you are if you're standing where the sword thrusts or the arrow plunges. Right, Dubhar?" he asked his black horse.

Cardden seemed to dismiss his modesty, changing the subject. "Have you lived hereabouts? I ask because you sound to my ear very like a local man, and not someone from the west at all."

"Do I?" was his reply. He had no ready answer to that, but after a while said, "I once worked near here. On an abbey."

"Why, you must mean St. Mary's at Melrose? My goodness. It's just this season finished, you know. Wonderful, immense place."

"So they did build it as swiftly as the king required. I suppose I should go have a look then, see if I can pick out the stones I shaped." He smiled as at a memory.

Cardden looked him over critically. "How old were you that you worked stone?"

"A child, really. Lost and then found."

"So are we all in this world who embrace Him."

He made no reply. He was at war with himself over what he'd already said—a fool to have linked himself with the abbey, however innocently, though fortunately Cardden had heard a different confession in his words.

And then they were out of the thick woods and into a green and wild land of copses and stone-speckled soil. Cardden pointed. "Here's where I'd recommend your oxgang start if you want to mark it. Surely for farming the better plot." When he received no reply, he turned.

The knight was pressed tight against his horse's neck as if they were racing along. He moaned.

"Soldier, what is it?"

Between gritted teeth he said:

"Where the coppice ends,
stones deep buried like bodies.
Plant me here and survive."

He slid from the saddle and landed hard on his back.

"Young man, young man." Cardden dismounted and waddled to him. "Tàmhas Lynn."

But Thomas hardly heard him, far away in space and time, on

Norman soil and in the thick of a battle that sizzled and cracked with
the lightning in his head.

Alpin Waldroup and he stood on a rise among two dozen others,
firing arrow after arrow upon Stephen's charging knights, who were
riding down the lines of foot soldiers rallied against them on the
plain below. The knights barely slowed against the assault; they held
their shields above to catch the descending arrows, and few got
through, fewer still did any damage.

"Now's the time," Alpin called through the thunder of war. "Use
your skills I've taught you." And then he ran to the right. Others
nearby broke and followed him. Did they know what he was doing,
or did they think he was running away and sought to do likewise?

No time to wait and see. Thomas drew three arrows between his
fingers and ran in the opposite direction, and found half a dozen
others pursuing him. He fired as he ran, and so did they. The knights
busily hacked away at the chaotic last lines of foot soldiers, cutting
the poor untrained men and boys down like saplings while trying to
keep those shields up against the arcing arrows ahead. Thus were
they unprotected from straight-flying missiles shot from their right
flank—arrows that pierced throats and thudded into the dark sockets
above chain coifs. Find, focus, fire, and flee—again and again until
his quiver was nearly exhausted. Their numbers decimated, the
knights who burst through the foot soldiers' ranks wheeled and sped
furiously toward him and the others around him, while those on the
far side of the field tore after Waldroup and his group.

Into the trees then and up another hillside, Thomas dodged
between boughs, kept his wits, and made each shot count, dropping
the nearest horsemen, his running aim assured and lethal now,
almost the equal of Waldroup's. So long as no enemy archer on the far
side of the horsemen tracked his distance he could keep ahead of
pursuit, lighter in his leather armor than the knights in their mail. A
sword would have cleaved him, but nobody was going to get close
enough to try. The others running kept up a similar barrage; the
knights, most of them, gave up, swung about and charged back
downhill for easier prey. They couldn't shield from both low-flying
and high descending arrows, but riding uphill toward these
marksmen was suicide; better to ride hard and weave through the

carnage, trust to luck and mail, and the inexperience of the enemy. Still a few, likely enraged beyond reason, spurred on up the hill at the archers clustered among trees.

When the surviving horsemen had almost reached the first cluster, everybody scattered across the hillside, and the knights were forced to pick their prey.

Thomas grabbed, found his quiver empty. He scrambled alongside the others, retreating higher up among the trees, where he watched helplessly as stationary archers below—some with arrows stuck in the ground beside them, ready to be grabbed—were cut down at close quarters, trampled, chopped, and those who did not flee fast enough were slashed or beheaded from behind. Satisfied at their handiwork, the knights abandoned those few higher up and near-impossible to get, soon turning to charge back down the hill, and Thomas immediately raced to the nearest body below, snatched up the contents of its quiver, and, kneeling, fired a volley at the retreating knights. He hurried to grab up abandoned arrows stuck one after the other in the ground, pulled and fired them as he went. Then he tore across the hillside, finally reaching the archers who'd held their ground. Most of them had paid with their lives. He replenished the quiver at his hip from those no longer being put to use.

By then Stephen's forces were in complete disarray, and Thomas and other archers across the hillside sent a new lethal barrage into the chaos. Finally, the remaining knights abandoned their return assault upon the foot soldiers and fled the raining reeds. The archers cheered and shouted rude catcalls. Thomas paused and located Waldroup on the far side of the rise among the group who'd run that way. Together, they walked among their fallen comrades, tended to the wounded, and collected arrows from the dead. A few men swapped broken or inferior bows for new and stronger ones lying with their dead comrades.

That rout of Stephen's forces was a good day. The survivors celebrated with stolen wine and a roasted pig over the fire that had been Stephen's army's encampment. But it was the end of their employment, too. King Stephen and the Empress Matilda had reached a stalemate, and, regrouping, would attempt diplomacy. He and Waldroup were paid the next day and released from duty, if such it could be called. He was given a script of scutage for two oxgangs of land should he ever manage to return home.

But that night he collapsed on his bedroll, drunk and grinning, his chin greasy, his arms aching, unaware that the morning would bring dismissal. They had expected it sooner or later, of course, and already had plans to head to Italia, where abbots were hiring mercenaries and stonemasons both. They'd hoped it would not arrive so soon.

Then it was Waldroup shaking him in the firelight, a look of wide-eyed terror on his face. He gripped his ördstone, which pulsed with sparkling blue lines. "Tàmhas," he called, a variation of his name that Waldroup didn't even know, because Thomas had only adopted it while on his ride back to Scotland.

"Tàmhas Lynn?"

He jerked awake upon a bed of straw. Wooden beams lay overhead. There were tapestries against the walls. Beside him sat Janet Cardden, who called out, "Father, he's awake!" Her face flickered in the light of a central fire.

He was inside Cardden's great hall.

Cardden appeared behind her, blanket-draped, and Thomas experienced one last moment that interposed Alpin Waldroup, similarly wrapped, coming toward him around the cooking fire the night after that battle, grinning and proud and drunk, a moment so splendid it almost brought him to tears.

Then Cardden stood over him, saying, "Had you a fit, son. Fell right from your horse, foam at your lips. Lucky your head didn't land on stone."

"Of course." His head did feel strange, and he knew why. "I was . . . I was wounded in battle," he lied. But he touched the scar above his right temple as proof. "I've suffered ever since with occasional fits. Not often, you understand. Bright light can sometimes cause them. Like the sparkling of a river through the trees. I didn't think to shield my eyes. Rarely does it last more than a moment or two. I . . . Did I say anything?"

"Well, ehm, it were puzzling, sort of a riddle, like. Something about 'bury me here if you want to be safe.' Or, no, 'twas '*plant* me here' and was the stones that was buried like bodies hereabout. I'm afraid till you fell I didn't understand what was happening. Thought you'd just fallen asleep against your horse, tired as you were."

"*Plant me here.* Did I say where?"

"'Where the coppice ends'? I think that came first. Was where we were when you fell. It coincides with the edge of the oxgangs I was about offering you."

He squeezed his eyes shut. "You said that was good land, yes?"

"'Tis. High enough the river won't flood it, and good soil."

"We needn't look farther, then. I promise when next we go I won't inconvenience you like this again." At least, he hoped not. It had been many months since the last fit. He'd dared to think he might be quit of them, but as every time he'd thought that before, he was wrong. This one had put him out for hours. Maybe it was the exhaustion or the fall, or both. Or could it have been the ördstone itself riddling through him? *Plant me here.*

He sat up.

Janet Cardden put a hand on his shoulder. "You shouldn't leave," she said. Her gray-green eyes were hard, insistent. "It's night now. We can't be sure you're well enough." She faced her father. "He must stay the night, visit his parcel on the morrow."

"I am well enough, thank you," he protested.

She bit back a reply, meeting his gaze. Her expression softened. "Then do it for your horses. They're exhausted. I doubt any of you has slept for many days if not weeks."

"My daughter knows horses, Master Lynn."

"Horses as well as soldiers. How does one so far removed from war know so much of its practitioners?"

She rose up as if his words stung her. "I'm acquainted with all sorts of animals," she said, drew her shawl around herself, and walked away.

He took care getting to his feet, but stood without dizziness. Nevertheless, she ignored him as she left. "I have said something regrettable, I think."

Cardden grimaced, slowly shook his head. "Naught you could have knowledge of. There was a local Roxburgh lad my Janet gave her heart to. Like you he went to war, but was ne'er heard of again."

Thomas leaned back. "Infantry?"

"Very likely."

"I saw those faces every day near and far, as many dead as living. I am sorry for him she lost." Then, "I must be a terrible reminder."

Cardden patted Thomas's shoulder. He said, "Come and have some food. Sleep by the fire on the pallet here tonight, we'll set out again in the morning to mark out your plot."

They ate, wood bowls of hot, mashed root vegetables along with a few hunks of warm bread. They spoke of livestock and planting—of when to plant oats and barley, which led Cardden to mention the miller of Oakmill, Forbes, who milled all his grains and would, of course, do the same for Thomas, and who, by the way, was courting Janet—or would be anyway once she stopped grieving for her lost soldier.

Janet herself did not reappear.

XII. Waldroup's Madness

A smith in nearby Roxburgh would build Thomas his plow, and told him to return for it in three weeks. He wandered through the town awhile, getting accustomed to the shops and goods there. There could be no returning to Ercildoun next time he needed something; Roxburgh was larger, busier, and far safer.

During those three weeks, he acquired two oxen from Cardden, which he drove onto his grassy shieling above the stretch of land they would shortly be plowing. The hut there wasn't much, but he collected bundles of heather and repaired the thatch topping to make it at least habitable and mostly waterproof. Later, down beside his oxgangs of land, he would build a cruck house of stone, but for now as he tended the oxen and grazed his horses, this sufficed. It was a better enclosure than had protected him on many a night the past five years.

His neighbors were a family named Lusk. They had three children and all lived in what could only be described as a hovel, a wretched thing of posted frame, with stone, clay, and here and there wattle filling the spaces between the posts; roof thatch that looked to have been piled together by someone unacquainted with the notion of how a wall could support . . . well, anything. To Thomas, one side in particular looked as if it might cave in with the next good wind and crush half the family.

He still had all his chisels, braces, and mallets. He and Waldroup had bolstered their income working as masons whenever there was no army to join. Fortunately, new fortresses and abbeys and churches were being built all across France, in Belgio and Paesi Bassi, and as far south as Italia, so he'd had ample opportunity to improve his masonry skills, working beside his friend. Waldroup was right—stonework was significantly easier and safer than the practice of war. And even if he and Waldroup could not speak the language, they understood the methodology of cutting and setting stone, and working treadmills and lewises, and once that was communicated they became immediately indispensable. He also beheld and undertook ways of constructing a wall that had not yet traveled this far north, apparently.

Thus, when he described how he might improve his neighbors' house while awaiting the building of his plow, and offered his services, husbandman Lusk did not refuse, and even gave him his twin ginger-haired boys, Kester and Filib, as assistants—no doubt seeing it as an opportunity for the boys to learn a trade.

First they cut down trees nearer the river and shoved new posts in to bear the weight of the roof while sections of the wall were dismantled and completely rebuilt. Thomas's plumb line seemed like something magical to Lusk, very like witchcraft, although Thomas convinced him it was *natural magic* and thus acceptable; the boys grasped the idea immediately without needing convincing, too young perhaps to have absorbed their father's superstitions. Many of the stones Lusk had used in piling together his wall were unworkable. Quite a few had simply been turned up in plowing, and were piled on without regard to whether they were the right shape for the space. More of these lay randomly along the sides of the fields. Thomas scrounged many useful stones there, and for the rest, he and the boys carried them up out of the river.

Fashioning a wall out of irregular stones was more like working a puzzle than the building of an abbey or church with its uniformly rectangular blocks. But Waldroup and the southern masons had taught him well, and he shaped the stones one by one, filled the spaces precisely, and shortly had a sturdy vertical wall between the beams that would keep the wind from whistling through and not fall over for anything short of a siege engine. By way of payment the family fed him most evenings before he climbed back up to the shieling, where he did nothing so much as simply collapse. Stonework was exhausting. It made his muscles and the skin of his hands hard, but it was a hardness he relished: Repairing Lusk's house felt like accomplishment.

Lusk must have said something to Cardden, as the tenant-in-chief turned up one morning, Janet accompanying him, to watch Thomas work. As Cardden looked over the mason's tools laid out, Janet told him in confidence, "We didn't entirely countenance your claim to have worked on St. Mary's. I see we were wrong to disbelieve you."

"Why would I have lied?"

She gave a little smile. "Many do lie about so many things in wanting to impress their betters."

"Well, my thanks, then, for the warning. When I meet my betters, I shall take care that I tell my story true."

For a long moment they stared each other down. Her gaze seemed as if it was trying to see him fully, to peer into the depths of him. Then finally she laughed, wheeled her horse about, and rode away. Her father remained, full of questions about the shaping of the stones, all of which he answered, for the benefit of the Lusk boys as well as his landlord, before returning to work.

To the remaining sides of the house, Thomas added small buttressing in two places. Lusk's home was now far less likely to kill its inhabitants while they slept, even in the winds of a storm. He left it to them to rethatch the roof.

And all the while, as he plowed and planned for his own house, he made regular nocturnal forays to the ruins of Old Melrose.

In the shieling hut he'd thatched, Thomas left a small fire burning in the center space, then set off on foot to the west, coming down from the heights beyond Lusk's property where he would not be seen. Farther on, he skirted the tiny village of St. Boisil, crossing the heights and then keeping to the river bank, which brought him in sight of the ruins and not too far from the corpse road bridge over the Tweed that he and Waldroup had taken once upon a time. The ruins lay abandoned, empty, the collapsed section if anything larger.

"This is a fool's errand, you know, little brother," Waldroup's voice whispered in his head. "Neither of us has the slightest notion how regularly they seek out a *teind*, much less if it's always from here."

Thomas glanced to where he imagined the shade of his friend walked beside him. "But sooner or later, they will. They have to."

And Waldroup replied in singsong:

"Below the living, with the dead
Sleep we gray and pale.
Find us you won't
Where a whisper can pass,
Nor where it's high and bright."

Thomas walked on in silence. It was a riddle he had spoken in a fit that overcame him in Italia. Waldroup had taken it to mean that the dormant Yvag would not be found in the ruins any longer. That much they agreed on: The ruin would let whispers, breezes pass everywhere.

After a time, Waldroup commented, "Took Onchu in the day, though, not in the dead of night. Even if they've come again, you most likely missed 'em."

Angrily, Thomas turned and argued, "What should I do, then? *Live* in the ruins, Alpin?"

There was no one beside him to answer, of course. Just moonlit shadows.

Something had been going on with Waldroup, but for the longest time Thomas didn't know what. By the time their participation in Queen Matilda's campaign had ended, the change was obvious—a twitchiness had begun to undermine Waldroup's calm and calculating way of preparing for and looking at battle. He lost his train of thought, got confused, contradicted his own plans. If they joined another military campaign, it was going to get him killed, and maybe Thomas along with him.

On the road, traveling through Paesi Bassi and then south, he woke on repeated nights to find his mentor sitting awake, features traced in a blue glow, obviously and surreptitiously contemplating the ördstone. If Thomas asked what he was doing, he confessed that he was fearful the stone might lead the Yvag to them, and that to be safe they should keep moving. Thomas wanted to ask, if he considered the stones so dangerous, why he didn't propose they bury them somewhere and go on without them?

They rode on south, through France and down across the German Empire.

One night as they lay exhausted side by side, Waldroup suddenly asked him, "What if ours is not the only world, Tom?" It sounded like a question he'd been turning over for some time.

Given what they'd already experienced at the ruined abbey, he replied, "We know it isn't. The Yvag—"

"Yes, the Yvag, but what if it's more than them? What if there's more than we know of?"

Thomas rolled over and, as he'd half expected, found Waldroup cast in the blue light of the ördstone, which he was holding up overhead as if placing it like a star in the sky. He probably should have asked then, but Waldroup tucked the stone away again, rolled onto his side, and said nothing more.

The night of the fit that brought forth the riddle about the "high and bright," they had been working for a month as masons on the abbazia di Santa Maria di Lucedio, a Cistercian abbey in northwest Italia. Another of the stonecutters, a thick-bodied and shaggy fellow named Gallorini, happened to be sitting there beside Waldroup when the seizure struck. He heard the riddle, and while he could hardly have understood many of the words, he crossed himself and instinctively backed away, obviously persuaded that something unholy possessed Thomas. He was hardly the first who'd attributed the fits to demons.

Despite their assurances to him that it was a sickness, not possession, in the days and weeks after that, Thomas often caught Gallorini watching closely, as if anticipating some further revelation or evidence of possession—another seizure at the very least. And all the while, Waldroup continued to grow more disturbed. The stone seemed to have wormed its way into his mind, embedding tumefying notions and doubts.

Finally, after one evening's meal, they were sitting alone when Waldroup abruptly asked, "What if you found out that Christ wasn't from here? That the real isn't real at all." His voice grew tighter and more frantic. "What if you pushed at the world with your hand, and it flexed and opened, and you beheld another, one that was a desert of blue sand with scattered moons across its sky? This other, suppose it proved so real you could smell it, and it smells nothing like here, and there are castles and fortresses like nothing we've ever seen or know even how to build, some so high they look to reach the moon—what if *that* turned out to be the real world? Or what if it opens onto another and that onto another, like doors inside doors inside doors? What if . . ." He sat trembling, unable to find the words to describe this vision and further.

Thomas hesitated before asking, "These are dreams you're having?"

Waldroup shifted, as if he'd just discovered Thomas beside him, then nodded tentatively. "Dreams, yeah." He met Thomas's gaze. "It feels like they're going to catch up to us, Tom. Like they know exactly where we are."

"You want to move on again when we have employment here, and no one is looking for us." He shook his head. He wasn't used to being the wise counsellor between the two of them. But now his friend had become so unstable, it worried him. "We fled the Yvag over a year ago," he said. "The stones have never been out of our possession in all that time, despite which, we haven't encountered a single one of their kind anywhere. None of your high-born skinwalkers strolled any of our fields of battle in search of wounded, did they? No one pursued us here, either. It's exactly as you predicted, Alpin—they don't know what happened at Old Melrose. We left them no idea where to look or who to look for. They're likely still hunting for us all around Ercildoun."

"Clacher knows we left. He'll describe us and not even realize he's told them."

"But he doesn't know where we've gone. He'd have told them we were returning after the winter, which means we've disappointed them sorely by not turning up." This was ridiculous—he was saying to Waldroup things that Waldroup had told *him*. It must be the Yvag's stone warping Waldroup, but he couldn't understand why. The stone he had taken from the alderman had had no destabilizing effect upon him. He didn't even believe he was dreaming peculiarly, certainly not dreams of other worlds or Yvag pursuers; if anything, between the two of them, after all that had happened, he should have been the one obsessed and paranoid.

Tempted as he was to ask Waldroup to let him carry both stones awhile, he was certain the suggestion would drive a wedge between them.

"We don't *know* if we've encountered them, Tom," Waldroup

rejoined. "The walkers look like . . . like everyone. There might be some hidden among the Cistercians. The abbot . . ."

"There might," he conceded, "but then they don't seem to have identified us, either, do they? We're just two itinerant stone cutters, same as all the others here. Nobody's come out of the forest and taken us at swordpoint. Nobody in that black armor. Think, Alpin, what it would look like if they had found us."

And Waldroup agreed finally that, yes, they were better off hidden among other stoneworkers and should stay put. That ought to have put the matter to rest, but of course it did nothing to address the control the stone was exercising over him. Reflecting upon it, Thomas conceded that they perhaps should have moved on, but he suspected that no matter where they went, the same thing would happen, the same visions and fears would plague his friend.

One night perhaps a week later, after they'd worked the whole day upon scaffolding at the level of the abbey roof, Waldroup sopped the last of his dinner gravy with a hunk of bread and abruptly said, "I've been thinking, suppose abbeys are built in places that were already seen as hallowed, long before monks came."

"What, like Old Melrose, you mean?"

"Mmm." He nodded vigorously. "What if it's the same here? If we asked the abbot, do you think he'd know if this place was deemed sacred and that's why we're building his abbey here?"

"I—it might be."

"Food for thought, innit?"

Without having to ask then, he knew Waldroup was planning something, and these various "innocent" questions were just a discursive path to that plan. He wanted to probe further, but squat Gallorini was watching from his one-legged stool near the fire, so Thomas concentrated on his meat and said nothing more. He glanced past Gallorini, at the other fourteen stonemasons, at the twenty distant monks leaving their beehive huts on the ridge to gather for *compline* before they retired. There were too many people hereabouts for Waldroup to enact what he seemed to be considering. But the two of them had practically lived in each other's skin long enough now that Thomas could guess what was coming. It came sooner than he expected.

Later that same night, he awoke to find Waldroup gone. Each of the groups—the French, Hungarians, Germans, Spanish, and Italians—slept in clusters with the cooking fire at the center. The two of them slept off to the south of it, a place where the hillside leveled onto a shelf just large enough for two people to lie comfortably.

The cooking fire was nothing more than embers now, and no one else stirred. Thomas quietly gathered his bow and quiver. He noted that Waldroup had left his own bow behind, but taken his knives. He guessed at which direction his friend had gone. He headed down the hill.

Many of the trees had been cleared on the hillside—most for the scaffolding they stood on daily. The true woods, called Locez, began at the bottom of the hill. Thomas paused there and drew a small leather pouch hung on a thong around his neck. He loosened the cord and reached in, taking out a small lump wrapped in wool. This he unfolded, then lay the stone upon his palm.

The blue glow of it was dull, but as he moved his arm to the left, the stone pulsed brighter, and for an instant the air ahead ignited with the ghost of the same glow, like a line of glittering spiderweb leading deeper into the woods. He moved his hand back to that point, and when the darkness glittered again, he followed the path it wove.

He crossed a shallow stream, one of many tributaries of the Po River, and kept going, deeper into the woodland, measuring the distance, speculating as to what Waldroup might consider sufficiently remote from the camp. The masons would see nothing this far away, and he anticipated that Waldroup wouldn't be able to wait very much longer.

Something crashed away from him, a stag or something as large, off to his left. In the thick of the forest now it was so dark, he could make out almost nothing. Branches brushed his face. He navigated by the thin blue glow of the ördstone.

It led him up a rise. He was cresting the top when, on the far side of it, green fire suddenly sparked, and above him the thick forest lit with thrown-off reflections and shadows, everything visible, sharply defined.

He ran over the top just as Waldroup, in a gully ahead and below, traced a diagonal line to the ground, and the line split into two and each half flexed outward until a ring formed. Waldroup laughed, like a child entertained by a simple trick.

The flickering, spitting light made the trees and undergrowth ahead seem to shift and dance. Within the ring, despite the color of the fire, lay a space the color of blood, the same as he'd beheld at Old Melrose. Waldroup tucked away the stone and drew his two knives. He stepped through the opening.

Once inside it he paused, seeming to peer at something distant.

Thomas half expected the circle to close up and seal him off. It would not have surprised him to discover that the stone was speaking to Alpin, inveigling, ensorcelling him all the while it was driving him mad with dreams and visions, duping him into returning it and himself to its homeworld. He waited for the circle to snap shut. But nothing happened, and the opening remained where it hovered in the middle of the forest, as stable and solid as a stone arch.

Looking around himself inside it, Waldroup shook his head as if to say "There's nothing here," and then walked on out of sight.

Thomas looped the bow across his torso, right shoulder to left hip, then ran down the slope and sprang through the circle after him.

XIII. Þagalwood

The space is like a tunnel, with creased and puckered sides as reflective as polished bronze but of a much darker red that seems in motion, flowing—or at least appearing to—all around them. It begins where Waldroup has cut the air, as if that cut formed the tunnel, not as if he has cut into something that was already there. Thomas, staring into its depths, remarks to himself, "This goes on for eternity." Running hard to catch up, he feels as if he's wading hip-deep through an invisible gelatinous current opposed to him. Finally, he reaches his friend, who turns, startled.

"Tom, what are you doing here?" Waldroup breathes hard. It's as much a challenge for him to push forward as it is for Thomas. The air seems thick as porridge.

"Did you think I would let you do this on your own?" He glances back at the opening. "Should we leave it like that, do you think?"

"Have to. If we seal it, how will we ever find our way back?"

"The tunnel is right here. It leads to this spot."

"But you go in deeper and look back, it'll look like every other tunnel."

"Every other?"

"There are hundreds. Maybe thousands."

This is not the first time Waldroup has cut open the night. The blue desert and sky full of moons weren't just random examples plucked out of the air. For now, though, he says nothing. That's a discussion for when they are back in their own world. Instead, he comments, "To me this all looks the same as where you carved an opening to send that Yvag home."

This far in, the tunnel is strange, queasy, as though at every moment as he pushes against the invisible current, he's about to stumble forward and fall. His grotesque reflection in the surfaces all around distracts, tricks his senses, even seems to move just before he does, anticipating him, as though time is stuttering, letting him get ahead of himself. It causes him almost to tumble forward, and so he tries not to look. Wonders if the tunnel is itself somehow alive.

Focusing instead upon the way ahead, he sees where the pathway vanishes and the blood-drenched tunnel seems to evaporate. He turns around again, looks at the exit, which ought to have dwindled but doesn't seem to have done—at least it's not receding as quickly as it should. He lays a hand on Waldroup's shoulder to slow him down. "It's as if," he huffs, "wherever we are, wherever we cut, we always enter . . . the same place."

Waldroup stops, while his asynchronous reflection still proceeds for an instant. "Believe me, we're not in the same place." But he sounds less than certain, and glances at the glittering stone he holds as if afraid to let go of it. "I mean, where's the dead Yvag I shoved in here, then?"

"That was a long time ago. They surely came and took the body away."

Waldroup shifts from foot to foot, obviously unable to wait. "We need to go farther. We can't waste this opportunity."

"But the ring—" He points back.

"No one can see it. I picked a good place, I know how to choose places where nobody will see."

Thomas bites back a comment that Alpin has certainly kept all of this from him.

"Come on, we'll be quick," he insists and sets off again.

Thomas wants to ask how they can be quick when it takes such effort just to walk forward. He contemplates using his own stone to go back and seal the opening, but Waldroup's point that they might never find their way out again prevents him. There's also the niggling prospect that they might open it up and find themselves back at Old Melrose or who knows where. Maybe in a world with four moons and blue sand. Maybe in hell—who can say this isn't the way into it, bordered by pellucid walls full of swirling blood? Anyway, why should one side of the divide be consistent when the other is not? Nothing is clear except that this is hard going.

He presses on to catch up with his friend again.

The unnatural thickness of the air proves more noticeable the faster he moves. The reflective walls lie just out of reach; when he angles over and stretches toward one, the surface eludes his fingertips, untouchable, as if it has slid away from him so that the tips of his fingers reflect in its surface but never make contact. Struggling that way again, straining, he *still* cannot lay a hand on the wall. He slips his bow off, ducking his head, and then holds it straight out from his side, even thrusts the bow at the wall that appears to be right beside him. It also contacts nothing, while the tip appears to glide upon the surface. Can the sides be mirrors made of air? Uneasy, he drifts back to the seeming center—or at least to where he is lined up directly behind Waldroup. Securing the bow across his body again, he glances around.

The green circle remains clearly in view, though still not as distant as it should be by now. Something small and dark seems to be moving about in the center of it. What if the Yvag are containing them, hemming them in? Well, he thinks, if so, he and Waldroup are surely done for. There is nowhere they might hide in this strange tunnel, following this hard and narrow path, itself like stone but seamless. Whatever this Ailfion is, they are at its mercy now, and will probably have to fight their way out.

Slowly, the red walls become less substantial, and reflection dulls as if they're veering away, until it's nothing but a mist, a sheet of fog hovering in the torpid air. Then slowly that, too, fades, revealing a greater depth, a suggestion of distance and of shapes in the darkness. Then, as if a cloud has drifted from the face of an unseen moon, he and Waldroup find themselves hemmed in by pale and leafless trees like none he has ever seen. They border the path on both sides. Neat rows of them extend away into the blank landscape, as if they were planted in rows, like a crop in a field. Receding into a black distance, the trees might be carved from bone. Patterns of knars and whorls cover their thick, deformed trunks; their branches fan out like enormous, elongated fingers.

As he walks, his position relative to the trees never seems to change—the branches remain in the same place, as if the trees are on spindles, turning while he trudges so as to keep the same side toward him. Again he has the sensation of slogging in place, and a kind of vertigo grips him as he follows the ossuarial branches overhead, where they link right above him as at some knuckle joint with those on the opposite side, forming a tracery vaulting over the path, a parody of every window, ceiling, and door in every church and abbey he's worked on. So intent is he upon this intricate archway, that he runs straight into Waldroup, who has stopped ahead of him.

"Tom"—the one syllable filled with terror—"where have we come?" However much the ördstone may have enchanted him previously, this skeletal woodland has Waldroup ready to bolt.

"You haven't come this way before?"

"Never saw nowt like this."

The nodose deformities on the trunks move then, warping in such a way as to imitate features: contorted eye sockets and distorted mouths, the toothless skulls of antlered giants stretched into tree shapes. All seem to have awakened at the sound of Waldroup's voice.

A whisper floats to them like a chill rising out of the ground. "Þagalwood." The word shivers. "Þagalwood. Lonely ones, come." He makes himself look away from the trees. Way off through the gaps between thousands of branches, something glitters distantly, tiny jewels sparkling. But at this distance, whatever it is must be huge. Is it someone's bonfire out across some darkling plain? There's no apparent sun, nothing to throw such a reflection. What can the source of the light be?

Waldroup's seen it, too. "What—" he starts to say, when from behind them comes a cry.

"Attendere! Attendere, streghe!"

Streghe? Witches? Are they under attack? Thomas swings about, takes his bow up, nocked and drawn this time.

Chugging along the path after them comes short, rotund Gallorini. He carries a sword in one hand and in the other a crossbow. How he's able to trundle along while carrying both, Thomas cannot imagine; but seeing the bow aimed at him, Gallorini goes wild-eyed, ducks his head, and dodges from the path and into the trees.

Thomas calls out, "Gallorini, stop, I won't shoot you. *Fermo!*"

But Gallorini has already stopped, rigidly.

The sword and crossbow slide from his grasp. He stands stiffened, arms and legs spread wide. Then he tilts back his head and pules, "*Io ho solo voglia*—I only want share in your treasure—*il tesoro!*"

Thomas starts for him but Waldroup grabs hold of his tunic from behind. "No," he says. "It's too late. It'll get you, too."

He yanks free. "What will? What treasure is he talking about?"

The trees whisper as if pleased, "Lonely one, yes, yes."

Even as he takes another step toward the Italian, Gallorini is taking root. The ground where his feet are planted is leeching the essence from him, transforming him. His clothing pulls, strains, and tears. It slides down his body, seemingly into the ground.

He screams now like a bear set on fire. Roars and screams as his skin, like the clothing before it, stretches tight and tears away, leaving glistening muscle beneath. His arms thrust high above his head, tissue and sinews unraveling. They slither down, until the arms are naked of flesh, the fingers extending, growing, branching, as his skull melts into his torso, ribs condensing, joining. His screams by now have curdled to a whisper; in any case, he is no longer Gallorini but a miniature version of the thousands of trees around him, his gasping wail mingling into their rustling call. "*Pagalwood.*" Now the never-ending agony threaded through that word is clear. Whatever the others were, whatever existence they once knew, this is their banishment, their doom, a suffering that has no end. And they were calling to him and Waldroup to join them in it.

Behind him, in the direction of whatever it is sparkling beyond this horrible skeletal forest, something rumbles, a thunder that doesn't die, but grows slowly, steadily louder. Pounding. They've been through enough battles to identify the sound of an enemy horde charging in their direction. That is the moment Waldroup yells, "The *stone!*" He stares first at his hand, then at the ground around them, dropping to his knees, and begins patting all around himself. "Do you see it? When I grabbed your shirt, it was in my hand. How could I—It has to be here, Tommy."

"Whatever's coming, it's closing on us, Alpin. We can't wait!"

Waldroup claws the dirt, stares wretchedly up at him, hands out as if imploring. "It glitters so blue, why can't I see it?"

Thomas doesn't know if he dropped it just now, or before, so in awe of the evil wood around him that he didn't even notice when he let it go. They don't have time to find out.

"Look," says Thomas, and he tugs on the cord around his neck. "We still have a stone to get us out. Come *on*." He tugs Waldroup to his feet, pushes him ahead, and they finally take off running.

The trees seem to be reeling in a gusting wind now that neither of them can feel. The branches clatter and knock all around them, excited by this chase or maybe directing their pursuers: *Here, here they are.*

They plunge into the fog again and it swirls away. Ahead of them, what has previously been a single circle spreads and divides, and divides and divides again, until there must be a hundred red tunnels, all identical, all receding into darkness, all pulling on him to go their way. Waldroup stumbles and tries to lead them off. "It's this way!" he insists, but even he isn't certain any longer.

Thomas hesitates, takes the ördstone from the pouch and holds it in his fist, concentrates. The many paths spin around them as if they're running on a treadmill spinning infinite ways to go. He holds up the stone, and the blue spiderweb flickers in one direction, aligns along one path—the only one burning with green fire like a tiny star at its end. When he focuses upon that star, the other ways collapse and fold together again into the untouchable, bloodred walls. The single line of blue gossamer light from the stone points the way. "Here!" he shouts, and drags Waldroup after him. He holds that flickering exit in his sight to keep from joining Waldroup in becoming lost. Somehow, Waldroup has caused the multitude of paths to appear; without his stone, he is the helpless quarry of this place. It would trick him, trick them both.

Far behind them the thunder has closed the distance. Beating hooves seem to be gaining every instant, while the green fire seems to be forever out of reach at the end of the tiny blue thread strung from the ördstone. Wheezing, he dares a look back, but there's nothing visible beyond the bloodred tunnel, nothing in the distant, receding woods, nothing galloping on the path behind them even as the sound roars down on them like a storm.

And then quite suddenly he shoots out of the green circle and falls.

XIV. Talking Stones

On the outside again, he tumbled, instinctively clutching his arrows so they didn't spill everywhere. He rolled upright onto his knees. Waldroup sprawled ahead of him, crying, "The stone, Tom! Quick!"

Thomas dropped his bow and drew the ördstone from its pouch. It burned cold as ice against his palm.

He lurched to the opening, and with the stone first touched the ground and then swept upward the way Stroud and Waldroup had done before him. The flaring ring collapsed along the line he drew, green fire sputtering to nothing below his hand as he got to his feet to finish. In the gap just before he sealed it, a helmed face rushed at him, eyes ablaze and fanged teeth bared. Quickly, he cut upward and jumped back, expecting an Yvag's sword to plunge out of the night and impale him. But the last sparks of fire were gone. Nothing emerged in the air.

Even so, he picked up his bow and aimed where the circle might open again. Held the bowstring drawn taut until his arms were trembling. He sensed Waldroup beside him, both knives out, similarly prepared for a sudden flare of green fire.

The gate had been erased; nothing cut it into being again, though surely the demon was just an arm's reach away.

Finally, Thomas lowered the bow. He turned.

Waldroup's features were strangely discernable. Thomas could even see the shine of his eyes, and behind him the treetops were rough dark shapes against a starry but lightening sky.

The monks would be up now for *lauds*. But that meant . . .

"How long were we *gone*, Alpin?"

Waldroup was staring at the treetops behind Thomas. "Can't have been but two hours at most. Not even."

"I'd agree, but the whole night looks to have passed us by. It's dawn now." With the arrow he'd aimed he gestured at the treetops. "Mayhap five hours gone or more." After returning the arrow to his quiver, he wrapped the ördstone in its wool cloth and tucked it back into the pouch dangling beneath his shirt. All the while he was watching Waldroup, whose expression contorted from something like pain into a look of utter grief.

Then he collapsed to sit cross-legged on the rise. He stuck his knives in the ground, crossed his arms around himself, and bowed his head. In a voice full of anguish, he said, "This is all my doing, my fault. I as good as killed Gallorini."

Thomas wanted to offer sympathy but found it difficult, as he happened to agree with his friend. How had an ördstone driven his friend mad when his own stone effected no pull upon him at all? "What did you do, Waldroup? Tell me, because I don't understand it."

"The stones," was all he said.

Thomas thought he'd misheard. "Stones. As in the one you lost and mine?"

Waldroup slowly looked up, and from that look it was obvious there was more he hadn't said. He stood wearily, retrieved his knives. "Come on. I'll show you."

They walked back through the woods. There was thin mist in the low wooded valley beneath the half-constructed abbey. Before they emerged from the trees, a herd of deer ran through, and Thomas shot a young one, which he then lifted and carried slung across his shoulders as they went on. "This at least makes it look as if we were out hunting this morning," he said. Waldroup agreed it was a good idea to appear so engaged.

As if to reinforce this, the first of the other stoneworkers they encountered on their way up the hill, Vasquez, asked if they had seen Gallorini. Waldroup lied and said they had not, and Vasquez smiled, replying that the young stag would make for a good feast tonight.

They went on their way up the hill, delivering their kill to the abbot's kitchen, where it was met with thanks. Everyone would partake of this bounty. "Now," Thomas said as they left the kitchen, "what is it you've kept to yourself, *big brother*?" He meant for the words to sting. Waldroup had lied to him—perhaps for their entire campaign across Europe.

They walked over to the small level space where they kept their things. Waldroup picked up his tool satchel and continued farther down the hill, well out of earshot of the others. As he went, he rooted around in the satchel, finally pulling out a pouch the size of a pilgrim's scrip. He started to unlace it, but his fingers shook, and he dropped it. Thomas caught it as smoothly as if he'd anticipated the drop. He began to unlace it. As he did, a strange pressure grew within him—an almost palpable presence pushing inside his head. He'd encountered such pressure before in the probing, stabbing thoughts of the Queen of Ailfion. He flung the bag down as if stung and took a step back.

Unlaced, the bag spilled open in the dirt—and there lay three flickering ördstones, their blue jewels twinkling in a weirdly coordinated way. The stones looked something like small encrusted oysters. In his head they were almost singing, a tune so discordant that it set his teeth on edge.

He stared into Waldroup's eyes. "Those dreams you described, they weren't dreams at all, hey, Alpin?"

Waldroup tried to smile, to make light of it, but failed. He sat heavily on the hillside. "When I went back into the crypts to look for the arrow you'd lost, I couldn't put it from my thoughts that the Yvag must *all* carry these, and maybe—and I don't know why I thought it—but I thought maybe the stones might somehow communicate with any Yvag who came after. You know, tell them it was you and me. I know it makes no sense. How could these small things tell anyone who we were? We slew the two that would know us, and, I mean, you don't know who's going to wake—"

"And if they can share what they've seen," Thomas interjected.

"So you thought about it, too, then."

"A little," he admitted. "Because in their heads, like a hive of bees they talked to each other, and talked to me that way, did the Queen."

"Each needs to cut their way home if their host dies, and I thought what if they can pass knowledge around, memory, experience? I couldn't let go of the idea." He gestured with a trembling hand. "So after I found your arrow I snatched them all."

"But why did you keep them, Alpin? Why not drown them? Throw 'em down a well?"

Even standing over them, Thomas could hear their skritching seductive susurrus enveloping his name. He understood now Waldroup's increasing agitation as the demons of the stones kept up their assault. Waldroup likely didn't even know he was hearing them, obeying them, twisted this way and that. Thomas found himself in an odd position, that of the wise counselor, schooling his mentor.

"How many times did you use them?" he asked.

"Twice. But they never took me to Ailfion. I kept opening other worlds. How can there be so many, Tom?"

What had he described? *Blue sand deserts and a night sky filled with moons?* Not here but not that awful forest of bones, either. "You went in?"

"Only as far as to see it wasn't all red. I thought for certain if I crawled in all the way, it would seal up and trap me."

"As it might." He nudged the three stones with his boot. "These are evil magic." He stared Waldroup in the eyes. "We have to be rid of them."

"Now, Tom, hold on—"

"Alpin, stop and listen to yourself. They've already bored into your brain like a brace and bit. They'll never let you be, nor me now. No one can be near these. We damned Gallorini, you and I. I won't do that to anyone else."

Waldroup's gaze fell. "No. No, we cannot."

"Then let me take them. I'll lose them somewhere no one else will find them."

"You'll not destroy them?" Alpin asked. Clearly, the notion worried him.

"What, smash them and release the demons living within? I wouldn't dare, and I wouldn't know how. I'm not certain either of us can."

"You think they are demons?"

"I don't know what to call them. Maybe they're the *fae*, same as that thing in the crypt, I don't know. But they're alive enough, they know we're near."

Waldroup only nodded.

Thomas folded up the pouch and tied off its neck, then picked it up. "Someplace we can always find them again if there's need." He turned and walked up the hill to the abbey. Waldroup took two shuffling steps, but stopped, tucked his hands in his armpits, and made himself stay put.

All the way up the hill, harsh whispering voices promised Thomas riches, rewards, whatever he wanted, much the way the alderman had slid into his mind in the crypt; maybe on account of that experience he could resist their enticements, even ignore them now. He wondered if the stones buried with the elven might be different in some way from the one Stroud had used, the one he wore around his neck right now. Could it be the stones that woke the Yvag in their tombs? Sly demons guarding the helpless sleepers, connected to their conveyances? Maybe they were indeed the *fae*.

The stones seemed to sense his purpose as he spoke to the artisan Gilleaux, who was even now sculpting the base of the abbey's baptismal font, circling it with figures of small demons and dragons, figures squashed beneath the weight of the purity and goodness of God in the form of that font. Its placement was already decided; the octagonal hole dug and full of rough gravel, surrounded by set floor stones. Thomas knelt and with both hands plunged into the gravel and dirt to make a deeper pocket into which he dropped the pouch. Ignoring the wailing of those demons, which faded as he pushed the little rocks back over the pouch, smoothing it so that no sign remained. Before day's end, the base would be set securely in the hole, and the cross-shaped font itself—large enough for him to lie within—placed upon it. Thomas was one of those laying the floor, and would be assisting Gilleaux in setting the font in place—after which the stones would never be heard from again. One way or another the purity of God would silence them. No dweller in Ailfion would ever hear their cry or learn what, if anything, they knew.

He stood stiffly, tired, and listened to the silence.

Waldroup had got it right: Those evil stones might have been able to identify them both. He didn't know how, but he didn't know they couldn't, either. So, although he'd nearly been driven mad for his trouble, Waldroup had been smart not to leave them behind.

Thomas walked back down the hill. The rest of the day afterward, it was clearly all Waldroup could do not to ask where and how he had disposed of them. Thomas tried to impress upon his friend how wise he had been—that far more men than Gallorini would have perished if the Yvag had tracked the two of them here. Maybe everyone at work on this abbey would have been slaughtered. Who knew what revenge the elven might take?

Thomas lay now upon a hillock overlooking the ruins of Old Melrose. Beyond, the Tweed sparkled with moonlight; but daybreak wasn't far off. Soon the sky would be lightening as it had done over that forest in Italia. They had stuck to their story of not knowing the whereabouts of Gallorini, a lie that tormented him to this day. But there was nothing for it; they couldn't have rescued the poor little man even had they returned like fools to the very same spot in the Þagalwood to hunt for Waldroup's lost stone. Had they strayed one inch off that path, they would have joined him.

So many questions remained: What sort of world was Ailfion beyond that wood, or was it all like that, a darkly haunted realm? If Gallorini transformed into so small a skeletal sapling, what race of creatures had been turned into the enormous tree things that vaulted the path, and whispered and sighed? Perhaps over time Gallorini would grow to their size. If that was so, then was the haunted wood what became of people the elves stole away as *teind*? He couldn't stop brooding on the possibility that Onchu had been there somewhere— one of the nine hundred eighty-seven bald bone tree-things edging the path.

He could not find out, didn't dare go back into the Þagalwood in search of answers. He doubted any answers at all awaited him.

He got up from the ground stiffly, stretched to hear his joints crack, then picked up his un-nocked bow and used it as a staff as he began to climb the Eildon hills back around St. Boisil and home.

"Another night, I'm sure," Waldroup whispered in his ear.

"I fear you're right, Alpin. Wherever they are, it's not here anymore. The crypts are all empty. I'm wasting my time."

"For a lad who pulled me out of that ensorcellment, you're giving up awfully easily now that it's just you on your own."

"Weren't you the one earlier calling this a fool's errand?"

"Me? I'm not even 'ere, am I?"

Thomas looked at the darkness beside him where Waldroup should have been. "Not even here, then keep your turnabout advice to yourself. If I'm to hope to survive, I have to identify the walkers before they identify me. Right, *big brother*? Or else get picked for their *teind* like *my* brother."

When Waldroup's shade failed to dispute him, he continued his walking alone.

"We need to know their number," he muttered. "I need to know what they've done with Innes."

XV. The New *Teind*

By the time his irregular vigils finally bore fruit, Thomas had planted his first crop of bere and beans. Lusk had shown him to divide his oxgangs into three sections, ploughing two of them, planting just one of these for now, and leaving the third fallow for a season. The second section would be for wheat and rye come the fall planting, at which time he would plow the fallow third.

Thomas had by then added four sheep to his shieling. They mingled with Lusk's herd, which the boys tended. They looked after both his oxen and sheep, so he let them stay in his shieling hut to which he'd added a small byre for the oxen. His bond with that family continued to grow.

During that time, Janet Cardden crossed his path repeatedly. It seemed that she often visited the Lusks and other tenant farmers; she brought them things, items as barter or trade for the bounty they provided—for instance, a shawl for Mrs. Lusk. He happened to be on hand for that, and asked her about her weaving.

"You cannot possibly care to hear about teasels and carding wool, sir knight."

"That's not true at all. When I was a boy, my sister sat at her loom for hours and hours. The way she worked her shuttle through the warp, how she altered patterns and colors, it all fascinated me. She made patterns out of nothing but what she imagined. Of course, I was a simpleton then. So maybe it wasn't as astonishing as I remember. A sunbeam could dazzle me for an hour."

"Is that why you chose war as an occupation? Because you were simple?"

But he refused to be riled by her needling. "I'm sure there's some truth in that," he replied. "I was good with a bow, and not much else."

"Oh, but you lie, sir. Your way with stone is most impressive."

He leaned back. "Have you just complimented me for something?" he asked.

Janet blushed. "If I did, it was an unfortunate accident."

"Unfortunate. Of course. Still, you must show me your loom one day."

"To remind you of your sister?"

"That, and to see if I'm still a simpleton."

She turned then and walked away. He followed. Outside, she had settled upon her palfrey, and pretended not to see him there.

As she rode off, Waldroup's ghost commented: *"What a long way you've come, little brother, from when first you met a lady and couldn't untie your tongue."*

"There's something in her unties it," he said, "and wraps my heart in her weft at the same time."

Waldroup laughed. *"Oh, off your head, you are, Tommy, and God help ye."*

"Off my head to return here, too, you said. But I—"

"Promised your Innes. I know. I know."

Thomas continued his nocturnal forays to the ruins of Old Melrose abbey. Talking to Janet had reminded him of Innes and his thus-far failed pledge to return to her. That duty overshadowed his brief and barbed encounter with Cardden's daughter, and he might have let the matter of what she stirred within him go, provisionally; only, upon one of his varied night routes to the abbey, he chanced upon her bathing in the Teviot where a hooking spit of land formed a deep pool. He'd fished from that very sandbar, caught bream for his supper, but not thought to bathe in the still pool it created.

He stood among the trees and watched her, a naked undine unaware of him. Had he not been making a point of not being seen on his way to Melrose, he might have wandered out, engaged her in more verbal combat, even joined her in the pool if invited. Instead, he dismissed such possibilities and reluctantly continued on his way.

Nevertheless, he felt as if she had somehow known he would turn up, though that was impossible, since even he did not know the route he would take. In truth he had little experience of women—just enough from his travels with Waldroup that he was lucky not to have the pox.

Then, waiting bootlessly in the gorse above the ruins, he found himself thinking of her, seeing the curve of her hip as she rolled in the pool. The image of Janet bathing even drowned the impish voice of Waldroup for a night. That was an accomplishment.

Time passed and he didn't encounter her again. The Lusk boys assisted him in building his house, gaining—as their father had hoped—some skill of their own with stonework.

As the house took shape, Janet turned up only in his dreams. He dreamt of her as a selkie, swimming gloriously naked in the pool while he crept down and stole her sealskin from off the strand. He awoke from the dream aroused and frustrated, the more so for having not encountered her swimming or otherwise. He suspected, perhaps feared, that Forbes the miller was taking up all her time.

He continued to make his nocturnal journey to the rocks above Old Melrose; more often than not he fell asleep in a bowl-shaped depression, exhausted, to awaken hours later soaked with dew, at which point he gave up and made his way home. Nights when it rained, he didn't bother going out; he doubted the ceremony of the *teind* would take place in a downpour. He no longer had any real expectations that he would behold anything. As Waldroup's gadfly voice liked to remind him, Onchu had been taken in broad daylight, not in the dark of the night.

Thus was he surprised one night to be awakened from his dozing by a sizzling sound. It was coming from below.

His head came up like a hound's on point. He rubbed at his eyes and sat upright, stared over the edge of the outcrop.

Below, in exactly the same spot where they had taken Onchu, a group of four figures stood gathered around a tall, gray-haired man who had just cut open the night. Brightly lit by the spitting green fringe of the portal, the man looked vaguely familiar. Thomas couldn't say where from, but guessed the village of Roxburgh. He hadn't been very many places since his return, and had been introduced to almost no one, but had traveled to Roxburgh for his plow and other supplies.

The three others clustered behind two black-armored and spiky Yvag soldiers on their grotesque steeds, and behind their new *teind*— a girl this time, perhaps sixteen. She had already obediently undressed. Yet, the nearest Yvag had her on a leash, as if she'd fought them hard and might yet try to get away. Where was the Queen? he wondered. She'd needed no leash for Onchu.

The girl's Yvag keeper stared at her, and she walked vacuously forward. He could see her clearly even through the ring, though it distorted her shape. Even so, she vanished the moment she stepped into it; by then he wasn't watching her any longer. The remaining three skinwalkers had come forward alongside her, their faces ardent as they neared the flickering ring.

His heart froze.

One of the trio was his father: older, thinner, and so tired-looking, but there could be no doubt of his identity.

The other two, a tall man and a woman, were unknown to him, but that didn't matter. He could not string his bow, could not strike them down. Of course it wasn't his father, not any longer, exactly as Waldroup had said years ago. Even while he acknowledged that, he could not make himself bring the swift retribution he'd intended for them. He'd sat up here all these nights for nothing.

He bowed his head, his course of action lost. No matter how he reasoned it, that was his father down there.

With Baldie and the alderman dead, his father was perfectly positioned to replace them both. There had been nothing he could do to prevent it. With him the Yvag required one less body in Ercildoun—he'd acquire the MacGillean property through Innes. The knowledge that he'd been right tore at Thomas like an Yvag's barbed blade; it was as if his words had cursed his father, and maybe his sister, too.

Waldroup's shade was back at his side. *"I know you feared this,"* said the ghost.

"Is he like Baldie, then? Some part of him still displaced within, unable to speak or appear to us while the monster moves him about?"

"Do we think they do it any other way?" asked the ghost.

They didn't. "Murdered and alive at once." The guilt he'd felt over his failure to rescue Onchu roared back as a kind of self-hatred.

Killing Stroud and Baldie and then running away—he'd cursed his father.

Waldroup's shade tried to talk him out of it: *"Don't you see, they'd have taken you and me, and still picked him?"*

His only consolation was that Innes wasn't there below, too. That offered a tiny hope to cling to, while it made more urgent the question of whether she was alive. Baldie had killed off every member of *his* family. Now with his own father turned by the elves, would she have been eliminated, too? Surely they didn't need to dispense with her, but how much did need have to do with it? If everyone already thought her mad, maybe his father hadn't needed to kill her. Might they have left her in that huge stone keep? Perhaps guarded. He'd wanted to know her situation all these months, but hadn't dared to show his face for fear that someone would recognize him, hadn't dared ask after her for fear it would identify him the way it had originally. Now that he'd identified the villains allied against him, his father amongst them, he became desperate to know Innes's fate. He'd promised her he would come back. He needed to protect *someone*.

At that moment, something like a horsefly buzzed right at his head, and instinctively he ducked, turned, and craned his neck, wary. Horseflies didn't fly at night, and this was improbably large.

The thing circled above him on the hillside. It was more like a tiny wren, or a bat with hummingbird wings. It dove and shot right at him again. Moonlight flickered silvery off the little thing. As it neared, its buzzing became a tiny, angry voice, like a deranged bee.

This time he didn't duck, but waited still, then slapped the air, smacking the creature hard enough that it spun against the rocks beside him. He grabbed it where it rolled, dangled it up against the moonlight by its tail.

It seemed to be *made* of moonlight; its head was like the cap of a tuber—rounded, with large ovoid growths to each side like bulging black eyes. The hideous hob came alert then, and the top of the "tuber" opened, revealing needlelike teeth. In his head, he felt the pressure of Yvag voices. The thing twisted and strained to bite him and let out a furious screech. "Shush." Thomas whacked it hard against the rocks, after which it dangled limply. He ducked down again. This was identical to the little nightmare that had flown out of the first crypt in Old Melrose. Waldroup had called it a *homunculus.*

One of the barbed knights was looking in his direction, scanning the hillside. The outline of its large eyes glowed green as the fiery, spitting ring itself. He could almost feel that glow sweep like a sunray over him in his hiding place.

The other knight shook its head and rode forward toward the ring. A moment later the first one gave up looking Thomas's way and followed. The green fire burned and the two Yvag knights vanished into the opening.

Thomas took the time now to memorize the others in the glow of the fire: the gray-haired man was broad across the shoulders though slightly stooped; he wore a red and black cotehardie. His nose looked to have been broken, flattened, at some point, and he had pouchy eyes. The woman was stouter. She wore a whitish wimple, which hid her hair from view, but her face was round, with fat ruddy cheeks. Her gown was dark. It might have been belted with a rosary, he couldn't be sure. *"She might be a prioress,"* said Waldroup. *"I'm sure they'd find that a useful placing."*

"Or a landowner's wife." He watched her awhile. "But where do they *lie,* Alpin? They're not in the crypts below any longer, are they?"

His ghostly friend recited from the riddle he'd spouted in a fit back in Italia, and which they'd picked over since: *"'Find us you won't where a whisper can pass, nor where it's high and the bright.' Didn't correspond with anything at the abbazia di Santa Maria di Lucedio."*

Thomas shook his head resignedly, but even as he did, something niggled at his thoughts. *"Below the living, with the dead*—that's the same as before, a crypt or a grave, but not here, not in the ruins. Nothing high and bright about it."

"But it says high and bright is where they aren't," argued Waldroup.

"So, not in towers then, not a castle."

"But someplace that has heights, otherwise why mention them at all?"

There was something Cardden had said to him when they'd first met. They had been talking about the Abbey of St. Mary at Melrose that he and Waldroup had worked on. "Just this season finished," Cardden had said. "A wonderful, bright place."

"'Wonderful, bright place' ..." Thomas muttered in sudden wonder. "Alpin. It has to be the new abbey of Melrose, St. Mary's. The east tower and transept. We didn't stay to see it finished, nor the glass installed. All the panes of the Catherine window when the sun lights them . . ."

"*High and bright,*" said Waldroup.

"And remember, Stroud's party who came to see the progress—Clacher said all they cared about was—"

"*The north transept, which wasn't done.*"

"But the steps down into the crypt and the crypt itself were dug out and marked."

"*No whisper passing in the dead air of a crypt.*"

"They just traded the new one for the old. But then why still cut the air here and not there?"

Waldroup made no answer.

He sat alone in silence and watched the three figures seal up the green fire. Their dark shapes moved away from the ruins, separating among the small markers.

The gray-haired man, it turned out, had a horse at the ready not far off. The woman went west on the path that led by the new abbey and on to Selkirk. His father plodded across the corpse-road bridge on foot and was quickly lost in the darkness and distance, heading back to Ercildoun. The horseman rode up the hill and straight past Thomas, who crouched down behind a stand of gorse. He watched the man skirt the heights of Eildon as well and disappear over the top.

The place below was empty now.

Thomas stood up with his unstrung bow. He held up the little monster he'd killed, to look at it again, but its body had melted into a dripping gooey strand through which a wiry core glistened, as if its skin had been painted upon an interwoven plait of hair. He flung it away, wiped his fingers in the grass, then headed down toward the ruins.

"*What's this development?*" asked Waldroup's shade, suddenly at his side again. "*Surely, you're not.*"

"I *have* to find out," he answered, and with such resolve that Waldroup dissipated. "If she's alive . . ."

He wouldn't need to come here again. The hunt had changed form: He'd met the foxes and was nearly certain of the location of their den now. But that was for another night.

He walked cautiously past the ruins, where there was no sign of anyone. After a few moments' pause to listen, he headed for the river bridge. The figure of his father was already lost to the darkness on the road ahead, and Thomas took care as he went not to catch up with him before branching off onto a smaller path, now mostly overgrown, that led west of Ercildoun and up toward the estate of clan MacGillean.

Castle MacGillean stood dark and forbidding, a sharp-edged silhouette on the rise ahead of him. The lack of torchlight was encouraging—if all of the household were sleeping, then it was unlikely any of them were involved with the Yvag. Nobody would be watching for him.

With his bow strung and fitted with an arrow, he cautiously approached the gate. It was, as it had always been, open. He eased beneath the bailey tower, pressed into the deepest shadows against the palisade, and kept it at his back as he circled around the yard.

Above, the keep was as dark as the various outbuildings, including the stables down the far end, everything appearing not merely empty, but abandoned. No one and nothing moved. He kept to the shadows until he reached the base of the motte. Then, exposed, he hastily ran up the steps to the keep.

The main entrance all but glowed in moonlight, and he strained his senses for the slightest hint of a sound, until he was listening to the roar of his own blood. He expected the door to be barred at least, but it wasn't. However, as he remembered too well, when he opened it, the hinges would groan like a mournful ghost. He tried not to push it very far, and slid through the narrow space, turned and aimed his bow at the main stairs. In this tomb-like castle, someone surely would have heard that door and would know there was no wind to push it tonight. But no one arrived. Something skittered across the floor. A rat or mouse.

He stood in place as long as he could make himself, just listening, then finally crept up the stone steps to the second floor, emerging into the corridor he'd last seen five years earlier.

The patriarch's room hung open and unoccupied. It smelled of wet ashes. No fire had been laid on here in a long time. The frame of the huge bed stood devoid of any bedding, its curtains in shreds, as if no one had ever slept there.

Across from it, Innes's door was closed. He turned the handle, then eased it open wider with his foot.

Her chamber, too, was empty. The bed here did contain a lumpy mattress, one stained with large dark patches that he guessed to be rusty blots of old blood. *Your blood or theirs*, he heard himself say. No Innes, no servant. The cradle where the grotesque "infant" of twigs and sticks had lain was still there, though of its inhuman occupant there was no trace. Would the glamour upon the room have lifted the moment Baldie died? He tried to imagine his sister and her nurse suddenly confronted with the leafy vegetative thing in the cradle where she had perceived a child only moments before. "He's so good and never cries at night," she'd told him. If the glamour had gone, then it was monstrously cruel, what he'd unintentionally done to her.

He retreated, searched along the corridor again, then back out and all the way to another door at the end. That opened twenty feet above the ground, an access for war, when the ground floor would be sealed up and only by ladder could anyone reach the upper floor. The entrance had never been used so far as he knew, but Onchu and Baldie had sometimes dangled him out it. He'd frustrated them by not reacting with proper terror, the same as with the tunnels and passages where they'd tried to lose him.

Finally he returned to the lower floor, the gallery, and great hall. The old moth-eaten tapestry still hung where he'd hid listening to Stroud and Baldie. The ashes against the wall were cold and clumped in his hand. Something fluttered overhead in the short chimney. Nesting birds most likely, or bats, coming in through the side opening. No screeching so it wasn't another of those horrible little Yvag *fae*.

Innes was long gone. Probably she'd gone soon after Baldie's demise. But what did it mean? Had they dispensed with her—had she become another of their tithes? Or had mother and father taken her back in? He tried to imagine how she would have reacted to the discovery that her baby had never been there. He was half certain he must have driven her mad. She would have fled from that room, from this whole malignant place, and if it had happened right away, then his father would still have been his father. But no doubt the skinwalker would want to keep an eye on her. Neither version of his father would leave her alone here, though for different reasons.

Beyond that, he had no idea. His mother, his sister—would they have been inconveniences to dispense with? Baldie had killed his entire family, but they would have stood in the way of controlling the MacGillean landholdings. Not so his own mother nor Innes.

Whatever the truth of things, he would not get his answers tonight. He was so exhausted already from the strain of this fruitless quest that he had to fight off the temptation to go back up the steps and sleep on her mattress in that cursed room. He made himself slip out the door, go down the steps, across the courtyard and away. There was too much chance that, if he departed in the daylight, someone would see him. If not here, then on the corpse road.

Cautiously, he traveled across the moonlit countryside toward the river.

"You know this could all be trappings of treachery laid on just to snare you," Waldroup's ghost told him.

"They don't even know I still exist."

"So you hope. Innes could well be no more than bait. You're so hell-bent on learning if she's alive. I tell ye, you pursue this further and you only deliver yourself to them. Or one of those Yvag midges will bite you, probably infect you with something."

Thomas laughed at the ghost. "Alpin, you don't hold me in very high regard after all you've taught me."

"Not I, it's them what doesn't. An' you don't know when this trap was set."

"Think I'm going to hand myself over?"

"I think you're obsessed and I think you'll take unnecessary risks."

"*I'm* obsessed. Which of us was it cut open the world time and again, and nearly delivered us both to the Yvag? Remind me."

The ghost had nothing further to add after that. He mulled over its warnings as he walked. Of course there was a risk he would deliver himself to them. Already someone might be watching him. Though he'd encountered no one, somebody might have been placed hereabouts to surveil Baldie's abandoned domicile—even, as Waldroup said, one of their "midges," if they could be released like a falcon to hunt. Every question that needed answering came with risk, and he was forever calculating odds, questioning who could be trusted and with how much. More than anything he yearned for someone besides an errant and probably made-up spirit as his confidant, whose opinion he might lay reliably against his own. Alpin was hardly anything. He wasn't even sure why he still heard Alpin at all, save that he couldn't imagine letting him go.

For five years he had lived a rough life with intervals of soldiering and stonework. Sleeping was a matter of laying something upon the ground and then yourself atop it, and—if you were lucky—when it turned cold, something over yourself as well. He could just barely recall the soft wool-stuffed mattress of his childhood, but no longer what it had felt like beneath him.

In the small new house he'd built for himself, the bed comprised a roped-together linen bag stuffed full of bedstraw and overlaid with an elk skin. Given the mercenary's life he'd grown used to, sleeping on bedstraw was like floating on clouds. Pure luxury. It had actually taken some effort to accustom himself to such indulgence. Tonight—and, more like, this morning—was going to take no effort at all. He prayed he would make it through his doorway and reach the bed.

That was how he stumbled into his house, discarding bow and quiver without hanging them on a peg, just dropping them upon the table, then stripping off his tunic and trousers as he went. He fell onto the bed, all but senseless, and the message that he was not alone (the scent of another filling his head) took an eternity to penetrate, to register, and at last to pry open his eyelids.

Fearfully alert, he lifted his head.

There in the darkness, he made out, atop the elk skin beside him, the very naked sleeping form of Janet Cardden—at which point he made a soft noise, almost a laugh. His exhausted mind wondered where she had shed her selkie skin. He lay his head down again, and the question chased him into oblivion.

XVI. Janet

From the first, she had denied that this errant knight could sway her in the slightest. Janet Cardden was still grieving the loss of her young love from Jedburgh whom everyone knew as Kenny. No doubt part of the continued grief stemmed from his death only being reported to them, an abstraction. There was no body, and no absolute certainty—only the word of a single returning soldier that Kenny had been cut down while besieging a castle in Lincoln far to the south. She had gone on believing for close on a year that he would return to her, just show up at their castle one day none the worse for war, while her father's friend, the miller of Oakmill, Forbes, had made his own entreaties for her hand, politely rejected over her father's protests.

The knight Tàmhas Lynn had ridden into the middle of that self-imposed exile from her feelings. He had struck her as impertinent but also guileless. For all that he had fought and traveled across places like Paesi Bassi and France, there was both an unworldliness and a sense of grief that seemed to run deep in him. It was to this latter aspect that she found herself attracted. He had suffered some sort of devastating loss that had worked its way down into the marrow of him. A pain the equal of her own.

Their conversations never touched upon this shared sense—she knew her father had told him of Kenny but he never asked, never pried, and never (unlike Forbes) swore that her pain would recede if only she would let him in. Instead, they teased and taunted, verbally jousting as if testing each other with every idle conversation so that no conversation proved to be idle. The interchanges left her strangely giddy. He spoke to her as an equal, as if it never occurred to him she could be anything else. The knight wasn't courting her nor attempting to. It was just who he was.

Then she and her father went to inspect the work he was doing for Lusk, freely shoring up and rebuilding the husbandman's house when he should have been plowing his own fields, tending his own sheep, and building his own abode. She watched him consider different stones, turning them both in his hands and his mind, discarding or chiseling them, tinkering, fitting, placing. He was a magician who saw a finished wall before it even existed. She found watching him to be captivating. And so without quite understanding what had happened, Janet Cardden gave Tàmhas Lynn access to her heart. He, of course, had no idea, which if anything simply increased the allure.

He stirred, opened his eyes, not yet truly awake but compelled by some force, which proved to be the pair of gray-green eyes considering him. Seeing them, he recalled collapsing on his bed. "Selkie," he muttered.

Brown hair spilled around Janet's prominent cheeks. Her jaw rested upon her hand as if she'd been watching him for so long that she had to prop her head up.

"I seem always to be waking up in your presence," he said.

Her mouth spread into a smile. "A most terrible fate. I'll go at once."

He rolled onto his side, his body mirroring hers now. He stared, voiceless, at her breasts and the sheen of perspiration on her skin, the tuft of hair in her armpit. "No, not terrible. But . . . why were you in my bed this night?"

"And in reply, I might ask why you weren't. Is there some secret love you visit past the Eildon Hills? For then I should truly leave."

When he continued to look upon her in silent wonder, she answered, "I went for a swim in the river, and then thought to come and see more of your handiwork. Husbandman Lusk continues to regale my father and me with tales of your skill at framing and stone—this thing you call a cruck house. I knew you were handy, but I'd only seen what you did in shoring up their walls." She gazed along the interior frame. "So you shape the uprights at each end like a pheasant's wishbone."

But he had stopped listening. "So I'm handy, is it?" He dared then to reach over and place one of his hands upon her shoulder.

For a moment, her eyes closed as if his touch filled her with seraphic bliss. She slid closer, glanced down between them where his stiffness poked at her thighs. Meeting his gaze again, she replied simply, "I trust you will be."

Their first coupling was clumsy and quick. He was her first and she cried out, which made him pull back; but she clutched him hard against her as if welcoming the pain, and he lost control almost immediately and spent himself.

She wept into his shoulder, but didn't seem sad at all. When they drew apart, he saw her blood staining the linen, and it caused him to recall Innes's abandoned mattress.

She asked what he was thinking. He could not explain about his sister. Instead he answered, "I thought you considered me an animal."

"I . . ." She lowered her eyes bashfully. "Sometimes I say too soon what I'm thinking."

"But you *were* thinking it."

"Yes, but then you fell," she replied. "I saw a gentleness in you when you slept and then woke that reminded me of someone I knew."

"Your soldier?"

She nodded. "There's also a sadness in you, corresponding to mine." Again, he thought of Innes but didn't want to speak of her just now, else get pulled down into the darkness in himself.

"Well, as to the falling, 'tis more a malady than a gentleness."

"You belittle yourself. You volunteered to help your neighbor. His daughter speaks your name with adoration."

"Sìleas is twelve years old," Thomas protested.

"Ah, so she's marriageable, then."

"You would tease this poor dumb beast."

She did laugh now. Her voice was like tiny bells. In that instant he recalled the fifty-nine of them woven in the mane of the Yvag queen's steed, and he might have slipped into dark melancholy then if Janet hadn't said, "You should know that sometimes a beast is exactly want one wants," as her hand stroked him hard again. In her laurel-green gaze was something he'd never seen before in any woman's eyes, and he willingly let it devour him whole.

※ ※ ※

After that time he slept again, waking to the sound of her moving about in his house. Dressed in her linen shift, she had built a fire in his hearth in the center and was stirring the pottery crock that she had just removed from the hot stones on which he cooked. He smelled oat porridge. Naked, he walked to her. On his table, he saw that she had rolled out and baked a flat oval of bannock. How had he slept through all of that? Sheer exhaustion after so many nights of hunting his enemy, no doubt.

She sensed him and turned, smiling. He drew her to him. They kissed. She pushed him back. "If we do, your porridge will grow cold."

"After, then."

She took a wooden bowl and spooned porridge into it. "Trading one appetite for another?" she teased.

He chuckled. It was the truth.

They sat and ate together. He had a jug of cider made from her father's apple trees, and rather than ale they drank that. The meal was more breakfast than he normally ate. He considered asking her about the miller who wanted her hand, but decided he was better off not poking that bear. Right now they were together in here and the outside world could stay out.

And then she asked him, "So where were you when I arrived last night?" and the outside world gained entry.

He had been wondering since he woke what he would tell her. Waldroup's ghost was nowhere to be found to advise him, leaving him to rely on his own instincts, stunted as they were from trusting no one other than his mentor, and nobody at all since Waldroup's death.

For all they had survived—the many battles fought, the dozens of accidents that could befall masons working lewises and balancing on scaffolds, not to mention foolhardy sidetrips into other worlds—the last thing that should have felled Waldroup was an ague, what the monk who tended to him called an *acuta febris*.

Waldroup seemed to know that he would not survive the illness. Thomas never quite admitted it: His mentor was so strong, so wise, and always a step ahead of his enemies in battle, that it was inconceivable he could be overcome by anything smaller than an army.

He lay upon a feather-filled bed in one of the four bays of the *firmaria*, his eyes darkly ringed and lips cracked and sticky with spittle. There were hours now where he didn't recognize Thomas, and periods where he babbled about trees that moaned and monsters who wore people like gloves. He insisted that he was already dead because he floated now "upon clouds, and isn't that the final proof?"

The monk seemed to pay none of it any mind, explaining, "Many a man thinks he's in the clouds because of the bedding here, the likes of which he's never known. It's quite common. Pray for him, my son. Prayer is the best medicine."

Thomas had to hope there was no skinwalker stalking the aisles of the small tapestry-cordoned infirmary who might understand ravings the monk dismissed. He pretended in the monk's presence to be equally uninformed and baffled by it.

Then, on the last day, Waldroup regained clarity awhile. "The devils didn't get us, did they, Tom?" he said. "We kept ourselves out of hell, we did. And you have to keep clear of them hereafter without me."

"I won't be without you, Alpin. Look how better you are than yesterday."

Waldroup closed his sunken eyes, sighing. "Don't trust no one never. Even the most decent of folk—*especially* the most decent. One misspoke word and they'll have you in their net, little brother. They got all the power, all the time to use it."

"Right, I know, I know that."

"You keep your own counsel."

"But *you'll* counsel me, Alpin."

He sighed again; it came from deeper in his throat. He said, "These *clouds*," then went still. For a minute, Thomas didn't truly comprehend the change. Waldroup had fallen asleep again, that was all. A few moments later, the monk returned, patted his shoulders, and recited something solemn in Latin. Then he knew.

And ever since, Alpin's capricious shade had counseled him, a voice in his ear that came and went, as if he, Thomas, were striding through invisible, folded, haunted layers of the world; otherwise, he had in all respects kept his own as promised. But here in this moment with Janet, he knew two things: First, that he would marry her, and, second, that he would have to trust her with the truth of himself if he did, starting with his adventures of last night, for she would need to know all that must never be spoken of. If she was to join her fate to his, then it must be in the full knowledge of who and what he was, and of the danger he presented.

He only wished he knew the scope of that himself.

XVII. The Christes Maesse

The most amazing thing about her, Thomas supposed, was that Janet Cardden did not flee for her life from "mad Tom" once he'd told her his story. To his own ears as he jabbered away, he sounded like a raving moonstruck idiot: the Queen of Elfland snatching his brother as *teind* (a debt or tribute of some sort, a tenth of something, the nature of which he still barely understood and neither he nor Alpin had ever entirely worked out), and monstrous things that breathed through holes in their sides crawling out of graves and crypts, trees that moaned and spoke, a stone that fit in his palm and sliced open the world—it was a mad concoction of magics well before he got anywhere near the admission that his own father was no longer human, but an Yvag lich who had helped capture a new *teind*, a girl this time, the very night before while he watched from hiding and could do nothing to stop it because it *was* his father and how could he bring himself to shoot down his father?

He showed her the ördstone while he explained what it did, but dared not demonstrate it for fear of creating a new entrance for the Yvag that would forever after lead right inside his house. He held it out on his palm, where it glittered, revealing the strange lines and symbols he could not decipher, but whisked it away when she reached for it, fearful suddenly that the touch of it might affect her the way the other stones had unbalanced Waldroup. All the while, he felt sure that his refusal to demonstrate or let her touch the stone only provided her with ample proof that he was indeed insane.

Perhaps Janet did not believe him that first morning, although she humored him—but then that's what one did with a madman. However, four days later the news of a missing girl from a Carterhaugh farm reached the Carddens. She'd vanished on the night Janet had slept in Tàm Lynn's bed. Her family claimed they'd heard a strange music in the night that must have put them all to sleep, and in the morning when they awoke, their daughter, who had been sleeping in their midst, was simply gone without a trace.

"Taken to Old Melrose," said Thomas, when Janet told him. "Led there by elven soldiers and human hosts."

"But why?" she asked, and to that he had no answer. Even the Yvag they'd cornered so long ago had not told him and Alpin the why of the *teind*. Why his brother? Why the need to kidnap anyone at all? They stole babies and left changeling things, bedazzled children and adults alike on some timetable he couldn't make sense of, and all for a purpose no one knew. He hadn't any idea, and he knew more of the Yvag than perhaps anyone else alive.

It turned out that the Carterhaugh girl's name was also Janet.

Janet Cardden had never heard of Innes Rimor de Ercildoun, though they lived within a half day's ride of each other. A day later, while Thomas was up in the shieling, she asked her father if he knew anything about Innes. He enjoyed local gossip, she knew, which was one of the reasons he was so fond of Forbes the miller, whose mill seemed to provide more intersection of tittle-tattle than even an alehouse.

No surprise then that her father knew a good deal of the elder Rimor and his holdings, and was able to corroborate most of the family's tragic history—at least what was said of it: Both sons had disappeared on the same day some years earlier, presumed drowned in the Yarrow, if he recollected right, by one of them. "An idiot, it is said."

The daughter, Innes, had married into another powerful family with which he was also acquainted, the MacGilleans.

"That family," he told her, "was if anything the worse blighted. The patriarch I knew quite well. We'd met at festival in Roxburgh, oh, when you were in swaddling. On a bone he choked to death, oh, eight years gone now? One son fell down a well, another his own life took, most likely in grief over his father's and brother's deaths. The

one Innes Rimor married, called Balthair, he was the youngest, and
the last of the clan. And then she, the poor girl, herself almost in
childbirth died, lost her babe within a week—a son, they said. And
as if that wasn't enough stones piled upon any family, Balthair, the
only family heir, a year later vanished in the company of an alderman
of Ercildoun, whom I believe you met once here. Stroud. A very
strange man, but also very influential. Powerful."

"I don't recollect him," she replied honestly.

"No, well, no reason you would do. About *that* event, all sorts of
stories arose. Two strangers at the time had in Ercildoun been seen
and nobody ever saw them again, so 'twas guessed they were
cutpurses who waylaid and killed the local men. And because on the
corpse road out of the town Stroud and MacGillean had last been
seen, well, it became the ghosts of the dead Rimor boys, or
MacGillean's brothers' spirits seeking him because, I suppose, for the
family fortune he must have killed them. It was even put about that
the men's bodies had been located among the graves of Old Melrose,
but in a state suggesting terrible dark magics. Of course that spot has
always been associated with magical goings-on. There were tales of
all sorts when I was a boy. Ah, but enough of that. Others think
somebody was digging up the old graves, hoping to find jewelry or
some such, and didn't bother with putting the bodies back, and that
someone else mistook them for Stroud and MacGillean, who,
accordingly, were never found. Masons there were, working on the
nearby abbey. Most had gone for the winter, but the remaining few
knew nothing of any of this. So many tales. Yet no one to accuse on
hand, and no certain thing to accuse anyone of—the sheriff never
even found their horses. But, you know, people love stories,
especially when you can fit them up with ghosts and murder and
magic. Soon enough, that girl from Carterhaugh will find her way
into some tale or ballad of elves and fairies when more likely she
wandered off or ran away with her lad. Doesn't need to make any
sense at all, so and it thrills."

She smiled patiently. "Yes, I'm certain, Father, you are right on all
of that, but what of Innes Rimor?"

"Oh, yes. She of course inherited the MacGillean holdings, once
Balthair was declared dead. That took another year, and in the
interim her mother died. And that, after losing her own child and

then her husband, well, the poor girl wisnae right in the head any longer. The holdings became property of the Rimors, and thus that family has come to own now more land hereabouts than anybody. Quite the power to be reckoned with. The father, he used to be a fine man, but he's turned cold and bitter, and, to be honest, quite distasteful. Well, I mean, he's lost both sons and wife, as well as the heir the daughter should have delivered. It's nae wonder he believes he's punished by God. As for the girl, Innes, well, he did the only thing he could. He sent her to a convent where she can be looked after. Cluny, isn't it? Old Rimor can well afford the beneficence. There's a hospital of sorts there. I hear they've even female surgeons, if one can countenance such stories. Not that the poor child is for the saw. What ails her cannae be cut out."

Janet drank it all in. Pieced together, her father's rumored events aligned remarkably with what Thomas had told her; she wondered both how many other stories of local families her father knew and had never mentioned, and how much she would have to withhold from him beginning this moment forward.

Cardden disrupted her thoughts by patting her hand. "Are you worried," he said, "that I might send *you* away, daughter, rather than permission give you to wed that knight of yours?"

Baffled, she stared at him, for a moment unable even to comprehend to whom "that knight" referred. Her father beamed proudly and rubbed his hands together, thrilled, it seemed, to know something else that his daughter did not.

"He asked me early this morning for your hand," he said. "Has he kept it from you?"

"No." She could barely get the word out around the knot in her throat. Her heart threatened to lift her up with the angels. "Not kept it at all."

Their first winter together, Thomas lived with Janet in her father's keep while he and Lusk's twins, Filib and Kester, worked together to enlarge the house he'd built for himself. The rear oak cruck became a middle support; he laid down new padstones on which new crucks would stand, and pushed out part of one wall to build a new and much larger hearth that ventilated through a chimney hole in the wall above it rather than through a central hole in the thatch—a version in miniature of the great hearth inside Castle MacGillean. It meant far less smoke wafting through the interior of the house than when the roof hole didn't draw well. With the central fire pit gone, there was space now for his wife's loom. Above their bed, on crosspieces, he laid boards for a storage loft and lay his bows and arrows there. He dug the original floor out, filled the pit with straw, and then laid planks over it. Separate from the house he erected as well a wooden byre beside the small stable he'd already built. In some ways he was simply creating a house he saw in his head drawing upon construction he had observed and absorbed in his travels. Not unlike his riddles and the numbers of things that came to him, he felt as if he was chasing after its meaning until it was framed and built, and he stood inside the low stone walls and low-hanging thatch, marveling at its assembly as much as anyone else did, though it came from his imaginings. Lusk and other neighbors came and admired the construction, asked him where he had learned such a frame. All he could do was reply, "Abroad."

"A visionary," one of them called him.

As Cardden's son-in-law he now oversaw all of the family's holdings and all of the other tenant farmers. The tenant-in-chief could not understand why young Tàmhas Lynn did not abandon work on this new house, however cleverly made, and live under *his* roof. There was certainly enough space in his hall, with two fire pits and plenty of beds behind screens and curtains.

Janet of course understood perfectly: Too many people lived at the castle, family and servants, baker and blacksmith, cooks, brewers, laundresses—a multitude who rendered it difficult to speak of too many critical things, and absolutely impossible to make nocturnal trips to and from Old Melrose unobserved. So constrained there, he would shortly give himself away.

That first winter, with his new duties and the house to enlarge, Thomas resigned himself to learning nothing more of the Yvag skinwalkers. Certainly, he could not investigate the crypts of the Abbey of St. Mary to discover whether he'd been right in interpreting his riddle. Moreover, being Cardden's son-in-law meant that he moved within a stratum of society surrounding Roxburgh that had been closed to him before. He didn't appreciate what this meant nor the danger it posed until the night Cardden held a celebration of the Epiphany in his great hall.

He spent much of the day at work on the rear wall of his house, and by the time he walked back to Cardden's, his bag of mason's tools hanging by his hip, it was late afternoon, the clouds glowing pink behind him. He was looking forward to a light meal and then tumbling into bed with Janet.

As he approached the main gate, a wagon with an arched frame covered in red cut across his path and rolled ahead, into the yard. The yard, it turned out, was full of wagons, carts, and horses.

Confused, he walked on toward the great hall. He was so dirty and ragged that Cardden's servant Rab, with his peregrine-sharp face, blocked his way at first. Then realizing it was Thomas, he blanched and stepped aside, saying, "Beg pardon, master."

"What is all this, Rab?" Thomas asked.

"The Christes Maesse," said Rab. "Did they not tell ye?"

Surely Janet would have, must have. What day was this? The work of enlarging the house had become so much part of his routine that all days had melted together like a string of tallow candles.

Before he could decide upon a course of action, Janet emerged from the brightly lit hall. "Oh, Tàm, you *did* forget." She wore a green gown, girdled with a long sash at the hips, and with wide, flared sleeves. Her hair was plaited in a ridge around her head, and one thick braid swept down over her left shoulder.

He tried to smile. "Only what day today is. I remember everything else, I think."

"We must get you clean, and right away." She took him by the hand and led him across the yard, between the wagons and their attendants, to the small ancient well. He drew off his shirt, watching his breath on the air, his skin rising in bumps like a plucked goose. While he drew up a bucket of water, she went into the stable and returned with a block of castile soap. "You wash. I'll bring you some thyme oil."

"And clothes might be helpful." He grinned. She flung the bucketful of water over him and he howled. She offered him the soap, and he snatched it and began rubbing it hard over himself as he hissed against the chill.

Janet said, "The stables," then hurried off.

He drew another bucket of water, then stripped off his braies and boots, and poured it over himself. As tired as he had been coming home, he was wide awake now. "Fourteen wagons, eleven carts," he muttered, "sixteen attendants, seventy-eight wheels, thirty-nine horses. And Rab." He poured a third bucket over himself before he was done.

Retreating to the stables, he paced, shivering. His own horse eyed him as if he were mad or dangerous. He huffed, told the horse, "Be in your own stable soon enough," then slapped at himself for warmth as he walked in circles. Wagons and horses—how many people was his father-in-law hosting, and from how far away? The wagons with their framed covers did not belong to the likes of his neighbors, the other tenants of Cardden's land. Besides, then Lusk would have known of it, mentioned it. Who attended a Christes Maesse? Prior to this, his every one had been spent sleeping on the ground, near an abbey or a castle or on a battlefield.

Janet returned with a pair of short pointed leather boots, striped hose, a linen shirt, and thick red V-necked outer tunic. She also had a small phial of oil, which she dabbed on him, and combed into his short beard and wet hair with her fingers. She parted the hair, smoothed it.

He belted his tunic.

"There," she said, "you look handsome."

"I look as if I swam across the Teviot to get here." He pushed his hair back above his ears. "I'm sorry I lose track of days."

She kissed him. "So long as you don't lose track of me."

"That will never happen."

"You promise?"

"I swear to—what should I swear to?—God Himself?"

She pretended to consider. "I imagine that's a high enough authority."

Arm in arm, flared sleeves tangling, they walked out of the stables. "So who is here with all these wagons?" he asked.

"People I don't know. Some are from Roxburgh, Melrose, and Selkirk." Her grip tightened. "You need to know, there are some from Ercildoun."

He stopped in his tracks. "Why is he hosting such a gathering?"

"The Epiphany. But mostly, I fear, it's for us. Our union is being celebrated as if the three kings had visited you and me. There was no talking him out of it." She looked him in the eyes, and he saw that there was something she had yet to tell him.

"What else?" he asked.

"The Ercildoun alderman is named Master Rimor."

He tugged his arm free and stepped back. "I can't go in there."

"You can. You have to. He won't know you."

He glanced at where Rab stood at the door, took Janet by the arm, and led her farther away so that they couldn't be overheard. "Because he is no longer my father, you mean? Are you willing to risk everything on that notion? He won't have come alone. Most likely your father's list will have included other skinwalkers, too. Maybe all of them."

"You think my father—"

"No." He gripped her hands between his. "I think as I've said— they're all high-placed. Inviting his influential neighbors, your father can hardly avoid them. And 'twould look strange if he did."

"But if Alderman Rimor's no longer your father, you're no longer his son, either. He has never seen you grown up, hasn't set eyes on you since you were a skinny beardless youth following your brother. That's what you told me. Isn't that the case? No one could recognize you after so long. You're the wrong age, and, well . . ."

He shook his head. "The difference of a few years becomes less of a distinction all the time, but say it is as you describe, what if I should succumb to a fit while in their midst?"

"Try not to?" She implored him, "If you don't appear, my father will seek to explain your absence, and what he'll say is—"

"—that I sometimes suffer seizures and spout gibberish. Yes, that should doom me well. Damn the yuletide." He pulled at his lip. "If even one of them finds out . . ."

She pressed herself to him. "They are not looking, my love. Let them see a local husbandman who fought in far-off wars and knows no one hereabouts, of no importance to them, just as my father with his lesser demesne is of little importance. They humor him, being here. Some probably laugh up their sleeves at him."

"May he never acquire enough land to make him of use."

"Play the part, Tàm. For me." She took his hands and placed them on her belly. "For us."

He read the meaning in her gaze, and for a moment all of his worries about the Yvag evaporated. "You're with child?" She nodded.

Thomas took her in his arms and swung her around, then pressed her to him a long moment, inhaling her thyme. "Now I must build the house even *larger.*" He laughed, but wished secretly that he were there right now instead of here. How many of those he'd watched from the hillside would be inside?

Across the yard, Rab watched them, a vague smile on his face as if he couldn't be certain whether or not he was party to a lovers' tiff. Thomas gave him a wave and Rab nodded back. Janet was right: There really was no choice. Stories would be told about him otherwise. With dread he tried to imagine what it was going to be like to look into his father's eyes and find a stranger there.

He'd never seen so many people in the great hall. Tables that usually stood against the walls had been carried closer to the middle of the room to form a single three-sided eating surface large enough to accommodate them all, with two strong fires. Only a thin haze of smoke hung over them all. Seeing him enter, Cardden came and took charge of him, sending Janet off so that he could introduce Thomas to the feasters. No doubt it let him feel important and proud.

He led Thomas around among his friends first—the sheriff of Roxburgh, named Gospatrick, and then the young mill owner named Forbes from near Selkirk. They had met on numerous occasions, none in which the bushy red-haired miller was anything but reserved. There could be no doubt that he hated Thomas for sabotaging his reasonable plans to ask for Janet's hand, although according to her there had never been any great pairing of spirits there—at least not on her side of the equation. She'd been grieving for her dead sweetheart that Forbes never quite grasped was an impediment and not an opportunity.

Trapped now in the Epiphany, Thomas welcomed a conversation even with such an enemy.

"Our Janet is well, then?" the miller asked him as if they shared her well-being between them.

"Oh, yes, quite well." They watched her together, Thomas deciding immediately to say nothing of her being with child.

A long pause followed.

Then Forbes added, "Well, I am not about to say the best man won, you understand."

Thomas, still smiling pleasantly, nevertheless winced a little. "Of course, though there really was no competition. I was not about seeking a wife."

"No doubt," Forbes agreed. "She was lost in grief over her soldier."

"Kenny."

"I should have seen it would take another such to draw her out again. I should have enlisted myself."

Thomas only nodded, saying nothing. If Forbes needed to believe all that, then there was no point in trying to persuade him otherwise.

He was about to take his leave when a heavyset woman intruded on their conversation. He knew the face from the group that had toured the abbey site. Forbes introduced her as the widow Mac an Fleisdeir of Selkirk.

"And who's this handsome young stranger, then?" she asked.

So, he thought, not a prioress after all, but the widow of a landowner, a woman with power the equal of the MacGilleans and the Rimors. She was ruddy-cheeked and seemed to be well into her cups. While Forbes was speaking, she gave Thomas a careful sizing up, a calculated look, then rubbed a hand over his shoulder familiarly as if he was a piece of livestock she might take home with her. She grinned loosely and with hardly concealed carnality. He eased himself out of her reach, then traded a look of recognition with Forbes. The redheaded miller's glance essentially said "You'd do well to stay out of her clutches."

She gave him one final open look of invitation, which he pretended to be too obtuse to read. Instead, smiling stupidly as though drunk himself, he toasted her and Forbes before retreating from the concupiscent widow. He wondered how her husband had died. An unfortunate accident, no doubt.

He put one of the two fires between them, then drifted farther away. Spying Cardden, he launched himself in that direction, only to find, seated close to his father-in-law, the vaguely familiar gray-haired man with the broken nose, the skinwalker who had directed the taking of the latest *teind* at the old abbey. For a fleeting instant he was watching the girl, the other Janet, walk forward on a leash and into the ring.

The man looked up at Thomas's approach, and stood. Cardden's gaze traveled from him to Thomas. The man said, "So you're the young farmer we're all hearing about. Old Cardden here can't stop singing your praises, you know."

The man's name was Baggi, and he referred to himself as a

magistrate of Roxburghshire. Among his duties he oversaw Gospatrick, the sheriff Thomas had met only a handful of minutes earlier. Baggi's wife, introduced next, sat across the table from the two men but seemed barely there at all. She said nothing when introduced, gave the slightest of nods of recognition, and observed Thomas through dark and fearful eyes that looked bruised from lack of sleep. The wine they were being served was full of sediment that needed to settle, but she drank hers down almost as fast as it was poured as if she might be able to drown in it. Everything in her manner hinted to him that she knew her husband had transmuted into someone else. She would have sounded insane, of course, had she voiced her fears, and he could not let on to her that he knew her secret, much less her husband's, though he would have enjoyed an opportunity to learn what she knew, how she had determined it. She was likely doomed, he thought. No way could he aid her nor even acknowledge that he understood, without dooming himself, too.

Baggi was watching him closely, his head tilted in perplexity. "I have to say, it feels to me as if we've met, Husbandman Lynn."

"I think not," Thomas said honestly. "Although I believe I have seen you about the town. I've gone there numerous times now, for a plow and other items."

"Ah, likely that is it, then. You were a soldier, you? Your father has been, ah, explaining."

For one beat of his heart, Thomas thought Baggi meant his real father. He'd not yet spotted Ercildoun's latest alderman, but took the moment of glancing around to cement his resolve. "I fought, yes, for King David, for the Empress Matilda." He borrowed the rest from Waldroup's story. "I was fighting in Wales and that ended in stalemate, so I sailed to France with others seeking more employment, and fought there until that was exhausted." At that point, Cardden stood, gave him a proud look, then walked off to engage with other guests. He knew this story already. Inwardly, Thomas was relieved that Cardden hadn't interjected how he'd worked on the new abbey. That was a problem he must shortly resolve.

"Well, and you survived with all limbs intact. That's rare good fortune for a professional soldier."

Thomas almost said that was because he was an archer, but stopped himself. An archer was likely still someone these creatures sought. "I was . . . careful," he said. "And even so . . ." He touched the scar at his hairline. "Just barely."

"You'll have witnessed many who were not, I'm sure," Baggi replied, his blue eyes solemn.

"What, battlefields sown with bodies? There is no other kind." He paused to drink some of his wine, pulling together his story before he continued. "But one of the soldiers had been a stonemason hereabouts, and between wars I apprenticed myself to him. A full two years we made our living working stone. He claimed to have worked on your new abbey."

Baggi cocked an eyebrow. "Your father-in-law said that *you* worked on our abbey."

Of course he had. "No, no," Thomas replied. "Then I've confused him with my tales of war. Janet—that is, his daughter and my wife—didn't wish to hear these things, as she'd lost a soldier of her own."

"Yes, I knew of this. But—"

"Things got a bit confused, because, you see, I didn't."

"Mmm. Tell me, Husbandman Lynn. This mason to whom you apprenticed . . ."

"Ah, well, he died, didn't he? In France."

"You returned to war?"

"We did. But, I don't know, the taste had soured for me. I'd seen too much slaughter. So I took my recompense from the king and came here, where I can plant something in the soil that lives instead of dies. My friend chose the battlefield again and was not so lucky this time. A shame, as he'd always hoped to return one day and see the new abbey. Truth be told, I haven't yet seen it myself. So much to be done."

Baggi listened, taking his measure, then responded, "That was well expressed, young man. I congratulate you on joining this good family through so lovely a maiden." He glanced Janet's way. "She is a prize."

Thomas had carefully outfitted his tale to place himself as far from here as possible, and could only hope that Cardden had not mentioned the fit he'd suffered or the riddle he'd spouted that day. Magistrate Baggi's reaction led him to believe that nothing had been revealed, and he'd now provided Baggi a dead end in the hunt for Stroud's killers.

He said, "Thank you, I think so, too, sir. And now I must meet the rest of my new father's guests."

Baggi and he went separate ways. Baggi's wife watched him dolefully over her cup but never uttered a word. He found himself circling near the widow again, and veered quickly away.

Between her and Baggi, he wove a complicated path through the room, into and around the many conversations taking place, none of which he truly cared to engage with. Maintaining his uncomplicated façade and covering up his gaffe with Cardden was proving exhausting.

Satisfied that Alderman Rimor must have departed, he sought Janet, and circuitously headed for her. But when he came around the tables once more, he found a man standing half-hunched over between her and Cardden. It was his father.

Alderman Rimor wore an overtunic backed with squirrel fur, an indication of his great wealth and standing. Up close he looked more withered and unhappy than he'd seemed from a distance at the abbey. His skin was gray, almost bloodless. Years had passed, of course, but this was more than that: a body wasting away. Either the encroachment of the Yvag was draining him or the creature had chosen to occupy someone already suffering from some infirmity. He guessed that his father was dying. Was it the loss of his sons? Probably that and the madness of his only daughter. Thomas thought of Onchu, of Innes, of his mother—all of them absent here because of the stranger lurking behind this ashen, familiar face.

He focused upon the center of that rich overtunic and only with great effort raised his sights to look into the eyes of his father. Those rheumy eyes met his squarely, coldly, without any hint of recognition, just as Janet had anticipated. Peripherally, she watched him with worry. He introduced himself to the alderman and tried hard to repress the keen awareness that something unholy stood before him, animating his father's corpse.

Rimor gestured to Janet. "You've married, um, this one, have you not?"

"Yes, sir. I have that good fortune."

Cardden interjected, "And they are to have a child!"

"Oh, well, then further congratulations are in order," said Rimor. "I'd not heard. I can still remember the excitement of making babies, mmm-hmm." His crooked smile was, in fact, lewd. His tongue moistened his lips.

Whatever the Yvag referred to, it surely wasn't any memory of his father's. His father, the widow—he wondered if all the skinwalkers were depraved by nature. He asked as innocently as possible, "And what became of your babies, sir? I imagine your children are all grown, no?" He glanced about. "Any here with you?"

"Oh, no, no. The boys—both taken, too young." He waved at the air as if dismissing them. "My daughter . . . eh, gone in another sense." And he placed a hand beside his head and twisted it back and forth. "We have severed ties, you might say: mine to her and hers to the world as we know it."

Thomas's hands, behind his back, curled into fists. "She is ill, then?" he asked calmly.

"What?" He blinked as if having lost track of the conversation. "No, I banished her to a place where she can keep company with other madwomen who've married invisible saints and demigods. Perfect place for her. She's of no consequence to me or anyone. No more babies coming out of her now or ever. Still, she did increase our holdings." His expression soured further. "For nothing. Our line is quite likely to perish when I do and that is that."

"Then I wish you good health, sir, in this new year."

The sagging face sneered. "Might as well wish a dog a good *kick*."

Thomas said, "Beg pardon, sir," and stepped back. He caught Janet's eye and shook his head that she should let him be. Then he turned about and crossed the hall.

He strode down the stone steps and out into the chilly night. One wagon was just departing. He stared after it.

What sort of creature inhabited his father, that it left not a trace of that kind and decent man he'd known? The Yvag seemed to loathe everything, as if, finding itself in a deteriorating shell, it railed against the short time left to grind a few more humans to pulp before it would have to depart. He would be doing it a favor if he slew his father's body, setting both free. What he truly wanted right then was to murder it. The urge took hold of him to ride to the Abbey of St. Mary's, locate their new lair, and slaughter all of the sleepers at one go. Having worked on it for more than half a year, he knew the abbey's layout, the entrance to the crypt. And why not? Why shouldn't he go and—

"Husband."

He turned at Janet's call. He had walked blindly past the well where a mere two hours earlier he had shivered, horripilated, and scrubbed himself clean. She closed the distance now.

"What is it?" she asked. "Your father?"

He told her, railing at the abominable things inhabiting the widow, the magistrate, but most of all his father. His eyes brimmed with tears, his rage boiling over. In that moment she placed her hands on his face and kissed him long and deep, as if she could draw the venom out of him; and somehow, miraculously she did. She must have felt him relax and let go. He threw his arms around her. "It's taken him away as surely as if he'd been marched through the green fire like all the *teinds*," he sobbed. "Everything he was is gone."

She let him wring himself dry. Then she spoke calmly. "You're as furious as a lightning storm, as you should be. But now, for my sake and your child's if not your own, please come back inside. If you disappear, if you go and kill some of these vile creatures, you tell them everything, and their suspicions will stick upon you as upon a target. They will *all* know, Tàm, and the consequences will ripple out."

He stood silently. Did not say that he'd been foolish to think he might have a life like any other's with her—a life full of hard work, harvests, and love. But he thought it. He regretted too late having pulled her into this. "I don't know how to pretend, go on and not take revenge for what that monster has done to my father. What all of them did to my sister. My whole family. And that poor girl from Carterhaugh—who'll avenge her?"

"If you die, you take no revenge at all, but you set them upon me and your child. Even if you strike and then flee as you did before with your friend, we'll be left here to pay for it. Tàm, you can't avenge everyone they've ever taken. How many would that be? Hundreds? Thousands? What if they've been here since the very beginning?"

He answered that someone had once told his father how Old Melrose was built upon a spot supposed to have magic, some sort of power, long before the monks arrived, that ancient rituals had been performed there on that spit of land. There had been a *maen hir* there, tall as a house and covered in ancient script. They had not been specific as to what rituals; nor did they say what had happened to that massive stone. It certainly wasn't there anymore, though plenty of others stood scattered across the landscape. Thomas had been an idiot child when he overheard the conversation, and now suspected it was nothing more than a local legend that had grown and changed shape over time, decades; it made him wonder, though, when the *fae* and the elven had first been spoken of, where the idea of these occult and magical creatures had come from if not from the intrusion of the Yvag and those flitting little monsters of theirs. His thoughts, wandering off into speculation, lost their fury. Janet replied that her father had cast that spot in a similar light although his stories of Old Melrose seemed gathered from dozens of sources.

He smiled at his wife for having listened to and calmed him. He asked her if she had met the unholy trio.

"I did. The woman acts inebriated. Magistrate Baggi grins and wheedles and would be everybody's friend. All three of them have a lecherous nature in common, and probably have their way most of the time because of their status if not their powers of persuasion, which serves to explain everything. Those who are used to giving orders expect to be obeyed. I also met a few other folk who know your father but nothing of the elves, and who insist your mother's death unhinged him—that he wasn't at all like this before it."

"Then you doubt their unnaturalness because there are other versions?"

"Oh, to the contrary, husband. They are like three psalteries plucked exactly so, ever in tune, so perfectly so that every note, word, and gesture plays false. The magistrate's wife is so terrified of him that she will hardly speak, and the widow, though she declares herself drunk, her eyes are not bleary. They shift and take in everything as coldly as a falcon might."

So, she had seen what he had. He saw also the wisdom of her advice. He took her by the hand to return to the keep, but she pulled him up short.

"How do they choose? They selected those three people out of everyone."

"You answered that yourself. Their status gains them great influence. No one is possessing a simple farmer or a shoemaker."

"But how do they realize their possession? Are they demons or ghosts, are they earwigs dropped in the sleeper's ear? What alchemy lets them steal the souls of the living?"

He shook his head. That was a question he had as well, a riddle he had never unraveled. How did they take over his father or the alderman before him, or Baldie, who was *dead* when they invaded him? For a long time he and Waldroup had thought that everyone they inhabited must have died, leaving an empty shell, but that meant the Yvag either waited about for the person to die or they effected such a demise first, which seemed too complicated and clumsy a process. And, anyway, some small part of Baldie had lingered within.

"I think it would be worth finding that out before you kill your leeches," said Janet, and he saw in her expression as much fury as he had felt before she calmed him. "It would end all of this if we could build a keep around our souls." She was certainly right. There must be a method. A poison imbibed, or a spell cast. Otherwise, they would simply have reached out and taken up residence in him and Alpin instead of confronting them.

He closed his arms about her and just stood there awhile, gathering peacefulness in her embrace. Then he let Janet lead him back to the festivities of the Epiphany. In all the tumult, no one seemed to have noticed their absence save Cardden, who patted Thomas on the shoulder and beamed at him. "Young love," he declared wistfully.

The rest of the evening, Thomas did his best to avoid the three Yvag skinwalkers by remaining at his wife's side.

XVIII. Morven & the Riddles

By the time their daughter, Morven, was born, Thomas had suffered half a dozen fits or more. Of these, many had occurred while plowing or up on the shieling, and whatever he might have uttered was lost forever. Even if he heard himself, he had nothing to write the words upon.

Three happened in Janet's presence.

The first took place in their house where Thomas and the Lusk twins were stuffing bound thatch into the new, extended rafters— the boys up above and Thomas on a ladder inside. He said, "Janet," then slid off the ladder and collapsed. She ran to him, and knelt, propping up his head. The boys looked down through the open roof as Thomas twitched and then suddenly, jerkily, began reciting. It lasted for only a few moments, and then he lay relaxed as if sleeping. Janet propped his head on some of the thatch, and told the boys to come down for the time being, all while reciting the riddle silently to herself. She had only to reach for her stylus and ink on the table above to write it out on a piece of parchment.

"I will serve when bent
To the will of my master,
Then I find my mark.
Upright I am unstrung.
Say my name."

The boys came in the door. Kester Lusk asked what he'd said, and she repeated what she had written. The boys listened, looked at each other. Then Filib asked, "Does it mean Tàm's bent to the will of your father, miss?"

"Possibly," she quickly replied, and left it at that. There would be no more work done on the roof that day, and she sent the boys home with pandemayne bread she'd purchased the day before from the baker in Roxburgh, as payment for their time.

Later, alone with Thomas, Janet read the words and said, "It's nothing to do with my father's will, is it? It's your bow it's describing, isn't it?"

Thomas nodded. "Sometimes the riddles warn of something coming. But most times, like this, they're like guessing games. What am I? Who am I? Name me. Some of those, I've never known what they're about. It's as if my mind's teasing me with questions to challenge me. Makes no sense, but why should it? My mind has never ever been sensible."

A second seizure struck one evening, following in the afterglow of their lovemaking when Janet was some months pregnant. She sat above him, and watched as his eyes rolled back and his body stiffened, then spasmed and jerked. Through clenched teeth, he said:

"So long as the Great Thorn Tree stands,
Fair Ercildoun shall keep its lands."

Foam flecked the corners of his mouth. But almost at once he returned to his senses. Knowing his own symptoms all too well, he asked what he had said.

They easily unraveled that riddle. The Great Thorn Tree of Ercildoun was well known to everyone. The riddle seemed to be a simple prediction of a time far in the town's future, as the tree was currently sturdy and healthy. But how the town might lose its lands, they could not fathom.

The third fit struck him down mere moments after he had held his daughter for the first time. Sìleas and Mrs. Lusk had been there for the birth, which had happened without complications. Sìleas had stayed after to help. Janet, exhausted from her labor, was holding the baby at her breast.

Thomas stood up from the bed but immediately shuddered and dropped to his knees. He put out his hands as if blind. His head twisted, and his mouth worked; his teeth creaked as he struggled against the lightning that was exploding in his head. He collapsed in the dirt.

Sìleas shrieked, but Janet hushed her. "Listen to him," she ordered, "whatever he says. Listen well." The girl stared back moon-eyed with fear. His jaw had relaxed. It worked as if some unseen presence was trying to make words using it. The words emerged softly.

"Striders 'cross landscapes, rivers and wild
None of them men, none e'er a child.
They who'll have all, their brows never ringed—
Counsellors to kingdoms, never a king."

Then he lay still and silent. "Quick, bring me my stylus and inkpot," Janet told the girl. "There." She pointed. Morven gurgled and whined as Janet set her aside. The babe resented her meal being removed from her grasp.

Sìleas handed Janet a feathered stylus and the small pot of iron gall. Janet repeated what she had heard, confirming with the girl that it was what he had said. Then she wrote it on the back of one of the skins piled on her for warmth. Reading it back, she muttered, "This one, I think, matters."

"What's it mean, ma'am?"

She shook her head. "I'm not even sure he knows. But we won't mention it to anyone until he's worked it out, all right?"

"He will be all right, won't he, ma'am?" Sìleas asked, and immediately feared she'd revealed her adoration of him.

"He will. But let's keep this between us," Janet replied. She was fully aware of Sìleas's infatuation.

Sìleas agreed, confused; but, superstitious, believing herself in love with Tàmhas Lynn, and in awe of the strange incomprehensible riddle, she went home and told her father of it. Lusk was aware of his neighbor's infirmity, having chanced upon him one afternoon lying behind the plow just after a fit had finished with him. He had no idea if Thomas had spoken that day nor what Sìleas's reported words might mean. Both of his sons listened to their sister as she recited what she remembered—it was already confused and tangling in her mind, since none of it made any sense to her. She described how it looked as if something invisible was making his mouth move and speak. The three children speculated that a devil took hold of poor Tàmhas Lynn, or maybe it was God, and the divine world touched him directly. Whatever the truth of it might be, they were more in awe of their young neighbors than ever.

That was true in particular for Filib. He had already asked if Janet might teach him writing. While that was not a skill of much use to a tenant farmer, Filib was developing ambitions beyond those of his more contented twin and his sister. He'd learned stonework and mortaring now, and how to plumb a wall; and he had begun to dwell upon the idea of the world beyond this tiny farm. Tàmhas Lynn had wandered through it and seen exciting things: battles, soldiers and kings, and many foreign places. Filib wanted to have such experiences of his own. "Striders across landscapes" probably referred to people like Thomas who traveled far and wide. People who advised kings—that's what the riddle said, too. "None of them men or children" couldn't mean just women. It had to be more like a reference to certain people who were special, different from the kinds of men who stayed in one place. That's what children did: They stayed in place. The message in the riddle, he thought, had surely been meant for him.

For Thomas, though, that night was his final seizure for a long time. Three years of peace followed, as though his daughter's emergence into the world somehow arrested the lightning in his head.

During that period, while his fits and riddles became more and more distant memories, in Ercildoun a ballad began to circulate about a lost young man with second sight who, because of his gifts, had been lured away from the world by the Queen of Elfland some seven years earlier. He was called Thomas the Rhymer.

XIX. Calligraphy

After three years of irregular practice, Filib Lusk could now produce nicely formed letters with ink and stylus. Janet provided examples for him to copy. These included some legal documents and a town charter, but mainly a bound copy of the Gospels so that he might come to recognize the words he drew. His sense of what any of it said came slowly. In part that was because in all that time Janet had provided him with just one large sheet of parchment. Each time he filled it up with writing, and they had discussed his handiwork, one of them would scrub the parchment with a paste of milk and oats, destroying the work in order to begin all over again.

His farm labor took precedence, of course, as did Tàm's and Janet's own lives. Between Tàm's management of all the land under Master Cardden's ownership, as well as farming and harvesting his own plot and the tending of his cattle, he seemed almost never to be about. Certainly, he never seemed to have an idle moment. Janet had to tend to their daughter, Morven, as well as help with the planting and harvesting. She participated in the sheep shearing, and had begun teaching Filib's sister, dark-haired Sìleas, how to weave on her loom, often at the same time that he worked on his letters nearby. He suspected that Sìleas's true devotion was to Tàmhas Lynn. She mooned over him whenever he was in the house with them.

Filib likewise had many duties to perform for his family. The result was that for perhaps an hour a week, he had opportunity to copy the shapes of letters and learn their sounds, and was only now beginning to understand the way that a string of them made words. From week to week it was hard to remember what he'd learned; still, the result was that he saw the shapes of letters in his head now and could sound out many of them.

He spent weeks perfecting just the writing of *Dilectus a Deo* from the Gospels. He wrote it up and down the parchment, covering every inch, to the point that he no longer needed to look at the original to pen the words. Janet explained the meaning of what he wrote. And he felt loved by God, too, now, though he couldn't explain it all to his siblings. But now he could write *Mattheus, Marcus, Lucas, Iojannes,* and count from their books *In Primo, In Secundo, In Tertio, In Quarto . . .* all the way to *In Decimo.* After three years, what he was doing had started to make sense.

One fall afternoon a few weeks after the harvest festival, Tàmhas Lynn was up in the shieling and Janet had taken Morven out for a walk along the river, leaving Filib alone at the table with Janet's stylus and inkpot to practice his lettering. Bored of copying the Gospels, he sat looking around for something else, and that was when he noticed the corner of a sheet of vellum sticking out ever so slightly from beneath the bed pallet. It was old and dog-eared, and had dirty lines from the boards underneath smudged across it. Under the dirt, in tight lettering, were grouped clusters of writing. There were different sizes of lines and shades of ink, which told him they'd been written at different times, sometimes with the stylus dulled and sometimes freshly sharpened; but all of it in Janet's hand. That much he recognized. What he couldn't decipher were the words. Whatever was written here it wasn't the Latin he was coming to apprehend. He peered at the grouped lines—sometimes two, sometimes four or more together. He sounded out "Ercildoun" right enough, but knew none of the words around it. He tried speaking them without much luck, but an idea took hold.

The clusters of lines reminded him of a riddle Sìleas had tried to recall one night maybe three years back, just after Morven's birth. He remembered she said that Janet had written it on the skin of a bed fur. He got up and returned to the bed, grabbed hold and flipped over the top fur. He began dragging it around and around the bed until he found the writing in one corner. It was faded, worn away in places, but it was identical to the last four lines written on the old sheet of vellum. The same words.

He placed the fur back as he'd found it, then returned to the table.

Picking up the stylus, Filib dipped it into the ink and began copying the letters as precisely as he could. One line at a time, he compared his marks to hers before continuing, and soon he had copied it all. He was especially careful with the last four lines, making sure each loop and stroke resembled the original as much as possible.

When he was satisfied with his work, he carried the vellum back and shoved it beneath the mattress. Then he sat and stared at what he'd written, concerned despite his care that it was not a good copy after all. He thought at first that when Janet got back, he would hand it to her and see how she reacted. Wouldn't she be surprised at his skill? He chewed on his knuckle whilst staring at the parchment, and began to worry. What if this wasn't such a good idea? She would know where the writing had come from, what it was, and would accuse him of poking through her house. No doubt the vellum had been hidden because she didn't want anyone to find it. Surely that was true. If she caught him, she would stop teaching him, maybe even ban him for seeking out this private writing of hers. He had the urge to scrub the parchment clean before she could see it, but he had no milk paste, nothing handy to clean his writing off it. At home he could make some, scour it there. That was a better idea. At least carry it out of here before she came back and saw it.

Filib rolled up his parchment. Leaving stylus and ink on the table, he hurried out of their house. If asked, he would say that his brother had come and got him to help with carrying rye to the miller Forbes. That's where Kester was right now, milling the grain they were going to sell in the town.

At home he busied himself roasting cakes of bannock on the firestone, and stirring the contents of the crock—whatever his mother was cooking for today—though that was Sìleas's task. It smelled like a stew of mutton. No one would ask him how his lesson had gone. No one understood what he told them when he did, nor comprehended the lettering if he showed it to them.

He could have used some of the oats and milk he'd mixed for the bannock to scrub the parchment, but now he could not bring himself to clean it off. Instead, he folded and slid the parchment under the pillow of his pallet on the floor.

Later, in the light of the fire, he took the parchment out and stared at it. Sìleas sat with him, her brow furrowed in concentration as she tried to make out anything comprehensible in all those squiggles. She asked what it was. "A copy," he said cryptically. She asked him what it said, and he shrugged and replied, "Dunno, it's just writing, innit, like on any other day." He didn't want Sìleas thinking it was special and saying something to Janet Lynn when next she was weaving, and he didn't want to admit he couldn't read it. He put the parchment away under his pillow again.

Eventually, he would have to scrub it clean or show it to Janet, or burn the parchment and pretend he'd been careless. He truly didn't want to do that. She might not give him a new piece to work with. He wanted now more than anything to know what he had written, even more intently than when he'd first started copying out the Latin words. But where could he go to have someone read it to him before his next lesson?

The answer came two days later when his father drove into Roxburgh with the sacks of milled barley and rye to sell, and Filib volunteered to go along.

"You just itching tae get out of chores, boy?" his father asked.

"No, sir. Done 'em, every one. Mucked out the livestock, too." With a nod, Mrs. Lusk confirmed this was so.

"Did ye, then? Good lad." Lusk threw his arm around his son's shoulders and walked him outside. "Well, then. Off tae market, and then we'll have us a wee stop at the alehouse after." His father winked at him.

Filib ran back inside, grabbed his parchment, and wrapped it around his forearm, hidden up under his sleeve.

In the alehouse, The Blind Fiddler, his father bought them each a mug, then settled him at a small table and abandoned him for some friendly, familiar faces farther back. Filib found himself seated beside the door, alone and regretting that his brother hadn't come along, too; but Kester had been in the river, fishing for their meal tonight.

The parchment up his sleeve began to itch. He needed to find somebody who might read it.

He was looking around when the door from the street opened, drawing his attention. Sunlight flashed for a moment before the door beside him closed. Filib blinked in the aftermath of brightness. He was staring up at a man who gazed down upon him as if in judgment an instant before striding through the room. There, he thought, went the perfect person to ask—a professional man, learned, and what was more they had even met, though he doubted the magistrate would remember. It had been in July when he and father were selling the wool they'd just sheared to someone at market who was buying wool to ship to Flanders, and the magistrate was officiating in the sales. Filib knew that he could read and write. He had to.

The magistrate continued to watch him while a mug was filled. Then, to Filib's surprise, the man came over and sat down where his father had sat, right across from him. "I know you, don't I?" the magistrate asked, smiling.

Filib nodded. Suddenly he could not find his voice. In the presence of one of *them* he always went mute. Men of power, class, and knowledge left him adrift upon the sea of his own inadequacy, knowing that if he spoke he would look the fool. It was the opposite of his own father, who spoke with such men as if they were equals even when both knew otherwise.

"Let me see," said the magistrate. "You are the son of someone, aren't you—well, how stupid an observation is that, hey? Of course you are. We all are." His blue eyes glittered.

"Filib Lusk," he managed to get out.

"Ah-ha. Your father is a tenant of Husbandman Cardden, is he not?"

"Yes, sir."

"Had you a good harvest, then? I'm guessing you aren't here to sell more wool, hmm?" He smiled, showing his crooked teeth. Filib wondered if they'd been pushed about by the same thing that had flattened his nose. "Oh, I see, *there's* your father. Yes, looks as if you have had a very good harvest. Let me stand you a second ale, son, and you can tell me about that thing up your sleeve." He rose.

Filib gaped. How did he know? Could he hear thoughts? Know the impossible?

The magistrate sat down again with a new mug for Filib.

"How?" he asked. "How do you—" He drew the parchment out a little.

The magistrate grinned. "Oh, it's nothing magical. When I came in, you were plucking at it unconsciously as if a flea was biting your wrist. Also, it does stick out past your sleeve."

Filib, feeling idiotic, now drew the parchment all the way out. "Begging pardon, sir." He slid the folded parchment onto the table.

Magistrate Baggi began to unfold it. "Goodness, this is your work?" He looked up, wide-eyed and admiring. "You are learning to *write*?"

Filib rocked a little, nodding. "Yes, sir."

Baggi's eyes flicked back and forth across the document. "Well, that is remarkable. Who is it teaching you?"

"The daughter of Husbandman Cardden, sir."

"And this." Eyes wide still, but different, ardent, the magistrate stabbed the parchment. "*What* is this?"

"I do not know, sir. I copied it without being able to read it as it's not Latin, but I think it's things her husband has said when he . . . when he falls down. He does, he used to, sometimes. Not so much anymore. I was hoping—"

Those blue chips of irises were fastened upon his eyes. "He falls down, you say? Her husband?"

"Tàmhas Lynn, sir. Our neighbor."

Magistrate Baggi smiled broadly then. He pored over the document, his lips moving as he whispered the words to himself. "'Who am I, brings calamity like weather? Best you don't know me, else drown in the torrent, your blood or theirs.' Dark words. My, my. Why, these read like imitations of this fellow they sing about in Ercildoun. Might you have heard a song or two by now—Thomas the Rhymer?"

"No, sir."

"Well, he's a famous legend there, it seems. Had a gift of prophecy. He is said to have warned of the flooding at Selkirk five years back. Riddled of the highwaymen who killed an alderman and landowner there. Oh, and predicted the storm that tore up the scaffolding at St. Mary's Abbey at Melrose—when was that, six years ago? Aye. In one song he even names that fellow who was killed that night—Clacher, I think it was. Buried him there, the very first grave at the new abbey. Such a shame." He smoothed down the parchment. "Oh, yes, these remarkable riddles are precisely like those ascribed to him. Might your neighbor by chance be writing his *own* ballad?"

"I don't know, sir," replied Filib.

Baggi looked Filib in the eye. "I don't suppose, then, you know if your Master Lynn would have been acquainted with this Thomas the Rhymer at some point? He disappeared, you see. Just up and vanished one day." He lifted his mug, but before taking a drink, set it down again. "Oh, but wait, I've met this fellow. At Cardden's Christes Maesse celebration. Seems to me he said he wasn't a local man. A stonemason turned mercenary, but taught by a local man. Arrived here with a scrip from King David. Where would he have acquired these?" He shook the parchment.

"I don't know, sir," he repeated. "They're just the things he says, that his wife wrote down."

The magistrate solemnly looked over the parchment again. "Well, your talent here is certainly evident, young man. If you continue in this vein, why, in a few years I might have a position for you. The ability to write is so rare. People outside of monasteries don't value it. Now, I'm sure this parchment is dear to you, but I'm hoping you will allow me to acquire it. What say I give you ten silver pennies, newly minted in Roxburgh, for this, hey? You can buy all the parchment in Scotland with that."

"But—" He tried to reach across for Janet's parchment.

Baggi held it out of reach. "If it proves not to be the words of this Rhymer fellow, I'll give it back to you. You keep the coins either way. And you keep practicing your letters on your *new* sheets of parchment. How's that?"

Filib stared at the profile of King David on the shiny pennies. This was real money. No one had ever given him real money before. And if he applied himself to learning his lettering well enough, the magistrate would employ him. His mind glittered with possibilities, and while it did, Magistrate Baggi folded up the parchment and tucked it away in his tunic.

"There, that's settled. Now, son," he asked, "how do you like your ale?"

XX. The Visitors

The pilgrims arrived at the house of Tàmhas Lynn on a cold wet October evening, four men and two women all bound for the holy isle of Lindisfarne. The men wore wide-brimmed straw hats and capes. The women wore wimples and couvre-chefs to protect their heads. All of them wore necklaces of scalloped shells. They had been following along beside the Teviot, their squat leader explained, and assuming that the husbandman had a byre, hoped that they might make use of it to keep out of the rain for a night. As they had come upland from the river, they would not yet have observed the byre and stables, lying in the darkness beyond the house.

"You're in luck," Thomas said to their leader. He stood outside the door. He leaned farther out and pointed. "Go around to the far side, you'll find a byre standing separate from the house. It's good and dry."

"Such a luxury to have it so, husbandman." He leaned heavily on a staff as though standing still pained him. A scrip bag rested at his hip. Just behind him stood a woman. The longer gown beneath her tunic was soaked and muddy at the bottom. The rest of the pilgrims hung back, seemingly out of politeness, but he could not make out their features in the gloom.

"I'll bring you some ale. No doubt you are all thirsty."

"Oh, most kind, thank you. We are, indeed." Leaning to one side and then the other, the pilgrim attempted to peer around Thomas and into the house. "You have family, do you?"

It was an innocent enough question. While the leader of the pilgrims attempted to hold his attention with his leaning to and fro, Thomas ignored him and focused on the odd stillness of the four who hung back. They didn't shift about at all as he would have expected of someone who'd spent the day walking up and down hills on tired legs. They might have been standing stones. He imagined that, somewhere in the gloom, a tiny winged monstrosity darted about and would have flitted through the doorway if he hadn't been standing in it. His windows were shuttered, too, keeping both the midge and their scrutiny out.

"No," he answered, adding carefully, "it's just me here now."

"Ah, you've lost someone, then?"

Instead of answering, Thomas said, "Tell me where you've traveled from, sir. I've never myself been on a pilgrimage, though I've met a few before you on their way to holy places and holy lands, and marveled at their stories."

"We? We hail from many burghs and towns, but we came together in Jedburgh because Bishop Ecgred of Lindisfarne founded the church what is now the priory there. It seemed an auspicious start for our small group." He gestured to them all as if to a group of players, and now they all moved, shifting about as if a cue had been given, which no doubt it had.

The woman behind the leader, though her face was much obscured by the draping of the couvre-chef, seemed to be reciting the pilgrim's words to herself as he spoke, her lips twitching ever so slightly, as if she could not listen to her companion without matching his speech. Thomas had the odd thought that if he listened hard he might hear whispered words inside his own head the way he'd once heard the Queen of these monsters. Instead, what he heard was Waldroup announcing the obvious: *"They've found you, Tom, and sooner rather than later. Where did you trip up?"*

"I'll bring you that ale," he said again, then stepped back and closed the door to the house.

He'd just witnessed a performance for his benefit. If they had already determined his identity, it wouldn't matter much hereafter how he played it.

The sleeping area was partitioned for warmth and he drew back the heavy curtain to find Janet seated with Morven on her lap, being happily bounced. But his wife was staring at him fearfully. She would have heard everything. Thomas put his finger to his lips.

At the foot of the bed, he opened the chest and took out a dark cape and hood that Janet had woven for herself. He closed the lid.

He laid down the cape. Then, drawing the curtain aside, he stepped onto the end of the bed frame, reached into the overhead loft, and pulled himself up among the rafters. His bow and Waldroup's hung from a peg there. He took his down, reached for the quiver belt and one of Waldroup's daggers.

"Those pilgrims?" she asked softly from below.

"Not pilgrims. Yvag. What I've always feared . . . I don't know what, but something has given us away. You have to go, you and Morven, to your father." He lowered himself onto the frame again, bringing his bow with him. He placed them upon the bed.

Janet had set their daughter aside, and Thomas leaned down, lifted her up. She giggled and grabbed at his hair. He nuzzled her and whispered to her, while her mother reached out and wrapped him in her arms. "Tàm, no," Janet pleaded. "There has to be—"

"There's no other way. My love, I don't know what I did that drew them, but forgive me. Doesn't matter now, it's done, and they've come." He kissed Morven's round cheek and finally handed her back. Then he picked up and draped her dark cape around her shoulders, kissing her, too. "When you leave, while I'm at the byre with them, walk straight out the door toward the river. Keep on that line until you're in the woods, then run home. Tell your father to arm his men and to kill any self-proclaimed pilgrims who arrive at his walls tonight. They will be no people, and the proof of that will be quick to behold. But he must show them no mercy."

He drew the small bag on its thong from inside his tunic. He untied the neck of it and slid the ördstone into his palm. Its jewels glowed bright blue as if lit from within and appeared to be flickering through some sort of sequence. "See?" he said. "It knows they are nearby with other stones."

"What will you do?"

"Take them their ale. Pretend ignorance of their true intentions."

"But they'll *kill* you."

He smiled reassuringly. "Not immediately, or they'd have done so the moment I opened the door. Anyway, they've tried before, and here I stand." *Alone*, he thought but did not say it. No Waldroup this time to cover him. No brother or sister, nor father or mother. *They* had taken all that from him, and now the elven would cleave him from his wife and daughter. There would be a reckoning; the only question, finally, was whose.

"Let me stay and fight beside you."

"Janet, if you were to perish, if they got their hands upon Morven, I couldn't live. I can lead them a chase far from here. From you." He returned the ördstone to its bag, slid it back beneath his tunic. Then he clutched his wife and held her tightly. "If I'm taken," he said quietly, "watch the ruins of Old Melrose for my return. It's there they'll take me through and there I'll come back if I get away." She started to protest. He kissed her hard, tasted the salt of her tears. She was trembling. He could not show weakness nor his own anguish now. He took a flagon from a shelf and filled it from a cask in the corner. A pity he had no poison to add to it. Beside the door, he left his bow and quiver before pulling on his fur-lined hooded shepherd's cape over his other tunic. "When you hear me speaking to them, then go. That will tell you no one's watching you." He kissed her again. He grabbed three small wooden cups and stepped outside.

The yard was empty. The rain had let up, and thin mist hovered in layers above the ground.

He circled around the house, looking for any figures crouched in the shadows, but there were none. He headed to the byre and stable. Beyond it, two cows stood inside the stone fold watching him, lit now by the flicker of a low fire.

The pilgrims had made the fire just beyond the overhanging roof of the byre. Three of them were seated before it; the other three stood in a cluster, everyone accounted for.

The leader had removed his hat. He turned at Thomas's approach. Thomas held up the flagon and cups. "I'm afraid I haven't enough cups for you all. I don't receive much company here," he said.

"We will share. Thank you for this."

The ördstone seemed to beat like a second heart against his ribs.

"I'm glad you found a way to warm yourselves. Wet business, striding through the rain." *Striders 'cross landscapes*—the words of his own riddle echoed in his head. "But for me, I'm exhausted from my day's work, so forgive me if I bid you a pleasant night's stop on your journey and do not stay and converse."

All the pilgrims rose as one and wished him a good night, one saying only "*Bon nuit*," which caused him to wonder from how far away this group had been assembled, how quickly the call had gone out. And why were the three locals not included? Were they cautious because of the disappearance of Baldie and Alderman Stroud? Suspicious that he knew their identities already? And where would the sleeping leeches for these six be hidden? Doubtful they lay in the crypt of St. Mary's, and that suggested more portals, maybe many scattered across the landscape, which made his small war seem all the more hopeless. Again he wondered how they invaded their hosts, how swift the process, how difficult. It must have been complicated; otherwise, they would simply have done the same to him or to Janet. So these pilgrims were likely not newly inhabited, but had been summoned like forces held in reserve because he would not recognize them. The only consolation he could take from that was how much they must want him.

He turned and walked away from the byre. He'd seen no weapons, yet at every step he half expected an arrow, a blade, something in his back.

He went back inside. Janet and Morven had gone and nothing had been touched. He took up his bow and quiver, then watched through the crack in the door. Perhaps they weren't absolutely certain yet, and this was a scouting party sent to ascertain his identity, perhaps hoping to find out how many stood with him. They couldn't be sure.

He closed the door. Yes, they wouldn't know that even if they were certain of his identity.

Suddenly he understood.

The pilgrims were being cautious. The one thing he knew for certain was that for every skinwalker there was a sleeping and helpless Yvag somewhere. They were like spiders all connected by webs of power and influence. When one fell, it tore the web, disrupted long-simmering plans, and the elven must begin again, selecting a new host, forging new connections as they determined who to inhabit. No, if they determined his identity, they would send for someone else. He thought he might know who.

Adalbrandr.

It soon came clear they had no idea yet that he'd sussed them. As he worked his way around the property, he encountered no one positioned to watch his house, no spies at all. He'd tied the bracer to his wrist, and belted his full quiver at his hip. His bow was strung and ready. He stayed alert, too, for any flying tubers with hummingbird wings darting through the air, but sensed none.

The light rain returned before he'd halfway reached his objective. It drove down the mist. The knees of his hose were soaked, and his leather boots. He pulled the hood of the cape up and worked his way around the far side of the byre. In the stable Dubhar and Waldroup's horse stood calmly observing the strangers next door.

There was a large boulder at the base of the rise that led up to the shieling. It wasn't far beyond the paddock that held his few cows. He nestled in behind it and waited to see what would happen.

For an hour, absolutely nothing did. The light rain sprayed the air. The pilgrims, save for their leader, sat so motionless that they became like carved objects. In his house, by now the fire would have all but gone out.

The leader in the straw hat drank some of the ale. When he did, two others drank as well, lifting their cups together, as if matching him. He set the cup down and they set down theirs. Then he got up, stirred the fire under the byre roof, and walked out into the rain. He began walking round and round in a large circle, until he'd created a muddy track.

Eventually the pilgrim stopped and drew something from under his round cape. Even at that distance Thomas glimpsed blue light reflected in eyes, coloring the pilgrim's face and the underside of the hat; at that point he realized that the other pilgrims had climbed to their feet and were approaching their leader, oblivious of the rain, all of them in unnatural lockstep.

They spread out along the line of the circle he'd trod, and when they had all taken positions upon that ellipse, the pilgrim raised his ördstone and cut the night. Green fire sizzled, blazed, unfolded, and opened.

How did they know? How could those waiting on the far side of that cut know where or when to be? If the stone was a beacon, then how had he and Alpin met no resistance? No one had been waiting at Old Melrose nor in Italia or the other places Alpin had cut into—and maybe no one would have come looking at all had it not been for Gallorini's intrusion. Were it a beacon, they would have been met, surely, when Waldroup cut open Old Melrose to roll a body to their side and when they blundered into the Þagalwood. Was it some part of the ritual, then? Or some secret in the stone itself? Maybe something the Yvag could do that he couldn't.

No time to puzzle that now. He expected to see warriors emerge on their demonic mounts as they had the day they took Onchu. Instead, the spiky black-armored creatures came through on foot, five of them, silently, black blades drawn. They marched straight out of the ring, and three of the pilgrims fell in beside them, striding past the byre and out of sight: a raiding party, it seemed, intent on swift surprise and a sure death for poor Tàmhas Lynn if he was home.

Three pilgrims remained before the crackling green hole in the night. Thomas, in shaping a plan, had regretted having to abandon Dubhar. Now he saw that he didn't need to.

Crouching, he darted to the circular stone fold, lifted the wood bars across the opening, and slid them aside. The cows watched him, shying away as if sensing his tension, but then they seemed to consider the gap he'd left them.

Thomas stood up. With three arrows in his drawing hand, he walked straight at the pilgrims and calmly loosed all three, so quickly one after the other that it seemed like one flight. The pilgrims dropped with hardly a sound, a red mist bursting from each. He ran then. By the time he reached them they were rotting like old gourds on the vine. He snatched up his arrows and raced for the stable. Dubhar was nearest, Waldroup's horse beside him. Quickly, Thomas fitted the bit in his charger's mouth and swung up on him. No time for saddling. He'd seen no bows among the Yvag but if they came around the byre, they could chop his horse's legs out from under him.

Dubhar took off with no prodding at all. They rode out and past the hole in the night. Inside its bloody circuit, another black-armored figure, taller than the others, stepped into view, then stopped as if guarding the entrance and raised one hand. Was it a greeting? It simply watched him thunder past. In the last instant, something might have darted from that hand into the night.

The cows bolted from the fold as he galloped around it and up the hillside. He took one final backward glance; distant figures charged about, lit by the green fire. Then he was over the hill and gone.

✤ ✤ ✤

Where would they trap him? Where would they expect him? *"Old Melrose,"* said Waldroup's voice in his head.

He rode instead for the new abbey. Cardden had said St. Mary's was completed, but he found that wasn't quite true as he made a cautious circuit around it. The east portion was—the great window, the choir and transepts, the nave and south aisle. But scaffolding still ran along the cloisters and the north aisle. Why, he wondered, had the work slowed? Clacher had seemed hell-bent to finish it upon the king's schedule.

Completing his circuit, he drew up and tied Dubhar to a tree some ways off. The rain had stopped again, and he stood and scrutinized the abbey from the shadows. No monks seemed to be about, no one at all, though a few lights flickered behind the stained glass windows.

Only four headstones stood in the new graveyard. Otherwise the distance to the abbey was flat and unadorned. He walked slowly, carefully along, the bow in his left hand, his finger holding the nocked arrow at the ready. He gave a glance at the names on the graves, then stopped short as he beheld CLACHER plainly carved on a pale marker.

Had the skinwalkers come looking for him and Waldroup among the masons? He could imagine how that might have gone: Clacher testily telling them to leave off troubling his crew, none of whom would have helped them in any way, and then in a day or two some convenient accident—a fall from a scaffold, or a stone slipping out of the pincer of a lewis. Another person who'd likely died on his account. Waldroup's ghost might try to argue him out of it, but he knew it was true as surely as if he'd been on hand and watched it unfold. And if they were going to murder his innocent friends, then they should expect no quarter from him. He walked to the east doors and went inside.

A few candles were lit in the choir and nave. No one was about. Would the monks have any idea what lay in the sepulcher beneath this floor?

He walked around in search of stairs. There must be stairs. Tried to recall the work, the layout, which must have anticipated them. Taking one of the half-melted candles, he walked deeper into the south transept. No steps there. He crossed to the north and came upon the steps like a hole into the earth. But nearing the top of them, he was overcome with a sudden desire to back away. He found himself turning to leave as if he had been instructed to, and had to make himself stop and turn around again. There was a spell in place here, keeping people out of the vault below. Yvag pressure pulsed in his head, urging him away. Perhaps one of the monks or the abbot himself was a skinwalker—someone who tended to the sleepers. Or maybe like the family in Carterhaugh who'd heard music, some sort of charm rendered them unconscious.

Thomas stepped forward. The spell shoved him away. He stepped back and it eased. So, it was as simple as that. Quickly, head down, he sprang down the stairs before his mind could talk him out of it. The sensation was like bursting through a great sharp-edged spiderweb. The contact stung and then he was past it.

Compared to Old Melrose the sepulcher under St. Mary's was an enormous space, with empty recesses all along the walls, and a row of vaults, open and waiting future abbots, or maybe kings. Who had built and installed these? Had they been here all the time he worked on the exterior walls? He never would have known. The north transept hadn't been finished, the steps and the crypt not dug. He wondered, was Clacher's death somehow tied to this construction? Probably he would never find out.

What he was looking for stood at the far end of the crypt—three vaults already covered with nondescript lids. From experience, he knew what he was seeing. The resting places of three insensible Yvags.

"Just as you saw, Tom," whispered the ghost in his head.

He set the fat, dripping candle on the edge of one of the open niches. The room glowed orange. "One of them's my father," he said.

Waldroup laughed. *"Not your father now, and you know it. We've been over this."*

"They'll take Innes next if he dies."

"Then again they might not. They've sent her to the nuns, and she'll not come back from there. More like, a distant cousin of the MacGilleans will magically turn up and take control of the land. Or maybe they'll claim to have married her to someone else, and who's going to ride to Cluny to confirm it? No, they won't leave anything to her. She's mad, so easily disposed of."

Thomas hoped Waldroup's opinion was sound, even if the voice in his head simply told him what he wanted to be true.

They had learned from Old Melrose: Start with the final crypt and save the first for last. He set his bow aside, then with effort pushed the lid from the last crypt. It tottered, fell on one corner, and broke in half. Warily, he peered over the lip.

Candlelight played over slick black armor that was neither leather nor metal, the long, cruel features, slender hands crossed in a parody of the carvings on top of sarcophagi he'd seen, of dead knights praying or clutching the hilts of their swords, perhaps as a final discouragement to any monk who somehow overcame the spell and decided to peek for himself. As Alpin had said, discoveries of these creatures no doubt explained all kinds of tales of ghouls and vampires. Like others they'd seen, it wore a dagger. He snatched that from its sheath.

The ördstone thumped against his chest. Setting the dagger down, he dug in, drew the stone from its bag. The jewels in it flickered and pulsed as he held it over the crypt. Gossamer threads of blue light ran from the stone to the gray-green creature, another ran straight across the sepulcher to the steps.

It sang in his head, but its piercing note rose into a terrible screech as a little batwinged hob came diving along that gossamer line, straight at Thomas. He grabbed the dagger he'd set down and swung it at the tiny monster. Even as he did, from the corner of his eye, he saw the sleeping creature open its eyes.

The Yvag blinked its golden eyes strangely, as if for a moment sightless, the circle of pupils expanding in response to the dimness. Then it saw him and lunged.

Its long fingers curled around his arm but he pulled away easily. It tried to drag itself upright, too weak still, those taloned fingers sliding along the lip. The hob came screaming in from behind him.Thomas whirled about and struck, slicing the thing in two. It plopped to the ground. Then he fell back, stuffing the ördstone away in the bag around his neck. The Yvag sat up and started to rise. Thomas dove in over the edge of the vault and stabbed its own dagger into its throat. The Yvag clawed at him and hissed. Its raging voice buzzed inside his head, drowning out Waldroup, drowning out almost every thought. One talon tore his sleeve as its fingers slipped from the lip of the vault and it fell back into the chiseled coffin and sank down. The sentinel had awakened it. And if it had awakened one...

"*Tommy, that thing's led them right to you!*" Waldroup's ghost shouted at him. "*Get out!*"

From the second crypt came subterranean rumbles; the inhabitant was awake and trying to get out. The lid thumped, raised a little, slammed back down. He aimed his bow.

"*There's no time! Leave it.*"

Screaming hornets filled his head, drowning out even Waldroup's urging. With no choice, he ran for the steps. Get to Dubhar, lead them a chase to the MacGilleans' and beyond, far away from Cardden's.

Across the floor of the choir sprawled monks who hadn't been on hand upon his entry. Were they summoned by the hob? But then why were they unconscious?

No time to puzzle that out. The hornet voices grew louder every moment. He hurried to the eastern door beneath that "high and bright" rose window. Pushed it open.

The murderous Yvag called Aðalbrandr stood there as if it had been waiting for him. He tried to raise his bow and the knight grabbed him by the throat and lifted him up off his feet. He kicked furiously, striking it once or twice, while stars began to sparkle all about him, merging with the sound of their chatter, the roar of his blood, then blackness.

He came to his senses to find himself being dragged through the nascent graveyard.

Aðalbrandr breathed with effort as it hauled him along. He noticed strange gaps in the black armor above him that flexed, opening and closing like inhuman mouths, deepening into dark red. It looked like a tiny column of the holes Waldroup had cut in the world, and he thought *I should have stabbed them there.* Finally, the knight dropped him in the dirt. Contemptuously, it considered him. Its buzzing penetrated his skull, hammering at him like a terrible headache. All at once the noise coalesced into a raw, orotund voice.

"Finally, you're mine," said Aðalbrandr, then reached down, clutched the thong around his neck, and tore it from him and with it the bag containing his ördstone.

Other Yvag knights came up. Their voices slid through his head, like stones sliding against stones.

"How far had he got?" asked Aðalbrandr.

"In the crypt, one of them."

Aðalbrandr nodded, glancing around, settling finally on Thomas's charger where it stood tied past the few graves. "Payment in kind, then." The Yvag stalked toward the horse, drew its black sword. As if knowing its intent, Dubhar tried to tear itself free until finally the reins snapped, and his horse bolted off into the night.

Run, Dubhar, he thought, *never stop running.*

Frustrated, Aðalbrandr sheathed the sword. "We'll find another way for you," said the knight, striding past him. "Bring him along!" They grabbed him under the arms and hauled him off to the east. He knew exactly where they were going. He tried to gauge whether he could get one arm free from the gray-skinned fiends long enough to grab Waldroup's dagger, glanced down and realized he'd already lost it. Someone had emptied his quiver of arrows, too. He strained to hear some advice from Waldroup, even the noise of his own ördstone; he managed only to fill his head with the buzzing of their thought-chatter. The breathing of the two dragging him was heavy, wheezing.

The Yvag knights trod the path along the river to the old abbey ruins, seemingly oblivious to the cold rain drenching them. Breaths steamed as from half a dozen chimneys, floating up from the holes in their sides. Thomas stayed limp, conserving his energy for whatever moment came. If any would.

Pretty soon they were weaving their way between old gravestones, and he knew where he was. He looked up to see, looming ahead, the spot where Onchu had been taken. He wondered why the pilgrims weren't there. Maybe they'd completed their part in his capture. He wondered what human host he'd killed by slaying that Yvagvoja. His father? Grief or joy—he didn't know how to react if that proved true.

As if it was nothing, Aðalbrandr sliced open the world. The stone he used looked to be twice the size of the one in Thomas's bag, leaving him to conclude there must be different kinds of them; no wonder Waldroup had poisoned himself in collecting the stones from the crypt. Those stones were likely never meant to be wielded by humans.

The moment the sizzling green line expanded to a circle, the Queen rode through on her mount. The effect was strange to behold—glaringly bright, she seemed to lunge through the opening, but then slow to a walking pace as she pierced the divide. The discordance lasted only an instant. It was as if she had rushed into a wall of water in the crossing.

She made no attempt to glamour herself to him this time. He beheld no beguiling Queen of Heaven in pointed cap seated upon her palfrey, but a creature of gray-green skin, the golden, canted sloe eyes, ringed with pupils, her hair the unnatural color of red-hot iron. Her elongated cheeks that he'd thought of as smooth as marble were instead mottled, even scabrous, more like the skin of a toad than a human. Her abnormally wide mouth contained rows of sharp needlelike teeth the same as all the other Yvag. She did not wear the same armor, but a gold-and-black cape or robe that covered her completely. He wondered if she breathed through her sides like the others.

Aðalbrandr bowed. She nodded to him formally, held one hand over his head as if blessing him. Then she turned her beast with its polished skeletal head to face Thomas. The beast came forward. The rain fell steadily.

The pressure of her mind probing his made him wince. "Oh, my pretty broken toy, it's *you*," her thoughts said in surprise. "You're our nemesis? This is how you repay my kindness, my generosity in stilling your discord?"

"This is how I repay you for taking my brother from me."

"Did we do that? Was it he who rode behind me, his arms around my waist? Well." There was hardly any sympathy in the word.

"Onchu—"

"Yes, I remember his name. I remember all their names. I had a look inside him. You know, he thought you a simpleton. Why would you even grieve for him?" When he gave no answer, her voice continued. "Besides, he has served our higher purpose. That is all that—"

"You mean, the *teind*."

She blinked at him. The ring of pupils shrank and enlarged in her eyes. "What can you possibly know of that word? Who gave it you?" she asked imperiously.

"It means he was your sacrifice. Something you pay."

"But you've no idea what or why, have you?"

"No," he admitted.

"No. You judge us without knowing the truth of us; then you murder us. We, who are but a breath shy of sempiternal. Comprehend you the cruel indifference of bringing death to an immortal?" She answered her own question. "Of course not. You are all mayflies. You live this long." She snapped her fingers. "You know nothing of what you steal from us. What you personally have stolen from more than one of us."

Even if her argument had merit, they had chosen his brother. Chosen his sister. Chosen his father. The Yvag that had been Stroud had told him Onchu was dead and that Innes's baby had been snatched from her so that these supposed immortals could "repopulate," whatever that meant. However terrible his perceived offense, they had brought it on themselves, stealing everything and everyone from him—the cruelty belonged to them. He wiped the rain off his face and stared her down, seething.

The Queen leaned back on her shiny black beast and regarded him anew. She had heard his every thought.

"You've come far from the addlepated boy I repaired." She smirked. "Do you riddle them all still? *All greenwood their enchantment?*" She laughed. The sound tinkled inhumanly.

He felt her, like fingers inside his head, trying to trigger a seizure in him. He cringed at the pain.

Then through it, Waldroup's voice whispered, *"Resist her, Tom."*

The pressure ceased abruptly. Now her eyes were wide with fury. "Who was that?" she asked.

He thought he'd made up the ghost. Was it possible that his insubstantial companion was real after all?

Thomas shook his wet, shaggy head. "No one known to *you*, Nicnevin."

Now her eyes narrowed, face drew tight in outrage. "Who has spoken to him?" she buzzed the Yvags all around her.

Aðalbrandr knelt. "None of us, Majesty."

Thomas recited a riddle Janet had written on parchment; until that moment it had been opaque to him:

*"True name spoken,
grants control.*

Say it full to
Own the soul."

She could have burned him with her glare. "That is enough of you, little man. I won't bother to joust nor justify what comes now. We need a new *teind*."

He glared at her defiantly.

"Oh, not you. I took possession of you already well before now and you are mine, *toy*. However, we've timed our taking of you to coincide with our culling." She turned to Aðalbrandr. "Where are the pilgrims?"

"They are coming," answered the knight, rising.

The Queen of Ailfion said, "Thomas Lindsay Rimor de Ercildoun, your family have indeed given us much. One final thing from you will settle our debt."

"My life?" he asked, his throat suddenly constricting.

She replied, "Why, mayfly, I have *that* already."

Slowly, out of the dark rain, the remaining three pilgrims emerged from around the ruins of the abbey, the leader distinguishable by his wide-brimmed hat. He held a rope that tugged a stumbling fourth party along behind him.

She said, "Tonight, we'll have your wife for our *teind*."

Thomas screamed but no sound came out. He wrestled to break free of the Yvag holding him, but his body remained still. She had spoken his name, his full name, his true name, and now controlled him exactly as his own riddle had surmised. The magic, it seemed, cut both ways, and he only knew a part of hers. Perhaps he had stung her, but he could not take her over, could not win against her.

Queen Nicnevin gestured with both hands as if pulling the air and re-collecting it. Something like a wind, a stream of energy, flowed out of the hole to the other world and into her hands, where it pulsed and glowed like a small sun. She threw it in his face and a searing pain roared through him. He fell to his knees, unable to resist. His mind seemed to crack apart, to scatter upon the night before it coalesced again, into something alien and confused.

Where he had stood, a shaggy ram had replaced him.

The Yvag who had held him knocked his skinny legs out from under him and he fell. He tried to shout but it emerged as a trumpeting bleat. The Yvags tore the remaining clothing off him. They bound his legs—his hooves—with straps, tight, secure. Another handed them a pole and they jammed it under the straps and lifted him into the air, where he hung upside down. Helpless.

Upside down, he watched a woman stumble forward on the end of the rope tied round her neck, a hood drawn over her head, her clothing sodden with mud, her feet bare despite the cold. Even as he took her in, she was pulled out of his line of sight.

He strained to no avail, bleated his rage. Tried to shout her name: "Janet!" It came out as another fearful blat.

The pilgrim leader handed the rope to Aðalbrandr. To the Queen he said, "According to our Yvagvoja in Roxburgh, he married his neighbor's daughter. But tonight that Yvagvoja is no more. He has killed it and lich both." The pilgrim pointed accusingly at him.

"Yes, we know. We must seek another to replace the magistrate."

Seemingly deflated by this dismissal of what he'd thought was a revelation, the pilgrim turned instead upon their captive. "We caught her sneaking back to the house from wherever she'd run, my Queen," he said.

Bending down, to Thomas the Ram, the Queen said, "This is what comes of meddling in our affairs. Even an idiot should know to stay away from elves and faeries." She was practically laughing at him, but mercurially shed her amusement, adding sternly, "You should have enjoyed what was given you, and not sought revenge for that which our need necessitated."

The pilgrims by now were circling Janet. He knew what was happening even before the chirring sound began, the strange chanting of the Yvags. Soon it stopped and he heard ripping, tearing. Rags of cloth were tossed away from the group. He did not have to see to know that his wife was now naked, spelled to walk to her doom, exactly as Onchu had done.

The Queen turned her mount about. "Bring them both, Aðalbrandr. We shall provide a family reunion. Briefly. And, you, seal up the rent after us." The pilgrim nodded.

The Queen rode into the circle and was immediately swallowed in the blood-drenched gloom of the other side. Again, for an instant her momentum appeared to hesitate, and then she was inside the other world. Thomas was carried toward it, helpless, her trophy.

Behind him another Yvag kicked Janet forward. Upside down, he could only see her stumbling feet behind him.

What had she done, left Morven with her father and then rushed back to aid him? He could not blame her for it, nor for anything. Neither he nor Alpin had heeded the danger, either. They'd challenged these creatures at every turn and it had become his obsession. Janet had been brave, that was all.

But bravery saved nobody.

PART THREE:
TYWYLLWCH LLWYR

XXI. A Road to Hel

The red road to the woods extends seemingly into eternity. A road through hell. It feels as if they float along it for days—*float* because no one seems to be walking and yet, hung upside down, he's swaying on the pole as the furrowed bloodred tunnel ripples past, recedes in the distance. It's as if the tunnel itself is compressing and expanding, moving around them while they stay in place. It's as if they're inside the body of an earthworm, an idea so grotesque he dismisses it. Was it like this before, with Waldroup? It was hard going, he recalls; they seemed to run in place and get nowhere but then to have traveled some distance. Now he can't be sure. Disoriented and dizzy, confused, he can't be sure of anything at all. Even of time: Has it been days or mere moments? Can it be both at once?

Awaiting the Queen on this side are five mounted knights. What's strange is that on this side their mounts and hers are almost luminescent: Instead of the polished blackness of their bodies, they are radiantly white here, forged from congealed moonlight.

Eventually, the red ribbed sides disappear and a darkness enfolds them as if they're journeying through a lightless cavern deep underground. He's sure he didn't pass this way with Waldroup. Not that it matters. He's helpless, however they go, wherever and whenever they arrive. He expects he won't die until then. Closing his eyes, he tries to insulate himself from the journey by concentrating on all the unanswered questions.

How do they pick their victims, and why? Is it a matter of convenience? Onchu from Ercildoun, and then many years later the girl from Carterhaugh—it seems they're careful not to select too many from one area, a notion reinforced by the pilgrims, who seem to have arrived at his door from multiple locations. And, of course, there's what Waldroup saw on the battlefield: how they pluck victims where no one will miss them. Thomas was lucky up till now. Once they arrive wherever they're going, though, if given the chance he will insist on taking Janet's place. She has a daughter, an influential father. She'll be missed. He won't. Let her go home to Morven. He'll be their *teind*. . . . Just please let them return him to human form again that he might bargain, exchange his life for hers. But what if they don't? The Queen can do anything she likes to him. He has no say in anything on this side of the veil. What *is* the fate of the *teind*? Thus far the only fate he knows of here is the fate of those who stray from the path and in among the Þagalwood trees. He and Waldroup speculated that Onchu had become . . . what Gallorini became, but there's no proof of it. Torment and torture might take a million forms among these creatures. He thinks of Janet, and has to fight down his terror. *Think!* he screams silently. Even upside down and helpless, he needs to think, but all he can think of is Janet being tossed in among those skeletal trees and the flesh ripped from her bones, while they stretch and twist into another hideous, spindly moaning form. The image makes him cry out, one more ragged inhuman bleat, and he panics, opening his eyes again, straining against his bonds to rock side to side, twisting his neck for a single glimpse of his wife. Of course it's near-pitch-black here. What did he expect? She was behind Aðalbrandr. At least this dark route is not that path he and Waldroup cut open in Italia.

He has just taken small comfort in this when out of the darkness on either side of him the spectral trees finally emerge; carried this way, he can't see the network of branches overhead. But having thought of Gallorini, he watches for that small bony tree.

When they pass it he almost gasps.

So this now *is* the path he followed with Alpin; they have connected to it from a different route. The way from Italia isn't the way from Melrose.

He is carried past Gallorini without slowing, which makes him hopeful that such is not the fate of the *teind*. Wouldn't there be more of those small ones by now—the girl from Carterhaugh who was taken would be here, too? And others, surely many others. Especially Onchu. Even deformed by this forest, his brother would be recognizable to him, he's sure of it.

The Gallorini tree itself is no taller than the last time he saw it, as if planted only yesterday, one tiny sapling among the tall and deformed trunks. And then he wonders if it's only been days or weeks here since that incursion. Time is some other measure in Ailfion. He and Waldroup were here for only an hour or so, while the whole night passed by in Italia. Who knows how many hours are racing by at home as they float along here? He cannot attune himself to it.

Around him, now and again, the Yvag knights speak to each other in that strange thrumming that he doesn't understand. It's like birdsong—he knows there's a conversation there, but its meaning is opaque.

There's enough light to see. He rocks and twists his head back again, and finally for a moment manages to glimpse Janet's muddy legs and feet on the red ribbon of road. She isn't lifting them any more than the knight ahead of her, isn't plodding along despite how everything around them flows past, and again he has the disorienting sense of the world about him compressing and expanding to move them all along.

All at once they come to a complete stop so abrupt it's as if time itself has ceased.

A ring edged in red flame appears ahead of them. He has to assume someone sliced it open. The other side of it, he can see upside down, is a broad, flat expanse of intricately placed stones or tiles forming some kind of a design wider than his view allows. Everything appears to have a reddish cast to it, the light almost as dull as it is here in the woods.

Straightaway they carry him through the red portal, but not before he watches three of the mounted knights turn from the road, leaving the Queen, to ride off into the darkness of the Þagalwood. No vines or roots rise up to clutch at the legs of their pale skeletal mounts the way they did Gallorini. The wood doesn't perceive them as intruders; the white polished torsos of the beasts are identical to the trees, would seem to be carved from them.

Then he has passed through the portal and is hanging above the mosaic of stones, which proves to be a great circular plaza surrounded by a low wall and, here and there, steps leading to a higher plain that seems to shimmer with heat—all of it, everywhere bathed in sanguine light. It's like the dying embers of a fire rippling the air even in the darkness. Ugly *fae* sprites swarm the air around the opening like gnats clustered above a wound.

In the center of the plaza stands another, smaller circular structure perhaps waist-high; the base seems to be constructed of marble and gems. Seeing it he can't help being reminded of that baptismal font in the abbazia di Santa Maria di Lucedio where he buried Waldroup's ördstones. But this font, this well, is capped by a brilliant, molten line of white-hot fire, its glow rising straight up into the night, a horizontal ring so bright it hurts to stare straight at it.

"Alpin?" he whispers in his head. The only answer he gets is a strap across his belly. His Yvag minder says something harsh. Did they hear the name in his mind? Or sense Alpin's ghost? He can't tell if the creature heard or is just enjoying itself by whipping the hanging ram. But the Queen heard him, didn't she? Thomas the Ram is carried roughly across the plaza toward the well. Now the knights, as if weary of supporting him, let his back drag across the rough stones, and when he bleats out at the scraping of his wooly hide, he's whipped again.

They come to a halt beside the well. The Queen dismounts her ivory white creature. Aðalbrandr assists her, and has let go of the lead attached to Janet. Thomas suspects she's spelled. She doesn't move, makes no attempt to run away—and where would she run if she could? With that sack over her head, she can't even see. Exhausted, Thomas dangles from the pole, his head lolling, overcome with despair, still asking how he gave himself away and to whom. Now these creatures are going to destroy his wife and he can't do anything to stop them. He wishes they would untie his wrists and change him back first. Give him his voice. At least he might die on his feet.

Across the plaza, another knight seals up the portal, turns, and kneels, drawing a spear as if from out of the ground. It has a bodkin head on it, four-sided and needle sharp. The knight climbs to its feet on the wall and takes its position, a wide-legged stance that Thomas recognizes from every military encampment in which he's dwelled. The edge of this plaza is a perimeter of some kind.

The tiny sprites flit about in every direction.

The Queen approaches Thomas, her voice in his head once more, though her fanged mouth doesn't move. At a signal from her his back is lowered to the ground and the pole slid from his bound limbs. The ropes are cut. His furry legs flop limp and useless. She pulls the air as she did before, and once more he experiences lancing pain as if knives have slipped into his joints to dismember him. He howls; the sound of it transforms with him from ram to man.

When it's over, he lies naked, trembling, worn to rawness by the pain, his wrists and ankles abraded and bleeding. He sprawls on the cold stones, passive, helpless. Breathing is difficult. The air here seems to be thick, almost viscid, and hot as if he's inhaling the air from an oven. He clears his throat. Above him is a blue-black panoply of stars and nebulae like a dome of almost-night, an impression reinforced by nearly invisible crisscrossing lines across that sky as gossamer as spiderwebs, describing something like the tracery of cells in a honeycomb, each offering a slightly different view of the cosmos. It's as though he's staring up at the night sky through the largest Catherine window in the world; in its center hangs a huge pulsing red-orange oculus, the obvious source of the dim light bathing this place. He absorbs it all, and under his breath thoughtlessly tallies the cells: "Nine thousand, seven hundred and sixty," he wheezes.

Nicnevin glances up at the sky. "You perceive the tesselation? That is remarkable," the Queen comments. "We shall be most entertained by your mathematical feats. For a brief time at least. Get up now, mayfly."

He stares up at her, wants to say that *she* is the one with the eyes of an insect. What he glimpses in her expression for one instant is fatigue. Has changing him worn her out? Then it's gone.

He manages to roll delicately onto one hip, expecting more pain, but there's none beyond the rope burns and the abrading of his back. Sensation trickles into his extremities, the sharp tingling as if a thousand of those little green hobs are biting him. He rolls to his hands and knees, brings up one foot, tests the knee as he rises, puts weight on it. It holds. Then he stands upright on both feet, unstable, swaying. Takes one lurching step to the side to better see his wife behind the Yvag entourage, but one of the knights steps forward, blocking his view, coming right up to him. Slender gray-green hands hold two jewels glowing blue the way the smaller dots in an ördstone do. One jewel the Yvag sets just above his collarbone in the center of his throat, while the other hand reaches around the back of his neck. There's a soft snick, and a strange force both circles his throat and pierces straight through to his spine, not quite painful but impossible to ignore.

The Yvag turns him to face the Queen again. He's too exhausted to care that he's naked before her. Too exhausted to run at her, strangle her, and not sure if in this heavy air he wouldn't collapse anyway.

But she gestures for him to come to her, and as if the blue jewels upon his neck are attached to an invisible lead, he staggers forward against his will, until he's close enough that he can watch the multiple pupils of her irises widen into single rings. Instantly she is in his head, and just as abruptly he beholds a world that's been invisible to him till now. Her voice: *Ailfion, I believe you've called this. And Yvagddu, which is fitting I suppose, as we do thrive in the eternal darkness of our red sun.*

The sparkling, shimmering welkin vanishes like a curtain pulled aside, revealing a plateau that seems to abound in colossal structures—glittering buildings the like of which he's never seen: great thin needles that might be made of solid air and stand tall enough to puncture the sky, next to helicoid spirals; obelisks of dark green jasper pressed beside complex stepped structures with some sort of foliage flowing out over their sides. Pathways through the air connect many of the structures. Here and there strange metallic tubes snake out of the ground only to curve back into it again elsewhere like the humps of sea monsters, in an interconnected pattern all the way to the horizon.

He thinks of puny Ercildoun in comparison to this vast and mighty conurbation, a town against an empire. The Queen turns toward the well; her gold-and-black robe streams above the stones. The incandescence that tops it is shot through with strands of red, blue, purple, and orange, all swirling. The bright rim makes his eyes water. Its flowing light bathes everyone in the plaza, makes their uniforms sparkle. Now that he's standing, Thomas can see that it's a ring hovering above the curved platform of marble and gems. The Queen's long gray-green fingers gesture at it and the bright fire winks out. The afterimage of the light stays with him.

What he's looking at seems to be the side of a well, if one were as wide as an oxgoad. He could leap into its center with arms and legs outstretched and not touch the sides. "Come," she insists, as if he has a choice. He follows her until he stands against the base, peering over the lip. It's depthless, but the emptiness is shot with more streaks of purple and orange, which seem to leap like lightning across the vastness of it. Far, far below, so far that he could cover it with his thumb, is what looks like a slaughtered side of beef afloat among the colors. There's something odd and asymmetric about it, though, and only after he's stared and stared does he realize it's a human torso that's been broken apart, extremities half-shattered into particles and spreading away from the center, the head looking like crumbs sprinkled out from it, an abstraction of a human head with long hair. He can only think of the girl from Carterhaugh who they took while he watched . . . and yet it *looks* like the pale-green torso of an Yvag.

"The mouth of Hel," says the Queen. "Few of your kind have ever beheld it. With few exceptions, only those taken as *teind* who feed it. I did once show it to a group of you creatures as a warning not to interfere in our business. If you thought yourself the first, you are not.

"I sent that group home—all but the one we threw in as an example. The next thing we knew, the fools had named a goddess after it and insisted that various caverns in your world led directly into her. They completely misinterpreted what they were shown, but that hardly surprises. Still, so long as she warns them off us, they can worship as they like."

He recollects caves where faeries, ciuthachs, and other hardly-ever-seen creatures are said to dwell, and a story about a girl and a frog and just such a well as this.

"The well of all worlds?" he hazards.

"Aren't you the clever boy? Correct after a fashion." She smiles to him, flashing those needlelike teeth. "For you, though, it is the answer to a question you have been asking awhile now."

"A question?" He steps back, no longer wanting to watch the body disintegrating far below.

"What is the purpose of the *teind*?" She glances past him, and he senses that someone has come near. He finds that his naked wife has finally been brought up close to him. Except—

"Remove her hood," the Queen orders.

He pleads, "No, stop, please, don't do this, what can I do to make you change your mind? I'll take her place, let me, please. She's innocent of this that's between us!"

Aðalbrandr, sneering, snatches the sack from her head. An explosion of dark hair cascades past her shoulders, and Thomas sucks in his breath, conflicted and trapped, unable to beg further and instead doing all in his power to wall off his thoughts.

"There are prices to pay for the many you've harmed in opposing us. This is the first, hardly the last. Bid your wife farewell, Thomas of fables."

He moans in a twisted agony while he suppresses as hard as he can even the awareness of her name, thinking "Janet, Innes, Sìleas" and more names lest the Queen hear it by itself. She is watching him, savoring his distress, not looking at the *teind*. "Oh, God, forgive me!" he shouts. Closes his eyes, puts his arms around her, and hugs her to him, flesh against flesh. She is compliant, insensible, and he whispers in her ear, "I'm sorry, so sorry." Then, as a hand falls upon her shoulder, he shouts again, loudly, "No, no, no!" Turns and swings wildly at Aðalbrandr, who knocks him backward hard. He flies through the air, tumbles on the mosaic, almost passes out gasping, but shakes the sparks out of his head and starts to get up again. The blue jewels light up and nearly cut right through his spine to crush his throat. He drops to his knees, choking, crawls forward to throw his arms around her legs. "Please!" he gasps. "Take me. Let her *go*."

"Now, Aðalbrandr," orders the Queen.

Sìleas Lusk is torn from his grasp.

Pulled back, she just stands there, slack-faced in her insentience. Aðalbrandr passes his long hands over and around her. Within moments she is no longer his neighbor's daughter. Sìleas has been glamoured into an Yvag, her skin that same scaly greenish hue, her ears pointed where they show through her hair that's now white as Carrara marble, her fingers and toes elongated, taloned, and everywhere—knuckles, shoulders, face—barbed with tiny spicules. Beneath the skin, however, is something other than ribs, other than bone; seemingly it's something tightly wound, as if her skin has become nothing more than a sheath, reminding him of the spun wire of the little homunculi sprites. It's an illusion, he knows—this is reverse-glamouring—underneath she's still Sìleas, still spelled.

Once the transformation is complete, she is lifted and stood upon the lip of the great well by two of the Yvag. For a moment she totters there. "Adalbrandr," says the Queen. The knight simply pokes one finger against her back. She does not scream, does not struggle, but flies outward in slow motion as if the air above that wide stone maw is thick as porridge. With arms wide, she sinks as slowly as the heaviest drop of treacle, as if eternity buoys her there. Then a jagged line of violet fire arcs across the opening and through her. Her body spasms once, and something like pebbles of her new gray flesh float out from her side, her fingertips, the tips of her toes, leaving behind ragged spots of red tissue.

He watches, repelled, horrified, doubling over to retch, filled with self-loathing to have hidden her identity from them. She's not Janet. They have kidnapped the wrong woman, but he mustn't even acknowledge that thought, must not allow the Queen to hear it in his mind. The guilt knots and squeezes him. On his account Sìleas is doomed. Even if he were to reveal their error, they wouldn't have let her go. They needed their *teind* now, and would still have sicced more fiends on Janet and Morven for the next sacrifice, or else they would have tossed his wife and daughter in amongst the Þagalwood. But at the moment he doesn't even let himself think these thoughts, clinging instead to his real and wrenching guilt, fans its flames, screams "Janet!" in his head and aloud to drown out the rest of what he knows, thinks. Folds his wife's name into his self-hatred that someone else has paid a price for his actions. Repeats it, sears his thoughts with it. His wife. *Janet.*

Why did you come back, foolish girl, why of all nights didn't you stay away from the house? But what if she hadn't? What would they have done?

He can't stop himself from thinking of his daughter. Where is Morven? But stops the thought from blossoming into being, pushing the words *She's gone, she's gone, she's gone!* around it, a shield to seal off his real thoughts. The grief for this girl who did nothing at all but is dying for him, cracks him finally. Tumbling Sìleas—*Janet!*—disguised

as one of the elven, will be slowly, torturously torn apart, and he can't
bear it. He collapses with one arm over the lip of the well as if he
might reach her to bring her back. The hungry forces within it grab
hold of his arm to drag him in after her. His hand stings. He snatches
it back to find blood from a tiny hole through the edge of it.

Adalbrandr laughs, grabs him by the hair, and hauls him back
from the well as if anticipating that he'll jump in, flings him down.
The Queen reignites the incandescence around the top of the well, a
whirling St. Elmo's fire.

He senses what's coming next; either the pain or the misery of
what he's caused has triggered the pressure. He dashes his forehead
against the stones of the well in an attempt to knock himself
unconscious before the fit overtakes him. The Queen yells, "Stop
him!" and someone kicks him, but by then the lightning is ripping
through him, blackness has swallowed his senses, and the pressure of
the seizure rolls in like a storm. The riddle spills as if from some
other's lips.

"I connect the here and unhere
My siphon steals life, the fire and the meat.
Return there can be none—
You are the rain of the Sluagh that feeds the Unseelie."

When the riddle releases him, he curls up with his hands
clutching his bleeding head as if to ward off another beating. The
blue jewels flicker at his throat but he's past reacting even to their
delivered shock. His eyes are open, but he might as well be a corpse.
His muscles fire without guidance, twitching. He drifts in and out of
awareness while the creatures stand stiffly around him, and hears the
Queen and Adalbrandr heatedly arguing. Most of it is just
incomprehensible drone. Only occasionally does he grasp what's
being said, and even then only makes sense of half of it, reminded too
well of his childhood self and the arguments that went on right in
front of him—parents, brother and sister—because his presence
didn't matter.

Censoriously, Adalbrandr says, "You'd take another? Is that wise?"

The Queen's response is as cold as a frozen pond. "Your lineage
may run as deep as my ... even ties to the Seelie court itself ... almost

as deep as my disdain of ungovernable lineal claims, any ... could promote ourselves through a connection to the throne. Even our changelings ... the *astralis* coursing through you ... all that matters."

"We do not know—"

"There are Yvagvoja among the court who could argue primacy over you. Two surviving heirs to your none ..."

Aðalbrandr thrusts an accusing finger at him. "This meat's *astralis* ... incompatible."

"... be altered."

"Majesty—"

"It is not your place!"

The chirring stops.

Above him, Aðalbrandr finally bows. Steps back. Even dazed, Thomas recognizes the rage churning in those alien eyes.

The remaining Yvag knights have stood motionless throughout, eyes downcast. He knows from experience, one does not meet a monarch's gaze.

Nicnevin addresses two of those knights then as if Aðalbrandr isn't even there. "Bathe him before you deliver ... to my summer house," she says. "He stinks like all of his kind."

She sweeps from view.

Aðalbrandr glares down on him and raises one foot. Thomas expects his head to be crushed, but the knight steps over him as if he's a log and is gone. Roughly, he is grabbed and hauled upright. His head thunders, his vision shrinks to a tiny lens, sparkling. He passes out.

XXII. Queen's Pawn

⽥

The ice-cold water of a perfectly circular pond snaps him back to
alertness. He splutters and thrashes while two disinterested Yvags
unseal their strange armor. The pond is in a different plaza, among
the spires and strange stepped buildings. The Queen and her
entourage have gone. The light is still the molten gloaming cast by
the dull red sun overhead, but the spires and towers seem to throw
off a glow of their own, much like the well did, like St. Elmo's fire.

Dazed still, and captivated by all that's strange, he sees but fails to
register how the knights' armor transforms—how its chitinous barbs
and spikes retreat, and it simply falls away like linen or silk. He
becomes transfixed at the sight of the two of them, wading in naked
after him for the first time beholding more than mottled hands and
faces, and thick metallic strands of white hair.

Their torsos are of tightly stacked, coiled rings of muscle, which
ripple in sequence as they move. A vertical row of circular slits
corresponding to the holes in their armor run down those coils
beneath their arms and enlarge and shrink rhythmically. He
understands that he's seeing them breathe. While their spiky limbs
and backs are all of the same greenish-gray color, their bellies are a
dull yellowish pink. Their arms are segmented, almost like
interlinked bulbs, capable of bending in ways that arms shouldn't.
Legs, too—their oddly jointed hips remind him of grasshoppers'
limbs. Recollects how he watched alongside Waldroup as one of them
climbed the steps of the Old Melrose crypt, its movements ungainly,
peculiar. Now he understands why. And while he's observing them,

those long fingers grow longer still and circle round his arms and throat, forcing him down under the water.

He comes up spluttering. One of the Yvags reaches for a coarse square of soap. The rings of torso muscle flow and let the body extend to reach it. Again he's reminded of the red tunnel itself, as if they have all traveled inside a giant version of themselves. They utterly repulse him. Their sex, if that's what it is, appears to be a bright yellow, hooked appendage emerging from flaps of skin.

Despite his revulsion and his attempts to pull away, the two Yvags yank him closer and begin scrubbing him with the soap. His skin reddens as if he's being flayed. His back already raw from being dragged across a plaza. He yowls and tugs furiously to be let go. They ignore him as if bored by everything he does, and work the soap back and forth in his long hair until a froth is running over his face. They might as well be scrubbing a horse, and in fact on the far side of the perfect pond another Yvag is washing one of those sinister beasts of shiny bone, but not with anything like the kind of force being used on him. Without saddle and caparison, that creature, too, is fully revealed, a body of peculiar horizontal ribbing, its pearlescent anatomy polished and nacreous as a nautilus. How is it black in his world and such a silvery color here? There is no skin over its rigid anatomy, either. It looks less like a horse than ever, and more like an assembled, artificial thing. Its empty eyes stare at him as if it hears his thoughts and is not impressed.

Head shoved under the surface again and held down, released, he comes up choking, spitting.

The two Yvag attendants haul him out and drop him on the stones. He notices their feet for the first time. Elongated like their hands, the feet are some cross between those of humans and taloned birds of prey.

Lying there, he sees that the Yvags who went wandering into the Þagalwood have returned. Little *fae* hobs dart around them. They carry with them bundles of hacked-off branches and larger severed sections of those moaning tree-things. It looks as if they've cut one down and split it apart among them. As they pass by, he realizes that the pieces have the same iridescence as the beasts, and that they are moving, slowly curling as if alive.

His two Yvag keepers have paused to watch the procession, too, but now step once more into their black-and-silver garments. Almost molten, the material flows over them again, reconstituting their solid shape within its breastplates, thorny helms, and greaves—armor that's not armor, is more like a shell encasing a lobster, but that, a moment ago on the ground, was something as squishy as a lobster's flesh. The black armor has molded their forms, in some ways disguising their true grotesqueness and making them more resemble human knights. Disguising seems to be something they're skilled at. *They remade Sìleas like it was nothing before they condemned her to death.*

For him, no outfit is offered. They pick him up and drag him between them. He looks for a destination in the weird landscape of star-shot spires, massive edifices, and sky-roads overhead, but they seem merely to be wandering along paths through an ever-nocturnal domain. Other Yvags observe him with mild interest as he's hauled past. Their costumes are strange and seem to flicker with color, but how much is clothing, how much glamour? No one says anything nor seems surprised by his presence in their midst.

At a point he fails to notice, they enter a field in the middle of the stepped towers and obelisks, and wander into wine-colored grasses as high as his waist. His hauling flattens the grass. It hisses angrily at him.

Ahead looms what at first he takes for a great mount of rock—a circular outcropping but flattened, something like Eildon Hill with the top sheared off. The sides are marked with runnels and crevices, many of which reflect sparks of light, of color, as if gems are embedded in the deepest recesses.

The entrance proves to be a cut to the far left, and passing through it they arrive in a curving atrium walled with polished onyx, reddish brown and lustrous. The scrape of him being dragged along echoes off the walls, echoes ahead of them on their ever-curving journey through chambers of different colors, textures, some brilliant and as iridescent as the bones of Þagalwood; others are blue or purple despite that there's no source for the light. Walls arise seamlessly from the floor, and the deeper the knights take him, the higher they reach, until all the ceilings are vaulted and ribbed. Because of the omnipresent dimness of the sky, it's awhile before he realizes that the vaults are transparent between the supports. He is seeing the weird

matrix of stars. He marvels at the construction of this place, so far
beyond anything he and Waldroup ever worked on or could have
imagined. The halls, however, are structured much like the framing
in his cruck house, and he wonders if the shape of it came to him
from the Queen or from his first contact with the portal, a ghost-
image lodged in his head, waiting to be used.

The final chamber is round. They deposit him on a great circular
tile in its center, then withdraw.

Overhead, the seventeen ribs all gather at one spot—a single clear
panel that mirrors the tile he's on; it's like an eye, a lens that magnifies
the reddish star of perpetual twilight hovering above, and its intense
orange radiance paints the floor around him. He raises a hand to
shield his eyes from the intensified light, recalling another time when
he did that—the day he first set eyes on *her* against the sun. The day
they killed Onchu.

"*Keep that to yourself, Tom,*" advises Waldroup's ghostly voice,
though he can't see the point—she already knows his identity. Keep
it to himself that he remembers?

"Why, Alpin?" he whispers. No response.

His deliverers have gone, left him alone, and he's beginning to
bake in the light. The tile, however, remains oddly cool.

He stands up. Immediately there comes a tug at his throat. When
he instinctively resists, it chokes him. He lets go, lets it pull him to the
left. He staggers off the tile, out from under that star's light, leaving
wet footprints across the great open space.

He thought he had entered through the only doorway in this
circular chamber, but it's as if the walls have rearranged. The door
he entered is gone, and what was a smooth wall panel previously is a
dark opening. Pulled along, he walks through another chamber, one
containing a silver throne adorned with carved faces distorted either
by anger or terror... it's hard to say which. From there he's drawn
through one after another parabolic arch, a long procession of them,
each with an alcove between the nacreous supports, so many arches
that it seems impossible he is still inside the same structure. Here
and there more branch off, more vaulted ribs, a confusion of apses
and transepts. Through some he spies more Yvags, some of whom
glance up, disinterested, at his passing. In one they're attending to a
seated figure in brown robes, a monk it seems. Then he notices the

manacles on its wrists and ankles, huge hands and feet. When he tries to walk toward it for a closer look, the pull on him turns to burning anguish. There will be no investigating anything. He stumbles on.

The concatenation of twenty arches end in an immense door made of glass or something like glass, but milky, impossible to see through. Pressing it opens the way into another circular chamber, something like a hemispherical chevet, with all the ribs of the vaults gathered in a dazzling array overhead. It's an architecture beyond imagining, a chaos of vaulting; at the same time it has a peculiar, identifiable symmetry. Vaults and walls are made of some iridescent blue-and-green substance that throws these colors everywhere. Waldroup's ghost whispers, "*No human hand ever fashioned this place,*" as if he wouldn't have realized that on his own. He feels it's a line from one of his riddles, one he cannot recall.

In the center of this terminal chamber, upon a round pedestal bed, sits Queen Nicnevin. She strokes the air, each stroke drawing him deeper into the chamber. She still wears her formal gold and black robe.

She drops her hand then and says, "Now you're here, come to me of your own accord. Show me your capitulation."

Capitulation means little if anything, he thinks. He couldn't find his way back out of this building, much less out of Ailfion, if he tried. If he was allowed.

He walks hesitantly forward, looking about him; passes a red onyx room full of additional small recesses. There are narrow copper mirrors, necklaces, gowns hung like draperies everywhere. No others from her entourage are here, not even Aðalbrandr.

In his head, her voice replies with amusement, "*Especially* not Aðalbrandr."

She stands and makes a slight movement with her shoulders. The robe falls to the floor. She is naked beneath it. Lean and strong, with coils of muscle like the ones who carried him from the pond, a physique that looks as hard and polished as marble. Her coloring is different—a flush of rose at her throat that runs down her torso, over the coils, ending in protuberances the two who bathed him lack. The joints of her arms and legs are also more brightly colored. Her ribbed abdomen swells along the vertical holes that open and close like gills.

"Very good," she says. But he can't hide his revulsion.

Standing on the dais beside the bed, she towers over him. He is certain she's taller than he is even on equal footing.

"I am. Does that concern you? It has caused others of your kind to tremble."

"No," he replies. He has fought larger men and won.

She laughs. "Good. And do fight me, if you can. It will make our game more challenging."

She reaches a long-fingered hand to his cheek, and he pulls back before she can touch him. She smiles slyly. Her forearm extends, and the pads of her fingers brush his cheek. He remembers how giddy he felt when she rode past him with Onchu—she touched him then, too, but not with such intent. A talon-like nail flicks to make the tiniest cut, and suddenly he's drowning in desire. This arousal isn't abstract—it's as if the blood in his veins has been replaced with the liquor of Nicnevin. She nods at the result. "I'll make this easier for you at first. In these our current forms, we're incompatible. You don't have the right equipment. But you will."

As she did at Melrose, she gathers the air around her. This time the energy seems to come from everywhere, and he expects he's about to be turned into an animal again. But instead, it's Nicnevin who transforms before his eyes, into the voluptuous human Queen of Heaven. She might have been assembled from his private imaginings and memories, an amalgam of Sìleas, Janet and every woman he's ever felt anything for in his short life.

"Glamour," he says. Tries to dismiss what he sees, but his mouth is parched with lust. "Only hides your shape."

"Ah, well, you weren't simply glamoured, were you, mayfly? You *were* a ram. Glamour is appearance. It lies in the minds of the perceivers. Reshaping is far harder to do, and far more exhausting to maintain. Waste not our time."

Her hand closes around the back of his neck and draws him up onto the dais with her. She catches her lower lip with those sharp white teeth, then leans in and kisses him. Her breath is like ice, her lips honeyed with some moist substance, more of her elixir. The taste of her makes him so drunk with lust that she becomes the only thought in his head. She turns him and pushes him down on the bed, then climbs upon him and without preamble fits him inside herself. "Take me for a ride by the longest route."

He arches himself to thrust as deeply as possible into her, and tries to maintain it as she moves. If he were coiled like her kind, he would stretch up as high as one of the many parabolic arches that compose this building. No awareness of sensation but where she holds him tight inside her, as if his mind itself has been gathered and stuffed into his prick. Her ride goes on and on, hours, perhaps days—he loses all sense of it. Knows he should have spent himself by now, and maybe he has. Maybe he has a dozen times, but she has hidden it from him so that he remains erect and straining, until she at last takes her pleasure. And that might be an eternity from this moment. If there were any speck of him left uncaptured, he might protest.

She tilts onto her side but doesn't release him. In that moment she becomes Janet, stolen from his mind, her face leering the way the skinwalkers all leered. Janet becomes Sìleas with a demon's face, lying across a blue sand landscape—another image stolen from his thoughts, memories. She steals a kiss off him, takes bites of his lip, his neck. He bleeds from a dozen tiny wounds, blood that she smears over him like paint and licks from her fingers. Each tiny bite only drowns him deeper in drugged, biddable lust for her. She could devour him like a mantis and he would hold with her until the last moment before he perished, never cry out; death would be sweet agony.

It might be that years do pass. Then suddenly he's released, the spell gone, the blood in his veins his own again. She has disengaged, and he is sprawled back, scratched and bitten, nearly insensate. With that abrupt release of his mind, the lightning flashes through his head, the pressure rises.

The Queen with Janet's face slides away to observe his thrashing. She listens to the storm in his head, and before the riddle can emerge, she commands it to cease. Her presence, like powerful hands inside his head, closes over and squashes the thing before he can speak it, pushing it down inside him while his body rocks back and forth, helplessly. Foam flecks his lips, but the fit fails to twist him up. Instead, it withdraws, a passing thundercloud. He collapses and stares up at her, hollow, consumed, unable to clear his thoughts. She shakes her head. "I have no interest in deciphering any more of your nonsense rhymes. That's not what I want from you, mayfly." Her fingers move in the air again. They brush his lips, then slide down to the jewel set in his throat. The sensation of it expands like something closing around his larynx. "Hereafter the choker will keep you silent while I take everything I want."

He doesn't even have to try to speak to know that she's taken away his voice with that jewel. She leans down and licks blood from a wound on his shoulder.

Studies him. Her shape changes to her true form. Yet even as the Queen, she tortures him with faces plucked seemingly at random from his mind. "Now let's see."

Agony scours him, shapes him, worse than when she turned him into a ram. His bones must be snapping. He clutches at the bedding, thrashing, in such searing pain that he can't lie still, rolls and crawls to escape it, but it comes with him. And then she's upon him, feasting, the liquor of her running in his veins if he has veins any longer. His body's on fire. Close by, she whispers, "I own you, mayfly, until you die of me."

Whatever she does next, it splits him apart until he's blind with pain and screaming.

"Again," orders Nicnevin.

XXIII. "Again"

✠

"Again."

It becomes the only word in his head, inflamed by her unappeasable desire. There are moments when the pain withdraws and he comes to his senses lying alone, unsure whether he was unconscious or just so lost in pain that his mind collapsed.

He has come to his senses in Yvag form, bound to her by some sticky substance wrapped around them both; he has come to his senses as she withdraws some appendage from him, feeling as if she's hollowed him out; he has come to his senses to find himself ridden by Janet, by Innes, worst of all by Sìleas.

They have been nose-to-nose, her golden eyes boring into his, with him pressed so tightly against her that he can feel her muscles coil and expand. It's like being pressed against a huge leech. Stretching, she flexes, and something sharp and well inside him burns as if thrust straight from a white-hot forge. It's a pain he can taste, while the liquor of her makes him crave it even as he writhes in agony. His own transformed body feeds him more exotic sensations that nauseate him. He can feel his gills dilate when he breathes. In this form the air may be easier to inhale, but he's only allowed moments to appreciate it before she starts on him again. His shape ripples. Arms and legs are bitten off, and he lies there helpless while something unholy feasts upon what's left of him until his screaming outlasts his lungs. Then comes a darkness filled with the stench of her, the corrosion of their coupling. It's the stink of decay, the reek of bodies on a baking battlefield five days after the war. And when it is done, it all begins again.

✠ ✠ ✠

When next he wakes, he finds himself alone in a small round cell made of the same nacreous substance as the massive arches he walked through however many days or weeks before. A smell of braised meat has awakened him; his stomach growls but also threatens to heave. What has been done to him?

He's lying on a spongy pallet, beside which sits a concave wooden paten containing a small feast. He swallows down his bile, leans over, and tries a small piece of the meat. His hand trembles so much that he barely manages to stuff the meat into his mouth. When it doesn't rise back up in his gorge, he falls upon the paten like a madman; meat juices run down his chin, his belly, which he's happy to discover is his own, and not coiled yellowish alien flesh. He's been shredded as if whipped, scored with countless cuts, colored with bruises everywhere. There's a scar on his side that looks freshly healed. He thinks he remembers knifelike pain there, but even now all of it runs together. Better to blot all of it out, focus on what's in front of him.

Where this shoulder of beef has come from, he doesn't care. He saw no cattle, no animals at all on the journey here, no crops, no farming. But elves are well known to steal from human farmers— cattle, sheep, crops, as well as babies. He's far too hungry to care how it got here. He drinks whatever is in the cup. It tastes wonderful, sharp and sweet both, and must be some sort of potent liquor, because by the final sip, he's barely able to sit upright, and falls back on the pallet.

Under the smell of the food, he smells her on himself. Even the meat juices can't wash her scent off him, that stink of decay.

He lies back, helpless, drunk and sated, staring into the twilight, with no clear idea of anything. *"Again."* The word rises unbidden, as barbed as an Yvag dagger. Time has tangled around him like threads off a loom. It's akin to being Thomas Lindsay Rimor the halfwit all over. No way to cling to any clarity; he can't even put the snippets he recollects in order, but mostly he doesn't want to look at what she's done with him, to him. If her goal is to torture him until he breaks apart, she may already have cracked his shell and put him back together again. He's sure she's not finished devouring him.

On the pallet, his fogged mind turns to Janet and Morven, to Sîleas probably pulled to bits by now. Soon he's curled up, sobbing for the poor girl who died because of him, wretchedly asking himself what he did to give himself away, how did he fail all these women? Was it that night over Old Melrose, the little homunculus he killed there? Had that *fae* given him away somehow? He gets up, stumbles on weak, trembling legs to the garderobe behind a panel in one corner, then crashes back to the pallet, where he finally passes out while thinking that what he wants is for Nicnevin to use him up. Let her kill him or throw him in that well—anything so long as he knows, feels nothing further.

He wakes up to two Yvag knights dragging him back to the pond for another scrubbing. There seems to be something in the soap or the water that kills lice and keeps his beard from growing out. Afterward he's deposited back in the Queen's chamber, shivering and wet. She must hear his despair, because upon arriving she draws back and observes him a moment. "Yes," she says, "you do dwell too much on past irrelevancies. So much so that you haven't even noticed how easily you breathe now in your own form. The *choker*"—she taps a finger on the jewel at the front of his throat—"also helps you to inhale our air. You see, it's not *all* punishment. Lying with me isn't punishment, is it?" She smiles seductively with Innes's sickly face. "Now . . ." She puts a hand to his cheek, and the flood of her carnal appetite offers to drown him in a mindless escape. He closes his eyes so he doesn't have to behold his sister so reduced. Her carnality drags him down regardless, an anchor pulling him to the very bottom.

No nights, no days, only the perpetual umbra above this place she calls her summer house, which is surely as massive as the greatest cathedral ever built and more complex than a fortress.

Time becomes like a lake and he like the stone skipped across it. Whatever's being done to him, he strains to reach the numbness that lets him miss most of it.

Then one day he wakes in his small cell, and grief has less pull on him. He half accepts what's happened—it has all been done *to* him, out of his control—and with that acceptance comes a moment of clarity, of reassurance: Janet is alive somewhere. His child is alive somewhere. He has saved them, though Sìleas paid the price. The fault for that belongs to the pilgrims and the elven, not to him. More than that, it's a reminder that these monsters do make mistakes.

He's still alive. Doesn't his survival indicate that Nicnevin doesn't intend to kill him—at least not immediately, otherwise why not use him up completely?

So, when next the jewels lead him to her massive chamber and her bed, before she begins, he signals a desire to speak. She considers him indulgently. "Something different, mayfly? Have you come to your senses enough to have questions?" She draws her robe around her and gestures for him to proceed.

He tries to speak, begins to cough instead. His inability seems to amuse her. Finally, in a raspy voice, he says, "You turn me to Yvag, yourself to human. Why?"

"Are my whims insufficient reason?"

He shakes his head. "I know—" He clears his throat. "It exhausts you."

"You know that, do you? I must not be using you sufficiently if you have time to consider *my* exhaustion. What can you possibly understand of my capabilities?"

He doesn't answer. It's only happened a few times, and only for a second. The first time was when she transformed him back from a ram; she didn't realize he saw the effort it took. The other two times, here, he has been at the point of collapsing himself. He can't be certain what strain he actually saw.

"You ponder the imponderable, I think. But you have asked politely, so I will tell you, though whether you can comprehend remains to be seen. As I've told you once before, the Yvag race is sempiternal. Effectively to you, we are immortals. Do you recall I asked if you appreciated the cruelty you inflict upon us when you kill us? Yes, yes, your brother, our *teind*, I know your perspective, and you're hardly the first to express it. But let me ask you, do you think about the life of a rabbit before you skin it for dinner? It lived to be your meal. You don't think about it at all. You—that is, your kind—exist to be a tithe we must pay. We choose not to pay with our own kind, because our numbers are insufficient. If we had remained the *teind*, there would already be none of us left. The price paid for immortality turned out to be our fecundity. Now only a small number of us have sufficient . . . well, you don't have a word for it. We call it *astralis*. It is the stuff of stars within us all, the spark that ignites life. When you slaughter our kind, you're not snuffing out a life, you're obliterating a memory that's existed since before your solar system even swirled together. Of course you don't know what that even means. The crime of killing one of us is unspeakable, and you don't take one, you take three and four at one go. If I listened to the likes of Ađalbrandr, you would already be flung into the well of worlds. But you see..."

She brushes his chin, pricks him with a talon. He is instantly burning with lust for her again. Watching it take over his expression, she grins. White, needlelike teeth fill his view.

She leans close to him and whispers, "The Queen wants an heir."

He seizes up. The pressure swells and lightning crackles in his head again, but she clamps down upon the seizure like the pincers of a lewis.

"Ah, ah, I told you, no fits, no riddles. You will give me a child, mayfly. We are not compatible species, but that I will fix. Either as a human, your sap mixing in me while *I'm* transformed, or else as an Yvag with such potency that your own rich *astralis* will roar through me like an ocean wave. You serve a far greater cause than my pleasure, though you serve that, too. Think on this—should your seed take in me, your offspring, our offspring, will expand our diversity, will outlive your own universe." She bites his throat then, a dozen tiny pinpricks, and sucks his blood. It trickles from beneath her lips, down his chest. She pulls back, grinning, licking her bloody lips. While sucking his blood, she has made herself human once more—made herself into a demonic Janet again.

She casts off the black-and-gold robe. "Now," she says, "again," and the word resounds as if chasing him down the plaza well.

The last thing he remembers is the glowing ribs of the arches overhead, toward which he, released from his body at last, seems to float. But try as he might, he cannot pierce the veil, cannot reach heaven. The Queen of Elves reels him back in.

"Welcome back, little brother," the voice in his head whispers.

He opens his crusted eyes. He has been returned to his cell. Food has been left upon another paten—smoking meat, some cheese, and a toasted barley bannock—and although it rouses his appetite, he makes no move. Just stares at it.

Alpin? Alpin, get me from here.

No answer comes. It might have been a voice in a dream, but it's set his thoughts awhirl with impossible possibilities: of tearing off the jewels of obedience, of escaping from this labyrinth and finding his way home again, even though for all he knows the Þagalwood, hidden on the far side of a portal, might be on the other side of the world. Unbowed by these obstacles, he conjures up a joyous return to Janet, and their flight to some other country, somewhere safe from skinwalkers, far from Ercildoun and Roxburgh, Yvagddu, and changelings. Surely, there must be some place where the eldritch creatures haven't intruded.

Eventually, he crawls to the end of his pallet and eats his meal with the eagerness of a man with renewed purpose. They have not killed him. They will not kill him. The Queen wants a child by him, as ridiculous as that seems. He's not done in, not yet. Sooner or later, there will be opportunity for escape. There must be.

It is as he's drifting off, surfeited, that he vaguely senses a presence in his room. He opens his eyes but otherwise doesn't move. A tall, darkly robed figure is picking up the round paten, the remains of his meal, its hands revealed to be huge and bone white. The fingers are long, weirdly segmented.

He raises his head. "Wait," he tries to say, forgetting that the stones have taken his voice again.

The figure pauses. From the depths of its cowl, two dull violet eyes glow. As though it's heard his thought and now considers him. Then it turns and rises all in one swift movement, and in turning away seems to melt into the shadows of his doorway—so quick and silent that he's not sure it was there in the first place. But the hands... they were like the overhead branches and twigs of the Þagalwood.

He drifts off again, dreams of a skeleton companion mocking him with Waldroup's voice.

He wakes while being dragged to the pond again, doused and scrubbed to death, then hauled back through the labyrinth. Try as he might, he can't memorize the route, almost as if the way transforms each time, as if the building is alive and altering itself. Then he's deposited with the Queen; she immediately alters him so that he drowns in pain, then infects him and her desire consumes him, blasting away his last mote of consciousness.

The routine of captivity defines his entire existence now.

He has never done anything else; it's as if that precious life he remembers scraps of is pure fantasy, concocted perhaps by the voice in his head that he calls Alpin. He can barely recall who that might be—random images of battles and skirmishes, of slicing stones. Has the Queen's plan worked? Is there something growing in her? *Astralis*. She told him what it was but he's lost track as he's lost track of how many times she's disjointed his body into an Yvag shape. Will she use him up or cast him aside? Clearly, she's unconcerned that he might try to escape. The choker never comes off, and probably won't for as long as he endures here. But in those few moments of solitude she affords him, he can barely walk across his small chamber without collapsing. The only escape he's planning now is to die, and it seems Nicnevin's in no hurry to allow it; she'll wear him to a husk first.

How many years will have passed outside? How many winters is he missing under the furs and skins with his sweet, warm Janet? Janet, whose memory has all but been replaced by the distorted, leering face the Queen has given her. So, too, Innes, with her sunken eyes and cracked lips, and Sìleas, grinning like a ravenous demon. These are the faces he sees each time the Queen takes him. Now there lurks a subterranean need for the feel of Nicnevin against his palms. Her lust is like a love-philter, and he's twinned and turned and helpless in its all-consuming sorcery. Thoughts of Janet as she was are like a sprinkle of rain after an ocean has dashed him against rocks over and over.

If his fate lies in the hands of the Queen, there's one matter that gnaws at him still. Lying upon his pallet, he keeps turning it over. Eventually, as if the ghost in his head has been watching and listening, Waldroup quietly intrudes.

"What difference will it make, Tom? Even if you learn the answer, it's not as if you'll be allowed to tell Innes."

"I know. It makes no difference, other than that I won't stare into the eyes of every one of these elves and wonder if that's the one."

"You want an answer, even at the risk of her spleen? If this is her kindness, her venom will split you wide."

"I know."

The next time he manages to gather his wits in bed with the Queen, in sweaty postcoital emptiness, he signals to her that he wants to speak again. After a moment, she flicks her hand as if it's a trivial matter, and releases his voice. "What now?" she asks.

He massages his throat, then in a raspy voice announces, "I would like to see my nephew."

Her pinpoint pupils widen into rings. "Your what?"

"My sister's child. Your . . . skinwalker, Elgadorn, swapped him for a pile of twigs, a glamoured forest thing. According to you, you took him to make a new one of your kind, which means he's here somewhere in your world."

"Undoubtedly to replace someone you murdered. Such as Elgadorn."

He closes his eyes so she won't see the simmering rage in them. "This was well before I put an arrow through any of your undercroft sleepers, so think again." Opening his eyes again he can see that her patience is running out. He goes on quickly: "Once upon a time this Elgadorn inhabited a drowned body named Balthair MacGillean, slew his entire family to place himself in charge, then married my sister and fathered a child off her. Afterward, he left her to rot away in her madness with a little horror fashioned out of sticks to suckle. Do you even know of the events that happen in your kingdom?"

She pinches thumb to her first two fingers and he clutches at his throat, unable to breathe. "Careful of the tone you take with me, mayfly." She releases the hold upon him and he gasps for breath. "I know all of this, half of it plucked from your own mind. And by your description alone, her child rightfully belongs to us. We had taken over the lich. So what is there to discuss?"

Now he's too tired, too furious to care what she does. "There really is no cruel act you can't justify, is there?"

With one swift gesture, she robs him of his speech again. Coldly tells him, "We are done now. You would do well to remember how small and fragile your position here is before displaying such contumacy again. You continue to exist entirely by my whim, and my patience wears thin."

He tries to plead, and she shakes her head. Nicnevin gets to her feet, so tall and steel-gray and muscled. She wraps herself in one of her black-and-gold robes, turns away, but stops and comes back.

She says, "This *kindness* you think you deserve is not within my powers. I do not sort one changeling from any other—who are they to me? They arrive here as human, male or female, and through ritual of cellular recomposition they become Yvag, of which there are four variant genders, including *Queen*"—she smiles slyly—"of which you have been three now. However, if so much time has passed—how many years has it been in your world, more than a few?—then the ritual has long since taken place, and he is now *we*. His own mother would fail to recognize him." She studies him coldly. "Did you ever even set eyes on it? On the meat, not the changeling."

He shakes his head.

She mocks him with a laugh. "Perhaps you'd like me to bring its mother here, to see if she can pick him out. What was her name, your sister?"

He knows she knows the name already.

"*Innes*. Shall we bring her? What say you?"

He shakes his head vigorously.

"Giving you voice is like keeping you from your bath for an extra day. It benefits no one."

Then she is gone. He is left with the poison of her lust still flowing through his veins.

"*Wasn't wise to goad her,*" whispers Alpin. Then, "*Felt good, though, didn't it? For a few moments were you free of her sorcery. Well, you'd best start planning an escape now, little brother, no matter the odds. Because between your ire and hers, you'll not much longer be in her company.*"

Whatever Alpin is, he's undoubtedly right about this. "Start planning your death, Thomas Rimor," he mutters, and lies back down upon the bed.

XXIV. The Royal Hunt

⚜

Now he is abandoned in his cell. Days, perhaps weeks pass—he can't be certain. Nobody hauls him to the pond. Nobody interacts with him at all. Without whatever substance was in the pond, his beard has begun to grow out, and he's aware of his own stink returning. There seem to be times when he is suddenly sleepy for no good reason, and each time he dozes he wakes to find a new platter of food has been left. It seems he is not to be given another opportunity to witness the Þagalwood servant that delivers and removes the food. Something puts him to sleep to ensure this. His time can only be measured by these meals. Is there one a day? Or two? How long is a day in perpetual twilight? He's given nothing to go by. When he stares up through the roof at those strange, incongruous swirls of stars, he feels as if he's melting into them. There is no escape. No windows in the little garderobe, and no way to scale the smooth, polished ribs to the transparent vault, assuming he could by some means penetrate it and climb out if he did. What's the likelihood the choker wouldn't respond if he got out that way? In this complete isolation he can't help imagining the worst—that any time now, the doors will be flung open and he'll be dragged out to the well between worlds, where he'll be ceremoniously glamoured and flung in. Probably they're just biding their time until the next *teind* is due. He has served his purpose (or failed to, he suspects), and Nicnevin is finished with him. Why not let go and escape into madness? What better place to elude her? Her sorcery can't pursue him there.

Then he awakens from one of these manufactured dozes, unable

219

to recall when he fell asleep. Instead of a meal he finds a pile of clothing beside him. A shiny material of their design, a loose-fitting gray article of clothing with sleeves and leggings, split halfway down the front. He steps into it, and the material comes to life. In a panic he tries to tear it off before realizing that, like the uniforms of the Yvag knights, it is simply adjusting itself to him. The sleeves flare, the shoulders extend out from his own into soft points. The gray shades into a blue-green with a diagonal stripe of violet. The leggings grow into soft boots that swirl themselves around his calves, ankles, and under his feet, which forces him to pull up each foot as the "growing" material pinches together. Around his throat and at the ends of the sleeves are bands of gold trim. The material grows up the back of his head, forming a hood. Thomas reaches up to feel it, fingers following it to a point behind him. He pushes the hood back off his head. The nondescript clothing has become a belted tunic above dark leggings and black boots.

This is strange; nothing like being the *teind*. Would they dress him up just to strip and glamour him?

Shortly, an unhelmed Yvag knight opens his door, gestures for him to come. Whatever awaits, he has no choice but to follow.

He walks the curving labyrinth, for the first time clothed and under his own power. Side chambers that have always been empty before are bustling with more of the elven than he's seen since he arrived, all costumed elaborately in lustrous, shimmering fabrics, in jackets and gowns, sashes and jeweled regalia, their silver hair coiffured, a hundred different styles, colors, patterns. Compared to their elaborate costumes, his own looks drab. His head fills with their buzzing, chirping conversations; all of them sound giddy. It's not about him—hardly any of them pay him the slightest attention as he passes by.

The knight and he walk the path through the field of waist-high grass and emerge above the plaza where he's been bathed so many times, but today the pool is not in use, and the plaza is full of gray-skinned, spiked and fanged Yvags, as if all the elves in creation have turned out, which may be the case. Overhead, goggle-eyed sprites flit to and fro, sweeping across the whole plaza like bats attracted by the light or the intense murmur. He's lost, almost invisible amidst this crowd. If anything, their costumes are more elaborate than what he's seen so far: high collars, puffy sleeves, multicolored leathers, and embroidered cloaks adorned with faces that change expression as they move and appear to be conversing with other pieces of clothing; a swallow-tailed coat covered with eyes that follow him with their gaze although their owners pass by without so much as a glance; elaborate metal breastplates carved into profiles of strange beasts that snarl; one cluster of elves sporting grotesque, lurid codpieces some of which represent, to his experiential horror, attributes of the three Yvag sexes. The chatter and buzz of the plaza fills his head so completely that their words must be spilling from his ears. A few do turn to observe him candidly as he passes among them; most look amused by his presence, or maybe by the knowledge of how he's being put to use. He recalls the name his mother called elves when he was small: the Sluagh. She insisted it was bad luck to speak their true name the way Waldroup so blithely says "Yvag" *(You're dead, Alpin, and I'm a prisoner here, so was she wrong to think so?)*. Beholding all of this crowded grandeur, calling them the Sluagh now seems fitting: a host, a multitude. Was it someone else brought here against their will, beholding this spectacle, who first applied it? There are stories, but how many humans have ever set eyes on this impossible landscape and lived to describe it?

Mixed in among the colorful costumes are others like his, the same color, stripe, form, a dozen or so mingling. The others are all young elves—younger in appearance than he is anyway. Might they all be changelings, his nephew in among them? They each regard him in his costume with a look of disdain. Around the perimeter, some knights sit upon their pale-boned beasts, which are also adorned in a spangling panoply of caparisons and chanfrons and crinieres like horses decorated for a pageant. The knights look bored. The one who led him here joins them, climbing aboard its mount. He looks for Adalbrandr, who despises him, but does not see that one.

Shrubberies surrounding the plaza sparkle, the berries in them throwing off light somehow. The pool where he has bathed glows from within as if filled with liquid fire.

On the far side of the plaza, the Queen sits upon a throne with a towering and elaborately carved back and a golden canopy at its top. For a moment, Thomas watches her and all of the others. Nobody is watching him, and he speculates how easy it would be to wander off between the various spires and towers, wonders how difficult it would be to escape from Ailfion entirely and vanish beyond the spire and tower landscape. The trouble is, he has no idea which direction, where to run once he has slipped away, or if he can get far enough from here that the choker becomes inactive rather than lethal.

Even as he considers this, the choker exerts a sudden strong pull, tugging him in the direction of the high throne. Although she has given no indication even of noticing him, Nicnevin commands his presence.

Stumbling his way through the crowd, he is drawn not to the throne but to a strange exhibit—a tall, circular containment as clear as fresh water but hard, solid. In the center of it, as far from all sides as possible, a strange creature in a threadbare brown cloak hunches low and watches them all. It is stocky, more strange beast than human. Black hair falls in thick braids from its scalp. The gray eyes are larger than his, and wider apart, with a broad, protuberant nose not unlike some of the Yvag codpieces styled as faces. Coincidence? He doubts it. He wonders was this the "monk" he saw chained up however long ago that was—weeks or months?

The creature's gray gaze fastens upon him, and it rises up on thick legs, treads heavily toward him until only the clear wall separates them. There is intelligence in the eyes, and something else: rancor. Whether it is aimed at the elves or at him, he can't tell; but it seems utterly disinterested in its Yvag captors, having come straight to him, the only other non-elven creature in the plaza.

The creature babbles something, words he can't comprehend. Thick, knobby hands press to the wall, smearing sweaty handprints on it.

Behind him, Nicnevin's voice intrudes. "She's asked you to intercede on her behalf." The Queen has left her throne, drawing a flock of opulent elves like a wake trailing her, including the huge and surly Adalbrandr. Her costume is unlike anyone else's: A blue crinkled fan surrounds her throat. Her head, adorned with a circlet of gems, seems to balance in the center of the fan, above a lighter blue and luminous bodice sewn from diamond-shaped panels edged in a deeper midnight blue. The high-backed robe she wears gathers at her waist, so whatever she wears below it is hidden in the folds of that black and gold cloak.

Me?

"You. She would have you take her place. Wants you to know how many children she has if you'd care to listen."

I don't understand. Take her place in what? In there?

"No, no, fool. In the Royal Hunt. First, I shouldn't believe her about the children. Trolls almost never tell the truth, and you are a human, famously gullible. Pots of gold, secret treasures, brief liaisons with faeries—you're notoriously easy to lead astray."

She . . . She's a troll. They're real.

"Tediously so. This was their world once, before we arrived. They were the dominant species, although no more advanced than your ancestors who dwelled in caves. I suppose most of the world still is theirs, however many of them remain. We have not reengineered it for *their* comfort, have we?

"You might recall my mentioning those foolish members of your kind who named Hel as their goddess? We were returning them to your world when the trolls made a rare bold move and stormed through the cut that had been opened. Cunning of them, distracting everyone as they did, stealing ördstones—a more coordinated effort than we gave them credit for. By the time we could seal off the portal, hundreds of them had jumped to your world. We're not certain quite how many; they are subterranean by nature—or have been since we remade the surface here for us. And they opened many portals, so probably spilled into other worlds as well."

She closes her eyes, smiling, as if recalling something wicked.

"*Your* sun, however, proved deadlier to them than our atmosphere. They quickly calcify in its light, becoming stone. If you didn't know what you were seeing, you would think you beheld a natural if strange formation of rock. Some, I think, managed to survive in your world by descending into deep caverns before the sun could torpefy them—we know this because one of our Yvagvoja heard and brought back some of the stories being told. Undoubtedly you've heard similar stories but have never met one before this." Then she quotes from something: "*Hvat's troll nema þat?*" Laughs quietly.

He looks off beyond her, recalling tales that some warriors recounted, that he and Waldroup thought were ridiculous and told by credulous men. *Trolls.*

"All that you really need to know is that today is a Royal Hunt, and our quarry is asking if you would willingly take her place. Would you?"

What, be hunted down and slaughtered by you and your knights? I think not.

"Wise choice." She hesitates, then adds, "Although, you know, if you were to succeed in eluding my hunting party, you would win your freedom, as will she."

Is he being baited or is she telling the truth? *How many have eluded you?* He studies the miserable troll.

"Oh, perhaps one in one hundred. But they *know*, you see. The hunt is something they understand. It can snatch them up at any time, which knowledge keeps them . . . in their place."

But if there's a world full of them beyond your . . .

"Our *sovereign state*? Ailfion?"

Why not use them *for your* teind? *Why take from our world?*

"The short answer is, they're of no use because they're impervious to glamouring."

And taking my kind is easy, I suppose.

"It was, before *you* came along." She stares a moment longer into the cage. "We only hunt *them* for sport. They are wild and clever and elusive, difficult to capture. Nor are they immortal. They wear out, the same as you, a little faster, in fact."

Nicnevin returns to her throne. He is drawn along as if on a lead.

"So, if you won't take her place, then you are hunting her along with us, mayfly. Which is why you're costumed as a beater. Can't have you running about naked—that's for my entertainment alone." She touches one sharp finger to his cheek, and even that contact makes him thrum with lust. She taps the stone at his throat. "Your choker is reconfigured to allow you to roam today. But as you've already contemplated this, don't take encouragement from that news. Your range is limited. And I would so hate for those twinned jewels to compress."

He is presented with a long, polished staff, tipped at both ends with gold caps, and ushered over to the group of young Yvags dressed in the same blue-green outfits as his. They regard him with scorn. Their conversations buzz and drone in a collective sneer. He studies the changelings: They are smaller versions of the white-haired, golden-eyed knights, dotted with budding spikes but mostly not the sharper spines adorning their seniors. They have wider, rounder faces, too, that he assumes will stretch and narrow over time, but right now still express their former humanity. None resembles Innes or Baldie at all. When he moves in for a closer look, one of them smacks him with their staff. He leaps back, and they laugh at him. Needle-sharp teeth grin at him.

Whatever signal is given, he misses it. All at once the clear wall dissolves into the plaza stones like melting ice, until the female troll is separated from her captors by nothing but air. The elves move aside, creating a straight line across the plaza, up a series of steps and toward a distant hill covered in some sort of purple heath.

Something like a trumpet sounds, its note echoing off the towers and spires. Who knows where it originates? The troll struts into the lane they've opened up for her. The Yvags watch like a pack of dogs beholding a wounded doe. He half expects them to fall on and devour her right here, but they don't. The troll reaches the edge of the plaza, climbs the steps; then with one final look at her enemy, she charges straight for the distant hill. The Yvags all cheer. The hunt, it seems, has begun.

The crowd do nothing. They return to eating, drinking, buzzing excitedly until another trumpet blast sounds. The troll has vanished over the hill.

The changeling beaters turn as one and march off across the plaza. Thomas watches. Then Nicnevin's voice rings in his ears, *You'd best keep up, mayfly. Your choker will punish you for* avoiding *your duty, too.*

The pressure at his throat is mild, but a compelling threat.

He runs after the other beaters. Before they've reached the crest of the hill, he has to stop. Hands on knees, he wheezes, his lungs straining at the heavy air. Without the choker filtering it, he can't imagine how he would ever get very far. He would suffocate.

Reaching the top of the hill, Thomas pauses to catch his breath again and looks back.

From here in the dusky light he can just make out the ambit of their *city*—counts eighteen plazas like the one below between the towers, including the one with the bright circlet of Hel at its center;

there's an outer ring of fifty sparkling spires, and between them, everywhere, more of those curious eel-like pipes that rise out of the ground in humps. They dot the landscape all the way to the horizon. The towers suggest a population a thousand times greater than the throng amassed below for the Royal Hunt. Did the Queen lie about their numbers or are these spiral towers the abandoned shells of a dying race? He wonders when they invaded this world, if they somehow brought the city with them.

The most distant towers seem to wink in and out of existence. He once beheld an island that floated on the horizon of the ocean and wasn't truly there. It likewise came and went. Are these towers like that—existing somewhere other than where they appear to be? In two worlds at once?

With a savage cry, the beaters race down the farside of the hill, drawing his attention back to them. Behind him, the Yvag horde in their finery at last pour out of the plaza and begin the ascent. Thomas rushes down after the changelings.

The landscape ahead and below is covered by midnight-blue gorse or something very like it—leathery leaves growing knee to waist high out of pale blue sandy soil, reminding him again of Alpin's blue desert.

The beaters spread out wider across the landscape and begin thrashing back and forth while ululating—a sound that would terrify anything. When he catches up, the nearest one points for him to take up a position beyond their far right flank. Silently, he falls in line, imitating them, whirling the staff and slapping the waist-high plants, though without the weird wordless calls and with far less energy. The nearest beater gestures for him to move even farther away. He finds a narrow path going in his direction and follows it.

Overall, their line must stretch for miles now. Soon he can just barely make out the next one over. The Yvag hunting party is nothing but a distant tumult.

Wherever the troll has gone, Thomas doubts it's lying on its belly in the night-blue heath.

He wanders down and up two more ridges with nothing much higher than the dark heather anywhere—no sign of the troll. Given what Nicnevin described, he wonders if it hasn't gone straight for a cave somewhere. Thus far neither caves nor caverns have appeared, and no forest of any sort, either.

When next he glances at the beaters, they've spread out so wide that he can't see the next one over now. The sound of the Yvag horde has faded as well. For all he knows, one of the changelings successfully rooted her out; then again maybe not, since the choker hasn't recalled him. How cunning is a troll? Surely at least as cunning as a fox. It's her land, her world, or was.

The next ridge is more like a broad butte or escarpment, a stony hill with a nearly uniform top to it. He circles down around the side, thinking that now he's finally going to find caves and caverns.

The far side of the escarpment is a sheer drop from above. He would never have been able to climb down. Beyond it the landscape is different. There are pockets of forest ahead. Nothing like the expanse of the Þagalwood—most of the trees are short, with blue-black needles and lighter trunks. In the wan light of the shriveled sun, it's like peering at a landscape cast in moonlight, and the path he's on appears as a pale meandering line through it. Once he's rested again, he descends the silty slope, crosses a small meadow of golden whin, thicker than the heather was. With all the rocky heights around him, for a moment it's as if he's wandered out of Elfland and back home. He stands at the edge of the meadow and takes it all in, before picking up the path again, and soon climbs yet another steep and craggy hill, this one topped by a tor, like some giant's cairn, and pocked in places by depressions, maybe even caves.

On the far side of that, the path leads straight to a broken, crumbling ruin of some earlier civilization: great stone pillars, some still supporting portions of roofs, buildings that were once five- and six-sided before parts of them collapsed, some foundations in rows like the orderly properties of Ercildoun, but two that were obviously larger and might have been palaces or temples. A civilization far closer to his own than to the shining towers of Yvagddu. It reminds him of Roman ruins he's encountered below the broken stone wall that separates parts of Scotland from the south. Those had similar sunken floors and pavings, too. This suggests Nicnevin lied about how advanced the trolls were.

If he were a troll, this is where he would go. The definable path suggests that some have.

The craggy descent from the tor is full of dark spaces that might be cave entrances, or caverns, or deep recesses good for hiding, places where Yvag hunters might not catch their prey.

Down the rocky slope he goes with one idea: to find the troll and somehow help her escape her hunters. He keeps such a close watch on the ruin, he doesn't even glimpse the thing that strikes the side of his head, dropping him in his tracks.

Moments or minutes pass—he can't be sure. He sits up, dizzy for an instant. Touches the side of his head, which stings, finds wet blood on his fingers. Looks around.

In a shadowy crevice he's passed, the troll stands motionless, watching. A simple leather sling dangles from its fist, fitted with a rock. The wonder is the last one didn't split his skull open. Thing is, it's not *her*. Not the hunt's target. It's an even larger, hulking male troll with a prognathous jaw and enormous yellowish lower teeth arranged in an expression that's not pleased to see him.

It says something, gestures at him—at his uniform in particular. Of course, it sees a beater wearing a glowing purple sash, an agent of the elves, and nothing else. But where is the troll he thought he was following?

Even as he wonders this, he becomes aware of a distant rumbling. It is the same sound he heard with Alpin the night they entered the Þagalwood, and he knows it now as he knew it then.

Something is coming.

"Run!" he shouts at the troll. It leans away as if his voice has shocked it. Spins the sling. He drops the staff and raises his hands to show it he means no harm.

The rumbling grows. He glances up the hill. The troll does the same.

Suddenly, coming over the side of the tor, an Yvag warrior appears. The bone-white charger's three-toed hooves explode the whin, making along the same path straight for him and the troll... except that the troll is gone, nowhere to be seen, vanished back into the shadows or into the earth.

The knight has drawn a sword and holds it vertically. The black blade scintillates. The pose is one he's witnessed on a dozen battlefields: a charging knight thundering in for the kill.

The troll isn't the target. *He* is.

He turns then, sweeps up his staff as he springs over a fallen pillar, over jagged chunks that were once part of a building, and races for the remains of a standing wall, knowing that he can't outrun that charging beast for long. He's in battle again, reading the landscape, noting perilous holes, craters that could break an ankle, gauging distances as he reaches the piece of wall and dives over it headlong, tumbles, gouged and cut by stones as he rolls. His uniform tears and instantly the color and form flicker and go out of it. It becomes gray, shapeless, spongy. He's up and dodging around a canted floor still halfway attached to another hunk of wall, the ground having given way beneath it.

The hooves overtake him while he's scrambling past the chunk of floor, nothing but another wall ahead. The blade sweeps the air like a scythe. He hears it and throws himself to one side, the blade cutting emptily past with a *whoosh*. Lands and slides on the slanted floor, falls among debris, tearing his palms, knees. His beater's stick clatters away, but he grabs at it, and picks up a stone in his other hand. He's gasping.

The grotesque charger rises up on its back legs. The black-helmed warrior's arm raises. Thomas, on his knees, flings the stone for all he's worth. The flat of the sword slaps it aside almost casually. Sparks crackle at the contact, but at least it isn't cutting him in half yet.

Backed into a corner of the low wall, he has nowhere to veer in either direction.

The knight's free hand drops the reins and pushes back the helmet, which becomes pliable and sacklike, folding around the Yvag's neck. Long silver-white hair spills out. Even in the ruin's shadows, Thomas recognizes the hulking Aðalbrandr. Grinning, eager for the kill. The Yvag dismounts, stands higher up on the canted floor, brings the blade up in both hands again with the cool certainty of the kill looking it in the face.

When it cuts, Thomas thrusts up with his beater's stick, catches the blade against the metal cap, arms vibrating from the force of the blow, and twists to shove it into the wall. The tip cuts chips out of the stone instead of out of Thomas.

He presses back. The stick might withstand one more blow, but he's trapped here and Aðalbrandr will never give him quarter. Then the harsh voice is in his head:

"Mayfly," she calls you. You think that's a term of affection? You are an insect. What does she even see in your kind? Your astralis is useless.

The sword comes up again, patient, determined. Thomas's only move now is to throw himself forward and under the cut across the tilted floor, but that will require such precise timing that he doubts he can do it. The canted floor, the wall—he's hemmed in and clutching at straw.

And then a chunk of the dark ruin comes to life, rising up on the broken wall behind Aðalbrandr.

Thomas can't help but look. The Yvag starts to turn. There's a whipping sound, and a stone flies into Aðalbrandr's forehead, knocking the knight half off its feet and back against its mount. The troll springs then and lands upon the knight's back. Large filthy fingers with broken nails curl around Aðalbrandr's head, dig at the Yvag's eye sockets. Aðalbrandr screams as one of the hands slips, and thick fingers rip down to tear at its mouth instead, but the other fingers gouge deep into its eye. Finally the knight drops the sword, spins about to throw the troll off, slips and stumbles onto the canted floor, where it drops down on one knee and throws the troll over its shoulder, into the wall. Thomas leaps out of the way. He grabs for the sword, but Aðalbrandr snatches it first, thrusts at Thomas, slicing across his bicep before whirling about to swing the blade at the troll. The creature bellows at Thomas. He doesn't know the language, but he understands the meaning, the same as his to it: "Run!"

Aðalbrandr chops into the troll's shoulder, and it roars, springs upon the knight again, both hands raking the gray-green face. The sword clatters on the tilted floor.

Thomas leaps past them both. He should flee; he knows how this will end. But he takes the beater's stick and swings it hard at the Yvag's head. Aðalbrandr stumbles and the troll pounds both fists into its back, dropping the knight to its knees. The troll snarls at Thomas, and bounds over the wall.

Aðalbrandr's face is a dark, bloody mess, one eye looks ruined from what Thomas can see. But it ignores Thomas now, snatches up the sword and charges after the troll. Both are swallowed up in the darkness of the ruins.

Certain that the knight won't forget him once finished with the troll, Thomas flees the ruins with the intention of finding a cave in this hill into which he can crawl. The choker hasn't activated yet, so maybe he can both disappear and escape the fate promised, at least for a while.

Before he can even begin to investigate the crevices, however, a full hunting party appears beside the tor above him. He's fully exposed here. If he tries to flee for a cave now, they will know both where he is and that he's attempting to escape. They will surely kill him.

The only thing he can do is wave the beater's stick in the air to signal them and watch them descend. He takes advantage of the time to get his breath back.

It proves to be the Queen's group, with three spiky knights in black, her in her finery, and a cluster of changeling beaters. None of the colorfully costumed Sluagh.

Before she reaches him, the Queen is already looking at Aðalbrandr's mount standing idly in the ruins behind him. She takes in Thomas's torn and bleeding condition, his ruined uniform.

"Tell me, did you manage to kill Aðalbrandr with only a stick? Impressive." Before he can answer, there's a roar from the ruins that ends abruptly.

Knowing what that cry likely foretells, he turns to watch with her.

"What is this situation?" asks the Queen, all amusement gone.

The truth seems like the best idea. He attempts to answer, then remembers he can't speak. He concentrates on thinking it out. *Your other beaters directed me here on purpose. In Aðalbrandr's employ.*

"Are they indeed?" She looks back at the changelings. They stand in a cluster, hanging back behind the mounted warriors. If they are trying not to look guilty, they're doing a very bad job of it. "He knew where you were, I see. His was to be a different trophy than ours, hey-o," she says, making light of his near-death. "But what I—"

Her question hangs as the figure of Aðalbrandr stumbles into view around the far end of the wall that had trapped Thomas. The knight's silver hair is matted against its head and shot with blackish blood. In one hand it carries the sword. In the other, it's gripping the severed head of a troll by the stringy black hair. Aðalbrandr's own face is blue-black with blood, particularly the left side.

"Well. Aðalbrandr has won the Royal Hunt," she says. "Whatever else he's done."

It's not the troll you were hunting.

"That is of no consequence. He'll have to share the prize with you as beater." She seems to find the idea extremely amusing. "That will be awkward."

Adalbrandr reaches them without assistance, wobbly but determined. The long gray face is pale and sweaty, twitching with what must be agony. Raises up the troll's head and manages to rasp, "Majesty." Bows unsteadily. The troll has cost the Yvag dearly. The skin has been half-ripped from one side of its face almost to the ear. The gore of the gouged left eye is a black runnel down its cheek. It drops the head and finally collapses before Nicnevin. Two of the knights and the beaters rush to catch Adalbrandr.

He plotted to kill me.

"Oh, we are in no doubt of it. It seems we have reached a discontinuance."

A what?

"We have reveled in your passion, mayfly. It has been fun to use. But all things have an end. A queen has duties beyond gobbling up the occasional human lover. And I surmise it's caused a rift in my court. I could punish the complicitous beaters, but it's simpler all around for *you* to accept the penalty. Besides, you've given me what we desired most, what we needed from you."

It's a moment before he comprehends her meaning, and the first word that comes to him is *Astralis?*

She smiles, fully exposing her sharp teeth. "Very good, mayfly. I will soon transition with child for the very first time. But don't worry, we do not expect you to share in raising them, though you will survive here long enough to see them mature. Perhaps long enough for them to get a child off you, too."

He glances at the unconscious Adalbrandr. *Is that why he came after me?*

"It's humiliating to him. Adalbrandr is so many things, as I've said before. Passionate, overweening, jealous. But sterile, most of all." Her strange eyes fix upon his. "Perhaps why he hates you most of all. A jealous consort—I wonder how long I will tolerate that."

She dismisses him with a look, then glances around at her entourage.

"All of you," proclaims Nicnevin, "the Royal Hunt is ended here, fittingly where trolls once lived. Time for us all to return to our city."

She signals the remaining knight, who takes hold of Thomas, while the others drag Aðalbrandr to the bone-white mount. The skeletal thing lowers itself that they might throw the Yvag upon its back.

"Ah," she adds, as if a thought has just occurred to her. "And we wish to see all the beaters when we return. I'm curious that you directed this novice to these troll ruins. I fear some of you have not upheld the standards of our court today. This shall be addressed." Looks of fear are traded among the changelings in blue and green.

She waves a hand to direct them back up the slope. Then she leans down nearer Thomas. "It is our race's affliction, sterility. It's the reason for changelings. We tell you this because we have enjoyed your passion, your terror and revulsion, mayfly, more than any human we can recall taking, and we have tried a few. If you do prove viable—and we'll have to wait for the chrysalis to crack to be absolutely certain—well, then, we will have a far more, ah, extended use for you among a greater part of the populace. We'll pass you around like a tasty bit of dinner."

She touches his face tenderly. For once this does not infuse him with lust of any sort.

"Goodbye for now, Thomas Rimor."

Something stings the back of his neck: the jewel. He slaps at it, but even in that moment feels himself twisting up, falling away from the scene and into a darkness that's been awaiting him all along. He thinks, *I'm in Hel,* and tries to claw his way back out, but there's nothing to grab onto, no sides, nothing but the void that will pull him apart. He calls out to Janet, but in the void makes not a sound.

He is tossed like a sack of grain across the nearest beast's withers in front of one of the Yvag knights, who, climbing up, as if by accident, hammers a spiny elbow into his face.

XXV. Taliesin

Thomas wakes to someone calling, "Helo, art *ti* present? 'Tis my belief I do hear *ti*."

He doesn't answer directly, instead staring at the dark domed ceiling overhead, how it smoothly curves into polished walls of a small cell. It's all seemingly as shot with stars as the strangely quilted sky, but these stars, jewels, whatever they are, flicker like candlelight, providing what illumination there is in this space, as dim as the daylight outside. The cell has been scooped out of some substance he can't identify. He brushes his hand over it—neither stone nor wood but hard, smooth.

He's lying on a pallet. Perhaps it's the same one as in the Queen's summer house. Is that where he is, a new chamber in that chaotic spiral of an enclosure? Beside the pallet stands a stone seat like a hollow toadstool grown right out of the floor; its shape suggests its function—another garderobe of some kind. The multitude of flickering spots throw conflicting shadows everywhere. He wonders why they didn't toss him into that all-devouring well, then recalls the Queen's suggestion of how they will put him to use if he has truly succeeded in getting her with child.

After a minute comes the "Helo?" again. The voice is harsh, an old voice, and it draws his attention away from brooding.

Thomas sits up, finds that he's still dressed in the torn gray clothes of the hunt. His hygiene ceased being of concern to the elves awhile ago, but now they aren't even concerned with the shreds of his costume, which says everything about his situation. So then...

235

He touches his throat. The jewels have been removed, front and back.

He jumps up. Approaches the doorway of his cell, another open arch, the same basic form that repeated everywhere in the Queen's summer house. There is no door, no bars, nothing obvious, just . . . a hand reaching around the edge, waggling fingers that end in thick horny nails.

He reaches tentatively out, expecting he doesn't know what—a stabbing pain, a shock, some sort of crippling punishment. There's nothing.

The reaching hand latches onto his arm. Untrimmed fingernails dig into his skin.

"Ah!" he cries, throat raw. Pulls his arm free while he begins coughing. He spoke. He can speak again!

The sound of nervous laughter. "Oh, so *ti* art not my imagination?"

"Should"—he clears his throat loudly—"should I be?"

A long pause. Then the voice, as if talking to someone else, says, "Do we tell him he might still be? That seems unnecessary if he is."

Still expecting to find himself in some other part of the Queen's house, Thomas wanders into the central space. It's another large circle, one ringed with seven identical arches counting his cell. An old man stands in the one beside him, but he ducks into each of the five others. Surely one must provide an exit, a way out.

The cells, however, prove to be identical right down to the garderobe seat in each, as if the elves anticipate five more human prisoners soon. Embedded stars light up and glitter as he enters each, but the spaces offer nothing in the way of hope. There's not another doorway or chamber or hall branching off any of them.

He returns to the center circle, and looks up expecting to find a trapdoor in the ceiling, something. There is no door, and not even a line in the ceiling. It's not an oubliette, either.

All the while the old man just stands there, at the front of his own cell, a sympathetic smile on his tilted face. He slowly shakes his shaggy head. "Na way out, yes, he'll see."

He is shorter than Thomas, bearded and covered with hair so thick it's almost a pelt. He looks like a woodwose, and up close he stinks like a wild man of the woods, too. His head has turned, tracking Thomas's movements around the ring of cells, but his eyes don't track anything, looking nowhere and everywhere.

The stinking old man is blind.

He argues, "No way out, but they *did* put us in here. I didn't just float in."

"I cannot say, for I did not hear *ti* arrive. As likely a way as any, floating." His words taper off into soft muttering.

Now he understands why they've removed the jewels. Where can he possibly go but around and around in a circle? He cannot pretend anymore, the way Waldroup's ghost has urged, that this is temporary, that he will seize upon an opportunity to escape. He's been removed from her court, her presence, permanently. She took what she wanted from him, and judging by the condition of his sole companion, he is as of now not even an afterthought. *Mayfly.*

While he frets, the old man reaches, pats his hand, then feels along his arm with both hands, more carefully this time, and continues patting at him, his chest, neck, face.

"Young," he says, "strong, younger than was I when she took me. Still likes her pleasures then. *Wrth gwrs,* she does. Too strong the thrum and quiver for her ever to leave lust behind." He chews on a finger, seems from his expression to be lost in fond recollection that all at once encounters a memory not so sweet. His expression blanches. After a moment, he recovers and asks, "What shall I call *ti*?"

"Thomas. Thomas Rimor de Ercildoun, sir."

The old man cups his hands over his mouth, and excitedly breathes, "Yes!" as if the name has great meaning for him. Then, trembling, he lowers them. "Ercildoun, is it? *Ffydd,* I think I know not the place. Na, na. Prolly came after my time."

"It was only just made a town in my own."

"The world is wide to us all."

"And what do I call you, sir?"

"My name is Taliesin."

Thomas blinks. "There was a poet Taliesin. People used to say in front of me I was like him because of the riddles that pour out of me."

"Riddles," says the old man in some dismay. "Not poems?"

He smiles modestly, realizes the poet can't see him, and says, "No one would mistake them for poems."

"Then you're nothing like him at all. Taliesin is a bard, a poet, a *seer*. Not a simple *riddler*." He says the word with great disdain, and then launches into a recitation:

"The Catraeth men rise with the sun,
Circling their prince, that raider of cattle,
Urien of Rheged is he.
The feast of princes is his charge,
For warrior Urien is of all about him lord.
Came the men of Prydain in their legions
To Gwen Ystrat, valley where battles sweep all.
No field there nor tree to offer shelter
When the two sides clash."

He pauses, tilts his head.

Thomas remarks, "You declaim well, sir."

"*Felly*, of course I do." He taps his chest. "I'm Gwion Bach ap Gwreang. I'm *Taliesin*." Then his attention seems to drift away again. "I wonder how Owen mab Urien made out—royal blood was Urien's son." His pale blank eyes shine. "Very long ago, if 'twas a day. Way time flows here, all's dust before the verse is e'en sprung."

Not quite following the poet's wandering thoughts, Thomas says, "I've passed through Catraeth once."

"Sure it will be different now."

"On my way north."

"And who is king in the north these days?"

"It's David. King David."

Taliesin shakes his head. "*Dafydd*. Na notion of that name. Be he a good king? Do the poets compose verses around 'im?"

"I don't . . . Maybe. On his account I fought, and after, I was given land to farm."

Taliesin claps him on the shoulder. "Come, we must upon every single thing discourse. *Ti* will tell me of the world passing by, because as you can see—as once I did—we've nowhere to go. Time has devoured you, Thomas Rimor, and this"—he points feebly to the central circle—"this is its gullet."

The first thing he learns is where to sit in relation to Taliesin to minimize the stink. The second thing is that Taliesin has only occasional lucid moments, and that Thomas has to listen closely to make any sense of them. Sometimes the poet drifts into verse and seems unaware of his presence. He babbles in Welsh, sometimes holds conversations with an invisible companion or two, sometimes Urien—even asking that unreal lord of Rheged's opinion—and sometimes another whose name he doesn't say. Thomas thinks, this is what *he* looks like to everybody else while talking with Alpin's ghost, so who's to say Taliesin is mad? And where is Alpin's ghost these days? Not answering again.

That first morning, however, Taliesin asks about the Queen, remarking that she turned him into various creatures "using her energy ball." He's sure he wrote it all down back when he could see, but now can find neither the parchments nor his quills. He's certain someone has stolen them. It's not as if there are places in the cells where things can be hidden. "One of the others," he says, which presumably means other previous occupants of these cells, of which Taliesin has mentioned a few. It sounds as if they were here when he arrived and subsequently died or sufficed as a *teind*.

Before Thomas can get more information out of him, however, he suddenly leans over and puts his ear to the floor, then climbs stiffly to his feet, backside facing Thomas, who instinctively leans well away from it.

Taliesin says, "Our meal is arriving." He drags a wooden paten out from behind the garderobe stand. It's the same sort that Thomas has been fed from while kept by Nicnevin. "Here, you must set this in the center. And we in our cells must be else they will not feed us. I learned that early on. Come, come, come. Go to yours now."

He shuffles back through the small arch and to his pallet.

Uncertainly, Thomas returns to his cell, waits just inside the arch, watching the central space to see how the food arrives, hopeful that this must reveal the way out.

Not a minute passes before the walls cease to glitter and deepest shadow absorbs him. The suddenness of the pitch dark catches him off guard. A brief low musical note sounds, stops. He stumbles a step in the blackness, but even as he does the walls glow again, and there in the circular center are two fresh wooden patens containing some kind of steaming meat over grains, what looks like barley, with a piece of honeycomb beside it, and a wood mug filled with water. How this has appeared, he cannot say—his mind is strangely muddled. The whole thing took only an instant, but how did he miss that instant? It's almost as if the food manifested in the dark out of the music.

Confounded, he walks out, picks up a board, and carries it to Taliesin, sets it down beside the pallet. "Here," he says, and guides the poet's hands to it.

"Most kind." Taliesin pats his wrist. "Mark me, *ti* must always eat. Never reject a meal here. They can be quite cruel if they believe *ti* to be disobedient."

Thomas returns to collect his own food, but he's thinking, *They can be quite cruel anytime at all.*

Time is impossible to measure. Is it a day after he's eaten and slept? The twinkling starlight only goes out when the meals come. Otherwise it never varies. He's long lost all sense of day versus night in any case.

After Taliesin sleeps, most times, he has to reintroduce himself. The conversations that follow are discontinuous. Taliesin claims to have been Nicnevin's lover, too. "*Wrth gwrs*, that was so very long ago I might as well have dreamt it." It's devastating to contemplate. If he is truly the poet who played for Bran the Blessed, then he's many hundreds of years old. Generations have come and gone while he's been a prisoner of the elves, and it's not lost on Thomas that this is his planned fate, too.

One time after the meal comes, he says suddenly, "*Chrimbil*—that's how they maintain their population."

"*Chrimbil*?" he asks.

"Changelings. They do steal babies to replenish the line when one of them dies. They are, most of them, infertile."

"So I was told."

"There's a golden green pool somewhere in the city where the babes are dipped and their—oh, how to call it?—their *composition* altered. Dunk, dunk, dunk, hey, presto, a new elf."

"They snatched my sister's child . . ."

"Oh, was it that pursuit by which *ti* came here? Avenging a gone-astray babe?"

"In part, I suppose."

"Well, *ti* are hardly the first. But all time and life ye've wasted. The child will already be reapportioned. They'll mature till they have known some fifteen of these summers. Is it fifteen? I think that's the number, but you know best," he says to his invisible companion. "Yes, fifteen of their summers. Hundreds of ours. Already your babe will be white-haired, sharp-faced, and spiny as a lobster. *Ti* nor I would know them for anything but Yvag, and e'en then we could not tell its sex. Three states they have, indistinguishable to us."

"So Nicnevin told me."

"She did not lie, but told *ti* true, True Thomas." He cackles himself into a coughing fit then. "Mind you, even after being dipped in the pool, perhaps one in a hundred fails to embrace the indoctrination. Something does not take properly."

"What happens to *them*?"

"Oh, various things. Some try to escape. Others have been known to attack their fellows, their preceptors."

"And?"

"They end up here for a while. I've had a few mad companions in my time."

"Where are they, then?"

"Oh, they're kept only until a new *teind* is due, or they kill themselves in their madness." He opens his hands as if to say there was nothing he could do to stop it.

Another day, Taliesin forgets who Thomas is, and tries to teach him the history of the elves. He explains how they have come here from another universe entirely, whatever that can mean, and that this is a temporary world to them. "It used to be home to trolls."

"That I know."

"You do. Well, I am impressed at that. There are still some of them alive in caves, holes in the ground, mostly far from the city. So many names for everything. What they really want, the elves, is our world."

"Why?"

"Have *ti* seen the machinery? Did she lead *ti* beneath the surface?"

"Surface of what? I don't understand."

"Ah, she didn't, then." He begins arguing with himself. "No, no use describing it when he hasn't seen it. It's enough that he know *of* it." Then to Thomas again: "I personally had expected something more bucolic. All the stories of Elfland are of such pastoral beauty, so perhaps it was the purples and the blues that amazed. Still and all, nothing like this had I ever heard mentioned. The gleaming city, sometimes called Ailfion, is only a tiny portion of their world. Most is hidden. Underground. They draw all their power from the world's heart, and are slowly draining it whilst they prepare to take a new one, one that they will make over to their liking."

Thomas works out to what he's referring. "Our world, you mean."

"A slow process. We haven't the machinery yet, but in time we will. They'll guide us to build it. And they don't care if it takes time, being immortal."

"But why take ours when they have their own?"

"Why?" His expression is one Thomas has seen a hundred times on faces confronting him—that of a person who's discovered he's simple. "To escape the Unseelie, naturally. They need to jump so quickly that the Unseelie cannot follow them."

"Who are the Unseelie?"

Taliesin shakes his fists in the air in frustration. "Have I taught you *nothing*?" After that, he doesn't speak again for hours. When finally he does, it's to calmly announce that the meal is coming again.

Coming how? How can he know?

Thomas listens, hears nothing. Once more he gets up and goes to stand in his doorway, ready to spring upon whoever comes; once more the lights dim and return, and he is tilting off-balance, falling this time. Hands out, he catches himself against the floor. New food, steaming, sits in the center. Whatever magic they're using, he's unable even to glimpse it. He knows he heard a kind of music, but what tune eludes him.

Wearily, he gets up, carries the board and cup to Taliesin, but then retreats to his own cell to eat alone. This is going to break him, sooner than later. He can't keep up with the volatile shifts in the old poet. Embedded in what Taliesin says, there are hard facts, no doubt important things he should know. But it's all maddeningly unpredictable. He needs a way out.

He needs to go home before everyone he knows has died.

XXVI. Beeswax

His discovery occurs because of an accident.

Meals arrive while Taliesin is so busy declaiming a poem of his in which trees march to battle—"I have beheld Caer Vevenir, where made haste the very grass and trees . . ."—that when the lights blink off and the food appears they both remain seated in his cell. The poet stumbles in his recitation then and comes to a stop, confused. Thomas stands clumsily. He retrieves the patens at which point Taliesin begins his poem over again. As Thomas approaches, Taliesin cries, "I have been an eagle!" and abruptly flaps his arms, striking one of the patens. It flips out of Thomas's grasp and lands upside down on the floor, skidding along on gravy and honey. The cup sprays water all around the center. Thomas scurries to scrape it all up, getting most of it back on the board, but a smear of gravy and honey remain across the floor of the entrance into Taliesin's cell. He gives Taliesin some of his water. They settle down, and Taliesin, never to be dissuaded, starts his "Battle of the Trees" all over yet again.

By the time he finishes reciting this epic verse, the smear of gravy has dried; the honey remains a sticky spot that Thomas avoids as he carries the two empty boards into the middle. He returns to his cell and lies down on his pallet.

The empty patens often disappear while he sleeps, but a few times he has been awake when the darkness descended. One time he crawled out afterward and indeed the patens were gone, as mysteriously as they had appeared.

When next he walks around to the poet's cell (expecting, as usual, that Taliesin will not remember who he is), he is careful to avoid the sticky smear of honey . . . only to find it has been cut in half along with the gravy stain. Both end now along a perfect curve. They simply stop. No line nor gap is visible. The floor looks as if someone has taken a wet rag and wiped half of the spill away.

He is still pondering this development when many hours later the next meal is served. He gets up from his own cell and retrieves the two patens, turns and discovers that the stains have returned in full—gravy and honey exactly as he left them after the last meal. The floor has been replaced and then returned. It's the only thing that makes sense. He wonders how many ways that can be possible. Floor and ceiling, are they interchangeable? Does the ceiling descend, replacing the floor, or the floor rise, to be replaced by another beneath it? One or the other? The cells remain the same, as borne out by the half of the stain that has not changed. No wonder the food will not arrive if either of them is in the center. They would be crushed or else whisked away to a different level of this prison. Critically, it means that another level to the prison exists!

He broods on this for days, or what he thinks of as days. At one point he doesn't put his empty paten out in the center, recalling that Taliesin had done the same once. He dips a finger in the cold remains of the food and draws a thin stripe across the threshold of his own cell on the floor while the smears at Taliesin's door are absent.

Soon he's established that only two floors are involved. The stains vanish and reappear with each plunge into darkness.

This knowledge feels powerful, exciting, a step of some kind toward escape; but the feeling doesn't last long. How can he remain conscious while the exchange of floors occurs? The darkness, the music—no matter how he tries, he cannot overcome them. On one occasion he waits on hands and knees to spring out the instant the lights dim.

When they do, he leaps.

He wakes up lying in the center, his chin throbbing, and this time there is no food. The stains also bear out that the floors have not been switched. He vaguely remembers hearing the musical note sound, but he was airborne.

When he explains what he attempted to Taliesin, the poet chides him. "Now we won't be served anything for at least a *day*."

Yet, barely an hour later, he's asking where their meals are, having no memory of the previous exchange.

Distracted both by thirst and by the imponderable escape while Taliesin drifts from topic to topic, Thomas remains in his cell. To him the poet's babbling is just noise, and most of the time he forgets halfway through what he's even speaking about. First it's Nicnevin, then the flitting little homunculi, which he refers to as manikins, then it's the elves having crossed by some means from one world to another and their attainment of a state of *athanasia*. It's a waterfall of words.

Then, in a lull, he suddenly says, "I must remember if I have not, to tell you so overjoyed was I when I heard you say your name."

Thomas blinks back into the conversation. He remembers how the poet covered his mouth with his hand, as if excited by the news. He stands, stretching, and walks out of his cell, stands before the poet's. "I do, now you tell me. Overjoyed at my name?"

"Quite some time ago True Thomas appeared in a prophetic dream. It was he who was to share this prison with me, he who would defy them."

"You saw me. In a vision."

But Taliesin has drifted into an argument with his unseen companion: "Yes, yes, it was someone else's vision and not mine, very well, does that make the claim any less valid? I will *not* this circumstance downplay, no." He huffs. "*All* of you have told me. There, will that do?"

Bemused, Thomas inserts himself into the conversation again. "You and your . . . companion beheld this True Thomas?"

"Him. And a few prior to him, not I. 'Tis his brother he refers to. You see, as a voice, like the others, he was a mere wisp at the beginning and will—"

"Onchu?"

Taliesin balks. "Why, yes, that is his name." Then to the invisible one: "He does know your name, just as *ti* predicted he would. Final proof, yes, yes, I accept it is he."

For a long minute Thomas just stares down at him. Then he says, "You're speaking with my brother?"

"Cannot *ti* see him?"

Thomas grits his teeth at this cruel jape. "There is no one there at all to see. You told me you spoke to Urien of the poem."

"And sometimes I do. If you can't see Onchu, then *ti* lack the vision. Nothing to be done about that. I've powers none." A blind man is telling him he lacks vision. It's too absurd, but the suggestion that the poet is conversing with Onchu while Thomas never has inflames and stings. Taliesin offers, "They come to me, you understand, for a brief time only. He'll be gone soon."

"*Who* comes to you?"

"Why, the *teind*."

Thomas draws a breath. "But the *teind* are all dead. They're thrown into Hel. I had to *watch*." Sìleas drops once more into the bottomless pit, disintegrating in slow motion right before his eyes. With all his will he wants to suppress the awful memory.

"Oh, they'll not return to this world, *ti* has sentenced that most direct and true. Their fall lasts an aeon, but there is a space in that infinity when their voice grows and grows until I can hear them and they me, and then, slowly, as they have arrived so they fade away. *He* is fading, I fear. Someone else will follow, for there is always another. The elves do not miss paying their tithe. But he and they assured me you were coming."

The old poet waits—he would say *eagerly*—for his reaction, but nothing about this constitutes a joyous reunion, nor any reunion at all. Would that Alpin's ghost was here right now to interrogate Taliesin's phantom. The notion gives him an idea, and finally he says to the empty space, "Onchu, if you're truly there, tell him something only we would know."

Taliesin's wrinkled brow furrows. "He says, there were two thousand nine hundred sixty-eight leaves on the black alder tree."

Thomas gasps at that, then laughs aloud. He sinks down onto the floor. It's a long time before he speaks again. His eyes grow wet. "What . . . what is it like, brother—Hel?"

Then Taliesin's aspect changes. He winces as if the response itself hurts, and his features pull as if his face is trying to recast itself. His milky eyes roll back in his head. "Agony," he says, and the voice has lost the Welsh lilt entirely. "Every scrap that were me coming apart, but ever the while distant. My suffering was spread across a black sky, agony shared with all the others who fall ahead of me. One by one, they've gone, and I'm now from meself parting, nearly gone, as well. Taliesin is a candle flame in the depthless pit of Hel, oh so dim now."

It *is* his brother. The cadence, the flow, the words belong to Onchu. "How did you know I would come here?"

"Hel. Hel folds time, past and future all together, your and my time together, and even long after that, Tommy. I ken ye when you first peered in, when the girl, Sìleas, was flung after me. I thought they would tumble you as well, but you retreated. Saw you brought low but not so low as the devils think, heh? Ye'll rise again, brother, hey-o, to count your catkins on the river bank. I swear I will be there to hear the tally when you do."

Thomas wipes at his cheeks, snuffles.

Taliesin sags. When he raises his head again, he says, "Nay, he's drifted off."

"Gone?"

"Oh, probably not forever, though it's difficult to be certain. I've spoke with hundreds. And one day they're simply not there anymore."

"But I have so much more to say to him. I want—I need for him to know . . ." He breaks off, shakes his head, runs his gray sleeve across his nose.

Taliesin asks, "When does the food come?"

"Don't know. Soon, I hope." He means it. He's just as ravenous at this point as the poet. "I wish I'd asked him how I escape. If Onchu can see the future, then he would know, wouldn't he?"

"Oh, but he did speak to that."

"What? When?"

"Before you asked him about Hel." Infuriatingly, he adds nothing more.

Thomas wipes his hands across his face. "Well, what did he say, poet?"

Taliesin blinks. "Beeswax."

Thomas stares, certain he's hearing more nonsense from mad Taliesin.

The poet is leaning on his hand, palm against the floor. He stiffens upright abruptly. "Food's coming," he announces. "Get to your cell, lad."

He has just entered the arch when the lights go out and a note sounds, and once again he finds himself tipping forward. This time the pallet catches him, but he bangs one knee on the floor.

Cursing, he gets up, hobbles back out to where the patens await, food steaming. As he bends down to pick them up, he looks at the honeycombs laid to the side and realizes what Onchu was talking about. They've been sucking the honey from these combs almost daily. The wax has been right in front of him. It's the answer to a riddle he hasn't asked yet.

This is how he will escape.

XXVII. Thomas Underground

As the time of the next meal approaches, Thomas tries to go over every detail of the escape plan with Taliesin. For Thomas to have any chance of escape at all, the old poet must maintain the appearance that he's never left.

"You'll have to eat double portions," Thomas explains, "or else throw the leftovers in the garderobe hole."

"Double rations sounds wonderful."

"Yes, I'm sure."

After a pause, the poet asks, "Will *ti* come back after *ti* determine where we are?"

"I can't. If I make it out of here without being caught, I don't dare return. Besides, if you aren't here to eat the food, they'll quickly discover our absence and neither one of us will live long."

"Yes, yes. Wise. I must divert them."

"Convince them I'm still here. That's all."

"But how will *ti* get out?"

"I don't know." They have had this part of the conversation twice already. The poet forgets nearly everything. How he's going to remember to eat both their portions . . . Well, Thomas can't do anything about it other than hope.

The old poet strokes his hairy chin, nodding to himself. "I will have to compose a poem about True Thomas."

Thomas bows his head, pats the old man on the shoulder. "If you share that with Nicnevin, they *will* toss you in Hel."

Taliesin munches on his beard awhile. "Care I?" He seems to consider it. "The only pity is, I wouldn't be here for me to speak to."

Thomas folds some sticky saved honeycomb, pinches and rolls it into a ball, then divides it in two. He awaits the poet's signal that the meal is coming. He knows he should wait and watch one time before taking the leap, but every day he doesn't act might be a year passing by back home, another year without Janet, and who knows how many have gone already? Ten? Twenty? More? Is she even alive? Is his daughter grown by now? Who's left?

Taliesin says suddenly, "Once you orient yourself, *ti* should head for that troll ruin again."

"What? Why there?"

"The trolls might assist *ti*."

"They might kill me, too; they tried to the last time. After all, I led Adalbrandr straight to one of their own."

The poet mulls that over before saying, "Yes, well . . . I've no other advice, except don't let them catch *ti*."

Thomas nods, says nothing. Regret is sinking in, wrapped in the realization that if this subterfuge works, they will never see each other again. Taliesin will die here in isolation, having thrust True Thomas like his own vengeance upon the Yvag. He may die considerably sooner because of his part in it, too. Either way, it's not the fate Thomas would wish for the old poet, even if, as he reasons, in some sense Taliesin died centuries ago. Surely, the loss of Waldroup is stirred in with the melancholy of the approaching moment. He's lost Waldroup twice now—first in life, then in death, the ghost who accompanied him silenced, it seems, by Nicnevin's use of him.

"Tell Onchu I love him and I'll—I'll count the catkins in his honor. Tell him—"

Taliesin interrupts: "It's coming," he says, finger raised, and turns to get up. Thomas watches him climb unsteadily to his feet and thinks, *You would never make it up even the first hill, old fellow.* The realization is so obvious, yet it stabs him sharp as a needle. How has he failed to appreciate the infirmity of Taliesin before this?

Thomas scrambles up and steps back into his space while stuffing the warmed and formed beeswax into his ear canals. He listens to the roar of his own blood, the only thing he can hear now. The twinkling stars in the walls fade to blackness, and in the same moment the musical note sounds, only he doesn't so much hear it as feel it in his bones, rising up through his feet, shins . . . rattling his jaw. He's gritting his teeth.

Right before him a wall begins to descend. Before it can seal off his doorway completely, he dives beneath it. He plummets, bracing like a cat, having no sure idea how far the floor is below. The fall knocks the breath out of him, and he bangs his forehead hard. The darkness sparkles.

The floor glides silently to a stop. Recovering, he rolls over. Above him in the shadows hangs the great arched ceiling he has always observed. Yet, surely it can't be there, must be an illusion.

Two arches lead obliquely away from the circle here—side-by-side tunnels receding as far as he can see. They are lit at seemingly random points and full of mist or steam. Directly behind him there's a smaller, scooped-out niche, as if a section of the wall has caved in symmetrically.

The floor thrums with some deep vibration. He rolls up onto one knee just as a great shadow comes marching along the right-hand tunnel. Thomas throws himself into the niche. The space proves to be shallower than his cell. He presses as far back as he can, hoping that the shadows will mask him. The empty patens left from their last meal together sit in the middle of the area.

Somewhere above, Taliesin will right now be calling out his name, determining that he has gone. The thought stings with a further pang of loss. He's bid the poet farewell and lost his brother again, this time forever.

Then the shadow comes marching out of the mist and into the empty circle and all such thoughts fall away. Thomas bites back his shock. The creature is bone white, formed—much like the beasts the knights ride—from the trees of Þagalwood. This one, like nothing he's ever seen, is made of living, flexing pieces joined together by some incomprehensible magical process. Its lower three-legged base flows out from a central spine. Higher up, eight pale arms dangle, seven of them ending in pincers that seem precisely designed for collecting food boards. The eighth arm has extensions like gelatinous fingers with which it anchors itself while it collects the empty pattens. Then off those fingers, it spins on its central axis and launches straight at him. There is no obvious head, no eyes or features he could call a face. Its upper section spins again as it backs in completely—at least he thinks of it as backing. Nowhere to hide and no way to escape. He presses against the curved wall, then crouches down and clasps his knees to take up as little space as possible. He would be invisible if he could, laments how short his freedom has turned out to be. Yet the thing takes no notice of him. The creature, like Taliesin, has some set routine in a mapped-out space. It's operating on instinct or memory. One of its legs presses up against one of his, cold as stone.

The digits of the creature's eighth arm flow to a point and press into the wall beside the opening, which shrinks to nothing, sealing them in. Then it's as if they're a leaf in a storm, spinning and falling all at once. Lights flow up and then across the door. He's sure if he were standing he would have fallen over by now. Then silently, abruptly, the compartment stops, the opening reappears, and the creature skitters away. For a second he sees other grotesqueries beyond it, but then he's sealed in again and falling. He grabs at the wall, certain he'll float up off the floor.

More lights blip past, faster and faster. It's as if he's plummeting to the bottom of Hel. He realizes suddenly that there might be sound but he can't hear anything, and with his pinkie tries to dig at the beeswax in his ears.

The next time the compartment stops and the portal opens, it's as if a forge bellows has been pumped in his face. The air is so hot it nearly sears his throat, but he flings himself out of the space anyway and collapses on the floor, dizzy, visible to anyone, but overwhelmed by panic that he'll be trapped forever inside the tiny space; he rises to his hands and knees, immediately confronts another Þagalwood-made creature. This one is two-legged and has a head of sorts at twice his height. With steely eyes it observes him without interest, passes by, folds itself down and ducks into the compartment he has fled. He recognizes how it fits exactly into the space, as did the creature before it.

The wall contracts, the opening erased.

He gets up and takes a shaky step out onto something like a crystal bridge that extends as far ahead as he can see. He has staggered into an incomprehensible space.

To either side of it are open pits that appear to stretch into infinity, with all kinds of ... what can he call them? ... upon the walls. They are like small windows, flickering lights like stars, shapes and bulges beyond his comprehension. Already drenched in sweat, he stumbles slowly along. The air is so thick, he has to rest every dozen steps or so. He won't survive long down here.

He dares to sidle toward the edge and peer down. Layers of other crystal or glass walkways extend below. Great globes of light go sliding up and down the walls. In places they connect with curious fluttering tentacles on the wall. Exotically woven Þagalwood creatures rise or descend all around him, like flexing jellyfish within a waterless sea. Far, far below, a fiery glow as bright as the sun pulses and throws off lightning-like discharges. Painful to look upon for more than a moment. He moves away from the edge, wipes the sweat out of his eyes, and gazes up instead to behold what seems like an infinity of walkways, of creatures, and twinkling lights overhead. Spinning blades, steadily turning gears, tubes and pipes and things he has no words for. There's not a single Yvag in sight anywhere. Perhaps they cannot tolerate this hellish pit either. If this is magic, it's a magic of creatures and machines more advanced than siege engines or mill wheels, which are the most advanced machines he can think of.

As he stands there gawping, another creature comes up silently behind him. It clamps one appendage onto his shoulder and turns him. Glowing red eyes, not human, not alive, like coals in a forge, glare at him from an otherwise featureless head. Another of its jointed arms clips onto his torn clothing, runs gently up and down the rip. The thing's head tilts as if assessing him. Then it reverses direction to drag him against his will back to the same niche. He's shoved inside. The creature squeezes in with him. One appendage joins to the wall. The portal seals up and the compartment rises and whirls. Dizzy again, he closes his eyes rather than watch the lights flicking past. When abruptly the movement stops, he pitches against the creature, so close it keeps him upright.

The portal reappears and the creature hauls him out into another vast space, this one with an actual floor of lighted pathways extending to the right and left, and still more crisscrossing those. The air is cooler, the light dimmer.

The creature chooses one path, dragging Thomas along. It releases him at a chamber filled with squat Þagalwood creatures of yet another design: two-legged and four-armed, with various appendages, some ending in a cluster of flexing needles, others in tiny pipes. One of the bone-white creatures turns to him as his captor glides away. Its "head," on a long, snaking neck, weaves around him, inspecting.

It reaches up, tugs at the torn garment, combs an appendage with needles over the tear, followed by an arm whose pipes discharge a thin bluish mist. Even before it has fully let go, the material comes to life, rippling along the tear; the garment thickens, extending new fibers across the gap, rejoining, closing, sealing the tear until there is no evidence that it was ever ripped. The beater's uniform shifts then from gray back to bright blue-green with the violet stripe; the sleeves flare out, shoulders grow points, and the leggings once more enclose his feet. As before, he has to raise each one up for the boot soles to weave across under them.

The creature has already turned back to its work, which seems to be the weaving of garments, although the looms—if that's what they are—look like nothing he's ever beheld. They flex and spin threads thinner than spiderwebs, glittering like rainbow dew. Not only beaters' uniforms but loose piles of shiny, almost oily, black—the armor of the Yvag knights, a platform heaped with them. Surely there are enough to equip all the current knights twice over.

The weaver continues to ignore him.

Watching it, Thomas hardly has to lean forward to grab the nearest pooled costume and snatch it away. The nearest loom, as if recognizing its absence, whirls to life and begins knitting more near-invisible threads. Everything in the space ignores him. Nevertheless, he backs away, then runs from the weaver until his lungs burn, and he has to stop and wheeze. Hands on knees, he feels as if his lungs are winching blocks of stone.

At a bend in the pathway, with nothing approaching from either direction, he strips off the beaters' garment and steps into the knight's uniform. It's far too large for him, dangling off his hands, flopping beyond his toes. Then almost immediately it springs to life and shrinks to accord with his body. Spikes sprout along the forearms; the pliable leggings become hard protective greaves below his knees, something akin to leather above them. A helmet flows up around his head while the sleeves shrink back into webbed gloves. Smaller spikes adorn his knuckles. Gingerly, he touches everything. The helmet sports a hard nosepiece but does not cover his lower face, his beard.

There's nothing for that, and he wishes he had an ördstone right now, though it would likely deliver him somewhere underground.

Balling up the now-gray beaters' garment beneath one arm, he continues on the walkway, trusting—hoping!—it will lead him somewhere he wants to go.

Soon it splits. One path leads to a space where Þagalwood creatures assemble and disassemble more of their own kind. Lying about, the pieces, like those he saw hauled back by Yvag knights, writhe and twist. They are like thick eels or snakes, he thinks, reminded painfully of how Gallorini became part of the wood, stripped of his very flesh. Thomas stays well back as he watches. Placed pieces unite with others, and flow seamlessly together. They appear to *know* what they are to become. Soon they are assembling themselves, limbs sorting through the collected parts, finding and adding more. One creature, fully assembled, skites right past him and heads back to the transporting cell. He backs up, turns, and keeps going.

He knows he's too short, too human-looking even in the black uniform to pass close scrutiny when and if he encounters Yvags, but what he's figured out is that they don't frequent the subterranean levels of their dazzling city. Never. The Þagalwood creations, like machines themselves, maintain it all. Once he reaches the surface, he'll have to stick to the shadows. Until then, he suspects that nothing will slow him down other than the air he can barely breathe.

Then, as he approaches a cross-tunnel, something flits past his head. Instinctively he ducks, even as he recognizes it as one of those *fae* homunculi. For a brief instant its buzzing fills his head. Then it's gone down the tunnel. He risks glancing back. What was it doing here, is it a guard of some sort? Did it consider him out of place? Does this mean he's close to the surface? Surely it must. But if that thing is reporting his presence, the best thing he can do is get out of here now.

At the next intersection, the narrow tunnel to his left leads toward a distant yellowish-green glow. He takes a step past it, but then stops. What was it Taliesin said? That somewhere in the city there's a "golden green pool" where changeling babies are turned into elves. He can't help but think of Innes's baby. Maybe it's futile, hopeless—both the Queen and Taliesin have told him so—and perhaps that light doesn't even come from that pool. But if it does . . .

He turns into the narrow tunnel and heads for the light.

XXVIII. Thomas Underwater

The golden light is cast by clear vertical cylinders, like two stretched-out tuns made of glass, one to each side of the tunnel and set back from the central path. In one, fluid is flowing down; in the other it's rising. The liquid itself is the source of the glow. The cylinders go straight through the ceiling and floor. Behind them are dark walls covered with more objects he cannot comprehend, lights that blink or pulse, surfaces dotted with rows of bumps like small bosses on shields, and etched with writing that looks like Ogham or runes, nothing like Janet ever wrote on parchment. The narrow gap between the cylinders ends in a wall of rungs extending through a hole in the floor and, above, through another hole in the ceiling. Even as he holds onto a rung and looks up, another skeletal thing is climbing agilely toward him.

Before it arrives, he's crouching on the far side of the cylinder again. The thing comes to a stop slightly above him. It has skinny appendages top and bottom connected to a central globe by a sort of spine that displays needle-thin and flexible ribs, reminding him mostly of the skeleton of a trout. The top and bottom halves are mirror images, the appendages end in curved claws that fit the rungs. Two of the flexing ribs stretch and curl to the wall to press on the bumps. Two lights, as yellow as the sun, wink on and off. The fishbone creature, as he now thinks of it, continues its descent, its claws clicking rhythmically out of sight.

He slips through the gap again to peer up the rungs. Nothing else is coming down, and the rungs don't appear to run much higher.

He grabs hold and starts the climb, becomes aware of a distant roar that grows noisier the higher he climbs. The liquid in the tubes behind him froths and churns; the sound intensifies, finally so loud that if someone shouted beside him he couldn't hear them.

The rungs end in a blank ceiling. He turns, one elbow hooked over a rung. The massive tubes vibrate from the churning within. So close, he sees that they're full of infinitesimal glittering, like sparks from a fire, one set rising, the other swirling down.

He pushes against the ceiling. And then again. On his third try, his gloved hand sinks into the solid matter above, and a circular lid, hinged off to one side, slides out of the way. The roar becomes deafening, and the glow intensifies. He tosses the beater's uniform ahead of him and climbs up through the opening.

Before him is a broad, curving, open window with a cataract of the incandescent liquid roaring past it. The chamber appears to lie behind a massive waterfall. Rungs like those below run in crisscrossing lines across the floor to a curving wall of more flickering lights beside strange little crystalline boxes. The fishbone creature, or something like it, must navigate everything via rungs.

All of the creatures are specialized; they are shapes that already know their tasks by the time they've been joined, and it all takes place out of sight down here. *They draw their power from the world's heart.* The Yvag live by a magic he cannot begin to comprehend; but he's seen it now, seen the glowing, pulsing heart of their world that somehow propels it: living branches, trunks, limbs, and twigs that flow into any desired form from knights' coursers to spidery, headless climbing things; the ördstones themselves; the beads that can crush his throat but also make it possible to breathe their clotted air; the well that shreds living bodies into a million particles, all while the elves drink and debauch and make sport of insignificant humans, trolls, of who- and whatever they like. Their magic is a cruel, labyrinthine system without mercy or care.

What would Alpin make of all this?

Abruptly, the lid slides back into place beneath him, with no trace of a seam. No backing down the ladder, then.

Right in front of him the waterfall roars, yet not a drop of spray enters the chamber. He puts his hand out, finds an unseen barrier preventing him from reaching it. The ceiling and the wall behind him look to be formed from molten metal that's cooled into layers, like a black sludgy bog standing on end.

The waterfall surely means he's no longer underground, and below him must lie Taliesin's magic pool where the changelings are taken. But how to escape? If there is a door, it's like so many others—seamless, hidden, doors that become doors only when touched. Or maybe where he pushes, a door is created, the way ördstones cut the world anywhere.

First he gathers up the uniform and stuffs it down against one dark wall. With luck no one will notice it, a dark rag in the shadows.

Then he presses his gloved hand against the rough wall, and indeed the section right beneath it becomes transparent, which flows up until it's become another archway. His hand passes through, as though the wall itself is the illusion. Beyond lies an enormous space, another of the elves' cathedral-like creations lit solely by the shimmering waterfall and whatever's below it. He steps through the doorway and it seals up as if it had never been. The chill of the space hits him instantly. He draws a startled breath, exhales a frigid cloud. Has he been imprisoned so long that winter has come to this Ailfion?

With the bright waterfall on the opposite side of this artificial height, he stands in the deepest possible shadow on a tier that appears to run all the way around it, overlooking more levels below, inside a vast open and empty nave. Its ceiling is—what else?—arched, the overall effect that of a giant centipede with immense innumerable legs curving to the floor on either side. The nave seems to have been built for the Sluagh, for a multitude that may no longer even exist in Ailfion. There are steps down to the next tier. He quickly descends, and keeps going.

From the ground he recognizes that this is a four-sided pyramid, a miniature version of tiered buildings he saw on the hunt. He edges cautiously around it until Taliesin's sparkling pool comes into view. Thin, translucent reeds grow around the base of the pyramid there. In the middle of the reeds stands a great statue of imperious Nicnevin, her arms extended before her, forming a circle. The waterfall cascades down four stories to pour straight through that ring, frothing and crashing around the Queen's feet.

The statue faces the far side of the pool, where a ramp emerges from it, extending up to scalloped doors that look as if they've been carved out of ice—believable in this frigid air. Beyond them it seems to be bright and sunlit, which must be an illusion. He knows this world now. There's no such brightness here. His curiosity gets the better of him and he steals toward the scalloped doors.

He has hardly started around the pool when the doors start to swing open, as if in response to his approach. That surely cannot be the case. Still, he hesitates.

Gleaming light pours out from the opening and along the ramp— morning sunlight spreading across a field. It's the light of home, of Ercildoun, the light of his house above the Teviot. He's so close he can taste the air.

The doors slowly shape a circular space like an ördstone's tunnel leading straight to a meadow that must be somewhere in his world, not theirs, not with that bright light. It's populated with children, babies. The babies are mostly human, pink and fat. The children are Yvag, human, or something halfway between, all of them tended by different Yvag handlers dressed in red flowing garments as if they are of his world, too. As the circle opens wide, a cortège of these handlers, moving as one, emerges, all of them clothed in those red raiments. They're like an order of novitiates from a diabolical church.

In a crouch, he retreats, circling back around the pyramid, certain that the gray-faced goblins will know him for a fraud the moment they get a close look at him. But coming around the far side now is a company of uniforms like his own, shiny black armor. They carry pikes and march in synchronized step. Are they looking for him? Did the vicious little hob sound the alarm? Do they know already that he's escaped? He can't take the risk, can't afford the confrontation, but he's caught now between two groups with nowhere to go in either direction. The company of knights will emerge from behind the pyramid in moments.

The only way left is into the pool. He dives into the growth of reeds, pulls himself deeper among them, then swims quickly beneath the turbulence of the falls, coming up below Nicnevin's statue, gasping for air and grabbing onto her carved heel to draw himself around to the far side of the statue. His breath steams, a yellow-green mist; his eyes sting from the fluid in them. It runs in rivulets from his hair. He hangs off the statue's foot and watches.

There's no green fire, but the group coming down the ramp do seem to emerge from an ördstone tunnel. If he could only run past them and through that doorway, he would escape into some place that's of his world. Even as he looks on helplessly, the doors close and the bright sunlight behind them fades. Now the icy doors stand dark and red like everything else here. There's no point in grieving over it. It's gone.

This pool is practically the size of a corrie loch. He could swim to the most distant side and probably escape unseen, but his vision is blurry with oily fluid, his mind confused as if the thunderous cataract has shaken it loose. He ignores how the water stings.

The Yvags in red meet up with the martial black entourage, which parts and turns aside, revealing in its center Nicnevin. She wears purple and gold, but the garment fits strangely. It makes her look as if she's grown enormous wings beneath it. Her face seems much thinner, even haggard, and she walks with effort. Is she ill? He wipes at the sparkling fluid on his face, but it's greasy. It smears. He blinks some more to clear his vision.

Nicnevin climbs up onto the ramp. Then the novitiates, as he thinks of them, bring forth an object they're carrying; it's a baby, a naked human baby. They hand it to Nicnevin. She holds it out, the way her statue above him is posed for the sparkling cascade. Two of those red novitiates draw off her cloak. She descends the ramp into the pool naked, and he can see why the robe fit her so oddly. It's not wings. On her back is a long translucent pod, a crystalline cocoon. It's attached, growing out of her strange ribbed torso, and there is something dark, something alive inside it, a chrysalis. He knows what it is. What he wouldn't give to have his bow right now, and an arrow to pierce that cocoon, to repay her for the horror of being so used.

A little unsteady, she carries the human infant into the water, lower and lower, coming straight toward Thomas. Her coloring has changed—the rose along her abdomen has turned violet, and wraps now around her sides, up into the cocoon. The ramp seems to reach all the way to her statue. He pushes back, circling behind the pedestal to look on helplessly as she immerses the baby, holding it down so long that she's surely drowned it, and still she strides forward.

He thinks of Baldie facedown in the river, of blue babies that never draw a first breath, of every imagined terror he endured while Janet birthed Morven—that Janet would die, or Morven would be stillborn or deformed—and the litany of prayers and promises he whispered, muttered, offered, to keep them both alive. The baby in Nicnevin's hands remains submerged for an eternity.

He has swum backward to maintain his distance from the Queen. Suddenly, he's grabbed and dragged under.

Torn free of the statue, he's sucked down into the pool, straight toward a dark hole at the bottom—it's the mouth of the cylinder, the tun with downward-rushing water. His hands swipe and slide against the statue's base, close on some of the reeds growing there. He tugs himself up. One of the reeds tears loose and immediately goes shooting down past him. He grabs another and pulls, and then another, until his hands are against the cold stone base again. The reeds part, and his fingers touch a rung. Desperately, he grips it and pulls hard. There are more rungs. No doubt some other Þagalwood creature uses them for something. Madly, he tries to climb up, to kick to the surface, his lungs screaming. But the suction catches him for a moment, long enough that his lungs simply give out. He sucks in the oily fluid, knowing he's about to die. To his amazement, he finds it *breathable*. He ought to be choking, losing consciousness, as dead as Baldie. Instead, inhaling it again, he pulls himself, rung by rung, around the base of the statue. He comes up against its rear side, the fluid burbling out of him as he coughs and vomits and sucks in air.

Whatever this fluid is, he's alive because of it. And it's cleared the last of the beeswax out of his ears.

He spits the last of the vomit from his throat. It floats away like a small half-digested island. His breathing returning to normal, he glances across the pool. Nicnevin is still holding the child immersed. Surely it's been a full five minutes. Then, quite suddenly, she lifts the baby aloft again and hands it to the novitiate in red who had given it to her, and who has followed her into the pond.

He squints to see. The babe is contentedly kicking and gesturing as if nothing strange has happened, but appears already transformed—its skin no longer pink, but iron gray. Sure and its wriggling fingers are longer than they were, too.

Queen Nicnevin's breathing holes flex and blow out more golden fluid. As she emerges from the water, one of the knights drapes the Queen's cloak over her grotesque form. The Yvag buzzing in response is so intense that Thomas winces where he is. With his eyes closed, he's seeing the sparkles in the liquid, the same as he saw in the cylinders beneath the pool. With them open, it's like trying to see through hard rain.

A shiver ripples through him. The air is still freezing cold. He needs to get out of this pond and away from here, but the ceremony isn't done, the novitiates surround Nicnevin and hail her. The loud buzzing coalesces into murmurs and then, abruptly, into actual comprehensible words.

"Fountainhead of our world now gone,
Mother of all children here,
Fill us, make us
Eternity's spawn."

Humpbacked Nicnevin opens her arms to them all, and they sigh as if an angel has touched them. Not a sentiment he shares any longer.

Then all of them, red novitiates and black knights, turn as one and go back through the scalloped doors, entering to a darkling plain, not the meadow. That escape route, if it was a portal back home, has closed.

That only adds urgency to his need for an ördstone. The trouble is, taking one from any Yvag knight will alert them all to his presence, not to mention probably require him to kill the creature. That will not get him out of here. At best, he'll be back with Taliesin and in chains this time.

When finally the creatures all leave, he crawls out of the pool directly behind the waterfall. The great space is empty.

He lies awhile, disinclined to get up, exhausted. He's not sure if he dozes. The spangling fluid seems to have muddled his brain as though he's been swimming in a vat of mead, crawled out as drunk as the warriors in *Y Gododdin* that Taliesin recited randomly all the time. He misses the old poet already. It's absurd, he thinks: If he does manage to escape back home, Taliesin will likely outlive him here.

When at last he does get to his feet, he is momentarily dizzy, drops to one knee and has to lean against the stepped structure awhile. Stares into the waterfall. Its roar combined with the way it glitters draws him hypnotically, and he has to fight off its pull. It's as if it wants him back in the pool.

Muddled, he stumbles out through the reeds at the edge, seeking an exit. He's surely making too much noise, but there's nobody to hear. The entire reverberating space lies empty save for him and the statue of Nicnevin before a cocoon grew upon her back. More than anything he needs to get out of this city, away from these insectile monsters.

He needs to go home.

XXIX. Escape

�֍

The exit is like a narrow narthex, edged with a kind of railing. Outside, it's warm, the way he remembers it. His shivering diminishes. He recognizes where he is: behind the Queen's massive summer house. Strangely, what was perpetually dim previously seems brighter now, as if their red sun has swelled while he was imprisoned. But one look at the tessellated sky—its mosaic structure clearer than ever—and he knows otherwise. This is some residual effect of being in that pond.

Around the far side of the Queen's house lies a broad field of purple grasses through which he was dragged time and again before and after his baths, and beyond it the plaza where the Sluagh gathered for their hunt. It's empty now, and in any case, not the plaza he needs in order to orient himself. He must find Hel. That points the way, or will once he finds it.

A phalanx of Yvag knights comes marching across the plaza, and he crouches in the grass to watch, studying their gait closely. He must imitate that stride as he pushes on, but he's still feeling mildly feverish, disoriented. It's an effort to stand and continue.

Down to the plaza then, past where he used to have the skin scrubbed off him. As he passes by other elves, they nod to him, but he barely acknowledges, hoping that Yvag knights are generally as standoffish as Aðalbrandr, which seems to be the case—at least, none of the others reacts oddly. Their tilted sloe-eyed glances appraise him, and their buzzing fills his head; as with the baptismal ritual he's just witnessed, the noise coalesces into words now.

"He's rather grand."

"A captain, isn't he?"

"Yes, like all such, no time for anybody else."

"I would love to try him out."

"Which would you be?"

"Oh, definitely the Þ_____. He's small enough to fit into my ʒ_____." Some of the Yvag words elude him but still drip with odious carnality.

"I suspect he's one of the changelings, not entirely transformed."

"Exotic, you mean. . . ."

After the third such encounter and overheard dialogue, he's wondering how they don't see his beard. Has the armor glamoured him somehow?

He wanders the walkways then, trying to recall the buildings, the landscape through which he was dragged. Half the landmarks that seem familiar he doesn't trust. No idea in what order he encountered them—he was trussed up, a goat, utterly confounded and upside down. All he knows is, keep walking, brave it out. Something will occur to him or else he'll walk all the way to Þagalwood even if it's on the other side of the world. He can't come this far to be thrown back into prison.

Three small shapes zip past him. *Homunculi.* Was one of them down in the underground? He might fool an Yvag, but these little monsters? Not a chance. He walks on, hoping they'll just go on wherever they were flying.

Yet, a moment later, he senses one of the sprites settling on his shoulder. Peripherally, he can just make it out. Resists the urge to swat it flat before it can sound an alarm. What would an Yvag captain do? Ignore it, he hopes.

It suddenly screeches at him. His fist clenches, ready to crush it. To his amazement, though, he understands its words: *"Reporting I, Captain, with nothing to report."*

Thomas nods. Thinks loudly, *Be gone then.*

"So, where you go, Captain? Assignment?"

Well, why not? He lets the word surface. *Þagalwood.*

"Raaa!" Its screech practically makes him jump. *"Teg can prepare you way. You see. Reward Teg. Take along Teg, no?"* It slues off ahead of him without waiting for an answer. He tracks its flight as it veers left between two curling spires. The hob knows where he's going even if he doesn't.

On the far side of the spires is the plaza where sits the well between worlds. Hel awaits him.

He remembers a guard taking up a position across the way as if at the perimeter of something. Thomas strides across the plaza, pausing at Hel long enough to glance over the white glowing rim. A body, far below, is disintegrating, half gone already. It's not Sileas. No sign of her. How long has it been, he wonders, that they've tossed in at least one more sacrifice? And when will Taliesin hear her? At what point in their eternal fall do they communicate to him? Onchu was years ago now. He leans against the well, careful not to touch the burning white fire, but otherwise momentarily confused, off-balance. What's happening to him? He's down on one knee. Thoughts jumbled.

Gets up, tries to march but staggers instead across the plaza. Are other Yvags watching him now? He rubs his face. Even through the glove he can feel the odd grit of his skin, thorny growths at his chin. There's no beard. *I am glamoured, but when?* He can't imagine the hob did this; no, it was reacting to him in this form already.

He remembers what Taliesin told him about the changelings that don't acclimate, that go mad because of the transformation. If other Yvags watch him now, maybe they think he's one such.

Across the plaza Teg squawks to a guard—the perimeter guard, posted on the same mound as before above a set of steps. There's another Yvag there, one in a long, flowing gown with whom the guard seems to be half engaged in something vaguely salacious. The guard has already taken out their ördstone and sliced open a portal, probably just to get rid of the annoying Teg. He can hear them urging the hob to go away.

Thomas clenches his teeth and strides purposefully, almost angrily, toward the green fire, hoping to pass right by the soldier.

At the last moment, however, the perimeter guard comes to attention; the one they've been dallying with edges aside, but looks coy as if a changeling captain might be more entertaining than a guard. He wonders how his rank is determined? The armor all looks the same to him.

Buzzing fills his head. "Begging pardon, Captain, sir, where's this hob gathering its information? We've heard naught on it."

Thomas stares at the guard. Reminds himself *I am one of you.*

"Meeting a returning"—Oh, what was the word Nicnevin used for them? Stroud had said it, too—"an Yvagvoja."

"One of our glorious heroes is returning? How grand to learn. It's just, *we* haven't been privileged to know what this gnat knows." Trying not to make it sound like a complaint, though it clearly is. He wonders what can happen to an Yvag who's petulant. Probably nothing. It's not as if they'll be executed for insubordination, their dwindling numbers all too precious to Nicnevin. This is being played out to impress the dalliance who's standing by.

"*Me go.*"

No, Teg, you stay here. His head is pounding.

"*But, Captain!*"

Reward on my return. Big reward for you.

The sprite flits about, grins with a hundred silver needle teeth. "*Big,*" it repeats, and settles upon the shoulder of the guard, who eyes it distastefully. "*Big,*" it tells him.

Thomas takes a careful step toward the burning portal.

"Captain, which *Yvagvoja* is it?" asks the perimeter guard.

Panic. He has no answer for this, has only ever heard a few names, and what if it's a trick to trip him up? *Janet*—he has to get *home*! Now!

He sees the guard's expression beginning to change, knows he's slipped up, and at the very least the guard suspects he's a deviant changeling. He punches the Yvag across the jaw, knocking it into the gowned one beside it, both toppling off the knoll, and Teg caught between them, at least for a moment. After that he doesn't know, because he's running hell-bent into the sliced-open tunnel to Þagalwood.

With each step he takes, the tunnel collapses the distance—that, or he's hallucinating. One second he's running down a bloodred passage, the next he's burst onto the path among the skeletal trees. Stumbles to a stop a moment to take stock. The trees whisper. *Intruder*, says one. *Chosen*, says another, but no indication of what he's chosen for. The axe most likely if they catch him.

Already he's realized his mistake. That guard had an ördstone. Why didn't he snatch it, instead of losing his grit? He could have sealed the way. Now he's trapped himself in the Þagalwood, and it won't be long before . . .

He doesn't even finish the thought before distant thunder echoes through the woods, a thunder of hooves. Exactly like the time he strayed here with Waldroup.

Something is coming after him.

He runs harder. Thinks: *What if I left the path?* Even knowing what happened to Gallorini, he tries to convince himself that this Yvag uniform will protect him.

Shortly, he passes the Gallorini "tree." Stops, turns back.

Gallorini had weapons, and Waldroup...Waldroup lost his ördstone somewhere here. Right here. What if no one's ever looked for it? Why would they?

He skids to his knees beside the path and claws at the soil. The Gallorini tree whispers, *Tomasso*, and in horror he stares. It has no mouth, no face he can recognize, but again his anguished name floats through the darkness from it.

The thunder grows. Thomas twists around.

The Yvag knight is but a speck in the distance, but will surely ride him down in less than a minute. The way everything collapses on itself here, it could be seconds.

No time. He casts about, pictures Gallorini calling *Strega!* after them, remembering what the poor man carried.

Across the reddish soil the glint of Gallorini's sword reveals itself; like a compass needle it points at him. He clutches the wide wootz-steel blade, pulls it to him. The sword's quillons catch and flip up the bolt of a crossbow, and then the stock. With a tug he drags both to himself through the dirt and the fingery roots. His whole body shakes as if from the thunder of hooves and the growing threat. Down the path, the knight draws a sword, holds it out, positioned to lop off his head as it passes him.

Training consumes his panic, takes over.

The bolt fits into its channel, kept in place by the whipcord bowstring. The Italians taught him the basics of the crossbow. He tugs the stock, unceremoniously falls back to a seated position, and slaps the crossbow down between his legs. The knight is almost on top of him. He shoves his feet against its sides, and inelegantly pulls the bowstring back by hand as hard as he can, nocking it. Tension boils out of him in a howl.

The Yvag is huge, surely larger even than Adalbrandr. It seems to grin impossibly wide at this easy, seated, defenseless prey, showing nothing but the white of those teeth.

In one quick motion, Thomas leans back, tilts the crossbow up and fires. Then, as the knight's sword slices straight at his neck, he throws himself back and to the side.

He rolls into the roots, which wriggle up. They don't grab him securely the way they did Gallorini, but he hacks them to pieces nevertheless. The chopped, bleeding roots slither back into the dirt, and Thomas pitches away, coming up on his knees just in time to watch the hulking Yvag knight crash down over the back of its moon-white mount, slam into the path, and then lie still. The bolt sticks up above its helm.

The pale beast the knight rode slows to a stop, looks back as if uncertain what to do next.

He gets up, walks unsteadily around the body, sword at the ready.

The bolt's driven into the skull from beneath the chin. The body quivers, and like some immense eel the shiny black uniform pulls loose, slides off the form, and pools on the ground beside it, leaving a wide strap attached to a hard scabbard for the sword. The thing is not Aðalbrandr, no, not even Yvag.

The body is bone white, the same as the beast it rode—another Þagalwood construct, assembled in the shape of a knight, with an elongated oval of a head and empty eye sockets. There's no mouth. What he took for a grin was the white bone of its face beneath the black helm. He can't even be sure it's dead, can he?

Gallorini's sword slices right through the neck. Thomas kicks the head away, off the path. The body never moves, but he still doesn't trust it. In any case, it carried no ördstone the way an Yvag might have.

How many other construct guardians of the Þagalwood are right now waiting to ride him down? Better not to find out.

Using the sword like a staff, he lowers onto his knees again and pats frantically at the ground all around the path, side to side, working methodically up the path from the body. How far did they stand from Gallorini? Farther than this, but Waldroup thought he'd lost the stone before the little Italian showed up. If not, Thomas will have to keep searching back that way. He scrapes across the surface with the sword blade, flipping up pebbles, bits of dead root.

Then, on the far edge, where his palm passes over the dirt, one spot suddenly glitters, sparkling blue. And there's Waldroup's ördstone.

He keeps the guardian's spiny black blade and the stone, puts on the strap so that the sheathed sword sits comfortably between his shoulder blades; he discards the boltless crossbow and Gallorini's fine sword. Blearily and without ceremony, he runs around the bonelike corpse, slices the air, then grabs the reins of the untended beast and hauls it after him through the fiery-edged portal.

Quickly stepping past the beast, Thomas knelt and sealed up the green fire. Then he turned.

On the hilltop above stood a Cistercian abbey, an immense silhouette rising against the early streaks of dawn sky, its shape all too familiar. He was in Italia.

In something like awe, he pushed back the helm and let the night air ruffle his hair and cool his sweat. He was with Waldroup again for a moment, having just survived their first encounter with the Þagalwood, about to discover that Waldroup had collected all the Yvags' ördstones from the crypt of Old Melrose. *They all need to cut their way home,* he'd said.

"Yes," Thomas answered the remembered words. "We all do."

The sleek monster beside him, black now, stood patiently, having nothing to do. Thomas gripped the ördstone again. His weird inhuman fingers shook and he feared he might drop it. He had been thinking of Gallorini and Waldroup and apparently had opened a doorway to the last place they had all been together. If he was right, the ördstone was somehow attuned to his thoughts, his memories: It brought him where he wanted to go.

He blinked sweat from his eyes, concentrated hard upon the image of Old Melrose, then carefully sliced the dawn air, ready to draw the sword in case soldiers came pouring out of the opening. None did, and there on the other side of the spitting green ring stood the ruins. No red reflective tunnel leading first through Ailfion, Þagalwood, whatever it should be called—this was a doorway between two places as if they stood side by side.

The shiny black steed waited patiently, and he swung up into the saddle. The beast didn't react, didn't try to throw him off the way a horse might have done. Maybe it didn't distinguish one armored rider from another. Maybe given how it was assembled, it had no allegiance to anything, simply knew its job. He didn't care. Home was right in front of him. *Home.* His eyes flushed with tears. "Janet," he whispered.

He kicked the steed into motion and they rode through the circle, from Italia to Scotland in four short steps.

With a sob of thanks to God, he offered a silent prayer to Taliesin. The old man had saved his life. He'd escaped from the inescapable prison. He had survived.

Now he must dismount and seal up the portal. He drew the beast to a stop and started to swing down—at which point something struck him from behind and dragged him to the ground.

PART FOUR:
RECKONINGS

XXX. Filib & Janet

Filib Lusk squatted in the overgrowth that was steadily devouring the remains of Old Melrose. He kept his hood up because it was cold: Winter was coming, and soon enough these nightly vigils would be suspended until the thaw.

Even with those iced-over months, in the time that Filib had accompanied Janet Lynn to watch for her husband's return, he had witnessed three occasions where people were taken by the elves as tithes. Twice the ceremonies had been conducted by men; once, by two men and a woman. All were people he recognized as powerful members of society, including landowners, a prioress, and even the previous sheriff of Roxburgh. Always one or two of the black-armored elves joined or accompanied them. He'd come to appreciate that his childhood notion of elves bore little resemblance to the sinister reality of them, and that whatever they were up to involved a conspiracy of his neighbors—powerful people assisting them. No doubt they received some benefit in return—maybe even the power they wielded. And no doubt if they spied him watching, his life wouldn't be worth a pence.

None of that affected him; Filib accompanied Janet out of more guilt than any threat of death could discourage. In showing his copy-work to a magistrate named Baggi, he had been the cause of both Tàm Lynn's and his own sister's abductions: They had both vanished on the very night that Baggi, seated in The Blind Fiddler, had abruptly clutched his throat and, in front of a dozen screaming witnesses, melted like a human taper. Some who hadn't run off immediately claimed that his heart had burst right out of his chest and taken flight. He'd had Filib's parchment with him still, but afterward nobody would touch it, covered as it was in Baggi.

He'd never told Janet nor anyone else about giving his parchment to the magistrate, and the guilt of that secret ate away at him. He continued to accompany the widow every night she chose to come here, even though he'd long since given up that they would ever see her husband or Sìleas again. Taken people traveled in but one direction—and that was into the ring of green fire.

Deep down in his soul he might have wanted revenge for his sister's absence, but he knew better than to act upon it. He was just a simple farmer, not someone skilled in fighting demons. He wasn't even a soldier like Tàm Lynn, who had proved no match for the elves in the end, either.

No, Sìleas had been a warning to him and Kester not to pry or interfere, unless they wanted to disappear, too. Aiding Janet Lynn had to be enough, and he thought probably it wouldn't be for much longer. She was ill, he knew, though she hid this well and never spoke of it.

Tonight would end the same as all the other nights. He and she would reluctantly depart with the sun coming up, knowing that they had done their duty to her husband's memory, to the promise she'd made.

Filib climbed up on stiff legs, turned to walk over to where Janet sat on the hillside, wrapped in heavy blankets. His back was to the spot in the moment that his shadow was suddenly thrown ahead of him in flickering green radiance.

Filib crouched back down. He looked about sharply for a nearby gathering, a new tithe being shoved nakedly into the clear space they watched, but no one was there below. No one had opened the way. The green line split and spread into a circle as if on its own, and moments later a lone knight in spiky black armor emerged, riding a huge black stallion—at least superficially in the dark it looked like a stallion. Closer observation revealed that it was one of *their* beasts, with smoldering red eyes. Odd, he thought, he'd not beheld one of them alone riding out before, though invariably some always seemed to be on hand for the ritual of the *teind*.

Unexpectedly, Janet flung off her blankets and crept down the hill. Filib didn't dare even call out for her to stop. What was she doing? Why was she taking this risk? He hurried cautiously after her, pulled his dagger, uncertain what he could do if she revealed her presence. Would he dare to kill one of the demons?

The knight turned the beast in a tight circle, then started to get down. He seemed weary, as if crossing between worlds had thoroughly exhausted him. His shaggy black hair shone in the moonlight, shadowing his face.

Then, before Filib could reach her, Janet Lynn charged out of the bushes beside the ruins and straight at the knight, who had one foot in his stirrup and was swinging his other leg over the gilded saddle.

She would get them both killed. Elves were known to be lethal, and this one wore a broadsword. Filib ran after her anyway.

Janet tackled the knight, who cried out, and twisted around, unprepared, his sharp gray face a mask of terror . . . Then suddenly her hands circled an enormous hissing serpent, writhing and squirming hard enough to send them both to the ground.

The saddled beast stamped and backed away.

Filib reached them just as the serpent became something huge, warty, and hideous like Filib imagined trolls to be. Janet clung round its thick neck—he didn't know how. This had to be excruciating for her.

The elf transformed again, into a snarling creature with huge teeth and a mane like a kelpie. Abruptly it was an elf again, this time with its helm pushed back and its gray mottled skin, and wild silvery hair uncontained, whipping about. It could easily have flung her off, but it transformed instead into a huge wolf, as though it couldn't settle upon any one form for long. The wolf swatted at her as she rode its back, then rolled upon the ground, rolled on top of her. Filib stood stupefied. Janet lost her hold and was thrown aside.

Clutching her side, she yelled, "Stop it, stop, my love! Please!" The wolf, facing her, took two steps and simply melted away, falling straight into her arms. And there, to Filib's amazement when he reached her, lay Tàm Lynn, dressed just like the elf knights who had escorted victims through the hole, his hair black again and matted against his forehead.

Disbelieving what he saw, Filib kept his dagger out. Twenty years. If somehow he had survived and escaped the elves, it was a miracle.

Tàmhas Lynn was weeping, shivering. His hands cupped Janet's face, smearing it with dirt, his lips kissed her cheeks, her mouth, and he murmured her name over and over as if he'd been starved of hearing it. Finally, he sagged in her grasp. She lay him down gently on his back.

She reached out to Filib. He tucked his dagger away and hurried to aid her. He helped her to her feet and remained to steady her. They stared down at her husband.

For all he must have endured, the clean-shaven Tàm Lynn looked as young as the day he'd vanished, younger than Filib himself. Would he know what had happened to Sìleas? Was she still alive and preserved on the other side of that green fire, too?

For the first time, Filib thought that they might rescue his sister.

As he lay unconscious at their feet, he shivered, and his body rippled uncertainly between states, from elf with long, slender fingers and sharp face, to serpent, troll, kelpie, wolf, and back to trembling Tàm. Steam rose off his skin as if on the inside he was on fire.

Janet worried, "What if he's fleeing them? What if they're chasing him right now?"

Filib saw the round and glittering stone in Tàm Lynn's hand, bent down and picked it up. He'd watched how those people like Baggi had opened and closed their fiery circles, just like the one Tàm had ridden through using something small and flashing with this same light. He got up and hurried past the beast. It regarded him warily, seeming to focus upon the stone in his hand. He knelt and just stared at it a moment in his hand. It looked like nothing but a polished and scalloped stone set with bright jewels, more like something he and his brother might have skipped across a pond than an object of magic.

With some trepidation, he reached out and touched it to the green fire. His fingers tingled. In his head was a humming drone. Squinting and ready to jump away, he started to draw it up, diagonally. The very bottom of the fiery ring appeared to pull loose and attach itself to the stone, sealing and then vanishing after it. Halfway up, he looked through the opening that remained; he beheld what looked like an enormous abbey cresting a hill. The sun was coming up there the same as it was here. It didn't look like what he imagined Elfland to be.

The abbey vanished from view. A few seconds later, the circle was gone as if it had never existed.

Filib found the beast still watching him with its dark red eyes. Its polished black head looked as much like a machine as it did a horse.

"I don' think anyone was coming after 'im," he said. "Prolly we shouldn't wait about to see, though." He glanced down. The unconscious Tàm Lynn seemed to have resolved into himself, finally. No steam poured off his unconscious form now.

Together they loaded his body across the beast's odd saddle.

Filib dropped the stone into his small purse, tied at his belt. Kester would surely want to see it. The beast was definitely watching it, too.

He took the reins and led the beast after Janet, remaining as far away from its black bony head as possible. Its three-toed hooves left odd markings in the ground, nothing like a horse's hoof. "This might be a problem," he said. Janet saw where he pointed. "Anybody'll see and follow these prints easy."

She studied the ground. "All right." After a moment she suggested, "What say we go up over the hills and come in from the east, over the rocky hilltops. Less likely to leave any tracks there. It might confuse them."

They walked on awhile before he added, "Still, they're gonnae come to my house, because it used tae be yourn. First place they'll look no matter where we send 'em 'ere."

"Then you must be home and sleeping and innocent. Give me the reins and I'll walk this beast. We'll come up far from you, far from where you enter. I won't tell you where. Then you cannot possibly know and none will find the knowledge in you."

That appeased him somewhat. They went on. He continued thinking it all over. "What d'you suppose happened 'im, makes him able tae change like that?"

"I've no idea. Something the elves did to him."

"We're sure it's him, then?"

"*I* am," she replied.

"Yeah." He thought a moment. "Maybe it's all glamourin', hey? You could ask yer father's friend, Forbes. 'e tells my wee ones all manner of stories of elves and fairies dancing on the Tweed waters by the mill."

Janet made no reply.

Probably it wasn't the best idea to bring up the miller Forbes. After all, he'd offered her his hand in marriage repeatedly since Tàm had vanished. She'd refused, but then as something of a consolation, after her father's death had allowed him to advise her on commodities. The last time he'd pressed his suit had only been a week ago. She hadn't yet given him her answer. So, then, not the man you went to and announced that your long-lost husband has returned. Besides, tales of faerie folk didn't mean he knew anything about anything. Everybody knew some tales. Filib had witnessed enough now to know that most were nonsense. There was nothing friendly or kind about the elven.

He'd begun by accompanying her on these vigils, doubting that she was more than a mad, grieving widow of a man who'd run off—until the night he'd witnessed a *teind* being taken. That had kicked him back on his heels. Thereafter, one of them—Janet, he, or Kester—had kept watch most nights. They'd all beheld people and elves splitting open a night and taking some poor lost soul through the green fire to nowhere—sometimes it was someone they knew. They'd all seen the gray spiky bastards, and understood that Tàmhas had not left of his own volition and so probably nor Sìleas.

She asked for the reins. He handed them over, but the beast snorted and tried to bolt. She gripped them tight, but the beast twisted away, as if it wanted to go with Filib. "Wait," he said. He opened his pouch and took out the odd stone. The beast calmed down. "Here, missus, I think you have tae possess this."

Sure enough, the beast tracked the handing over of the stone. Janet pulled the reins lightly and the creature started walking docilely behind her. She stopped. "Thank you, dear Filib," she said, and came back to him. "Thank you for never quitting on me. I know perfectly well you and your brother have thought me mad all these years." She leaned forward and kissed him.

He smiled stupidly, blushing. Quickly, he waved her off and walked away, headed up toward his house, the house that had been built by Tàmhas Lynn more than twenty years ago. He could never tell her the real truth, which was that he'd been in love with her since she'd first placed her hands around his, enclosing a stylus that together they pushed across a parchment in his first attempts to write.

After reaching his home, he lingered beside the byre and looked out over the hills, but she and the beast had disappeared. He had no idea what path she'd taken. Janet had found her Tàmhas again. Full well he knew that nothing good was going to come of it.

XXXI. Glamouring

There were beams overhead, and tapestries hung against the walls; a fire burned brightly in the hearth he had helped build, that ventilated through a hole above it in the stone wall, the same as in his own house. Had he dreamt everything in the grip of the seizure? Any moment Cardden was surely going to lean over and say, "You had a fit, son." He'd lived through all this before . . .

Turning his head, he spied Janet asleep in a high-backed wooden chair beside him, a fur pelt pulled close around her. The firelight played over her, the face he adored, but strained now, hollowed and lined with years lived in his absence; her hair was striped with white. Her hands looked dry and cracked, the nails short, broken—years of working the fields and tending the sheep without him.

Not a dream then, not any of it. She *had* called his name as he tumbled off the Yvag beast; she *had* brought him back to himself from a spinning storm of madness worse than all the lightnings and fits and riddles combined. Had he really transformed like that? He peered beneath the blanket.

The images in his head, the sensation of his body contorting, swelling, stretching—he was amazed anyone could offer a way back from that maelstrom. But of course his Janet had.

He saw that he still wore an Yvag's armor. That memory was real, too. All of it. They would be coming after him. Might be here already. He mustn't be found with Janet, mustn't be found here. And *Morven*—where was his daughter? She wasn't in this room, here in Cardden's keep. But how many years had gone by? She could be a wife herself by now.

283

He sat up. There was no time to waste. He should be on his way right this minute, before they were all caught together.

His body ached as if his skeleton had been pulled out and stuffed back in, but he'd slept off his exhaustion. *How long?* He went and knelt beside his wife, touched her hand. She flinched and her eyes opened, focused upon him. "Tàm," she said, and tears flooded his eyes: A voice he'd never expected to hear again, so much love in his name when she said it.

They clung together in the firelight, one body never to be sundered. "I never gave up," she whispered against his face. "I knew you would find your way home." She kissed his forehead.

"No, and I never gave up, either. When I was allowed to think at all, it was of you and Morven."

"And Sìleas?" she asked quickly.

"Sacrificed." He explained how the Yvag pilgrims had caught her on the way to their house and assumed she was Janet. There'd been nothing he could do to spare Sìleas: They were making his wife their *teind*, making him watch, as a punishment for his opposition.

"Had I breathed a word, I'd have lost you and Morven, and they still would have murdered Sìleas."

"Their kind are about e'en now," she said. "Filib and I have seen them. Kester, too. But they've not come inquiring after me."

"On the other side they all believe you are dead. The new skinwalkers would believe that, too." He glanced around then, asked, "Is your father here?"

She shook her head sadly. "Dead four years. This is *our* home now, Tàm. I'm the landlord."

"A woman of importance and influence." He grinned. "And the house I built?"

"Filib Lusk and his family live in it. Kester's in the one you repaired for them. It's never fallen down." She tried to smile with him, to lighten the reunion.

"They're like to seek me there first. Filib's sure to be in danger. They will make him tell. Sooner or later, they'll put it together."

She stroked his hair. "He knows. People have come up to him and Kester over the years, inquiring after Tàm Lynn. Some of those might be harmless, but they've been cautious. They don't know what happened, that the house, the land was given them by the landlord, my father, and that the previous tenant vanished. They both have kept faith with me all this time while I watched for you, Filib most of all. Watching for your return, we witnessed the new helpers of the elves delivering their tithes. We learned who to be wary of. Filib was on hand tonight when I caught you. Between us, we made sure nothing leads from Old Melrose to his house." She eyed him sidelong. "Your beast leaves strange tracks."

"Straight to here?"

"No, I kept to the heights, the rockiest parts. If anything, they will think you rode to Jedburgh. After that I descended to the Teviot shallows, and stayed in the river until we were close."

"What did you do with the beast?"

"He's in the stables. He was passive and easy to manage once I had this." She held out the ördstone.

He let out a deep sigh. "I didn't lose it, then. Did I seal up the opening?"

"Filib. We've watched their opening and closing it enough times; he simply copied what he'd seen." She passed the stone to him.

"Then, if they haven't come through already, maybe we do have a chance," he mused. "Taliesin might be able to keep up the illusion I'm still in my cell for days, perhaps even weeks." He had to have been glamoured somehow. Nothing else could explain the guard's reaction, or that of Teg the little hob calling him "captain." A changeling gone mad, then. Taliesin had said "one in a hundred" became unhinged. How long would it take the Yvags to realize none was missing? How long to find the slain creature on the path? And then how long before someone thought to look in the prison? Every hour, every day's delay in Ailfion, could give him days, weeks, maybe months here.

"Who is Taliesin?" asked Janet.

Instead of trying to explain, he looked at her a long while in silence. He did not have to reach far into his memory to find her, then to blend that memory of her with Janet now, compressing—or trying to—the distance in time. Changes large and small, he smoothed as best he could. Then, his voice tight, he asked, "How long have I been gone?"

"Nineteen years almost to the night."

"Jesu. Morven, is she . . . ?" He looked overhead, as if he might see through the beams.

Janet bowed her head. "She's at the Abbey of Our Lady of Fontevraud."

"A *nunnery*?"

The question seemed to deliver a blow to Janet. She sat again.

He realized how accusatory it had sounded. He hadn't meant it that way, had he?

In a voice thick with grief she explained how the night they came for him, she took Morven and fled as far away as she could, exactly as he had stressed, across the water to friends of her father in Lussemburgo. She refused to stay with them for fear that, should she be caught, they would suffer as well. She moved into a small house in Brittany for a time. Someone had mentioned the abbey, and she made inquiries. Her father wanted her home. His health at the time was not good. He wrote her assurances that no one had come looking for her at all. She decided to return home, but because there remained a remote possibility that her father himself might be turned, she first placed Morven in the abbey. "It's a—a good place," she said, "and she's *safe* there away from me." But the tears running from her eyes told him the true toll this decision had taken on her.

He said, "No, you made the right choice. They wanted her as much as they wanted you. They would have turned her into one of them— too horrible to imagine." He had imagined it enough for them both.

She wiped furiously at her cheeks. "When I returned," she said, "I learned that a magistrate named Baggi had died the same night you were taken. He'd melted like a candle in a tavern in front of a dozen onlookers, who spread at least that many versions of the story. Most everyone concluded he was a witch and the devil had claimed him."

"Not my father, then," he interjected. "He didn't perish."

Janet shook her head. "He endured another two years or so after I returned here. Father had installed the Lusks in our house by then. I was forever fearful I would encounter him somewhere and he would remember me. I would be found out. But we never crossed paths. Then a distant cousin of yours arrived in Ercildoun, and shortly after that a story traveled to us that your father had stumbled into a well and drowned. A story trickled out that a rope had brought up bones to which the flesh barely clung any longer, as if he'd been down in the well for years."

"Same convenient way Baldie's father died," he said, fairly incredulous. "They are fond of wells."

Janet replied, "Your convenient cousin, who just happened to be on hand, took over all your family's holdings and the MacGilleans' as well. One 'Ainsley Rimor of Alwich.'"

He thought, *Alpin, you had it just about right.* "I have no such cousin. We've no family in Alwich. So, that's one skinwalker we can be certain of. You've spied others at Old Melrose?"

"Yes. Alderman Threave of Jedburgh. The widow Mac an Fleisdeir of Selkirk, who's still grossly alive. And the assistant to Abbot Waltheof of Melrose. He's called Ranulf—named, I am told, after Ranulf de Soulis, a friend of the king's."

"By Melrose you mean St. Mary's. The abbey I helped build."

She nodded.

"The assistant, of course, not the abbot himself. Always behind the tapestry," he muttered grimly. With him out of the way, the crypt was secure again for the Yvagvoja.

"Filib and I have watched Ranulf twice assisting when people were taken through that terrible fiery hole they cut open," Janet said. "And Kester and he witnessed another. I didn't know it was Ranulf until I attended a Christes Maesse at the abbey last year and saw him."

They had repopulated, of course they had. It was safe to do so once he was gone. Nobody remained who knew about them. And Ranulf was in the perfect position to keep everyone out of the crypts. His spell would be as strong at the very least as the one Thomas had encountered before, turning aside anyone who thought about descending those steps. All the walkers would be there—five tombs if he recalled right. His blood surged with a hunger for revenge upon them all; it came upon him so intensely that, for a moment, he ceased to see Janet or Cardden's keep around him.

"Tàmhas?" Her voice seemed to come to him from a great distance.

"*Tom!*" Waldroup's shout rang as if from the balcony above.

He came back to himself on his feet, one stone-gray long-fingered hand reaching as if to clutch at something. Janet had backed away from him.

It was a roaring, impotent rage, the kind of madness that overtook some mercenaries in the field—he and Waldroup had witnessed instances of it. Berserkers. Men who lost themselves in a lust for carnage, and though they usually managed to achieve plenty of it, they were invariably struck down by some enemy who kept his wits about him, if not one of their own protecting himself. In the end, madness lost every time.

He glanced at his hand; it was his own again. Without asking what she had seen, he apologized: "They took so much from me. I've lost twenty years with you and Morven. It's them I want to . . ." He finally gave up, unable to find a word to contain all the vengeance he wanted to deliver. With huge effort, he swallowed it. This rage would neither disappear nor be hard to find again. His soul was wedded to it.

Knowing that, he banished it all, took her hand.

"Forgive me," he said, "I am here with you, and I won't waste another moment of this precious time being somewhere else in my head. I've been somewhere else for far too long."

He held her close, his head bowed over hers. Whatever monster's face she had seen upon him, it wasn't enough to make her fear him, but he would remain on his knees so as not to terrify her further. Clearly, he did have some sort of ungovernable power now. It was not his imagination, and it hadn't ended with his escape from Yvagddu.

She closed his fingers in hers, then drew him after her. They left the hall to the servants and retired to bed. The bed had been warmed with a stoneware pig, and multiple furs lay piled upon the linens.

He knew her, knew every inch of her, but even so she was undiscovered country to him. He was tender and cautious, holding back until she was clearly enflamed before he let himself fall away as well. It was perhaps a little clumsy, but far better than their first time together had been. They still remembered each other in bed.

"You know how you first sneaked into my bed and then I didn't turn up till morning?" he asked her when they were lying together, entwined.

"I did not *sneak*. You weren't home, so you've no right to characterize it as such. I was quite brazen, if you want to know, undressing beside the fire in the middle of your house when you could have opened the door at any moment."

"I might have been with friends."

"You really didn't have any," she said. Her gentle eyes bored into his. "Oh, the Lusks, perhaps. But you were strange and isolated. I knew something had happened to you, something had marked you."

"And yet you climbed into my bed," he teased.

"Oh, ho, that something had marked you just made you that much more alluring. You were a great mystery to me, Master Lynn. You'd experienced more of the world than anyone I know e'en now. No one hereabouts travels much farther than Selkirk their whole lives. You were such an adventurer, like someone out of a story."

"Like the one about Thomas the Rhymer?"

She grinned. "Especially that one." She pulled his face to her so she could kiss him again.

This time they spent themselves slowly, savoring the moments. At the same time, he noticed throughout that there were instances where she winced or made a tiny gasp, and it seemed to have to do with where his hands touched her. There was a spot on her left side that caused her a discomfort of which she was not speaking; he knew her well enough not to ask. She had no mind to tell him, nor at least to let it interfere with the joy of their reunion. But he would not forget, either.

Finally, lying wrapped around her a second time, he decided to trade one line of inquiry for another.

"What did you see," he asked cautiously, "when I was seething with rage downstairs?"

She stiffened in his arms, drew her head back to look him in the eyes. "You don't know?"

"My anger misplaced me. I only glimpsed—"

"Is that how it was at the portal, where you came through?"

He thought about that. "I know that I rode the beast out from Italia, but not much else. It was like when the riddles come. I know I'm speaking but hardly ever what I'm saying. I could sense how I was changing but not what I changed into. As with the riddles, I'm left with the echo of it all and no more."

"Well, I recognized your profile in the moonlight," she said. "When you rode through, you had your back to me, but you turned about. Even with those many thorns or whatever they be, I could see you in that face. My jumping must have terrified you awfully. You thought it was them hunting you."

"I'm sure it must have been just as you say."

"You turned into such creatures, monstrous things, but I knew it was you still and I clung on. I don't know when I finally called your name, but you became yourself. It took such a toll that you collapsed."

Glamouring—the word echoed again in his thoughts. But this wasn't glamouring; it was the more complicated process, the Queen's *reshaping*. She'd said it took far more energy. It wasn't masking, throwing up an illusion; it was transforming, and it exhausted Yvags and him alike—the reason they needed skinwalkers for long-term impersonations. Transformations exhausted even Nicnevin.

He sighed deeply. "Well, at least I didn't become a ram."

"What?"

Shaking his head, he replied, "Nothing."

The greater question was, how had he come to do it at all? Had his being altered by the Queen gifted him with some power? That didn't seem right. Wouldn't he have transformed when the two Yvag fiends dumped him in his cold bath? His rage, and the shock of the icy water were surely the equal of his rage and surprise when Janet tackled him. And his fight with the troll, with Aðalbrandr—if the power had been his then, wouldn't he have changed? It couldn't be exposure to their world, nor coupling with the Queen, else he and Taliesin both would have been masters of such transformation. It had to have come after.

And that left the waterfall and the changeling pond.

Breathing those oily waters, floating beneath the surface whilst the child was being reshaped, held down past drowning, and him beneath the surface even longer, drinking deeply from the fluid as he hid from the Queen and her entourage. Droplets of the stuff had resorbed into his skin, coated his eyes, filled his lungs. It wasn't the ceremony, it was the liquid itself that turned babes into elves and drove some of them mad—which he now appreciated firsthand. Merely touched by Janet, he'd gone mad. If she hadn't called to him to stop he might have slid helplessly from shape to shape until he wore out and dropped down dead. . . . For all of which, it did not appear he had become a changeling, his natural form hadn't become that of an Yvag. He could only wonder what the long-term effect would be, and how long it might last.

He didn't want to explain any of it to her. He did not want to speak of how the Queen stole her image to drive him mad and encourage his lust, tortured and tormented him. Even less did he want to mention how he might even have fathered the thing growing on Nicnevin like a great glass cocoon. Her lust had owned him as surely as a seizure, but he couldn't imagine a way to speak of it that wouldn't shame him. The only thing such disclosure would accomplish would be to hurt Janet needlessly, and at a time where there was apparently a competitor for her hand, the miller Forbes, who'd had twenty years to plead his case. Thomas tried very hard not to resent the fellow, even as he remained amazed that she had held out, trusting that against all odds he would return.

In any case, Forbes's affections would not matter for long. He and Janet must sell her land, take whatever monies they received, and never return here. They would go live with Morven, far away and safe from these monsters.

Finally, he said nothing, and put his face against her neck. He drifted off to sleep with her name on his breath.

The last thing he heard, at the edge of sleep, was Waldroup's ghostly voice: "*Pray it's far enough, lad.*"

In the morning, he checked the beast in the stables. Its red smoldering eyes viewed him indifferently. He wondered if it would have been so calm if he'd lacked the ördstone. Could it sense the changes in him? That was a concern to test another time. Right now, he needed to hide the creature should anybody come looking. How did glamouring work?

He stepped closer to it, placed his hands upon the cold, sleek hardness of it. Closing his eyes, he imagined Dubhar, the horse he'd ridden back from the wars.

Dubhar had died eleven years ago. Nevertheless, when he opened his eyes, there stood Dubhar before him, black and sleek and blinking as if nothing odd had occurred at all. The memory of his charger had been enough to transform the creature.

There was no guaranteeing an Yvag wouldn't see through this glamour. He couldn't be certain of that just as he had no idea how long a glamouring might hold—the glamouring of Innes's chambers seemed to have lingered for weeks. At least this would hide the true nature of the beast from any casual glance into the stalls. He left it there and set off on foot to track Janet's route backward.

Tracks led from Cardden's to the river. Armed with fronds of goat willow to obscure the three-toed prints where he found them, he carefully brushed away all evidence of the beast's passage.

"She would have led them right to your door."

"Alpin! I thought you were lost, devoured by Nicnevin."

"She weren't welcoming and that's for certain."

"But you're here again."

"I'm here, wherever here is. Don't know for how long, but then I never did." And with that Thomas could feel him withdraw, as if a mouth whispering in his ear had drifted away.

With the last of the prints wiped from view, he stood on the banks of the Teviot and followed it until he found the place where she had entered, then backtracked those odd three-toed prints up into the rocky heights. The rest of her own misdirecting had indeed been cleverly executed. Anyone who managed to follow this far from Old Melrose would be pointed in the direction of Jedburgh, and with the rest of the trail erased, they had no reason to change course.

Satisfied, he walked back down from the heights, passing in sight of his own house and that of the Lusks, but avoiding them both. He circled to the far side of the planted oxgangs and strode into the woods beyond. He arrived at the pool where Janet used to bathe, where he used to catch glimpses of her like some selkie who thought herself hidden. Whether or not she'd believed herself to be a selkie, her enchantment had captured him.

He walked out onto the curving spit of land that formed the pool and tossed the goat willow branches far out into the water. The river carried them away.

He knelt then and looked into the nearly still water of that accidental pool. His own face looked back, haggard and rawboned but essentially the face he knew.

How was he to do this?

He needed to control it rather than be surprised into changing every time. In fact, that would surely be his undoing. What would Taliesin advise? He focused upon the old man in his mind, recalling the sharp rebuke that Thomas was no poet if all he spouted were riddles. It made him smile. He threw off a great shiver. Leaned forward. In the water, Taliesin stared up at him. He tilted his head and Taliesin did the same. Looked at his hand, and it was liver-spotted and scaly, as hairy as the old man's. He drew back. The sensation of change was slight this time, less than a shiver. When he looked again, he was himself.

Had it been his imagination? He'd been thinking of Taliesin, but had he really seen him?

What would prove it? What about—

He didn't even complete the thought before his body shook fiercely, and he found Alpin Waldroup looking up at him. "No. Alpin." He reached for the water, shook again with a momentary ague, and was returned to himself before his fingers even brushed the surface. He felt suddenly drained and wanted to sit down. But Janet had seen something else, not a friend pulled from memory. And his hand, when he'd seen it, had been like theirs. That might prove a critical glamouring if he could do it. He must try once more.

This time he concentrated not on who, but on a general idea of the elven, in particular the ones who'd dragged him to the pool each day for bathing. He had seen hundreds of others, but those two he'd seen closely, their gills and strangely contoured annelid bodies. He squeezed his eyes shut.

He shook this time from head to foot, every inch of him twitching, so hard finally that he almost collapsed. The effort threw him forward onto his hands, splashing. When the water stilled, the face of an Yvag stared back at him, blinked with him. Its metallic white hair hung straight, almost to the water. He had only to glance askance to see the hair, no illusion. His fingers in the mud were thin and gray, the knuckles sharply pronounced and spicular, the extra joints and curved nails undeniable. He pulled up his shirt to find gill holes along his sides. He breathed and they flexed open; cool air rose in his throat.

He laughed, and his spiky twin laughed with pointed teeth, thorny cheeks, and an axe-blade-sharp chin. He climbed to his feet, studied the inhuman ripples of his torso; he lowered his shirt, which now fit him poorly. This was what Teg and the perimeter guard had beheld. This is what had crawled out of that glowing pool. Not mere glamour but reshaping. Once more he closed his eyes and strained, growing light-headed; when he looked down into the water again, the face and body were his. Then, just to make sure, he imagined that face again, passed his hand over it, and found himself with the features of an Yvag. He shook his head, and was himself again.

Glamouring was a spell cast to alter the perceptions of the beholder—the beast in his stables was still the beast, but anyone seeing it right now would perceive Dubhar. Innes's "baby" had been a thing made of living twigs, but she saw her own child. Simple glamouring took little effort or energy. He could conjure Taliesin and Alpin over and over, even the Yvag knight. But reshaping was exhausting from the outset. What Nicnevin had performed on him seemed to be what he had undergone when Janet caught him. Shifting his actual shape repeatedly had left him depleted and helpless. But both skills might well come in handy against his enemy. He could be anybody now, or anything—at least for a short while.

When at last they did come for him, he wouldn't have to hide. He would be neither Thomas Rimor nor Tàmhas Lynn.

He would be *them*.

XXXII. Preparations

The Master Lindsay who purchased two dozen arrows from the fletcher of Roxburgh was a short, corpulent man with the bulbous reddish nose of someone given to drink. He certainly did not look like the sort of man who spent much time at archery. That was why, he explained, these arrows would likely last him at least twenty years.

The Master Thomas who visited a fletcher in Kelso was thin, tall, and balding, with red patches of excema on his face. Although he looked vaguely familiar to the fletcher, he claimed to be a traveler, on his way now to London, and looking to protect himself and his goods on the road. By his own admission he was a "middling" shot with a bow and had used up his last sheaf, hence the need for thirty true-flying shafts. He hung them from their tips on his belt.

And then there was the dark and unsavory-looking villein named Land, an ex-soldier dressed in leathers and furs, who visited the fletcher at St. Boswells before heading off into the highlands for the winter. He wanted twenty-four good and true arrows because "when ye live way up and by yerself, ya live by yer wits—an' whatever purses ye can snatch nor snatches that'n be pursed, hey?" He grinned lewdly at the fletcher's wife.

The last anyone saw of the unpleasant Land, he was heading north toward the Tweed with a large pack and longbow. His coarseness invited no company; he vanished into the landscape and was not seen again.

Thomas Rimor arrived at his old shieling alone; there, amongst a large cache of quality arrows, he slept for hours. He'd glamoured himself twice; for villein Land he'd reshaped into a soldier he'd known in France. He had to admit to a certain enjoyment in acting the parts.

Filib Lusk and his brother stood up the target they'd roped together. It was lumpy and more of a deformed oval than a circle, but the canvas was as tightly bound to the packed straw and reeds as a good mattress. The bull's-eye was an oblong stain of rust. They stood it end-on with the hillside at its back. Thomas had explained that for the first days if not weeks, they would spend more time chasing after their arrows that missed than they would collecting those that struck home. Kester in particular rejected this idea, and just to prove it, he fired off four quick shots, not one of which touched the oblong target at all.

Filib made no comment. His brother had always been hot-tempered. Not only had he missed the target, he had not properly laced the leather brace around his wrist, so that the bowstring had burned an angry welt along it. Cursing, he sucked at the welt as he stormed off to retrieve the arrows. He'd grown thick over the years, a result of too much time spent in taverns. The bald crown of his head gleamed in the sunlight as he hunted up the arrows.

Kester had never gotten over the loss of Sìleas. He'd been closer to her as a boy, the brother she ran to when she was in trouble. He felt that in some manner he'd let her down, that it was his fault she hadn't run to him the night she disappeared. He was convinced he could have saved her, and picked apart every remembered syllable of their dialogue (some of which Filib doubted had even been spoken). In his cups he railed about how he would have cut down anybody who tried to steal her away. He was sure it had been those pilgrims who'd passed through. He convinced himself they had caught her and done terrible things to her before burying her somewhere or tossing her body in a river. Over time he was left with nothing but that black unhealable wound, around which all of him had stitched itself. The news that it had been elves changed nothing.

Kester was still collecting his wayward arrows when Tàm Lynn emerged from the shieling to meet them. Where three nights before, Filib would have sworn that Tàm hadn't aged a day, now he saw distinct changes—streaks of white in his dark hair, more white sprinkled through his short rough beard, lines and creases in his face.

He looked near as old as Janet Lynn now. Filib suspected the transformation. Perhaps what he'd seen was a face smoothed by moonlight and memory, but he doubted it.

Would Janet have told Tàm of her ailments? Maybe. Tàm Lynn looked stony and cold, a fair distance from the friendly young knight who'd shored up their little house and laughed with the boys and their sister. His was an expression as dour as Kester's while nursing his festering guilt and anger.

"Men," called Tàm as he leaned his bow against the stone hut and took off his belt quiver. They came walking, Kester with his four recovered arrows. "Let me see what you've bought."

They each held out their bows. "Target bows," he said. "Good. That's best for you right now. Decent arrows, and that's more important."

"What's the difference to your'n?" asked Kester.

Tàm reached over his shoulder and grabbed his bow. Right away it was obvious that it was taller, and smooth throughout its curve, lacking the grip in the center that each of theirs had. "For one thing, a war bow is for shooting at a greater distance." He took Filib's bow and laid it upon his palm. "Every bow is different. You want to find its center, its point of balance." He floated the bow on his hand. "You try it. Just feel." Filib took it, and Tàm asked for Kester's. He winced at the red raw skin along Kester's wrist. "Kester, didn't you purchase a bracer?"

"Aye, but—"

"There's no 'but.' Put it on, keep it on, or you'll peel your wrist right down to the bone. We're like to have only days before they come. I can't turn you into bowmen in two days, but I won't be able to teach you anything at all if you're spending all that time growing new skin on your arm." He held up his own arm, with the long leather cuff and the loop that ran between his index and middle finger. "This. Come on, then." He glanced at where they'd set the target. "Our target's not on the level, but that's probably good. Nothing that happens will be to your liking or advantage. The enemy won't stand on a nice piece of flat ground on a sunny day and ask you to shoot them. Once you get the distance, then we'll try standing on stones, or maybe even halfway up this hut."

Kester looked doubtful.

"You don't think so?" asked Tàm. He picked up his longbow, and drew three arrows from the quiver. Two dangled from between his knuckles as he held the bow. He stepped past Kester, but turned around and fixed them both with a look. Then he walked back to where one rocky outcropping jutted over the hillside. He took a step up onto it. Turned and fired, leaped down and started running. Halfway to the hut, he fired again and then sprang past them onto the curved wall of the hut and loosed the last arrow.

All three found their marks in a straight vertical column. If the target had been a man, he had shot it through the neck, heart, and belly. He set down his bow and walked past them to retrieve the arrows. Kester gaped. Filib nodded to himself. This was the knight who had fought in battles, become a mason, a farmer, but most of all an enemy of the elves. *Of course* he had the skill.

"You want to be able to shoot accurately," he told them, "no matter the situation. Even if you're running for your life. Especially then. Because most likely you will be."

"How much *can* we learn?"

"Well." He slid his arrows back into his quiver. "That's what we're here to find out."

Filib glanced at his brother again. Kester's features had curled with a kind of demonic glee. Where before he'd been the brooding brother desiring a revenge he could never obtain, now he'd beheld a way to exact it many times over. "We want tae learn everything," he said.

"I know," Tàm replied. "So did I."

After four grueling hours of aiming and shooting, aiming and shooting, while Thomas shifted their stances, pressed on their elbows, and talked them through shot after shot, their arms were aching, and the hint of skill they'd begun to display in the third hour began to deteriorate. Thomas called a halt. "We'll take this up again tomorrow morning."

But Kester refused to quit. He faced the target and fired again. The arrow hit it, but low. The second shot fell short, skidding in the dirt and stopping just shy of the target. He made a noise of rage, pulled and fired, compensating too much. The arrow embedded in the hillside above the target. Kester threw down the bow and stormed off to get his arrows.

Thomas walked up beside him. "Kester, stop now."

"You don't know, Tàm Lynn," said Kester. "Ye don't know how long I've waited tae be able to do *something* for Sìleas."

"Don't I?" He stopped and let Kester go ahead and retrieve his three arrows. Then, as Kester sullenly returned, he asked, "Do you want to know how your sister died?"

That brought him up short. He stared hatefully at Thomas. "I suppose *you* know?"

Thomas hesitated, but there seemed nothing for it now. He said, "They were hunting that night—hunting me in particular, pretending to be pilgrims so they could get near, find out how many people were around. How many they were going to slay. Me, Janet, Morven at the very least. Sìleas wandered into the middle of it all. She knew no cause why it was different from any other night she went a'walking. They grabbed her, took the two of us back to their world, their kingdom. It was me they wanted, but she was to be their *teind*, yeah? To punish me. They stood me up and made me watch her die, your sister who'd done nothing to them. It was the same way they'd murdered my brother near thirty years ago. They wanted me to witness it. They wanted me to know the fate planned for me, for Janet, for Filib's children. For you. For whoever they pick."

Kester's expression seethed. "Tell me it."

"They dropped her into a well, one that has neither water nor bottom, one where time slows down so that death seems to go on and on and on for years while the well pulls you apart."

"Jesus," muttered Filib.

"I doubt she knew what was happening. They'd glamoured her, placed a spell upon her. But not on me. And not on you."

Kester hung his head. He had imagined her death a hundred ways. Before now it was as if she'd been lifted into the air, gone. He would have liked if she'd become an angel, but his mind had gone elsewhere, shaping her death at the hands of villains. He knew how girls disappeared in the world, and it wasn't from God carrying them aloft. Thomas knew only what Filib had told him of Kester's grim obsession, and doubted that the facts would do the young man any good. And even telling them these facts, he could never have brought himself to reveal that their sister had died because she was mistaken for Janet. What could they have done with such information? It would only have shredded their guts, as it had his. No one else deserved to share that burden.

"But why?" asked Kester. "Why do they need sacrifices—why do they need *us* to be their sacrifices?"

"Us," Thomas replied, "so that none of them has to." He stopped then, realizing he didn't know why they needed the sacrifices in the first place, either. *The Unseelie*, Taliesin had said: the Yvag wanted to escape from the Unseelie. But then he had never explained what the Unseelie were. What could be so fearful to the elves that they routinely threw bodies into the well of all worlds to ward it off? He wished now that Taliesin hadn't been so mercurial. *What were the Unseelie?*

But Kester was waiting, and Thomas needed to cement his loyalty. He said, "When you tell me you want vengeance for your sister, just remember that I want it for her, too, and for my brother, and for a girl they snatched from Carterhaugh years ago. And for the ones you two have seen taken since then. We three and Janet are the only people who even know this is happening. Now, I—"

He seized up then. His arm flicked to the side. Lightning shot through his head and his vision narrowed until he'd gone blind. "Not now, not now!" he thought he cried aloud. He collapsed, writhing.

The other two looked on helplessly. Kester took a step. Filib said, "Wait. Don't touch him." A moment later, Thomas flipped onto his back, arms twisted out above him as if warding off an unseen angel, and he choked out the words:

"Armed against death,
It's death you will rain.
Betrayed by a compeer
And the one who'd lay claim."

The brothers exchanged glances, recalling the last time this had happened. They'd been patching the roof on Tàm Lynn's house when he'd collapsed on the ladder below them. Janet had never told them the meaning of that riddle, if she'd ever figured it out; Filib had copied it.

Thomas lay unconscious in the grass now as they wrestled with this one.

"Sounds like us, he's speaking of," Kester said. "We'll rain death on 'em. The elves—those are the betrayers, innit?"

Filib thought this over. "But what about 'the one who'd lay claim'?"

"Claim to what? Our houses, our land?"

"I dunno, maybe all of it, everything. When he comes to, we'll tell him what 'e's said."

"Think he'll understand?" Kester asked.

"No idea."

"Someone's going to betray us." Grimly, they sat down then and waited.

XXXIII. Forbes

Inside the seizure, the words he spoke reverberated as if off the walls of a cavern. The lancing, violent streaks of light slowly subsided like a storm moving off, and then his words were gone, and it was the voice of Waldroup echoing in his head, Waldroup looming in the settling dark of the aftermath: "*Hey, little brother. So you're not done with riddles and you're not done with me. I think maybe we're both part of this, what happens to you. But you need to wake up now. Time is short. Get on!*"

He opened his eyes to find himself inside the tiny shieling hut. The brothers must have stuffed him in there, which meant he hadn't awakened any too quickly. He crawled out again to find that a mist had set in on the heights and dusk had arrived. The punctured target had been laid up like a piece of roof thatch against the shieling. No sign of Filib or Kester.

He'd foolishly thought the fits were done with him. The Queen had somehow silenced them. But now, outside her influence, they were back, along with Waldroup. It seemed too unlikely to be coincidence.

What had this one been about? He recalled only the voice of Waldroup telling him time was short. He would have to ask the Lusks, but tomorrow. Right now he needed to go home. He worried that Waldroup's ghost knew something that remained opaque to him, and Janet would be growing fearful that the Yvags had found him already.

In fact, Janet wasn't thinking of elves at all. She was detaining Forbes the miller, who had come to hear her answer regarding his hand in marriage. With Thomas's return and the complications attending it, she'd forgotten Forbes's promise to pay a call for her answer tonight. She wanted only to let him down as gently as possible, but let him down she must.

Forbes had carried a torch for her from the very first time he had come to do business with her father, who delighted in the idea of a miller for a son-in-law. Janet herself had always been the obstacle to that union. Redheaded Forbes would pay his quarterly banalities and then find some excuse to remain after. Sometimes he was invited to share a meal in their company, where he and her father both talked around the edges of a union, ignoring that Janet already had a suitor in foolish Kenny, who thought he would win great honor or a title in battle but instead only won a grave somewhere far from home. She had not given Forbes a reason to think she shared her father's enthusiasm for their union. He pursued it on his own, smitten, although too shy and uncertain to confess what was in his heart, fearing—rightly—that she would say no. When the lad failed to return, Forbes did not press his suit right away, else things might have been different. He might have attracted her affections. Instead, he let her grieve and waited to see what she would do. That was when Thomas showed up, and despite (or perhaps because of) the danger of him, she joined her fate to his.

Then Thomas was taken, and she absented herself and her child. She supposed to Forbes it was as if she'd been kidnapped, too. She did not return until her ailing father wrote her to come home. Knowing nothing of the true circumstances of Thomas's disappearance, Cardden had tried to convince her to give up waiting for her lost husband. "These men of the world," he told her, "they often cannot be persuaded to settle down for long, daughter. You mustn't blame yourself. Sometimes the quiet, reliable man is the better choice in life." There was nothing she could say in response except that she wasn't ready.

After Cardden's death, Forbes remained steadfast, assisting and advising her on the business of running his demesne. He knew she'd sent Morven away, and that the child was still alive, but never inquired any further.

Thomas was gone, and so finally Forbes asked for her hand. She rejected his suit, which he seemed to expect. Then a month before Thomas returned, he asked again. And she, aware of something wrong inside her, had been ready to say yes, to stop fighting the inevitable and live however many months or years she had left in *someone's* loving company. He didn't know that—or did he? Had he sussed her capitulation? Her acceptance that Thomas was dead? He must have done. Unfortunately, life was not simple and followed no straight path; she'd asked for a little time to think about it and he'd granted her that. Now here she was, receiving and fending off poor Forbes while her resurrected husband failed to appear in order to establish, at the very least, that he had actually returned and she wasn't fabricating an excuse just to delay or put the poor man off again.

"I know you met," she told him. "Long ago it was."

He nodded. "At a Christes Maesse event here. In this very hall. Surely twenty years if it's been a day." He tried to look bright, happy for her, but the smile collapsed in on itself. "Where did he go? All this time?"

She tried to fashion an excuse. None had been necessary when everyone thought him dead. Now that she needed a story, an explanation, she could find nothing to put forward. She touched the flagon on the table. "Would you care for more of this Spanish wine?"

"No, thank you." He seemed incensed by the offer. "I would care for an answer. You owe me that."

She could find nothing, no alternative to the truth.

So she told him.

"He was taken by elves, twenty years ago."

His stare seemed to pass through her as if he was looking into the night itself. "He's escaped from *elves*." Disbelief dripped from the word.

"They *do* take people." Even to herself she sounded absurd, insane as some demented auntie.

Forbes brushed the feathery red locks on his forehead. "There are stories, I know. I remember a family in Carterhaugh. Their daughter—"

"Yes. Her name was also Janet."

He blinked a few times, then nodded slightly. "How do you recall that?"

"He saw them take her, my Tàm did."

"You know, you shouldn't put that about. It might make certain people suspicious of his having a hand in her disappearance." He raised his own hand. "I don't mean that I'm one of them, you understand. That is..." He sat, hands on his thighs, and seemed to search his own thoughts and memories. "And so, because he saw them do this, they came for him?"

"No," said a voice from doorway. "They came because they had taken my brother years ago and in return I killed some of theirs, and they do not forgive or forget."

Janet and Forbes both turned. Thomas stood there, glamoured to look as if he had aged alongside them.

The miller looked from him to Janet and back. "My God, really return you did."

"No thanks to Magistrate Baggi or the widow Mac an Fleisdeir."

Forbes stared at him a moment longer, then laughed. "Oh, Christ, I haven't forgotten her."

"Who could?" The two men shared the memory in traded smiles.

"Baggi, now—his death I remember. People claimed he dissolved right in front of them. But the widow—an elf? I mean, she's the size of Eildon Hill."

"She probably lives beneath it." Thomas strode into the room. "It is good to see you, Forbes. I know you cannot say the same for me, and I understand that, I do."

The miller nodded once, a ruined smile on his face. "You could have been much more convenient."

"Or less inconvenient? And on more than one occasion, as my wife will remind me later."

Forbes said, "A captive were you, then, all this time?"

"Was, but that's done and we should share a meal and talk of things yet to come."

Forbes responded to the melancholy note in that and rose to his feet. "What things?"

Thomas and Janet traded a look. Her eyes told him to trust this man.

"They aren't done with me, these elves. They aren't happy little creatures hiding in amongst leaves and tree boles, as you've no doubt concluded. And they have every intention of returning me to a cell forever and letting me rot."

"They're coming after you again, then."

"And anyone dear to me."

Forbes glanced at Janet. "Morven," he muttered. "Ah, I understand now."

Now both men were looking at her. Uncomfortably, she replied, "Do I have any say in this? Or are you two going to plot out everything for me?"

Thomas answered, "None of us has a say. I'm hoping to have delayed them. Still, they'll come, and we need to be away by then. We thought you might help, Forbes, with the selling of all Cardden's holdings. We would go abroad, perhaps ride for Italia. In any case, far from here. Safe, if such a thing exists."

"And if you haven't gotten away?" Forbes asked.

"If we haven't, then Janet needs to be elsewhere, as before. Your mill—it seems like a good choice. No one knows to hunt for either of us there. And if they take me again, then . . ." He was about to tell her that she should marry the miller with his blessing, but the words caught in his gorge. While the Yvag knights would never let him go a second time—would more likely kill him outright—he couldn't yet acknowledge the idea of his wife bound to this other man, however good and kind and reliable. He could even have been ungenerous and complained how the elves' hunt for him was all to Forbes's advantage, but he buried that thought like a burning coal under ashes.

Instead, he gestured to the miller. "Come, let's eat something, Forbes. There is food prepared, yes?" Janet nodded. "And we're in a feast hall. Let us discuss what needs discussing." He leaned down and pressed a hand to her cheek. "All of us."

A flagon of wine stood on the table. At least their guest might enjoy it.

XXXIV. Fortnight

In bed beside Janet, tucked up under the coverlet, surrounded on two sides by hanging tapestries and one small candle lamp on a chain, Thomas lay on his side and watched her sleep. Despite that she was asleep, he maintained the appearance of his older self, matching her years. He hoped she would forget that he hadn't aged alongside her and accept his older self. Eventually perhaps his appearance would catch up to hers. Give it ten or fifteen years and he would be an old man.

The meal with Forbes had revealed the flaws in their plan to sell off Cardden's holdings before leaving. As the miller had stated plainly, "A *davoch* this size is going to catch the attention of all the people you suspect of being elves. I could certainly avoid a widow Mac an Fleisdeir just by not soliciting buyers in Selkirk. But you're saying we can't be sure of anyone, including the largest landowner around, that Rimor of Ercildoun. How do we keep the information from him? I fear that you would have to transfer all of your holdings to me or someone else who can be on hand and withstand the scrutiny, while you are long gone."

It made sense. They needed to draw up papers, to name someone. Thomas considered the Lusk brothers. It was going to take more time than he'd hoped. He doubted he would ever know a good night's sleep again.

Since his return, he'd slept only in short bursts—a few hours at a time interspersed with periods of keen alertness, his thoughts rattling like stones inside his skull. It was as if his mind was stretching, listening for the distant sizzle of the world splitting open and Yvag knights pouring like beetles out of the opening. Kester or Filib, on watch for the portal, would alert him, but he couldn't help dwelling upon the idea.

His dreams now seemed to be full of ghosts: of Waldroup teaching him to shoot (no doubt because he was teaching the Lusks and drawing upon every lesson his friend had presented him); of Clacher shouting, "Day's end!"; of Taliesin whispering from the next cell, "They're coming!," a phrase echoed by the ghost of Sìleas, who blew away to dust even as her warning awoke him. These nocturnal foretokens were the company he kept now. Nevertheless, upon awakening from one of these respites, he crawled out from beneath the embroidered coverlet and linens, slipped past the tapestries, and went to the shuttered window, where through the slits he peered across the yard and out the gate until he was shivering with cold. Only then did he give up his vigil and climb naked back into the bed again.

Then, with a stubby candleflame fluttering, he watched his wife sleep, stung by the quiet desperate yearning to insert himself into all the years they had been apart. The yearning never left him; even when he wasn't thinking about it, he walked in the company of a phantasmal existence that hadn't happened: a daughter he hadn't seen grow, a partner who'd endured without him. It was as though he was trying to memorize her life backward, seeking places he might add himself to create a new past. It was not so different from the nights in Ailfion's prison when he'd strained to imagine what she might be doing at that moment in their house, certain he would never escape confinement nor see her again. Imagination was all he'd had. He was determined that he would never again leave her side. He would die in battle with the elves before he would let any harm befall her or be dragged back through the green fire.

She shifted, winced in her sleep, and changed position again.

Some ailment troubled her, of that he had grown certain. She did not seem to know the cause of the pain, and behaved as if untroubled by its existence most of the time. She had visited the infirmarer among the monks at the Abbey of St. Mary, who had given her a slender pharmacy jar of ointment, of myrrh and cannabis and poppy. It offered her some comfort. Mostly it made her drowsy. The monks had prescribed prayer above all.

Janet assured Thomas that it was a minor affliction—strained muscles, something of that order. It did not keep her from her day's work, so it couldn't be too serious. He doubted her reassurances, unable now to escape his own terrible fear that fate intended to take her from him again. And so he watched her sleeping until she stirred at dawn and met his gaze.

She mildly admonished him. "Oh, Tàm, you need to sleep."

He could only shrug as if to say it was out of his control. They lay together then, touching, kissing. He talked of the plans for when the Yvags came. He knew she didn't want to discuss it—it was too much like the last time twenty years before when they had planned how she would take Morven and flee. Now it was to Oakmill and Forbes she must go. The servants would be told an altogether different story, of course. This time, afterward they would leave Scotland and not return.

What they did not speak of was Morven. She was a hole in both their lives. He had done his grieving over her in the Yvag prison, and the sadness accompanied him always, the way Onchu's death remained forever with him. Janet grieved for the child she hadn't raised, the life she'd sacrificed to make sure their daughter was safe from any retaliation.

His and Janet's was a frail and insular state of existence. He prayed there would be time to sell off Cardden's land, to flee to France and resume a life with their daughter. If only Taliesin could keep up the appearance of two prisoners and the Yvags did not become suspicious. Perhaps they might live unchallenged for years.

In the end, they had just over a fortnight.

Filib Lusk watched Alderman Threave of Jedburgh lead three other horsemen up from the Teviot Water to his door. Late sun cut across the landscape, edging the five men in gold and throwing long shadows off them as they approached.

Threave was a tall, somewhat stoop-backed man with a weak chin and a sharp nose that had been broken and badly set at some point in the past. He had humorless hazel eyes. He wore knee-high boots, an embroidered orange wool cloak, and a hat with a padded brim that pushed his hair down over his ears. The three following him all looked like soldiers, but with mismatched helmets, and cloaks of various lengths and colors worn over darker tunics, as if they had been pulled from three different armies to accompany the alderman. What was oddest about them, however, was that the black chargers they rode looked identical, and identical to the one Tàm Lynn had ridden out of the green halo. The light was too low for him to make out the hoofprints, but he knew what he would find.

While he and his brother had practiced their archery up at the shieling, Filib's eldest son had kept watch at Old Melrose. As the day darkened, a green fire had flared up out of nowhere just as the boy had been told to expect, and nine of the elves had ridden out of the slice in the world.

Now Filib's boys and wife were packed off to friends in Kelso, safe from harm, so he took a risk and left his bow leaning against the wall inside the door as he went out to meet his visitors. Armed and defensive would be foolish, and proof of complicity. It would give away everything. Besides, two of the soldiers held crossbows. The four of them would finish him long before he could cut down even one. So he stood at his door in a clean tunic and leggings, unarmed, and dissembled that he was surprised by the approaching party, nor recognized the identity of the alderman himself.

Filib nodded respectfully to him as the foursome neared, and said, "What might I help ye with, yer honor?"

Threave leaned back in the saddle, straightening his bowed spine. "Husbandman Lusk, isn't it? Yes, we are seeking information about one Tàmhas Lynn, a man who used to live in this very house you occupy."

"Used to? Ho, been nigh twenty years 'n I heard that name last— 'twas from another gentleman such as yerself. Indeed, I know well enough Tàm Lynn lived in this house. Helped him build it, I did, after he'd shored up our own o'er that way where my brother still lives. He were a good man, but long gone from 'ere. One morning 'e just nae turned up, an' ne'er came back. Why be his name resurrected now, if I may ask, yer honor?"

"There is . . . new concern, Husbandman Lusk, a belief that the villain has returned to his old haunts. We have reports of him, and it falls on me in my duty to ascertain if these prove true, and arrest him."

"Sir, who has reported his like, an' where was he seen?"

"That is not important," Threave told him.

"Well. A villain, then. That I didn't know. I can tell ye he has nae tried to move back intae his house, if that's what you're askin'. Ne'er set eyes on him again in all these years. I thought sure an' he was dead. Was given this house by Cardden, the tenant-in-chief, who give us the land tae work, too. 'E's dead some years himself. His daughter runs it all now. If ye're wanting answers, you should go ask her, yer honor, that's what I'd advise. If anybody knows, it's she. But if you've doubt, you're welcome tae come in, look around, poke in the byre if ye like. He could be hiding, I suppose. Could be 'e's up in the shieling." He turned and pointed. "Nobody's been there for weeks. . . ."

Tàm had told him to blather long and hard. Talking made noise in and out of his head; it pushed his speech to the forefront and masked any thoughts he was blocking and didn't want them to hear. The Yvags would try to prod at his mind. Babbling a defensible version of the truth would protect him. So he prattled on repetitiously, almost idiotically, about raising sheep and children and crops, until finally the alderman raised a hand to silence him.

"Well enough," Threave said. "As you seem ignorant of the fellow's whereabouts, we'll leave you. But I warn you, Husbandman Lusk, if you harbor or aid him, however kindly your regard, there will be a severe penalty, paid by your whole family." The alderman wheeled about, the silent soldiers following.

Filib nodded and stepped back into the darkness of his house, closing the door. "Right," he said, "and then yer arse fell off."

He knew the matter was far from done. Once the four had ridden out of sight back toward the Teviot, he rolled his quiver and bow up in a small rug and then walked calmly to the byre on the far side of the house as if going to check on his animals. He noted the hoofprints in his yard where the soldiers had all sat: one actual horse, the rest queer three-toed prints. They could glamour the beasts, but not the ground itself, exactly as Tàm had said.

The Yvag knights led by Alderman Threave regrouped with another four beside the Teviot. Thomas and Kester had climbed into the nearby trees before they arrived to keep watch on this group while the alderman visited Filib. Thomas knew Threave was not making the decisions, and that Filib would give him no reason to act in any case. Had he any doubts, the soldiers themselves had already erased them. While most would have walked their horses, or at least gotten down and strode around to stretch their legs, these knights sat immobile and silent, more like statuary than men. Now and then, the pressure from their thrumming voices pressed into Thomas's mind, but hardly even that. They had little to say, and were far enough away that their communication was wisps of words. Two tiny insect things zipped around them—the hobs. Hidden in the branches, he was more concerned about being discovered by one of those sprites, but so far they swarmed and buzzed around the soldiers. He wondered if one might be the imp called Teg.

Only when Alderman Threave and his entourage rejoined them did the knights show signs of life again. The drone of their speech increased, though Threave did not contribute much. Either he did not communicate well in that way, or he was taking his orders rather than giving them. He spoke comprehensibly to one glamoured knight in particular, who sat tall and looming, with blond, bearded features that were hard as chiseled stone. The knight wore a dark leather eyepatch over its left eye. This was the true leader, the deadliest. Thomas had no doubt of its identity: Aðalbrandr.

Threave said, "Lusk claims to know nothing of our prey, claims not to have seen him since he was a boy."

"Is that a likely story?" Aðalbrandr asked.

"Who can say? His family did not move in until some time after we snatched this Tàm Lynn. 'Twas long ago here. Rethfreza, who was on hand then as now, already confirmed that much. And the babbling Lusk presented unarmed. He did not seem aware of the threat looming over him."

"Nevertheless," the one-eyed knight replied. "Make an example of this one and his family loud enough to call out the riddling idiot. Let us remind Thomas Rimor that everyone else will pay so long as he absents himself."

"But will he hear our message, Lord Aðalbrandr? You said yourself that from where he emerged in Italia he might have cut a hundred different exits, gone anywhere. And we found no tracks here. I am concerned—"

"Be as concerned as you like. I know him. He will return to what's familiar. Alwich hasn't seen him at the family home. That leaves these places that were part of his life after the Queen meddled with him. We've hunted him before and will do so again. You and I will go visit this landlord whom Lusk says grants him the land. This Cardden woman. Learn if their stories match. I expect we will hear more lies, and if so we'll cut her down along with this Lusk."

"*Someone* here must be hiding him," Threave said.

The knight's look smoldered. "Yes. That demented old poet's treachery gave him weeks to prepare. *That* was carefully planned, an escape that should have been impossible. He's clever. But he couldn't know when we would arrive. Tell me, how would you prepare for your doom?"

The alderman answered, "I might enlist the aid of . . ." He shrugged. "Someone."

The blond warrior chuckled. "Twenty years have passed here. All this one can hope to find now is a rumor of himself, mayhap a handful of old men who've lived long enough to recollect a fabled version of his story. We killed his brother and made use of his sister. His father became one of our liches. And he keeps tally." He shook his head. "But there are no warriors to come to his aid here. No soldiers. We will shortly sort him.

"Tocrajen guards the gate to ensure he does not cut a way out. If we turn him up here, he might attempt to do so. You three, return to the home of the man Lusk. He has family, you say? Haul them all out and slaughter them. Set fire to the house. Kill the livestock. Let Rimor know that we are here and he can go nowhere. Anyone who harbors him dies, and any place he hides burns. I want him to *know* we've come for him. If he has run, it won't be so far that news of the slaughter doesn't reach him."

Threave's three soldiers turned and headed back through the forest again, riding directly beneath Thomas and Kester. The other three joined Threave and the glamoured Aðalbrandr, and rode off along the river toward Cardden's keep. The flitting hobs went with them.

When all had gone, Thomas and Kester dropped from the trees as quietly as leaves, and both with their bows. Thomas wore his Yvag armor beneath an old moth-eaten green shepherd's cloak. He pulled up the hood of the cloak, leaving the helm of the uniform down around his neck.

"Did you understand any of that noise they were making?" asked Kester.

"Some of it. Didn't Filib's boy say there were nine of them?" he asked.

"Nine, yes."

"And Threave wouldn't have been one of those coming out the portal."

Kester stuck out his lower lip. "Where've they got to, then, the other two?"

"One's guarding the gate at Old Melrose. But that still leaves one missing. Be on your guard. And let's go before they get too far ahead."

As they ran, Kester asked, "What about your wife?"

Thomas shook his head. "Gone to Oakmill already and taken the beast I rode. The servants have been told that she was meeting me to assay a property north of Ercildoun. It's all they know. Therefore, they'll be telling the truth."

They emerged from the woods and raced across the fields. Kester glanced his way. "So who's this Thomas Rimor, then, Tàm?" he asked.

The knights kicked in the door of Filib Lusk's home but found no one inside. They'd shed their glamour. They wanted their true nature recognized for the terror it would cause . . . except there was no family on hand to terrorize.

"The out-buildings," said one. "Byre and stable."

"Burn both," said another, who'd assumed command. It carried an elaborately carved crossbow. "We're to set it all ablaze anyway. Easy to burn straw. Start with the stable." It gestured at the fireplace, and the third one leaned down and picked up a flaming log.

Then in their spiked and shiny black armor they marched out into the yard, one with a drawn sword, one the crossbow, and one the burning log.

They made it halfway to their target when the arrows struck from two directions: The first came from ahead, from the shadows of the byre. The arrow slid up the arm of the Yvag knight with the log, splitting its hand down the middle. The Yvag screeched and snapped its hand back. The log spun away. It clutched its wrist, but before it could even turn, an arrow from behind battered its helmet so hard that the helm receded. The Yvag stumbled. Gripping its wounded arm, it could not reach and replace the helmet before a third arrow drove through its neck side to side.

The remaining two Yvag had scattered away from the log-carrier. They quickly re-glamoured as human soldiers. "We represent the law!" shouted the one in command. "Lay down your weapons in the name of—" but got no further as two different arrows struck at once. One in the belly merely gouged the glamoured armor harmlessly. The other shot straight through its mouth. The Yvag seemed to leap froglike backward to land unglamoured and dead.

The remaining knight tossed down its sword and went to one knee. "Mercy!" came the plea, hands clasped.

Kester, with a nocked arrow, walked straight up to the figure and tried to tear off its helmet. Finally, he thumped a fist into the forehead and the whole of it drew away. The "man" beneath had brown hair and blue eyes. The terror in them might have been real enough. Kester said, "Mercy, is it? Here, then, I'll grant you the same mercy you were gawnae give my brother's family. Absolutely, I'll gi' yah that."

He shot the soldier through the face, then kicked it over. Before the body hit the ground, it was gray-faced and spiky, and black blood spattered its white hair, which floated out around the shaft of the arrow protruding from one eye.

"And that's for mah sister, you mingin' bogie." He spat on the creature.

Filib and Thomas walked up, gathered beside him. Thomas reached down and tugged at the black armor. He slid his hand inside a hidden cavity and drew out an ördstone. Janet had taken his in order to control the glamoured beast she rode.

He straightened up. "Drag them into the byre. Let's see if we can catch their mounts." He held up the glittering black stone. "See if you can find one of these on their bodies. It keeps the beasts docile." He had no intention of mentioning what else it could do, although Filib, and probably Kester, knew it would open and seal a portal. "Right now, I need to stay ahead of the others."

"Others?" Filib asked.

Kester showed his teeth. "Oh, aye. They're visiting the House of Cardden at the moment with your alderman."

Thomas said, "And when these three don't show up, somebody

will be sent. Maybe the one that rode off to Old Melrose, or maybe the one that seems to be missing."

Filib's brow knitted. "There's one missing?"

"One of you should stay the night in the byre. Protect each other."

"I'll take the byre," Kester said venomously. "I'll wait the week if need be."

Thomas saw that Kester would never stop now. He was wedded to the vengeance. He would imagine his sister's death over and over, until he screamed for revenge. The desire to erase these creatures from creation burned in him. If he mastered the ördstone, he would likely slaughter as many as he could in Ailfion before they cut him down. "*Berserker,*" whispered Waldroup's ghost. "*Not your fault, Tom, they turned him the night they took Sileas.*"

In Kester, Thomas saw only himself in the days when Waldroup was training him. All he'd wanted was revenge for Onchu. *I dreamed of killing them all, too.*

Waldroup might be right that he wasn't responsible, but the absolution brought him no pleasure.

XXXV. Return to St. Mary's

There was a hillock where fractured stones and pieces of scaffolding had been piled up into a mound of detritus—the leavings of the construction of the abbey. It had been considerably smaller the last time he'd seen it. Now it offered a perfect place to hide his mount from view. He tied his beast there, left his unstrung bow and arrows hanging off its saddlery, and took with him instead the ornate crossbow he'd collected from the dead Yvag at Filib's. The crypt would be tight quarters, and a crossbow easier to aim.

How much time he had depended on whether the servants at Cardden's keep convinced Aðalbrandr to ride north and capture him at a place he hadn't gone. He was counting on the servants' sincerity in relating the story they'd been told.

He crept up until he was in sight of the east entrance. Even in the darkness, the finished Catherine window looked magnificent. In the dawn it would surely spray the whole of the choir with light and color. He wished he had the time to see it.

The graveyard and surrounding area appeared to be deserted, but with one Yvag unaccounted for, he took no chances and pressed to the abbey.

There were no monks to be seen anywhere. What was the name of the abbot's assistant? Janet had said it. *Ranulf.* Wherever he was, he had been given plenty of time to prepare. Who then had warned him? Threave and the hunting party hadn't had time to come here; that left two skinwalkers—the widow, and Rimor of Alwich—and the absent Yvag knight. Whatever the case, surely they all expected him here this time. The sleeping elven leeches provided an enticement he couldn't pass up.

He wished he knew over what distances they communicated.

At the east entrance he paused. He was already wearing their armor. He touched the piece at his neck, which flowed up and over his head, disguising all but his sharp and thorny gray chin. That took little glamouring.

Thomas opened the door and went inside. The closing door echoed and reechoed after him as if down an endless hall. There were no monks by the door, and none in or around the candlelit choir, either. No doubt Ranulf had put them all to sleep. Likely, the monk would be awake and lurking somewhere.

He crossed the choir and turned to the north transept, where the stairs to the crypt lay. The spell hung there, potent as ever, urging him away. He could almost visualize it this time, like threads of mist crisscrossing the transept. He stood still and listened but nothing moved.

Taking one of the candles to light his way, he plunged through the warding-off spell, started down into the crypt. After only a few steps, he stopped and crouched to peer into it.

Though it was dark, nothing seemed to have changed: Tombs like huge boxes neatly lined the length of the chamber, dust-and-cobweb covered. Impossible to say how many were occupied by something other than moldering corpses.

He waited, patiently listening again as he took it all in. He sensed Waldroup's ghost holding its breath, too, although how could a ghost hold its breath? He was about to accept that the crypt was safe when Waldroup whispered in his head, "*Third pillar, near the ceiling, Tom.*"

He squinted. It appeared to be a shadow, a smudge, no bigger than his thumb, but Waldroup had seen the hob right. It wouldn't be there alone.

He went another step down, crossbow at the ready. The smudge shifted slightly. His head filled with a sibilant drone as if it was attempting to communicate to him. It wouldn't be a sentinel out of the tombs . . . unless something else had already climbed out, which didn't appear to be the case. It must be one of the little wretches that had arrived with Adalbrandr's knights.

Where do you think, Alpin? Behind a tomb or one of the pillars?

The ghost in his head didn't answer. Instead, the hob's noise crawled into his mind. "*It's an us.*" Then at him directly: "*Us on steps, who you?*" What was the name of the one guarding the gate? Aðalbrandr had said it. *Tocrajen.* He thought loudly *Tocrajen.* The hob replied, "*Us no Tocrajen, no.*"

So much for that idea.

Pressed to the wall, he descended another stone step. The light from his candle now dully lit the crypt. Only one step remained above the floor. The hob had received no response to its original identification of him as an "us." Whoever paired with it was waiting, withholding its location, as he would have done in the circumstances. The Yvag would have heard his response to the hob; between that and the candlelight, it would know where he was. But the hob's alarum had been directed his way, even before it probed him. It wasn't communicating with anything behind the pillars or the tombs ahead. Only one likely place.

If he stepped out into the aisle now, he would present the perfect target and go down dead as a stone.

The space between the pillars and the open niches was narrow, but not impossibly so. As Thomas stepped down, he flung the candle to the right over the nearest tomb and sprang left. The candle hit the tomb lid, sizzled and flared. Something shifted in the darkness beneath the curving stairs. He squeezed through the gap, dropped to one knee, and slid around the pillar, crossbow already lifted. The candle went out, but he'd already seen what he needed.

The Yvag knight stood in the deep darkness, but Thomas's gambit had caused it to take half a step forward, anticipating a shot it hadn't been able to make. For a fraction of a second the flame had revealed it, the deeper black form within the shadows. It saw him now and swung its own crossbow toward him. He fired an instant before the Yvag did. His bolt struck it square in the belly. Its bolt glanced off the pillar before stabbing him in the side. He fell back, gasping at the pain. The deflected bolt had pierced his armor nearly to the depth of the arrowhead. Gritting his teeth, he tore it out and let the bolt clatter on the floor.

He made himself stand. His side burned as if coated in pitch. His long gray fingertips pressed at the tear in the armor, trying to stanch the blood that flowed out of the hole.

He would have abandoned the glamouring then, but for the boom of a door closing above. He slid back behind the pillar again, lowered the crossbow to slip one foot in its stirrup, pulled the drawstring back and armed it. He picked up the bolt that had wounded him and set it in place.

Footsteps scuffed along the floor above. Thomas drew back and at that moment, something tiny whizzed past his face. Screeching, "Gaaaa!" it sliced his cheek. He snapped his head back hard enough to strike it on the pillar, cursed and wiped at his cheek, feeling the blood there. He gazed all around. In the darkness the hob with its little claws was almost invisible. It could spend all day and night stripping bits off him if it liked.

Candlelight glowed above the stairwell. The hob zipped at him again, but he ducked and swatted at it this time. He lowered himself down, set the crossbow on the floor, and sat rigidly pressed against the pillar. He wished he had one of those barbed Yvag daggers Waldroup had used on the very first of the little monsters.

The candlelight was now moving downward—someone descending the steps—but far slower than a group of Yvag knights come to finish him off. He tried to watch everywhere. Each moment more light bloomed in the crypt. The tiny monster dove at him again; the glow of the candle inadvertently revealed it as it bore down on him. Still he didn't move.

"*You no Tocrajen!*" the hob raged. "*You no* anything!"

It went straight for his face again. He made himself hold still. Let it come, let it cut him.

At the very last instant, he shot out one hand and snatched it from the air. Its claws feathered along his cheek, but he whipped it away and with all his might smashed it against the end of the nearest vault. It came apart in his hand, left him holding a gooey, dripping, lifeless coil of threads and wires ending in disks edged in hooks. The goggle-eyed head had exploded into nothing. He dropped it and lifted the crossbow again, leaned around the pillar. A white-robed figure peered into the crypt.

"Casseov?" the voice called softly. "Are you there?"

No doubt this would be Ranulf. Thomas pushed himself to his feet once more and stepped cautiously into view.

"Ah, good, good. I believe someone has entered the abbey." Ranulf had a deeply creased face under a shaved furze of orange hair.

Thomas nodded. He gripped the tiller of the crossbow, gestured with it under the stairs, and projected his own name.

"Really? Rimor? Have you killed him?" The monk hurried down the remaining steps, holding his robe up so as not to trip. The candle fluttered, then steadied as he reached the corpse. Even facedown as it was, the armor identified it. "Oh, but he looks like ... he's—" He set down the candle on the nearest tomb and turned the body over. "But ... *this* is Casseov." The monk looked from the body to Thomas as understanding dawned. "You're *him*. But how can that be?"

Pressure invaded Thomas's head, the sensation of the monk attempting to scry and take over his thoughts.

"Listen, now," Ranulf said as he rose. *"Listen to me."* The words of the spell swirled with allure, seeking purchase.

"Not this time." Thomas fired the bow. The bolt passed through the monk's robes and into the stone wall beneath the steps. The monk hardly moved, as if made of gossamer, as if magically unharmed.

The pressure in his head continued as Ranulf tipped to one side, reached over and placed a hand on one step. Then a red mist burst out of him, leaving a bloody oval like a target on the robe. The monk sagged forward, his head like a rotting gourd barely attached by sinew, and the robe collapsed, as if it had been held up by twigs. The pressure roared over and past him, evaporated.

"Just like the alderman," muttered Waldroup.

"The trick doesn't work anymore," he replied. "They can't take hold of me."

"Yes, but they don't—"

There suddenly came a pounding from the third tomb along, and Thomas calmly reloaded the bow.

The lid scraped and slid aside. Yvag arms reached up, clutched the edges, and pulled the knight halfway out. "Ranulf!" it managed to wheeze. Thomas fired as he strode toward the tomb. The Yvag was flung back with its arms thrown over the side. On its left it wore a dagger, the handle an elaborate T-shape. *"Ask and ye shall receive,"* Waldroup said. Thomas reached to tug loose the blade.

The sheath wasn't belted; when he tugged at the handle, it all came away. He couldn't see how it attached, but when he pressed it to his own uniform, the weapon locked into place as if it knew exactly where to be. Gingerly, his fingers explored upward toward his wound. The armor over the wound seemed to have knitted itself back together. He could feel the inside of the black casing slip, slick with blood against his skin, but the hole in his side, if it remained, barely stung where he touched it, as though he was knitting just like the uniform.

"Time to move," he said.

He pushed aside the lid of the next vault and slew one more of the leeches and then another, but left the first tomb closed. In that one there would be a guardian sprite, and he had no interest in dodging and grabbing for another of the little monsters just now. Let the sleeper lie. The two dead would alert his enemy if they all weren't on their way here already.

He left Ranulf's candle burning on the lid of the first tomb and climbed swiftly up the stairs and out of the crypt. Even as he pushed at the north entrance door, however, tendrils of communication invaded his head—half thoughts increasing to harsh orders in some disarray, urgent thrumming announcing the imminent arrival of the Yvag knights. Someone had died in their midst on the road just now. He drew back inside the transept, dodged through the nearest archway and into the north aisle. That narrow passage paralleling the nave lay all in darkness, made seemingly darker still beside the candlelit transept and choir. He pushed his white glamoured hair back and drew the helm up over his head again, then tucked himself into the corner nearest the arch, pressed against stones he had helped shape, and waited.

The north and south doors thundered open in almost the same moment. No doubt the invaders hoped to trap him between them in the transepts, nave, or choir if not the crypt.

Watching and listening, he counted four knights in all. Something flitted between them. It buzzed around the choir, then down the length of the nave, at which point a call rang through his head as someone ordered it to precede them into the crypt. It sped on dragonfly wings past the aisle where he hid and down.

Thomas leaned toward the archway as much as he dared, and was able to catch a reed-thin glimpse of the soldiers passing by in the north transept. They all looked human. But where was the one-eyed blond one?

The hob returned, and hovered in their midst. *"Dead out of box,*

Captain. Ranulf voja dead in one. Threaves voja, mac an Fleisdeir in others."

He knew that voice. *Teg,* the only hob that might recognize him on sight. He kept his thoughts tight and small.

"And Alwich?" asked the nearest soldier.

"Sleeping, let be."

"Did we drive him off, or . . . You're certain there's no one hiding down there?"

"Raaa!" the little monster screeched in annoyance. The sound echoed in the stairwell. A minute passed before its voice answered again. *"Gone, Captain. No one."*

"All right, then. We search everywhere. Belamex, go below. Guard the crypt better than did Casseov. You two come with me, scour this abbey, and the grounds. Our diktat remains 'kill him on sight.' Do not hesitate or you'll join the Yvagnajat who've perished this night. Come!" the Yvag snapped, and the hob flitted up beside it. They marched down the nave and toward the monks' scriptorium.

Thomas leaned back into the darkness and allowed himself a moment to breathe. It was time to go. But where the devil was their leader? Something here was wrong, and he could not see the shape of it. He'd anticipated all of them showing up eventually; another few minutes and he would have been set to lead them away. At least he knew now which three of their skinwalkers he'd slain. His false relative, Rimor of Alwich, remained alive. Nothing for that just now.

The Yvag knights were searching the far end and the south side of the nave. The one called Belamex suddenly buzzed from the crypt: *Casseov is regenerating.*

Regenerating. It was something he'd half expected to hear, given his own remarkable healing abilities since escaping Alfion. It meant, too, that an arrow through the middle was no guarantee with these creatures.

The disembodied voice of Waldroup whispered, *"Time to be gone from here, Tom, else it'll be five instead of four."*

He crept out of the aisle. The transept, glowing in candlelight, lay empty. He walked fast past the crypt entrance and pushed open the north door, paused, then turned about and let it close. The boom would echo throughout the abbey and keep them from knowing which door it was that had opened.

He raced through the trees for the tethered beast. As he went, he unbound the magic that made him look Yvag, pushed back the helm, and shook out his dark hair.

He worried that Aðalbrandr might have returned to Filib's house and taken on the Lusk boys personally. If so, Thomas feared for them. Aðalbrandr was a lethal enemy, and for all their nascent skill with a bow, that Yvag would surely slaughter them with ease. But if so, Aðalbrandr had taken them on alone, which seemed unnecessarily risky for the Yvag. He wanted to go and see, but didn't dare lead these four to the Lusks if they weren't under attack. The die was cast and he had to follow his own plan, and hope to draw all of the knights away.

The beast stood as still as the pile of discarded stones beside it, as though it could have waited a century and not been bothered. His longbow and belt quiver still hung from its saddlery. He discarded the crossbow and quiver of bolts. It was a risk, choosing his own skill with a bow over the penetrating power of the bolts, but he hoped to work at more distance. Besides, the Yvags would bring him at least one more crossbow when they came.

Agitated buzzing filled his head. They were looking outside now, circling the abbey. Soon enough they would expand the circle and find him here, but right now they were in disarray.

He turned the beast and rode out of the trees and off down the road for the bridge across the Tweed. Behind him, the knights' buzzing intensified, and one tiny sprite hissed in fury.

Follow me, you bastards! he shouted in his head.

He reached the bridge and then slowed, turned to wait; then, seeing them and, more importantly, ensuring they saw him, he charged ahead up the road in the cold moonlight until he reached a smaller path that led away from Ercildoun, across country and toward his true destination.

XXXVI. Oakmill

They had finished their meal of loin of boar. Forbes was being extravagant, although his tendered excuse was that Tàm and the Lusk boys would be famished when they arrived.

He sat across from Janet, having poured them each a cup of ale, which he had brewed himself. One of the benefits of operating a mill, he maintained, was the availability of grains—barley, rye, even wheat in the warm fall they'd had. He'd also made a science of collecting and pairing the different grains with bittering herbs. For most of their meal, he babbled away about shaping the flavor of ales. "This one," he told her, "is reliant on broom for its dark flavor." He set aside the jug, adding, "Bet I you weren't expecting your meal prepared by an *alewife* like me." He was grinning, and she laughed. Forbes was certainly no alewife. If anything, he seemed far too cheerful in her company tonight, given the circumstances that had brought her here. She dismissed it as a man trying too hard to impress and entertain a woman he'd come within a hairbreadth of marrying, as if he might yet through his conduct change her mind. She well imagined that on some level he secretly and sincerely hoped that her husband and the Lusks would never arrive. Had he admitted this to himself? He'd known to expect her—not necessarily today, but almost inevitably soon. Her greater concern had been whether she would expire before the elves came. Neither Tàm nor Forbes knew the extent of her affliction—the sharp-edged pain in her side. There was no point she could see in sharing the whole of it. They could do nothing but worry, and Tàm had outlined plans for how they would sell Cardden's holdings and leave before the devils arrived, how they would collect Morven from Fontevraud and be a family again. She let him have his fantasy. She knew her part in it would be short-lived.

She'd visited the infirmarer at the abbey numerous times now, and his provided potion did help with her pain. She'd learned to balance the effects of the medicine against the presence of her husband, but she had no illusions that it was curing anything. It stilled the pain but did not heal her. Even the infirmarer had said as much. She wasn't sure, had Tàm not returned, if she wouldn't simply have taken enough of the medicine not to have awakened again, and while his presence meant that she didn't have to answer that question, it left her asking another: how soon was she going to lose him? All the years the elves had cruelly stolen from her—and now their time was short. She could not pretend, nor could she forgive herself. She had given her daughter to Christ, her husband to the elven, herself to . . . what? Hope everlasting? God's will?

Forbes had wanted to marry her two decades ago and she had refused. They might have had a sound and agreeable life, but she had put him off instead as if she'd always known that Tàm would return. She wished she could say so, but it would have been a lie. Much of the time she hadn't believed, more nights than not she'd thought him dead, and in some sense he was . . . or at least he was wedded to this war with the uncanny, and it would always take precedence, because how could they stop the elves from coming for him? The creatures had boundless resources, it seemed, and all the time in the world to finish what they'd begun. The kingdom of elves corresponded to nothing in her world save her husband. She didn't know what had been done to him, but she recognized, for all his own newfound powers of glamouring, that time had not passed for him as it had for her. It had kept him from aging as she had done. He was pretending otherwise as a kindness. And poor fool Forbes, secretly hoping the elves triumphed and took or killed Tàm. She would not long survive the outcome, and Forbes would find himself tasked only with laying her down and burying her.

She drank more of his ale. It was stronger than what she was used to. The bitterness of broom was actually quite pleasant.

Then he was speaking again and his statement caught her off guard. Had she heard right? "I'm sorry, Forbes, what did you say?"

He paused, gave her a look that seemed to assess her, to weigh the outcome of the conversation not yet spoken, his lips pressed flat as if unable to decide upon a smile or frown.

Finally, he repeated, "I said, you have no idea truly for how long I've been looking after you."

It was such an odd sentiment. She hadn't returned a month from Fontevraud before Forbes had begun finding excuses to visit his landlord. It was Cardden himself who'd pointed it out to her: "He's hoping that Tàm's gone off to the wars this time forever."

She replied to Forbes, "Oh, I think I've a very good idea, practically down to the day."

He shook his head. "Not what I mean." Stared into his cup while he swirled the ale. He seemed to be making up his mind about something. Then he said, "About you they knew more than you ken. You and the Lusk brothers both."

Suddenly everything was still. The air in her lungs turned to ice. "Who knew more?"

"The Yvag . . . Yvagvoja." He said it with difficulty, sounding it out as if he'd never spoken the word aloud before. "What your Tàm calls *skinwalkers*." He made a face then, an expression she read as regretting he'd admitted this, as though recognizing how much more he now must confess. "They, ah, believed that Sìleas Lusk was the wife of Tàmhas Lynn, that she was you."

"Yes, I know that now."

"You disappeared at the same time, and your Tàmhas, well enough he hid it from them, too, but the widow Mac an Fleisdeir had met us both at your father's Christes Maesse. He didn't manage to eliminate her, so that when your father called you home, she soon heard gossip of your return. She probed your father. You mustn't blame him, for he only expressed his worry for you. He knew no better. She told what she learned to Threave and old Rimor."

She had no fear for herself. If they took her now, she would go willingly. What could they do that wasn't occurring already? Her fear lay elsewhere. "What about Morven?"

Now he smiled, beneficently. "That is what I wanted to say." He poured himself more ale. "I kept her from them. The gossip was, she had died, hence your return alone. You did not speak of her, and I promoted that story to them. Kept them from knowing anything else.

Your husband, they swore to me he wasn't coming back, but you and she needed looking after all the same. They had to be reassured, you see. So I protected you. Both of you. I made pacts. Your father, too. They'd wanted him over Threave, saw him as a lock upon you, but I convinced them that he lacked the affiliations they preferred."

She lowered her head, offering a prayer that her daughter remained safe. "But, Forbes, how can you . . . how do you . . . I don't even know what I'm asking. You are no skinwalker yourself, then."

"No. Were I, it wouldn't have gone your way. The rider would know everything I know, and you—" He seemed to blanch at the unspoken thought. "It was all an accident. I want to say how it was. Alderman Rimor, he came to me years and years ago and asked me to advise him, to provide him a little information from time to time about people who used the mill. I thought it was just the price of doing business with him, and the information seemed harmless—who delivered grain and how much, things of that sort. In return he sent more business my way. Oakmill thrived, which meant I could always pay your father. And for Rimor's patronage I did very little at all, because what concerned him underneath the innocent questions was that there was no one to take up Tàmhas's mantle and kill the elves."

"But you spied on me."

"No, my dearest, hardly any of it was to do with you. Mostly others he asked about." He shifted agitatedly. "Passed things along—I admit, a few things. In truth, mere confirmations of what already they knew or suspected. But I kept Morven hidden in what I shared. I *protected* you. You don't know. When you first returned after so many years, old Rimor wanted to drag you off to Ailfion. But I assured him you and I would wed and that would be crueler—letting Tàmhas know how you were living a life without him. He was forgotten. I promised you would never be a threat. Knew they that you watched their activities, but you never interfered, you and the Lusks. So they decided to leave you be." His eyes pled his case, a look begging her to see that he had served her better than Tàm, even standing between her and the elves. "I *hoped* our union would come to pass."

She turned over the empty ale cup. "They take children, Forbes. Do you know that? As changelings, and for tithes. The tithes they murder."

"I've none to do with that. I look after you, my darling. Only you.

I kept *you* from being their tithe. I can't save Tàmhas, nor any longer the Lusks, but you can still go forward without fear of reprisals—"

"Oh, Jesus have mercy, you're a damned fool. You've condemned us all in return for, what, a little help with your business? A little wealth for you?"

"Condemned?" He was suddenly confused. "*No*, shielded you, I have. And I'd do it a thousand times. I *love* you, Janet. I always have."

Before she could answer him, the door to the mill opened. Both, with different expectations, turned.

Up the wooden steps came a knight in dull gray mail and a black surcoat. He was powerfully built. He untied the chain mouthguard and pushed at the helm on his head. To Janet, it seemed to vanish, and the hood beneath to retreat into the mail at his throat like a high stiff collar. He was blond and wore an eyepatch. Forbes relaxed at his presence. Clearly, he'd been expecting this knight, who said nothing, only glanced at their mostly uneaten feast. How many, she wondered, had he invited? Coming to wait for her husband? She swallowed, and considered the carving knife that lay in the center of the small table.

In that pause the knight seemed to shimmer, almost like a dog throwing water off its coat. When the shimmering stopped, it had a face and elongated hands that were rough as sand and gray as iron. The surcoat had vanished, leaving instead a smooth and shining black armor that seemed fluidly molded to its body; its broad jaw ended in points like thorns; long silvery hair fell straight about its face, but somehow odd and not like hair at all; the eyepatch, no longer leather but metallic and beaded with blue jewels, remained. The other eye was golden or orange, and there was something wrong about the iris.

When it finally spoke, the Yvag's voice seemed to vibrate inside Janet's head. Its scarred mouth moved not at all.

"Have you another cup, Miller Forbes?" it asked. "Before we make any hard decisions."

XXXVII. Castle MacGillean

Like a great jutting cairn, the moonlit keep of Castle MacGillean rose into view on top of its motte, and Thomas pressed the Yvag beast to faster speed. He pushed down the chirr of pursuing Yvag. Their fury made his head throb and told him nothing he did not already know.

They were coming after him.

As had forever been the case, the gate at the outer bailey hung wide, unattended. The MacGilleans had never been attacked, never had to defend their stone tower, despite all the precautions they'd taken—tunnels dug, passages built into the walls. He was counting upon all of these.

As the beast reached the gate, he grabbed his bow and quiver and sprang from the saddle, rolled and came up running along the outside of the bailey wall, then broke away, down into a ravine. A spattering of saxifrage directed him up the other side of it in the darkness. He wove a course along the higher ground even as an ineffectual bolt struck him hard in the back. Stumbling, he kept going. The crossbows hadn't the range to stop him, but, breathing in, he winced, the pain suggesting that the force of impact had bruised a rib.

Thomas reached the saxifrage-covered hillock and dove over the far side. The wide stone lay there undisturbed. He pushed it aside and there was the hole, hardly larger than a fox's den. On elbows and thighs he wriggled into it, arms extended, poking his bow like a staff ahead of him. In a moment he was in the tunnel and crawling for his life. The hole would be visible to them all. They would come after him. He hoped as much.

As a child he'd crawled the other way—from the keep out. This was the exit, created for a time of war that had never occurred. Onchu and Baldie had stuffed him into it once, expecting him to scream in terror of the dark and close space, but he'd disappointed them and crawled straight out, even plucked some of the little flowers upon exiting—twenty-seven of them. He'd counted. Tight spaces didn't bother him, as it happened. He'd spoiled their game.

It wasn't long before the tight shaft widened. He knew where he was, and shoved the bow hard. It clattered in the dark. With both hands he reached ahead, found the lip of stone, and pulled himself out. Kegs had once stood before and below the opening; they were no longer there, and he fell the short distance to the floor, dirt raining down around him. He patted about until he located his bow, and, hunched over, quickly strung it. The space wasn't quite high enough to stand upright, so he turned in a half crouch until he was facing the way he'd come, took an arrow from his quiver, and laid it there upon the lip of the tunnel. Then he waited, stretched his mind out, listening. The silence pressed close around him. And then it broke.

Through the small tunnel a distant sound of scrabbling reached him: someone was crawling his way in pursuit.

In numerous training sessions Waldroup had blindfolded him, to teach him to hear how sound bent around solid objects—for instance, the difference between Alpin talking to him from in front of or behind a tree—and to find targets by listening. He'd tied little bells to the center of one target, and eventually replaced them with a few dry leaves that scratched against one another in the wind. *Hearing is as good as seeing, often better. You should be using it even when you think you're not.* Now that training took over and he listened. Abruptly, ahead of the shuffling, dragging sounds, an angry buzzing drone grew audible.

He snatched up the Yvag dagger and held it up in the center of the hole, edge-on. Not two seconds later, the hob flew straight into it. The bisected creature spattered against him, and plopped to the floor. He wiped off the dagger and stepped back.

The noise of crawling drew nearer. He pulled on his wristguard and fingertab, took and nocked the arrow, aimed straight into the hole, then waited. From the sound he could identify two of them crawling now. The nearest cast out *"Tont-tu, what's there?"*

Thomas drew back the bowstring and let fly.

The *thwock* of the arrow overlapped a clipped yelp. Then silence for a moment. Then came a new unanswered call, first to the bisected *tont-tu* and then to the Yvag who'd preceded it. That was followed by more sounds of scuffling and scraping, this time in retreat. He couldn't imagine backing out of that cramped tunnel, but no one else would get through it now. That left three that he knew of from the abbey. But where was Aðalbrandr? Inside the keep and waiting for him? He must assume so.

Turning, he crouch-waddled through the cramped storage room to the far wall with one hand extended to catch himself. He smoothed his palm along it until his hand felt the opening in the wall. There was a narrow path between jutting rockfaces that led him to a larger opening on the other side. A flight of stone steps went up on his left, the darkness of another low tunnel showed to the right. At the base of the steps lay six more arrows, wrapped in a skin. He'd placed them here more than a week ago, and added them now to his quiver. Then he carefully ascended the tight steps.

The exit, in the stable, lay in a clever niche between the upright posts of the outer bailey and a matching section inside. Viewed from the inner yard, it appeared to be a single line of posts without an opening.

Thomas crossed to the edge of the stable roof overhang, and stood behind a thick supporting upright that kept him in the shadows. The keep stood before him, on top of its motte. The yard and hill appeared to be deserted except for one of the Yvag beasts, possibly his own that had wandered as far as the yard and now stood as still as a statue.

He wondered, had they not come in, or were the remaining three inside the keep already and waiting for him? If he tried to climb the motte and they were in the keep, they would slaughter him. Slowing down attackers was the purpose of a motte.

Then a knight came running through the open gate. Dust and dirt flew off it, and Thomas guessed this was the second one that had crawled into and backed out of the tunnel.

He carefully drew back the bow as the Yvag started up the hill, then called out, "Ay!" The knight turned, confused, and Thomas fired three arrows in quick succession. The first caught the Yvag in the head. The second and third bounced off its armor. At the same time, a crossbow bolt *thunk*ed into the upright not an inch from his own head. He jumped away on instinct. Something moved in the doorway of the keep, probably the crossbowman reloading its weapon. They didn't dare come down the hill now, but he was satisfied he'd been right not to cross the yard. They would keenly focus upon the stables awhile. It was time to pop up someplace else.

He'd left another bundle of arrows at the top of the passage steps. He didn't need it yet, so left it in place but carefully slid aside the wall panel, then stepped in behind the musty tapestry. He stood in exactly the same place where he'd listened to the skinwalkers of Baldie and Stroud discuss his imminent demise. With the panel open, however, the tapestry was now fluttering as air was drawn around him and into the passage. There was no point in waiting. They would shoot him through the tapestry. He stepped out, bow drawn.

The great hall lay dark, save for speckles of moonlight that penetrated through the torn parchments covering the windows. No fire in the wall niche, no candles burning. He crossed to the niche and knelt, put his hand in the ashes.

As cold as winter.

He listened. From the doorway below, a whispery discussion pushed into his head—two Yvags, though he couldn't make out what they were saying. No other communication flowed to or from anywhere else in the keep. No sounds came from the upper floor. It was all too simple. It was as if these knights were expendable, were here to lure him in or keep him occupied.

If Aðalbrandr wasn't here, then there could only be two other places the Yvag had gone. The Lusks might seem the most obvious, but that one-eyed knight had a personal desire to make Thomas suffer—and the conclusion he was coming to terrified him more than anything. It meant that the elves had known the truth of him, of Janet, of Morven, or at the very least they did now. It meant that the mill and the miller were compromised, not safe at all, and he had to get out of here as soon as possible. The longer these two inhuman stalkers kept him in the castle, the more horrible the carnage elsewhere. Moment by moment he became certain of it. Aðalbrandr hadn't needed to know his plans, only to know what his plans were not. You don't pursue someone who will deliver themselves to you anyway, and more the worse for wear. Thomas, leading these creatures a chase, had become his own diversion.

He crept across the great hall. The main door lay below him, down a straight flight of stairs. The two knights there focused upon the bailey palings. He stepped out and took careful aim, at which point something struck him from behind hard enough that he stumbled. His shot went wide, skittering along the wall.

It was at his hair, tugging. It bit his neck. It screeched. He furiously batted at it. How had the damned hob sneaked up on him?

"The tont-tu has him!" came the unvoiced cry from below, and a crossbow bolt punched into him just below his left shoulder, knocking him sideways and onto the floor. The bolt remained in his upper arm, a strangely cold pain as if it had frozen his biceps. The vicious imp clawed at his face. He grabbed it with his other hand and flung it away.

Footsteps came charging up the steps. Thomas slapped one arrow to his bow, gritted his teeth. He sat up and fired.

The iron-tipped arrow caught the ascending Yvag in the forehead and flung it back down the stairs. Thomas dropped quickly flat as another bolt whipped over him close enough that he felt its draft on his face. He fired his third arrow blindly, rolled, and got up. He fled across the great hall and back beneath the tapestry. In close pursuit, the angry chittering hob thumped against the heavy drape, battered at it, then tried to pull the tapestry aside. Thomas grabbed another arrow from his quiver and stabbed straight through the rotting material. The battering stopped. He peered out.

The little monster dangled lifeless and dripping, impaled upon the shaft of the arrow.

In the same moment, the remaining Yvag stepped through the doorway. Thomas's bow was beneath the tapestry, useless. As the knight brought the crossbow to bear, he jumped back into the passage and tried to shove the panel closed. A bolt suddenly split the panel and drove into the stone beside his neck.

He gripped the blood-slick bolt still in his arm and pushed it through, roaring at the pain. In that moment only the narrowness of the passage kept him upright. There was nowhere to fall, but he sagged against the walls. Stars spangled and danced in the darkness.

He thought he would vomit. His arm felt like a dead thing hanging off him.

Then the Yvag knight was slapping at the tapestry, seeking the way in as if it thought the tapestry might evaporate and let it through. Thomas came to his senses. Hardly a moment had passed, but the knight had finally shoved its way behind the tapestry. It banged on the secret panel. Thomas let go his bow, drew the barbed Yvag dagger. The knight started to pull the panel out of its way, and as the wood slid aside, he thrust his blade in hard, pierced straight through its armor. The creature's buzzing screamed in his head, as loud as his own voice, but he gripped the blade tight and tore it upward, slicing the armor like mutton, opening up the creature's entire left side. Something long and wet flopped out around his hand, dangling from the breathing holes—surely one of its lungs. Black blood coated his arm. Thomas clutched at the tapestry, which tore, carrying him and the ripped tapestry onto the elf. They both crashed to the floor of the hall. The Yvag wheezed, and its thoughts raced frantically, overflowing with terror. Death to it was an alien notion. Even though it had watched and heard comrades die, it had imagined itself impervious. Its panic now assaulted him, almost as if by being inside his head it could hold onto life. It pleaded with him for something he could not grant. The whirling thoughts began to slow. He floated within them like someone lifted by an ocean wave and tossed against a shore. The whirl diminished and finally dissipated. He rolled upon the imagined beach alone. The wave had receded, never to return.

Thomas groaned and rolled over. His own left arm was slick with his and the Yvag's blood, most of it invisible upon the slick black armor. He summoned the energy and made his elbow flex, grimaced as the armor pulled at his wound. He'd been stabbed through but nothing had been severed, thank God. He could still use the arm. With difficulty, he returned the dagger to its sheath.

Whether or not he and his armor would knit as before, he couldn't lie here and wait to find out. The real targets by now would be imperiled if not murdered. He'd given Aðalbrandr more than enough time to strike.

Standing, he clung to the shredded tapestry, resting his face beside the goggle-eyed *tont-tu* dangling off the shaft of the arrow. It suddenly kicked and flailed, its thoughts screeching at him: "*Kill you, you. Not one of us. You a lie, a trick!*"

He almost let it be. But the specter of Waldroup whispered, "*It'll tell them who you are, Tom.*" "Too late for that, Alpin." He lowered his head, groaned. "They already know." Nevertheless, he grabbed the hob and yanked it back down the shaft, letting the arrowhead slice it cleanly in two.

XXXVIII. Aðalbrandr

Janet sat paralyzed. The elven knight had done this to her as Forbes sought a wood cup for the ale. The scarred elf had reached over with its long inhuman fingers as if to pat her arm and before she could pull away something stung her. Forbes didn't seem to realize it had occurred, but made nervous conversation with the iron-skinned creature.

"How . . . How go your efforts, Lord Aðalbrandr?"

The knight accepted the cup and allowed Forbes to pour ale. "Oh," it said, and the word rang in her head. It wasn't speaking, yet she heard its voice clearly. "We have every expectation that Thomas Rimor"—it faced Janet and all but leered—"Tàmhas Lynn, will prevail and we shall lose four of our own in the bargain. A great loss to our sempiternal multitude," it added, yet the notion did not seem to bother it in the least.

This close, Janet observed four perforations down the side of its armor, which flexed open and closed. They reminded her of a salmon's gills laboring to keep it alive out of water.

Forbes clearly didn't know how to react to his "guest."

How had he bound himself to these creatures? Everything he'd told her disagreed with the implicit threat that pervaded even the thoughts of the thing. Forbes tried a smile but lost hold of it, his expression clouding. "Believe you he'll prevail against so many?"

The knight continued to stare at Janet. "Your husband is, let us say, gifted in evading capture."

"But you caught him before," Forbes interjected.

"Indeed we did. And we assured you never would you see him

341

again. We placed him in our inescapable prison. And impossibly he escaped, and did significant damage to our realm in the process. He is resourceful." Its one eye fixed on her. "He sent you, mistress, away to this place of safety. Unfortunately for him it was not safe, which he couldn't know. As you didn't. All of what *we* know suggests he has planned and prepared for this night, and for that reason, we do not expect our knights to best him. Four more eternals gone. Four more against his name."

By now Forbes was watching Janet, too, and with a worried expression. "Janet?" he asked. She tried but could not respond. He turned to the smug creature. "What did you do to her?"

"Nothing of much consequence. I need for her to be still now until the way is opened." It reached over and placed something on the table between her arms. She strained to glance down, to see a strange object, an inverted pyramidal box, four-sided, balancing impossibly upon its point.

"What is that?" Forbes asked.

Adalbrandr faced him. "You want her to stay here with you when we take her husband, don't you?"

"Of course." His eyes darted back and forth between the knight, the queer object, and Janet.

"Then do not interfere."

"What is it you're waiting for?" Forbes asked, but the elf addressed his response to Janet.

"Yvagvoja. Your husband has once more slain our paragons, those who walk in human guise to watch over and guide our interests. In so doing he has killed those human hosts in which they dwell. We now await word of new volunteers who will make the sacrifice for our continued working of this world. It used to be that none had cause to fear this undertaking in the service of our race, but your husband has changed all that, killing Yvagvoja as they lie helpless. Imagine if we cruelly murdered you in your linens as you slept the sleep of the dead. They were out of body, all of them, guiding their hosts for our benefit." The elf sipped its beer as if pausing in telling a common tale.

"We're certain you do not appreciate how difficult it is for us to exist in your atmosphere, your air. If we are to emigrate—and we *will* emigrate—we must change it to suit us. This will take a thousand or more of your years, whereas we will hardly notice the time passing.

Your lives are small and inconsequential. I say this not to diminish you. It is simple fact. The universe will miss none of you when we reestablish our homeworld here for the next five billion years."

She wanted to spit her reply: "Except Tàm will stop you," but no words would come, her lips wouldn't part.

Forbes looked more and more distressed, and she guessed that he had never until now appreciated the undertaking in which he was assisting. Maybe he had simply preferred not to know. Various rich landlords and officials had benefitted him personally and that had been enough.

A quiet intermittent humming broke the silence, emanating from the Yvag. It slid a hand into a hidden seam in its armor and drew out a black stone covered in glittering blue gems, very slightly larger than the one Tàm had showed her. A strange pressure invaded her head. Forbes was reacting as well.

"Ah," said the Yvag. "We've arrived at the abbey. Two new volunteers are come through." It then passed a hand over the inverted pyramid and the little trinket began to spin, throwing off a mild green light.

Two. Her helpless horror swelled.

"Shortly, conveyance will take place and all shall be well again." The pupils of the Yvag's one eye enlarged and joined into a black ring. The creature smiled and removed its jeweled patch. Its left eye, though slightly cloudy in regenerating, seemed to see well enough. The ringed pupils focused on her. "That's better."

Some understanding of what was about to happen must finally have penetrated Forbes's willful ignorance—more than he could bear. He shouted, "I won't let you destroy her! You promised me!" and tackled the knight. The ördstone flipped across the table and rolled across the floor until it struck the steps up to the grain storage loft and the grindstones. Janet wanted to get up and run after it, but couldn't move.

Forbes got both hands around the Yvag's throat. As casually as shoving aside a branch, the creature brought one arm up between them and thrust him away. He stumbled wildly back against the stairs and nearly tumbled over the side of the milled-grain bin. Barely righted himself.

The Yvag stood to retrieve the ördstone. "It will all be over in a minute, Forbes," it said. "You'll still have her with you. But she will also be with us. And if you interfere further, we can easily add another volunteer. And then you'll be the closest of friends with her and her husband, though you won't of course be you any longer. Now, step away."

Forbes defiantly raised his foot and brought it down to smash the stone. He winced and stomped again. When he lifted his foot, the stone remained unharmed, twinkling. He whimpered, then looked around for anything, his gaze lingering at the grindstones above. He reached down to grab the stone and the Yvag caught hold of him and tossed him past the wooden bin and against the low stone wall that supported the axle from the waterwheel outside. Bending down, Aðalbrandr swept up the ördstone. "You're a fool," it said, and started back toward Janet. Pressure swelled inside her head. She would have screamed if she'd been able. "Now, let us be—"

The door to the mill opened. Everyone stopped where they were. For a moment, Janet hoped Tàm had arrived to rescue her. That hope died as a figure stepped out of the darkness, and the candlelight portrayed a second Yvag knight, this one armed with a crossbow in one hand and a longbow in the other. She recognized that bow as Tàm's. The thing had brought it along as a souvenir. Her hope died then. A tear flowed out of her right eye and down her cheek.

Aðalbrandr seemed more surprised by the arrival of the knight than anyone, but quickly flashed a triumphant grin. "Ah, Belamex, he has been defeated, then?" it said.

The knight kicked the door closed behind it and started forward. She saw that the creature was bleeding. Black blood dripped off its arm holding his bow. At least her husband had cost it that much.

"Defeated?" the knight said. "Oh, yes. All of them."

Casually, it raised the crossbow and shot Aðalbrandr straight through the chest. The bolt pinned the Yvag to a loft post. The villain snarled, raged. Black blood dribbled onto the floor. Then Aðalbrandr took one hard step forward, forcing its way down the shaft of the bolt, roaring at the effort.

The wounded knight had thrown aside the crossbow and taken up the longbow. Three arrows hung from its fingers. Its shape shimmered, becoming Thomas, his left arm drenched in blood. It dripped from his wrist guard.

Aðalbrandr bellowed, "Too late, mayfly!" It held up, then closed its hand around the ördstone. "Let's see how you enjoy murdering your own wife." The little pyramid sped up; the light it cast intensified. The beam it threw off began playing over Janet's upper torso, rising, tightening at her throat, spinning faster and faster.

Thomas aimed and fired the first arrow. It skewered Aðalbrandr through the throat, slamming the Yvag back against the same post. The iron tip sizzled in its neck.

"No!" screamed Forbes, and flung himself across the table, knocking aside the wooden cups. Janet sat frozen behind him. The green pyramid whirled ever faster. Forbes shoved Janet out of the way and she toppled like a stone.

Thomas raced to catch her, but Aðalbrandr snapped off the second arrow and charged him before he could reach her. The Yvag swatted him with one arm, then with the other fist punched him where he was wounded. He yelled in pain, rolled and fell back against the table; then, levering against it, he kicked with both feet, knocking Aðalbrandr away toward the door. The table tipped onto its side. Cups and food spilled across the floor. Still clinging to his bow, Thomas managed to get off a second shot. The arrow pierced Aðalbrandr's thigh, and the Yvag dropped onto one knee. Black blood smeared the wooden floor. Clumsily, Thomas grabbed Janet and carried her into a corner farthest from the mill wheels. Barely able to move her lips, she whispered, "Help him."

Forbes, fallen onto the stool Janet had occupied, sat spellbound. The spinning thing remained where it had been, hovering in the air, flickering over and over his body so fast that it became a continuous green radiance in his shape now, shrinking to his head, expanding out, shrinking again. His eyes had gone black and empty; his face seemed to come loose, the skin sagging as on a corpse. Lacking whatever paralyzing substance had anchored Janet, he began to shake and spasm where he sat. Foam leaked out of his mouth.

Thomas jumped forward and slapped at the green pyramid, but his hand passed through it like through a flame and he cried out as the leather fingertab and his palm scorched in a perfect triangle. The leather smoked. The intense pain caused him to lurch back from Forbes at the very moment that Aðalbrandr, with barbed dagger held high, leapt for him again. Thomas's erratic stumbling confounded the attack; instead of stabbing him cleanly, the dagger slashed through the armor at his back and cut his right side. The Yvag sprawled against the upended table. Thomas, back bowed, face to the roof, howled and fell against the upright below where his two arrows hung, dripping Yvag blood. Aðalbrandr rose up, staggering, once again, and Thomas sprang away, ducked around the low stone wall supporting the mill wheel axle, and up the four steps to the grain loft and bin containing the grinding stones. By the time he turned back he'd nocked one more arrow and lifted the bow, but Aðalbrandr already had one foot up on the four steps below him, dagger raised.

Thomas shot the knight through its recovering eye. The arrow snapped Aðalbrandr's head back and the Yvag's feet tripped off the stairs; it reeled against the vertical mortise wheel, struck its forehead against the heavy cogs of the horizontal wheel above and, dropping the black dagger, slid across the axle, where it hung, finally lifeless, the head of the arrow protruding from the back of its skull.

Thomas collapsed beside the grinding stones. He let go the bow. Reached around and patted at his back. His fingers poked into the deep cut. His hand came away shiny with blood. He was sure he'd been sliced through the ribs in his back. He leaned to the other side, away from the cut, groaning as the move pulled at the wound.

Janet lay on the floor across the room, seemingly unconscious. He called her name, but she didn't move.

Focusing all of his energy on her, he made himself get up. He slipped in the scattered grain on the floor, maybe in his own blood as well, and had to try a second time. With care, he navigated the four stairs down. His vision narrowed and he leaned against a beam to gather his energy. It felt like only a moment passed.

Forbes sat at an angle, face devoid of expression. The strange pyramid lay now on the floor, inert. When had it stopped spinning? It no longer glowed, looking rather like some arcanely devised metal box he could cup in his palm. Raised symbols or runes that he couldn't decipher decorated its five surfaces.

Carefully pushing off the beam, he inadvertently kicked Aðalbrandr's ördstone against the low stone axle-support wall. Its blue jewels still glittered. There seemed to be some sort of pattern, a repetition, to their glittering. He didn't dare bend down to grab it, but noted where it lay and kept going, left leg leading, right side in agony.

Janet! He shouted her name in his head, saw her eyes flutter. He dropped to his knees beside her. Stroked her hair, her cheek. His hand streaked her face with blood and he pulled it back, trembling, not knowing how to touch her otherwise.

She opened her eyes and met his gaze. "Tàm," she whispered, then lay her head down upon his leg. He touched his unbloodied fingers to her lips . . .

"Tommy!"

His head snapped up. Had he drifted off? "Alpin?" But even as he replied to the ghost in his head, Thomas saw why it had called his name.

Forbes was standing. He was studying his hands, arms, the room about him. He leered, an expression never worn by the miller.

Forbes leaned down and picked up the small pyramid. Tossed it between his palms. Dropped it and seemed to take pleasure in the sound of it *thunk*ing against the boards as it bounced and rolled, like Morven as a baby playing with blocks. "What sensations are these?" he asked. "I want them *all*. The bodies and their flesh, all!"

He turned around, saw Thomas watching.

"You." The word filled the mill and echoed inside his head.

"Forbes?" he asked. He knew it wasn't, but couldn't help himself.

Forbes shook his head, then carefully began to recite his full name: "Thomas. Lindsay. Rimor—but you're dead by now, surely. Aðalbrandr—" He looked around himself again, beheld the body hanging over the axle. "Oh," he said in disappointment. "Am I among the dead twice over, then?" He laughed at the idea.

Thomas carefully moved himself away from Janet and let her head rest gently on the floor.

Forbes faced him again, scowling. "Do you have any idea what you've done to us, Thomas Rimor?"

"Enlighten me."

"You contaminated the *pool*."

Not what he'd expected—he'd thought the miller was going to tally how many Yvag knights he'd killed. "The pool?" he asked. He could only think of the pool where Janet swam.

"The *changeling* pool. The *filth* of you contaminated it. Not one changeling has successfully transformed since you swam in it. The poet told you to do this, didn't he? He knew. We found your discarded uniform above it." Forbes tried to walk, but wobbled and had to wait. "We know how you escaped," he said, "but how much did it change you? Enough to glamour. That I see." The miller tried again, jerkily walked over to pick up the black Yvag dagger Aðalbrandr had dropped.

Thomas climbed, painfully and unsteadily, to his feet. The air sparkled for an instant, and his vision shrank, darkening around the edges. He fought not to pass out, to pay attention.

So they'd discovered that he had swum in their pool and thought that Taliesin had provided him with the knowledge to do so. Poor demented Taliesin. Maybe once upon a time he'd known how to poison that pool. If they thought that, no doubt they'd dispensed with him. Another cruelty inflicted, another death to be avenged. By somebody. He wondered what had done the job—his regurgitated meal or the hair and sweat and dirt off him after so long in their prison. Maybe both. Maybe the Queen's ritual was more than a performance. A necessary purification?

Cautiously, Thomas shuffled away from Janet, keeping the overturned table between himself and Forbes. With affected casualness, he leaned against a post to keep him upright, his legs from trembling. There was no chance he could maneuver past the skinwalker, up the stairs, and grab his bow from the loft floor. If he ran for it, he might fling a stool; it might serve to keep the miller at a distance for a moment, but he would surely pass out from the effort. The only thing in his favor was that Forbes's new owner was unused to its body just yet; leaping over the table might be more than it could achieve. What he needed was time to heal. He let his hand drop to his own dagger in its sheath. When Forbes attacked, he would only have one chance.

As if in command of himself, he said, "There's a message I want you to take home with you."

Forbes seemed fixated upon the dagger, turning it over, weighing it in his palm. Finally, glancing up with a grin. "You're sending me home? You think so?"

He went on. "I was going to give it to *him*." He gestured to where Aðalbrandr's corpse hung over the waterwheel axle like an emptied bag of grain. "But he's dead so you'll have to do."

The creature animating Forbes could not hide its unease then.

"First, tell your Queen. Tell all of them. For my brother, for my sister, for my father, I will kill every one of you that emerges through Melrose hereafter. You have wrung my family dry and I am shorn of pity for your kind."

Forbes blustered. "We'll come after you whatever you do."

"Then you'll die. I'll cut you down before you're through your gate. Interfere with my sister, my family any further, and I will slaughter you all without mercy. With all the ördstones I have, we'll slice into your world from a dozen directions, and you'll lose count of the immortals I bring down with me."

The skinwalker wearing Forbes barked a laugh.

"I've learned," Thomas said. "Your kind have gates all over. More than I might seal up in a lifetime. I'm only the slayer at this one opening. You go elsewhere, and stay out of my family's world, I won't even know of it, won't care. But come here again, next time I will mount an army and bring the fight to your side."

The miller covered his fear by sneering. "Bring the fight?" He tossed the dagger from hand to hand. "Why, you can barely stand up, Thomas Rimor."

Then Forbes charged. Across the edge of the table, Forbes thrust his dagger. With a swipe, Thomas knocked it aside, then scooped and trapped Forbes's arm under his armpit, locking the two of them close together. They stared at each other, scant inches apart. "I'm sorry," Thomas said, and plunged his own dagger into the base of Forbes's neck. When he drew it out, blood jetted into the air and he stabbed again. Forbes careened back and tried to slap one hand over the gushing new wounds.

His face went ashen. He pawed loosely at the table to remain standing. His arms shook.

For a moment, like Baldie so long ago, he was Forbes the miller again. His eyes met Thomas's, and he wheezed, "Janet. Tell Janet—" Then he crashed down onto his knees. Red mist exploded from his chest. It sprayed the tabletop, and evaporated. The dagger fell from Forbes's fingers, clattering on the boards, and he fell against the table and slid down onto his face.

Thomas leaned heavily on the table and stared down at the miller Forbes.

Within a few minutes, the latest Yvagvoja would climb out of a crypt it had barely begun to occupy and flee back through a hissing green portal with his message on its lips.

"He saved her, that one."

"I know, Alpin. Please shut up." He collapsed then against the table beside Forbes and just succeeded in not passing out completely.

Awhile later, he lifted his head again, crawled over, and gathered Janet to him, kissed her. She moaned.

He tried lifting her, first up on one knee, then climbing to both feet. His back burned along the line where he'd been cut, but he could tell already that he was healing.

He placed her on the stool where she'd been sitting, then hauled the table upright so that she could rest against it. She watched him, returning to herself slowly. "Tàm," was all she said.

Leaning close, he whispered, "Yes," and shushed her.

She nodded, and lay her head against the table. The contact seemed to make her flinch. He knew there was something wrong with her that wasn't obvious, as if she'd been stabbed and it had left no mark. Something inside her had plagued her since his return, and he knew where.

He slid one hand up her side until the aberration thrummed beneath his palm like a deeply embedded stone he could feel. Then he slipped his other hand around her side, against her back. What energies he controlled, he still didn't comprehend, but he felt a heat burning between his palms. It pulverized the malformation between them—a back-and-forth flow. He kept this up for as long as he could, but it exhausted him finally, and he sank down on the floor. This time he didn't resurface.

Upon waking, he found that he lay on Forbes's bedding beside Janet. She was watching him, and he couldn't help smiling as he remembered how often he'd lain beside her and watched while she slept.

He sat up in a panic then, but the body of Aðalbrandr still hung over the waterwheel axle. It hadn't reanimated. Sighing, he lay back down.

They kissed and whispered intimacies to each other. He reminded her how he'd thought she was really a selkie bathing in the Teviot and he must give her back her magic skin. She described how he used to tilt his head to the side when she said something that caught him off guard. They spoke of Morven, the Lusk brothers, her father, finally of Forbes, who'd protected her from the Yvags.

"He protected you for years," he admitted. "Even sacrificed himself to keep them from wearing you."

She shivered at the thought. "Are they coming back?" she asked.

"I don't know. I hope not."

She rolled onto her side, then leaned up. Her eyes unfocused and he could tell that she was listening to her body, a look of wonder on her face. "It's gone," she said. "Oh, Tàm. How?"

He sat up beside her. His back ached somewhat, but did not burn this time. He reached around and rubbed one hand against his back. The black armor, where it had been sliced in two, was whole as well. He hugged her to him. *The changeling pool*—its peculiar oiliness, how it felt in his lungs, the million spangles in the water that wasn't water. Somehow, it had suffused him, and given him miraculous healing power—enough to heal Janet.

Waldroup crept back in: "*Mind, they can still cut off your head an' ye won't heal from that.*"

"I'll deal with that when it happens," he said.

"Deal with what?" Janet asked.

He shrugged, and got to his feet. "These. The pieces of their plan."

He collected Aðalbrandr's ördstone and the strange inverted pyramid box.

Waldroup said, "*Solution's in the grindstones, innit, Tommy?*"

He nodded, climbed the four stairs, and dropped both items through the hole in the center of the grindstones. Then, taking his bow and quiver—just in case more Yvags had been sent after him—he went back, lifted Janet to her feet. Together they walked outside.

At the end of the sluice, Janet sat on the small knoll beside it. Thomas hauled up the gate, and river water poured into the narrow channel. The mill wheel began to turn, slowly, steadily, picking up speed. The grindstones would be revolving now, the two Yvag objects trapped in the hole between them. With any luck, both would be ground to bits.

He walked over to his wife. "I suppose I should gather Forbes's body to deliver to the abbey for burial. That would be best, no?"

She nodded.

He'd taken but two steps along the sluice when there came a loud crackling noise and the millhouse itself suddenly threw off beams of green and blue fire. They emerged from the windows, and pushed through joints in the stonework.

As if connected to the display, a jagged streak of blue lightning burst inside his head. He stumbled into the grass, heard Janet cry out his name. Then the lightning spun him away. Distantly, he heard himself proclaim:

"I blends with we in the warp of battle
Never with they, wounded by iron
Who breathe not our air
And would curse our world their way.
Noble shed souls,
Race of healers, in the well of forever.
Warriors, we fall together."

When he came to his senses again, he was lying with his head in Janet's lap. She stroked his hair. He wasn't certain she was even conscious of what she was doing. She was staring tearfully past him. He rolled over.

The mill was gone. Only the stone foundations, part of a side wall, and the mill wheel itself, canted on its sheared axle, remained.

"What did you do, Tàm?" she asked. There was awe in her voice.

He had no words for the magic he'd released, nor how he'd chanced to release it. Even Waldroup's ghost had nothing to say for once.

They held on to each other on the knoll with a fierceness that said no one would ever pry them apart again.

That was how the Lusk brothers found the two of them when they arrived at midday.

XXXIX. Alwich

The snow was half-melted when the two strangers rode up to the palisade gate of the Rimors' motte castle. They might have been spied earlier, but the piebald steed on which they sat almost blended into the speckled landscape.

The leading stranger wore a heavy brown cloak edged in squirrel, with a liripipe hood over his tunic, and dark blue hose. He had shaggy blond hair and wore a dark bejeweled patch over his left eye.

Riding pillion on a green cushion behind him, in a heavy hooded cloak, his passenger remained unidentifiable save only that, from the way she sat, she was female.

In the center of the bailey, the stranger dismounted, then led the horse to the fenced paddock beside the stables. People there and around the well eyed him suspiciously. There was something in his manner that spoke of soldiery, or maybe it was the terrible scars beneath his eyepatch. One could only imagine how he'd acquired them. And it was odd how he left the woman on board the horse.

He walked across the mucky yard toward the main hall, located in the center of various outbuildings, barracks, the bakery, and the cooking house. Smoke poured from the hole in the center of its roof.

On the scarp, above the flying bridge to his right, the wooden keep stood half disassembled, surrounded by piles of stones, two small treadwheels, and a half dozen masons. The old wood keep was in the process of being rebuilt much more grandly in stone.

The stranger asked a woman outside the baking kitchen where he could find Ainsley Rimor of Alwich, and she pointed to the hall next door. The stranger thanked her and, after a final glance back at his passenger, he entered the hall and closed the door after him.

A fire blazed in the central fire pit. A bent old man tended it. Nearby, seated on an ornate leather stool, Ainsley Rimor of Alwich leaned back against a long table and listened to a recitation of the *Chanson de Guillame* by a scholarly performer, possibly a poet, who stood before him. The stranger paused, taking in the room, and to listen. He nodded along with the romance. This was the first part of it, where William of Orange, Vivien, and Gui battled the villainous Saracens. That it was being recited suggested that Rimor of Alwich did not himself read French. Beside him sat a girl of perhaps seventeen years, dressed only in a dirty linen chemise. She hugged a green woolen cloak about her shoulders for warmth. Rimor of Alwich's left hand appeared to be busily at work between her legs while he listened to the recitation. A chessboard with spilled pieces and a game of tables lay farther down the table, as if the players had grown bored with both games.

Elsewhere around the room stood ornate, boxlike chairs with cushions, and tapestries, small tables, numerous pallets on raised frames, and one curtain-enclosed central bed for the lord of the manor. A red gown or bliaut with blue trimming lay over the side of the bed, probably the girl's. The furnishings had all been moved out of the wooden keep above.

The stranger strolled over to the old man tending the fire, who was sprinkling lavender seeds over it to scent the hall.

Softly, the stranger said, "Seumas, it's been such a long time. How are you?"

"I am...well enough." He squinted at the stranger. "We are acquainted?"

The stranger smiled and patted his arm. "Long ago."

Seumas McCrae cocked his head. Perhaps this one had been someone's child who used to run about inside the castle. Many children had come and gone in his time, beginning with the children of the original lord of the manor. The scarred face no doubt kept the stranger from being recognizable to anybody.

The girl turned her head to stare at the stranger, and this movement caught the peripheral attention of Rimor of Alwich. He raised the hand that had been between her thighs to silence the recitation of *Guillame*, then stood. He was a squat and solid-seeming man with graying ginger hair and beard. He resembled no one in the close family of Rimor de Ercildoun.

"Begone," Alwich said to the scholar. "We'll continue this later, tonight perhaps." Ignoring the girl, he walked toward the fire. He limped somewhat. His hip gave him trouble in the cold weather. "You go off now, too," he told old Seumas. "The fire will tend itself awhile without you *poking* at it." He had the snappish manner of someone easily irritated. He waited then while the scholar and the old man left the hall, and presented his aching hip to the fire. The girl continued to stare at the stranger as if sizing him up.

Rimor of Alwich acknowledged the stranger's observation of the girl. He smacked his lips. "Like the courtesan, do you? Ranulf acquired her for me in the Bankside stews when he traveled to London. He's a randy old thing, isn't he? Well, we all are in these fleshy vessels." He plucked at his tunic. "They lead such lives of filth and squalor. You want a bit of her first? I shouldn't blame you." The stranger said nothing. "No? Well, all right. Just being glamoured like 'em, you don't share the appetites of these liches, do you? Of course.

"I'll tell you, I expected to hear something from Ranulf days ago. Thought surely *you* would be back through the gate by now. How has he eluded us again? What *is* our situation, Lord Aðalbrandr, hmm?" Contempt colored his voice, suggesting he did not have a very elevated opinion of the one-eyed stranger, who simply continued staring at the courtesan. "Oh, yes, all right, all right." Alwich turned to her. "Shoo, go off now. Go put on your clothes and dawdle in the yard awhile."

They both remained standing, facing each other, while she pulled on the bliaut, tucking her chemise into it, then shoes. In the meantime, Alwich attempted to communicate silently, but the knight wasn't having any, and threw the probe back at him. Clearly, Alwich's sharp tone had not been well-received.

The girl clopped across the room and out the door. "There. Now you can tell me, *have* we achieved our goal?" asked Alwich.

The knight replied, "If you mean, are there any remaining who know of your transformation? Aside from us, there are not. Even the miller has been dispensed with."

"Oh, but I thought—"

"Ranulf, I should tell you, is also a casualty. He won't be acquiring any more courtesans from the Bankside stews for you, so you might want to treat that one better."

Alwich waved off this news. "Pah. We'll just have to confiscate some other monk, and hopefully this one can protect the crypt. It has been compromised twice now. We really should relocate the Yvagvoja, hmm? Don't you agree? Anyway, what about the Rhymer himself?"

"Nowhere to be found."

Alwich pushed out his lips. "Well, how am I to take that? Is that good news or bad?"

"Is it good news you want? Our Casseov recovered from his wounds in the crypt and returned through the gate, the only one to survive an encounter thus far."

"The only one not shot through the head, you mean," Alwich replied sourly.

Aðalbrandr drew closer. "That's exactly what I mean. What I am wondering about is the condition of the sister. The one called Innes. She is—"

"Still being cared for by the nuns of Cluny. I visited last spring to be certain. She remains a nameless madwoman there. They take in all kinds, even lepers. Who can say if some pestilence or other won't finish her for us? For all I know, her nose has rotted off already. Of course, if it's your preference I can speed matters along, use a *dight* and bring her into the fold. One of us riding her would look like a miraculous recovery to the world, and old Ainsley Rimor of Alwich could retire from the scene after his years of service."

The knight nodded thoughtfully. "So she does inherit if you, say, were to fall down a well."

Alwich blinked a few times, then tittered. "Well, she would, yes. Of course, the widow Mac an Fleisdeir would quick find us another suitable 'relative,' hey?"

"Oh, did I not mention that the widow's *Yvagvoja* also perished in the tombs of St. Mary's?"

"No. No, you didn't. What, did he wipe us all out?"

Aðalbrandr grinned. "Not quite."

Alwich rubbed at his aching hip. "Well, then, um, why don't I have some mead brought in and we can drink to our having survived him—unless, of course, your tastes are a bit more wanton, in which case I'll call the girl back. Or perhaps something else for you?"

"Perhaps in a bit."

"As you wish." Nonplussed now, he didn't know what to say to Lord Aðalbrandr. The Queen's consort did wield a fair amount of power, whatever *he* might think of him. He said, "Did you see the work being done upon the scarp? We're replacing the wood keep with one of stone. Going to have hearths on every floor. In all the rooms! Carved-out niches in the walls with holes above so the smoke is pulled out. It's remarkable to be on the cutting edge of change in this primitive society. Of course, MacGillean did it first. I'm not even sure that was *our* influence. Ahead of his time, though nothing compared to the perfect gleaming heights of Ailfion."

Aðalbrandr walked over to the fire and warmed his hands there. Without turning, he said, "I noticed you were listening to a recitation when I arrived. Did you know that the bard Taliesin wrote a poem about mead? *Kanu y med,* he called it."

"Why, I had no idea you sampled their poetry, Lord Aðalbrandr. Did you get him to recite it for you from his prison cell?"

The knight stared silently at him for a moment. Then: "You were going to have Seumas bring us some?"

"Oh, yes, yes, of course." He thundered to the door where he shouted out toward the kitchens that a jug of mead must be brought immediately. He closed the door and limped back to the fire. "These bodies—even the weather hurts them."

After a minute the door opened, but instead of old Seumas, a woman in a hooded cloak carried in the stoneware jug and two matching cups.

"What is this?" Alwich asked.

"A surprise for you. I mean, with Ranulf gone, you can hardly visit the Bankside stews yourself, now, can you?"

The woman poured out the mead.

Alwich glanced at his guest with new appreciation. "Well," he said. "Well, what can I say?" He hurried over to where she stood. She flinched as he neared but held her ground. He threw back her hood.

She stared defiantly at him. Her dark hair was shot through with gray but mostly hidden beneath a couvre-chef. Lines were etched under her eyes, around her mouth. Her cheeks were hollow, the eyes bright and maybe tinged with an edge of madness. She wore beneath the cloak a long blue belted gown.

Alwich just stared, trying to puzzle out why she seemed familiar. He looked to Lord Adalbrandr for some explanation.

"I had her brought all the way from Cluny for this," the knight told him. "You know, no one in our family is from Alwich. But I suppose that was the widow's idea. Who would there be to contest your claim?"

"My claim?"

But Adalbrandr was warping and reforming. Blond hair darkened, thickened; he removed the eye patch, tossing it in the fire. The scars beneath it vanished altogether, and a weary Thomas Lindsay Rimor de Ercildoun stood there in Yvag armor. He'd had to reshape himself as Adalbrandr, and then placed a glamour upon that form. "Your claim," he said coldly.

"It's forfeit," added Innes Ni Rimor de Ercildoun. Her gaze met her brother's. "We just wanted to tell you that. And to say, don't come back." Thomas nodded and they walked together to the door.

Pausing there, Thomas told him, "Goodbye, cousin." Then he opened the door, allowing Innes to depart before Filib and Kester Lusk, each armed with a bow, entered. He stepped outside and closed the door after them.